BEYOND PAIN

PAIN

kit rocha

Beyond Pain

Edited by Sasha Knight

ISBN-13: 978-1492201182
ISBN-10: 1492201189

For Alisha Rai.

And cookie butter.

1

RACHEL WAS DANCING again.
From her vantage point behind the scuffed bar,
Six had a decent view of the stage even with men standing three deep on the opposite side. A lot of them were
tall fuckers too, the kind that towered head and shoulders over Six, but the floor behind the bar was high
enough to put her at eye level with the biggest brutes.
O'Kane—or someone close to him—clearly understood
the advantage height could give a bartender who had to
face down a room of horny, drunk thugs.

Usually those drunks were crowded around the bar,
jostling for booze or attention, but Six hadn't poured a
single shot since Rachel's act had started, and she didn't
think it was the novelty of having a new dancer that held
these men captivated.

No, it was the fact that Rachel had lost her damn
mind. She was grinding to the music as she peeled off
layer after layer of perfectly respectable leather to reveal

the lacy white garments beneath. Men stared slack-jawed as she rocked and swayed and ran her hands over her body, lost in a haze that fascinated and repelled Six in equal measure.

She was an object to these pea-brained cavemen, nothing more than the picture they'd hold in their heads when they stumbled back to their hovels and took their dicks in hand. The way they watched her should have made her weaker. *Lesser.*

It should have, but the men crowding the stage were nothing to Rachel. Flies to be swatted away if they got too close. Grubby children with their noses pressed against the dirty glass of the bakery, dreaming of something they could never have while hunger gnawed in their guts.

Rachel was oblivious, and somehow that turned the men into the weak ones. The ones who were less than.

Six saw it over and over, every time an O'Kane woman took that stage. Power in the place of helplessness, pride where she would have felt sick and exposed. There was a secret in these women that went deeper than the ink around their wrists, and sometimes she thought if she watched for long enough, she could unlock it for herself.

Of course, watching could be uncomfortable for other reasons.

Rachel slipped her fingers beneath the ruffled edge of her underwear, and Six turned her attention back to the bar. The low throb of the bass rhythm was harder to ignore, its steady beat vibrating up through the floor. In Sector Three, they'd made do with passable musicians beating on already battered instruments, but the heart of Sector Four was a marvel of miraculous old tech.

Maddox had shown her the speakers that lined the walls, but Six still had a hard time believing that such bone-rattling sound could come from those tiny, unremarkable boxes. The O'Kanes took these luxuries for granted, but some days she felt as slack-jawed as the drooling morons hovering around the bar.

"God, this place is insane tonight." Trix dropped a tray on the counter and took a deep breath. "At least it's slowing down—for now."

For now, Six agreed silently, carefully not looking at the stage. As soon as the crowd broke free of Rachel's spell, they'd be eager to get back to drinking—maybe even more enthusiastically now that Trix was behind the bar. The newest member of the O'Kanes was everything Six wasn't—voluptuous, fashionable, *gorgeous*—and she spent every night drowning in admiring gazes and generous tips without doing anything more seductive than smiling as she poured whiskey.

Six tried to smile, but she felt like a stray dog showing her teeth in warning, and the men seemed to agree.

She swept up a rag and rubbed at a spill on the counter. "I should probably stick around until it clears out. If this keeps up, Dallas'll have to schedule extra help on the nights Rachel dances."

Trix shook her head as she eyed the stage. "She's making mad money, you know that? She doesn't play to the crowd, either. She ignores them, and they get off on it."

A stripper cocky enough to ignore a crowd in Sector Three would have to be quick with a knife to avoid some frustrated bastard determined to fuck the bitch out of her. Of course, a lot of dancers at the Broken Circle *did* wiggle and preen for the audience. The girls who got away with being above it all had one thing in common—intricate tattoos around their wrists, with the gang's symbol front and center. Everyone who belonged to Dallas wore those cuffs, and nobody in Sector Four would lay a finger on an O'Kane.

Six rubbed her thumb over her own unmarked wrist before glancing at Trix. The other woman had already taken ink, which put her beyond danger. "Are you thinking about doing it, too?"

"What, dancing like that? I'm a little more old-fashioned, I think." Trix began to line up fresh shot glasses on the bar. "You ever hear of something called burlesque?"

It was stupid to feel defensive when Trix wasn't the kind of person to poke at her ignorance, but Six still tensed. "No. Sounds fancy."

"It's kind of like the stripping, only not about getting naked. It's about the show, the spectacle..." She seemed to be struggling for words. "The joy."

If you believed the O'Kane women, everything up to and including fucking each other on stage was about the joy. And maybe it was, but it wasn't Six's kind of thing. "I'd put on a show if Dallas would let me in the damn cage. Can you imagine how much I could make betting on myself? The odds would be crazy."

Trix started at one end of the line of glasses and poured them full of whiskey, straight down the row. "If it's what you want to do, make it happen. Fight for it."

Easy for Trix to say. She was official now, a member of the gang in her own right, but Six was still...hell. A prisoner turned reluctant ally turned awkward guest. "I guess I could," she hedged as she bent to retrieve more shot glasses. "But it's not that important."

"Suit yourself."

Across the room, Rachel writhed on the floor and kicked her filmy panties—her last remaining scrap of clothing—off the side of the stage. As if it broke some sort of enchantment, the far more familiar hoots and shouts echoed through the room.

Even safe behind the bar, Six shivered. This was the part that twisted her guts until nausea made the room swim. Rachel was naked, her pale skin bare and vulnerable under the colored lights. Her tattoos did little to harden her soft curves, and every inch of her was on helpless display as she taunted the men by tracing her fingertips up the inside of her thigh.

The shouts got louder. Tension and anticipation built until the air grew heavy, and Six found herself struggling to take even breaths, to keep herself from dragging them into her lungs like each one could be her last. She busied herself with a second line of shot glasses, placing each glass precisely, its rim an equal distance from those on either side.

On the stage, Rachel moaned in pleasure.

A glass slipped through Six's fingers, and she lunged to catch it before it hit the floor. Ducking behind the counter spared her the sight of a gleeful Rachel with her fingers in her pussy, or rubbing her clit with so much enthusiasm you'd think getting off for three dozen strangers was the best fun she'd ever had.

Getting off. *Actually* getting off—no faking, no games. Six had done lots of things on stages. She'd been the entertainment, both willingly and unwillingly, clothed and naked. She'd fucked and stripped and bit her lower lip through floggings that left her body scarred. But she'd never, *ever* given those bastards the satisfaction of one unguarded moment, of one glimpse at *her*.

Rachel would work herself to screaming release right there in the middle of the Broken Circle. She wouldn't think twice about sprawling, naked and open, her heart and soul as recklessly displayed as her body. Every time she did it, she pushed a little further, came a little harder...

And Six had to choke back horror as the watching men lapped it up, taking something that should have been for Rachel alone.

Trix bent and pulled the shot glass from her shaking hand. "I'll handle things here. Go, if you want."

Six hadn't even realized she was still crouched behind the bar, and embarrassment joined the ugly jumble of revulsion and fear turning her inside out. "I can stay," she whispered, knowing it was a lie Trix could hear, but she couldn't help it. Pride wouldn't let her escape easily.

"No, you can't. And that's okay." Trix tilted her head toward the back exit. "Go on. I've got this."

Grateful, Six squeezed the other woman's hand and abandoned any pretense of dignity. The thick wooden door was marked STAFF ONLY, and she didn't look at the stage as she shoved through it, spilling out into a dark hallway. Doors to either side opened into extra rooms, closets used for storage as well as the small office where Rachel kept records of beer and booze sales.

A staircase to Six's right led up to the second floor and the employee lounge, but she skipped it and plowed straight for the exit, needing the fresh night air more than pitying looks from whatever dancers might be awaiting their turns on the stage.

She burst through the back door and into the comforting shadows of the parking area. In spite of the crowd inside, the lot was half empty tonight, with only two rusting cars and a cluster of motorcycles near the entrance.

She studied the bikes out of habit, looking for the familiar marks that would have indicated friend or foe in Sector Three, but nothing stood out. Nothing would. Most of the enemies of her old life were dead, and even the survivors wouldn't venture here, into the lion's den. Now that Dallas O'Kane ruled sectors Four *and* Three, she was as safe within the walls of this compound as it was possible to be in this life.

That was the story, anyway. Her racing pulse and queasy stomach weren't buying it. She sucked in a few deep breaths, forcing herself to calm through stubbornness alone. The fear and panic were still there—they always were—but it had been a long time since she'd let herself give in to them. The O'Kanes were making her weak already, as soft as some city twit who had time to whine about her *feelings*.

In Three, fear was everywhere. You lived with it or

you died from it, end of options—and that was if you considered dying a viable option. Six never had.

As soon as her heartbeat steadied, she stopped to get her bearings. Two large buildings loomed out of the darkness; to the east stood the warehouse where the O'Kanes held their weekly cage fights, and to the south sat the garage where Dallas stored his collection of lovingly restored cars. The living quarters lay beyond that, but that wasn't why she headed in that direction. Instead, she slipped through the gate and then through the side door of the garage.

The knot of tension between her shoulders unraveled when she saw the familiar figure bent under the hood of his car. "How's the work going?"

"Not bad." Metal clanged against metal as Bren straightened. "Finally got the carburetor rebuilt."

The words meant little to her. She'd never seen a working car up close before Bren had shoved her into one. "How long before you can drive it?"

"A while. It runs, but not well, not yet." His grease-smeared forearms flexed as he wiped his hands on a rag. "How was your shift?"

"Busy." Habit drove her fingers into her pocket to check the tightly rolled wad of bills, tips she'd managed to score from the perverse bastards who got off on being scowled at. "Rachel did her thing again."

"I know."

If she tried to talk about the panic that had sent her running, he'd listen. He'd watch her with those eyes that saw *everything* and probably understand parts of her she couldn't. It was too much exposure for one night, so she sidestepped the moment by hoisting herself onto the worktable. "Is it hard to learn how to drive?"

He tossed aside the rag and pulled two beers from a bucket next to the table. "Depends on how good you are at turning off your brain and letting your body do the work."

From anyone else, the words would have sounded like a lewd, clumsy come-on. From Bren, it was a straightforward answer, one made all the more ironic by how her body reacted to *him* any time she was foolish enough to turn off her brain. She was painfully aware of his graceful movements, of the appealing, subtle shift of muscle under skin as he held out a bottle.

"You should know," she retorted, taking care not to let her fingers brush his as she accepted the beer. Maybe her tart tone would cover her confusion. "If I could stop thinking, maybe I'd actually beat you in a fight one of these days."

A rare smile curved his lips. "I've had years of training when it comes to fighting, and decades of practice on the not thinking."

Those smiles were dangerous, and not only because they made her tingle. They were dangerous because she couldn't *not* smile in return, her lips tilting up to ruin her scowl. "That just makes you old. I *will* put you on your ass next time."

"That's what I like to hear."

"Sure, grandpa. Tell me that after I beat you."

He laughed as he leaned against the table beside her. "Cruz and Trix have their ink, but they've still got to drink in, make it official."

Rachel had explained the process in vague terms, something about having a new member do shots of all the O'Kane liquors before welcoming them into the gang. It had taken Six a month to realize Rachel hadn't been keeping gang secrets—that really was all that happened. No beatdowns for the men, no spreading your legs for the women. Just booze and celebration.

A few dozen city blocks separated this compound from Sector Three, but she might as well be on the moon. "It's an O'Kane thing, I guess," she said carefully, unable to keep her gaze from his wrists. Dark ink swirled around his muscled forearms, stopping above his broad

hands. The gang's signature cuffs, proof that he belonged.

"An O'Kane thing," he echoed in agreement. "Do you
want to go?"

"Am I allowed?"

Bren shrugged. "You'll go with me, like Jasper and
Noelle's party."

Maybe it was that simple. Dallas O'Kane was the
most powerful man in the sector—one of the most powerful men in their world—and Bren was part of his inner
circle. Rules didn't seem to apply to him, or to her when
she was with him.

Which didn't answer his question—did she want to
go? "How much like Jas and Noelle's party will it be?" she
asked, her cheeks heating at the memory of how quickly
that celebration had turned into a shameless fuckfest.

"More like a fight night," he hastily explained. "People might be getting it on in the corners or grinding on
the dance floor, but it's not— I mean, it's different."

Six covered her embarrassment by nudging his leg
with her boot. "So, no wall-to-wall fucking?"

"No, just people drinking and having a good time."

"Okay. It sounds fun." She nudged him again, more
for the excuse of contact than anything. He'd encouraged
her to ask for physical affection when she wanted it, but
she liked sneaking in teasing touches. Liked knowing she
could, and that he wouldn't hurt her for taking liberties.
"Thanks for including me."

"You're not a guest." He watched her intently. "This
is your home."

Home. Longing hollowed out her chest, a craving for
a concept she could barely fathom, because it started
with safety. "I don't know if I've ever had a home before."

Bren nodded. "A lot of people here haven't. You're
not alone."

She knew what he meant—that she wasn't alone in
being overwhelmed—but the words resonated more

deeply. Maybe it was because her panic from earlier had faded under the quiet warmth of his undemanding presence.

Or maybe she really was getting soft.

Some part of her trusted Bren, for better or worse, and that made his words true on every level. Closing her eyes, she leaned in until her shoulder touched his. She wouldn't be able to ignore her body's shiver of reaction forever, but tonight she focused on the satisfaction of friendship. "No. I'm not alone."

"So, how 'bout it?" He hesitated. "I can't skip the party, but you could, if you wanted."

She considered it for a moment, balanced the loneliness of being the only person on the compound not celebrating against the awkwardness of being the only outsider at the party.

Except no one treated her like an outsider, not with Bren around. "I'll come. I want to."

"Good. Trix'll want you to be there."

Something he'd been careful not to mention until after she agreed, just as he'd kept any hint of encouragement from his voice. Smiling, she clinked her beer against his. "Then it's a deal. As long as I can scowl at Ace if he tries to make me dance."

Bren downed half his beer in several long swallows. "Scowl at Ace for whatever you want. He probably deserves it."

"Yeah, but he probably likes it, too." At least he'd stopped tossing her those flirtatious smiles, the ones that were all charm and dirty promise—and all the more alarming because she didn't think he did it on purpose. "But he's not so bad anymore. Did you tell him to stop hitting on me?"

"Might as well tell the sun not to shine, sweetness."

She laughed. The sound was so foreign it still startled her sometimes, another way her body turned traitor around Bren. The warmth and the tingles and the smiling and now laughter. Low and a little rusty, but it was *real.* "Are you almost done working?"

"Yeah." He pulled down the metal rod propping up the hood and let it slam shut. "Want me to walk you to your place?"

"Sure." She slid off the worktable and tried not to let her gaze linger on his shoulders. This was always the most dangerous time, when she was loose and relaxed enough to remember a time when sex had been more good than bad, when she'd appreciated a man with a hard body and beautiful shoulders.

White looked good on him, especially with all the engine grease. His T-shirt clung, the sleeves stretching wide over flexing biceps. Aside from his O'Kane cuffs, his arms were free of ink, but a black swirl curled up his neck from beneath the fabric, hinting at the tattoo that covered his entire back.

She loved watching him fight in the cage, watching all those muscles move together so perfectly she thought the prissy bastards in Eden must be at least partly right about their God. Only a higher power could have created something as graceful and stunning and deadly as Brendan Donnelly.

He turned and caught her staring—he *must* have—but he didn't call her on it. Instead, he finished off his beer and held out his hand. "Come on."

Exhaling, she slipped her fingers into his. His hands still bore smudges, the kind that would rub off on her skin as tangible proof of contact. She knew she'd stare at it later, at the dark grease on the back of her hand that marked the spot he'd rubbed his thumb over, and she'd remember the way it felt. This jolt, the way his touch shivered along her nerve endings as if her instincts couldn't decide if he meant blissful safety or delicious danger.

Her gut already knew. Her body was safe with Bren, but her mind, her heart, her *soul...* Hell, Wilson Trent

beyond pain

had shattered her into a thousand razor-edged pieces, but Bren could grind those shards into dust.

If she had half a brain left, she'd run.

2

S LUMS WERE SLUMS, no matter where you went.

Bren ducked a low-hanging clothesline and marked the progress of the footsteps behind him. Quick, too light to belong to someone his size. Nervous, like a scurry.

He stifled a sigh and slowed. He knew better than to wear his normal clothes on an errand like this. He didn't dress fancy, but O'Kanes could afford quality. Forget the silver he wore or the cash in his pocket, his leather jacket alone could feed a desperate kid for a month.

He should know.

The scuttling steps drew closer, and Bren spun in time to intercept the arm swinging at him. Dirty steel flashed, and he twisted his wrist with a jerk, flinging the knife into a pile of trash heaped against the nearest wall.

His attacker was just a girl, no more than thirteen or fourteen, but she looked older under her dirty, matted hair. The features youth should have softened had been starved into sharpness, and her eyes were flat. Not hard, not quite, but dull. She stared up at Bren, who could have snapped her neck like a twig, but no fear materialized. No worry, but no hope, either. Like it didn't fucking matter what happened to her, she was finished either way.

That was what decided her fate. "You need to pick your marks better. Cash is worthless if you're too dead to use it."

She bared her teeth at him, but even that gesture of defiance stirred no emotion in her exhausted gaze. It was a challenge born of stubborn habit, like her words. "What, you some kinda do-gooder?"

"No." He didn't release her. "But I know a place you can go."

Suspicion tightened her features. "If you're a pervert, you're too far east. The cribs are on the other side of the city center."

Her conclusion was too logical for him to find it amusing. "No, no sex. I'm on my way to visit a friend. You can come with me, get something to eat."

It must have been days since her last meal, long enough to make the tiniest scrap of hope worth risking everything. She stopped trying to wrench free and stared up at him in silence for one second. Two. "Okay," she muttered, looking away. "Whatever."

"The concrete building past the tunnel access. Do you know it?"

She nodded, silent and wary.

"Good." She'd be able to find her way back on her own. "Come on."

Bren didn't slow down for the girl as he continued on to Cooper's building. She kept pace, undoubtedly accustomed to moving fast through the packed alleyways. "What should I call you?" he asked. Not her name, just *something.*

Her gaze rested heavily on him. "Syd," she said finally. "Call me Syd."

"I'm Bren."

"Bren," she echoed, like she didn't believe him. "You don't make any damn sense."

"No?" He stopped in front of Coop's door and pounded on it with the side of his fist, watching the girl out of the corner of his eye as his jacket sleeve rode up to bare the ink around his wrist. "I'm from the sectors. Four."

She'd stared him right in the face with the threat of death hanging between them, but the sight of his O'Kane tattoos widened her eyes. She inhaled sharply and tensed, as if she might bolt, but the scrape of the door caught her attention.

Coop was old and grizzled, his once-powerful body stooped with age and the ache of joints that had suffered too much punishment in his youth. But his eyes were still sharp, and he snorted roughly as his gaze jumped from Bren to Syd. "Good thing I had Tammy cook extra. This one looks like she'd chew her way through my boots if I gave her the chance. Bring her on in."

Bellyaching aside, Bren knew the old man would take care of any strays he dragged along with him. He urged the girl through the door and followed her. "Cruz couldn't make it, but he sends his regards."

"That boy's not flexible enough to travel between worlds," Coop said, only pausing long enough to let Bren bolt the door before leading them both down a narrow hallway. "Wherever he's standing, he puts down roots, and that's all there is to it."

He was right. Cruz had settled in to Sector Four and life as an O'Kane, but only because he'd thrown himself headfirst into work. Running jobs for Dallas wasn't that much different from being a high-level, decorated military police officer in Eden. You did what your boss told you to do, no matter how ugly or dirty.

A soldier was a soldier.

"He still thinks about you, though." Bren pulled a

credit stick out of his jacket pocket and pressed it into Coop's hand.

Coop tucked it into his pocket as they passed through the open door and into a warm, brightly lit kitchen. "Good. Maybe next time you come around, he'll unbend enough to visit."

The busty blonde bent over the stove turned with a smile of greeting that froze when she caught sight of Syd. Cooper's housekeeper wasn't much older than Bren, but she had a maternal streak a sector wide and a backbone stiffened by years of dealing with Coop and his protégés.

Syd didn't stand a chance. One second, she was still eyeing the hallway as if considering a bolt for freedom. In the next, Tammy had pressed a warm meat pie into the girl's thin hands and was sweeping her toward the stairs with the promise of a hot bath and clean clothes.

Coop watched them disappear with a look of fond amusement. "Suppose it's just as well Tammy's living here full-time now. She's good with the wary ones. Doesn't take any shit, but she doesn't scare them like my busted face seems to."

Survival—the strongest drive of all. "A hundred bucks says you still catch her trying to rob you tonight."

"I hope so," Coop replied heartily. "Those are the ones who have a chance. The ones who ain't done fighting."

"The ones like me?" Bren hit the living room first and dropped into his favorite chair in the corner.

Coop handed him a bottle of beer before claiming his spot on the throne-like recliner. "No one's quite like you, boy, and thank God for that. You wouldn't have stopped until you'd taken everything that *was* bolted down."

"I brought it all back." And so would this girl. She was beaten down, but not broken to the point of cruelty. Not yet.

He cracked open his beer with a glance at the label. Liam Riley was still the only brewer in town, and that wasn't likely to change. Rachel made plenty of beer in Sector Four, but her brew stayed in the sectors, where it wouldn't compete with her father's.

As if he could sense the thought, Coop lifted his own bottle. "How's Liam's girl? Still sitting snug with O'Kane?"

"Yeah." Bren skirted the news of her dancing and of her brief involvement with Cruz. None of those things were his to discuss.

"You come across the wall just for a visit, or did you have business in the city?"

Business. Bren busied himself with his first gulp of beer, anything to postpone the inevitable answer the man wouldn't want to hear.

But Coop had always been good at reading between the lines. "Miller, huh? When're you gonna finally put a knife between that bastard's ribs?"

"When the time's right." A quick, easy answer, as if Bren hadn't spent hours trailing him. *Years* biding his time, waiting for the perfect moment to strike.

Lieutenant Russell Miller—Bren's former commanding officer, the man responsible for his banishment from the city. The mission had been simple: plant some contraband on a mid-level executive at one of the biggest import companies in Eden, a man suspected of embezzling funds. The resulting investigation would include his financial records, making the evidence-gathering process easy for his employer.

Simple, except the man hadn't embezzled anything, and he hadn't gone easy. He'd gone *public*, and Miller had denied ever giving Bren the order. Instead, he'd sacrificed him to the nonexistent mercy of a perfunctory military tribunal.

Bren tried to imagine Dallas doing the same, abandoning one of his men instead of owning up to his own failed maneuvers, but he couldn't do it. Miller was a man without conscience, without *honor*, and one day he would die for it.

"Hey." Coop snapped his fingers. "You goin' down the rabbit hole or something?"

"No." Bren drank more beer. It was smooth, with none of the bite Rachel brewed into hers. It made him miss home. "You heard about Three? The other sector leaders put Dallas in charge of cleaning up the shit Trent left behind."

"Is that what's going down?" The old man grunted. "Heard a hell of a lot of rumors, but they're nothing compared to Gareth Woods turning up with his throat slit. Been fifteen years since someone managed to murder a councilman."

Bren swirled the amber liquid in his bottle. "It's a mystery, all right."

"Ain't it? And that fancy lady from Two on the hook for it, and not a whisper of your boss anywhere."

"Maybe he wasn't involved." It wasn't exactly a lie, since Lex had been the one to take Woods down.

Coop grunted again. "Just as well. I hear Eden's got their fancy knickers in a twist over a whole mess of things."

Of course they did, because the sectors were in upheaval. Power fluctuations were unstable, dangerous. Maybe no one gave a shit that Gareth Woods—a councilman, one of their own—was dead. The man had been crooked, even depraved. But with the sectors in flux, they'd be watching anyway.

Bren changed the subject. "Anything else I should know? Word on the ground?"

Coop nursed his beer for a moment before nodding abruptly. "A lot of eyes on the sectors, but it's more than that." He hesitated. "The whole city's got a vibe, like something bad might go down, but we don't know what it is yet."

A warning, loud and clear. When the men with the helicopters and explosives got nervous... "Everyone's waiting to see what happens next, and whether they need to blow it all to hell and back."

"Wouldn't be the first time." Coop fixed him with a steady gaze. "You just make sure you're not standing there when it does. I put too much effort into you to have it all go to waste."

"I'm an O'Kane now. If it comes to that, you know exactly where I'll be."

Coop sighed. "I know. At least you've got Cruz to watch your back now. That's something."

It wouldn't be a visit to his friend and mentor, his surrogate father, if he didn't ask. "There's a place for you there, you know. No questions. Tammy, too."

"I know, but I still have a few comforts inside these walls. And Tammy's tough as nails, but she's an Eden girl to her bones." Coop's smile returned, amused and a little self-mocking. "She gets flustered at the idea of kissing before marriage. You O'Kanes would give her a heart attack."

"Could be. But I think you'd be surprised how fast that fades when you get outside of these walls."

"A lot of shit does," the old man acknowledged. "You look good, Bren. You happy out there?"

"I'm—" He had everything. Power, security, the kind of family he'd have killed for as a child on the streets in the slums of Eden. Not a damn worry in the world.

Except for Six.

His lips formed the words without his thought or consent. "You've had a lot of kids come through here. How broken is too broken? How do you know what you can't fix?"

Coop didn't answer right away. He twisted the beer bottle in his hand, staring at the label as he picked away at the edge. "No one's too broken. But you can't fix a damn thing. All you can do is figure out which ones want to fix themselves, then give them the tools to get the job done."

Wise words, and it was just as well. Bren wasn't the man anyone called to fix things. He tore them down, ripped them apart. Killed them and disposed of the evidence.

He wasn't a man meant to build things—Eden had made sure of that, both with his childhood and his military training—but maybe he could stand beside her while she picked up her pieces. And the truth, something she'd definitely never heard from Wilson Trent's lips—about her situation, about Bren himself—he could give her that, too.

Surely it would be enough.

Bren was used to being called to Dallas's office. The man handed out orders from behind his wide desk, inhabiting the space with an assurance that spoke of power.

The woman at his right hand, though... That was new.

Lex studied Bren as Dallas poured a round of drinks. She had stepped fully into her role as queen, all right, but it was obvious she didn't intend to plan parties and serve as eye candy on her man's arm. She was *in* it, advising Dallas every step of the way.

"Bren can handle it," she said finally. "And if he can't, he'll let you know. He won't let his ego choke the shit out of him."

"You hear that, Bren?" Dallas grinned. "Rare fucking praise, indeed."

Bren held his answering smile in check. "I didn't know I had an ego. What exactly am I handling?"

Dallas stabbed a finger down on the map spread out between them. "Sector Three."

Bren stared at the lines marking out the sector. So far, Dallas had sent the usual suspects over to Three—

him, Jasper, and Mad. "Why me?"

Lex downed her whiskey shot. "Don't ask questions I already answered, Donnelly."

"There's what she said," Dallas agreed. "But it's also time. Lex and I need to focus on the bigger game. That means Jas is stepping up here in Four to cover more of the day-to-day shit, and I need someone I can trust keeping an eye on Three. Then there's Six." His lips twisted. "The girl. Not the sector, and that's fucking confusing. Don't suppose you've gotten a real name out of her yet?"

Bren arched an eyebrow.

Dallas sighed. "Fine, I'll deal with it. But *you* get to deal with *her*. I figure she can help you cut through a lot of the bullshit over there. She knows who's who, the lay of the land."

His first instinct was to refuse. She was still on shaky ground, barely trusted him, and maybe the last thing she needed was to go back there. But to not even allow her to make the decision for herself? Unacceptable. "She's not an O'Kane, not yet. If she says no?"

Dallas opened his mouth—then shut it and looked at Lex, who laid a hand on his shoulder and answered. "If she says no, that's fine. She can answer questions and provide information without budging. But if you're going, she'll want to go with you."

"Probably," Bren allowed, dropping his gaze once more to the map. "What's my objective?"

"Information, to start." Dallas bent and resurfaced with a second map, which he unrolled on top of the other one. It outlined Three, but large parts of it had been sketched vaguely with pencil, while other parts remained completely blank. "Ace pieced this together from the intel we have, but it isn't much. We need to know what's over there, who's got it, and who might try to take more when we're not looking. And if there are people in a bad way, people who could be loyal if we threw a little help in their direction... Well, I want to know that too, so I can take advantage of it."

Lex snorted. "It's not quite as mercenary as all that. Dallas O'Kane takes care of his own, and that now includes Sector Three."

Dallas glanced up at Lex, his lips twitching, but the look in his eyes was something Bren had never seen before. Quiet, peaceful satisfaction. "If the queen commands it," he murmured, the words carrying a teasing edge.

She threaded her fingers through the short hair at the back of his neck and held his gaze. "She does."

A private moment, but Bren couldn't bring himself to look away. All the kicking and fighting had come down to this—two people who knew each other inside and out, well enough to speak without words.

It was Dallas who broke the spell, quirking an eyebrow at Bren. "Stick to people who need our kind of support, but make a list for Mad. He'll coordinate all the feeding of the hungry and healing of the sick with his cousin."

"Got it." Bren rose. "You want me to head out after the party?"

"Sometime in the next few days, yeah." Dallas rolled up the map and offered it to him. "If you want something a little less unwieldy, Noelle's been working her way through my stash of tech. You can probably snag a tablet, but everything goes on the map. I want a hard copy."

"Understood." He tucked the paper under his arm. "I know this is about intelligence gathering, but what do you want me to do if I run into something really fucking wrong?"

That fast, Dallas made the transition from love-struck man to ruthless leader. "I want you to clean house."

They'd made a few contacts in Three already, people who would be more than willing to help him eliminate the worst offenders. "I'll take care of it."

"Anything else you need?"

A clear dismissal, made clearer when Lex eased onto Dallas's lap. Bren nodded to them both and turned for the door.

"Bren?"

He tossed a look at Lex over his shoulder. "Yeah?"

"Don't get dead."

kit rocha

3

THE LONELIEST PLACE at a party was on the fringes. The edge of the crowd, just on the other side of belonging. That's where Six had expected to be, drifting off into invisibility while the O'Kanes hooted and hollered and welcomed two more into the fold.

She hadn't expected Bren to park himself next to her.

"You don't have to stand with me," she told him quietly as they watched Cruz down two shots of tequila and slam the empty glasses next to the four that had held whiskey and vodka.

Bren just stood there, arms crossed over his chest, watching the spectacle with a small smile. "I don't mind."

He hadn't lied to her yet, so she took the words at face value and watched Cruz start his way around the loose circle of O'Kanes. He'd done the same after each of the previous pairs of shots, accepting hugs and kisses and Ace's too-enthusiastic back-pounding.

27

beyond pain

By the time Cruz had passed the spot where Six and Bren were standing, Rachel had poured another shot of tequila and offered it to Trix. The redhead grimaced comically before letting Mad pull her into a warm hug of welcome.

It was a world away from life in Three, and not just because Trix was being welcomed as a full member. Mad's brown skin would have barred him from the ranks of Trent's gang, no matter how skilled he was. "Dallas doesn't care, does he?" she asked Bren, following Trix's progress around the circle. Mad wasn't the only one who would have been excluded. Ace, Lex, Flash, maybe even Cruz—and those were just the names she knew.

"Care about what?"

"What color people are." It hadn't mattered on the farms, but the street kids in Three grouped together with others who looked like them, piecing together scraps of identity from the lucky few who remembered having parents. And Trent had never grown past it, even when it hurt him. "Cain had valuable farming contacts, and Trent *still* almost didn't let him in his gang."

"Because he's black?" Bren shook his head with a snort. "No, Dallas doesn't give a shit. Hard to believe there are people around who still do."

"Dumb people." Six couldn't help her wry laugh. "They still care if you have tits, too. Dumb people care about lots of silly things."

"Yeah, they do." His last words were almost drowned out by the roar of the crowd as Cruz took his next shots.

"Do the guys always have to drink more than the women?" she asked, eyeing the man's progress. He was still pretty steady, but she doubted he would be with twelve more shots sloshing in his stomach.

"The men are bigger," Bren answered simply, then laughed. "Don't worry, you can do both shots if you want. Sometimes the ladies do."

As if there was no question at all that Dallas would

28

accept her, like the only thing standing between her and a family was the technicality of time. Funny how the knowledge could be soothing even while it made her feel trapped. "I could get down sixteen shots, but I might not be walking back to my own bed afterwards."

"Neither did Rachel. She loved the whole world for about twenty minutes, then she threw up all over me and Jas."

Six pressed her lips together as firmly as possible, biting the inside of her cheek until the urge to smile had passed. "I hope Cruz doesn't puke on us."

Bren said nothing, but the tops of his ears grew pink as a blush crept up his face.

Oh, God. *He'd* thrown up.

She could bite her lips bloody and not hide her sudden grin, so she tipped her head forward and let her hair sweep down to shield her expression from him. "That's okay. I've heard booze hits old men harder."

"Smartass."

"C'mon. You can't be the only guy who couldn't hold down sixteen shots in a row."

"He's not," Lex cut in, easing between them. "But Bren doesn't spill secrets. Unless, of course, they belong to Rachel—who's gonna kick your ass, by the way."

"I know," Bren said mildly.

Six tucked her hair behind her ear and glanced at Lex. The female leader of the O'Kanes was dressed down—for her—but she still made a statement. Her pants alone were worth a month's wages, the leather so supple it hugged every curve and moved when Lex did. Lush, especially when compared to her tiny white tank top, but that scrap of fabric had a different purpose: to barely cover her tits while framing the pair of tattoos that shouted her status, with Dallas's name across her abdomen and his mark around her throat.

The O'Kanes said everything that mattered to them with ink. It made her feel naked, sometimes, having none at all.

Lex didn't seem to care. Her gaze tracked around the room instead, and she shook her head. "Things'll get pretty wild around here tonight."

Six couldn't tell if it was a warning or not. "I thought all your parties got a little wild."

"Some wilder than others. Right, Bren?"

Before he could speak, Trix whirled around, laughing dizzily. Lex caught her with a smile and brushed a kiss to her cheek. "Steady, love."

"Sorry." Her face was flushed, her chest rising and falling with quick, elated breaths.

"Nothing to be sorry about." Lex guided her toward Bren.

He kissed her temple and whispered in her ear, and something ugly and dark twisted in Six's gut, a feeling unpleasantly like jealousy. She jerked her gaze away in time to watch Lex fist a hand in Cruz's short hair and lick her way past his lips.

Jesus, these people had no boundaries.

Lex held the kiss, her tongue sliding over his, while he kept his hands out at his sides, as if he didn't know where he could safely rest them. Six didn't blame him— Dallas O'Kane was a scary fucker.

But when his voice came bellowing across the crowd, Dallas only sounded amused. "Christ, woman," he called out. "Pace yourself. He's barely halfway there."

"Technicalities," Lex murmured as she pulled away and patted Cruz's cheek. "Enjoy your party."

The man might be six-foot-four and carved from rock, but Six swore he blushed as he stumbled to the next person in the circle.

At least she wasn't the only one out of her element.

She tried to fake a casualness she didn't feel as Trix and Cruz worked their way back around toward Rachel. "What happens when they're done with their shots?"

"If they're still upright?" Lex raised both eyebrows as

she backed away into the crowd. "Anything goes, honey."

Six couldn't bring herself to look at Bren with the words hanging in the air, vibrating with promise. "Anything, huh?"

He stepped closer, his arm brushing hers. "She's exaggerating, but not much. If it makes you uncomfortable, we can go."

"Not uncomfortable yet." Six bumped her hip against his. "I didn't get it last time."

She felt his stare, intense and focused. "Get what?"

She watched Ace give Trix a friendly slap on the ass that earned him an indulgent smile in return. "That they don't wanna fuck me if I'm not into it."

"Not even a little bit." Bren gestured around the room. "Everyone in here is into something different. Mad likes to have as many people around as possible. Flash used to dig the groupies before he hooked up with Amira. Jas and Noelle are together, but they like to play a little, too. Dallas and Lex are... Well, they're them. But no one in here gets off on forcing anyone."

"But it's not just that. I've met plenty of guys who aren't into force but are fine with a woman who'll close her eyes and put up with it." She'd expected Dallas to be one of them, but maybe she'd been selling the arrogance of the O'Kanes too short. None of these men would tolerate being *tolerated*.

Bren's words confirmed it. "Doesn't sound like much fun to me."

If it had, he would have already fucked her. She shifted her weight, and the warm skin of his arm pressed more firmly against hers. "Must be nice to be such hot stuff you can hold out for the good sex," she said lightly.

He brushed a lock of hair off her cheek, and her stomach dropped out as his fingertips grazed the shell of her ear.

She dragged in an unsteady breath and shoved both hands into her pants pockets to keep from reaching for him. "Cheater."

"Why?" His hand lingered near her face. "Because you like it? Or because you want more?"

Bren didn't ask rhetorical questions. He asked blunt ones and expected honest answers. Worse, he acted on the things she told him. If she said she didn't like it, he'd stop, even if he didn't believe her. There was no safe evasion, no closing her eyes and protesting too much and secretly hoping he'd keep going.

Honesty—especially about sex—tasted odd on her lips. "I like it," she said carefully. "I don't know if I *like* liking it. It's dangerous, isn't it?"

He nodded. "I wouldn't do anything you didn't want, but it doesn't stop there. I wouldn't do anything you weren't really fucking sure about, either."

Her heart pounded as the full import of his words slipped through her. The precarious balance of their relationship had tilted. He'd given her the power to ask for more, had painted a magical picture with deceptively innocent words.

Do anything. So mundane, but easy to imagine them lower, rougher. Whispered against her ear, they'd paint a different picture.

I want to do things to you.

She shivered. "If you wait for me to be sure about anything, you really will be an old man before you get the good stuff."

He turned toward her, leaned closer, his bulk and the look in his eyes blocking out the rest of the room. When he spoke, it wasn't against her ear but her cheek, hot and gruff. "What qualifies as the good stuff? Tell me."

This time it wasn't a question. It was an order, an out-and-out command. As hot as his lips were against her cheek, she *would not* tremble like some city girl who'd just gotten her first glimpse under a man's clothes.

She pressed her hand to his chest and slid it down, past the thick leather of his belt, until her fingers found the firm bulge of his half-aroused cock.

At least she wasn't the only one getting hot and bothered.

With a shred more confidence, she traced the outline of his growing erection before pressing her palm against it. "Every man I've ever met thought it was getting this inside me somehow."

He swallowed, his throat working, and the barest hint of a groan escaped him. "That's not what I asked you."

"Then I don't know." She needed to release him, but feeling him harden under her touch carried a dizzy sort of power. How long had it been since she'd wanted a man to feel good when she touched him? Long enough that she let her fingers fall away. "The only good stuff I know about is getting off, and I never needed a man for that."

The back of his hand grazed the button on her jeans. "No, I guess you don't."

She hissed in a breath and tried not to picture his fingers sliding down the same path her own had taken so many times. "Do you get what I'm saying, though?"

His touch vanished. "No, but I get what it means. It means not yet."

From the shouts and whooping cheers behind him, Cruz and Trix had made another pass. Six felt bolted in place, held captive by nothing more than his gaze and her own confused longing. "What do you think the good stuff is?" she asked, desperate to prolong this quiet oasis of brutal honesty.

"Fucking? That damn sure counts." A tiny smile tilted one corner of his mouth. "But so does everything else."

Without taking her eyes from his, she touched his shoulder. Strong muscles flexed enticingly under her fingertips as she slid her hand down his arm and finally twined her fingers with his. "Even this?"

Bren's smile faded as he raised their clasped hands and pressed a kiss to her knuckles. "Especially this."

The sudden burn in her chest scared her. It wasn't arousal, but something far more insidious, more dangerous. Affection, digging hooks into the painful scars on her heart, and she had to laugh it off to keep from flinging his hand away and bolting. "Then you're easy, Donnelly."

"I know." He looked away, and the moment was broken.

But she still had his hand, his grip firm and reassuring. So she clung to him as the O'Kanes celebrated their newest members, and almost felt as if she belonged.

Almost.

She liked to watch.

It wasn't the first time he'd caught Six staring at a scene of carnal decadence. Tonight, however, Bren was ready to chalk it up to his imagination, horny wishful thinking at its worst. But the third time her gaze drifted toward Mad and Trix and lingered, he knew it was true. Not morbid curiosity or detached interest.

She liked to watch.

Mad had sprawled on a couch with Trix astride his lap. Her hands were tangled in his hair, and his were lost under the skirt of her dress. Their kiss might have seemed tame if the frantic, hungry movement of her hips hadn't suggested that Mad was being very, *very* clever with his fingers.

When Trix tossed her head back with a sharp moan, Six jerked her gaze away, color rising in her cheeks, her pulse pounding at the base of her throat.

Bren pressed a drink into her hand and watched as Mad shifted position slightly, his arm flexing. Trix whimpered this time, the sound quickly choked off by the shudder that wracked her.

"God." Six stared at empty space as she took a drink. "It's not safe to look anywhere after a few drinks, is it?"

"Lex warned you, and so did I."

"Yeah." She laughed breathlessly. "I don't know the rules. It's not like they're putting on a show. They're all just..."

"Doing what they want." And getting off on people watching. "If they had problems with being seen, they wouldn't be out here."

"Yeah?" She sounded dubious, but her attention was starting to drift again, this time toward the corner where Noelle was on her knees in front of Jasper, unbuckling his belt with slow, teasing movements.

In the shadows, but not quite hidden, which was part of the game. Jas and Noelle were into the exhibitionism, all right, but sometimes this seemed to turn them on the most. The thin veneer of privacy, all too easily pierced by prying, hungry eyes.

Bren slid behind Six, directing her gaze more firmly to the couple. "Now, *that* is different. They don't just not mind. They want you to see."

"Oh," she breathed, as if she hadn't meant to say anything at all. Her body was primed, and the battle between tension and arousal left her trembling as they both watched Noelle free Jas's erection. Noelle's face was blissful as she stroked her fingers up his shaft, and Six's hand constricted around her glass until her knuckles turned white.

Jasper's groan echoed in Bren's chest, but he held it back in favor of quiet, careful words. "What about you? Do you want to watch?"

Noelle used her tongue to taunt Jasper into sinking his hands into her unbound hair, his fists twisting tight. Six made a muffled noise and leaned into Bren. "I guess I'm a freaky pervert, after all."

He rested one hand on her hip to steady her. "It's not a joke, not any more than the blowjobs or the whips or anything else. It can be something you *need*."

"Do you need it?"

beyond pain

He tried not to tense. Not that it mattered—it wasn't like his predilections were a big secret. "It's hot, but the only thing I'd call a need of mine is the pain."

She didn't reply, not until Noelle's lips were stretched wide around Jasper's shaft. Six's free hand fell to cover Bren's, her nails digging into his wrist as she shifted uncomfortably. "I couldn't do this," she whispered, and it sounded like a warning. "I couldn't let them watch."

He shivered at the bite of her nails in his skin. "So?"

Her grip tightened, threatening to break the skin. "It's not rude? To get all cranked up and leave to take care of it?"

As if Jas and Noelle would expect her participation in a scene they hadn't discussed with her first. "They're not doing it for your benefit, not like you think. Not so you'll return the favor."

Noelle's hungry moan rose, dragging more eyes than theirs to the corner in time to watch her cross her wrists behind her back in willing, submissive invitation. Jasper teased her by going slow, rocking his hips in short movements before thrusting deep without warning.

"Fucking hell," Six muttered, losing her grip on her glass. Bren didn't have time to catch it before it hit the cement floor with a sharp crack, the glass shattering into a dozen razor-edged pieces.

Six flushed and twisted to face him. "Crap, I'm sorry. I didn't—"

He laid his finger over her lips and slid his free arm around her waist. "Watch the glass."

Lifting her over it was easy—too easy. She'd been in Sector Four for a couple months now, but she was still too thin. Almost delicate.

But she was warm. Her breath was warm too, puffing against his finger with every quick breath. Her nipples were hard little buds he could feel through their clothes, clear evidence of her arousal.

He had to get her out of there before he broke all the careful promises he'd made.

Her body rubbed against his as he lowered her, and he gritted his teeth until her boots hit the floor. "I'll take you back to your room, if you want."

She stared at his chest for a tense moment before nodding.

Her hand was shaking when he wrapped his fingers around hers and pulled her through the crowd and out the side exit. The heavy metal door swung shut behind them, blocking out all the music except for the dull thud of the bass.

She inhaled deeply as the cool night air enveloped them, but didn't speak. Usually she seemed as comfortable with not talking as he was, but tonight their silence was more tense than companionable. She clutched his hand as they crossed the cracked asphalt, not letting go until they reached the building that held the O'Kanes' living quarters.

"You can go back to the party if you want," she said abruptly. "I'm okay."

He kicked open the door and held it for her. "I'm not going to shove you down the hall and run for it. I'm taking you home."

"I won't get jumped between here and my room," she retorted, rolling her eyes, but there was no heat in the words, and her fingers brushed his. "Hell, no one's jumped me in months except you, during practice. I'm probably getting rusty."

"Will you just let me do this?"

She fell silent again.

Anger had lent his words a brusque edge, and he knew she'd assume he was pissed at her, at the world—anyone but himself. "Sorry."

Six shrugged uncomfortably. "I'm a pain in the ass."

He never broke his word. He never lost *control.* "I promised I wouldn't go there, and I shouldn't have."

"Wait." She grabbed his wrist and hauled him to a stop. "Go where?"

"The party." Except that wasn't quite it. "The sex."

Her brows tugged down in confusion. "What, watching other people have it?"

He felt worse. "You wouldn't have if I hadn't pushed you to, and now look at us."

"You didn't *do* anything." But she released his wrist and took a step back, crossing her arms over her chest in a way that screamed defensiveness. "I'm not some sheltered city girl who's never seen a guy getting sucked off before."

"But I promised—" And then it hit him, a thunderclap of understanding. She wasn't a city girl, no. But she'd been sheltered, because she had no idea. "You don't know, do you? How close we were?"

Those dark eyes were so wary. "To what? Fucking?"

He closed the space between them. He couldn't help it, just like he couldn't help the way his voice roughened. "Fucking. It doesn't start when you get naked, not the way I do it."

She stiffened, but even with him crowding her space, she didn't shrink away. She didn't look away, either, just stared up at him as her uneven breaths pushed her tits against his chest. "How does it start?"

"Like this." His hands itched to slide up and cup her flesh so he'd know what kind of noise she made when he pinched her nipples between his fingers. "When we both start thinking about it. When we both want it."

Her gaze dipped to his mouth, and her tongue darted out, wetting her lower lip. "Maybe that's how it starts, but it shouldn't count until you're trying to get in me. So you didn't do anything wrong, okay?"

Bren scoffed. He was so hard it hurt, and he'd bet cash money she was so wet he'd have to fight to keep his fingers from slipping on her thighs as he positioned her for that first thrust. Maybe it shouldn't count, but it sure the hell did.

Didn't it?

He stepped back, putting a solid two feet of distance between them before meeting her eyes again. "You wouldn't tell me if I *did* do something wrong, though. Would you?"

She blinked, as if he'd broken a spell, and her features twisted into a scowl. "If you did something I didn't want, I'd knee your balls halfway to your throat."

Which didn't mean she wouldn't let him lead her, talk her around to something because she trusted him to know what was best. To treat her kindly. "Come on." He resumed his path down the hall. "It's getting late."

She trailed behind him, silent as a shadow until he reached her room. She paused with her fingers on the doorknob. "You don't have to go back to the party to get off. We could—or I could. I mean, if you want."

Oh, Christ. "I'm not going back to the party." And he'd be damned before he let any woman, much less a traumatized one, throw him a pity jerk.

"Oh." She pushed open the door, but didn't cross the threshold. "But you don't wanna mess around?"

It was his own fucking fault for jumping the gun, for the mixed signals of putting his hands on her. "Maybe some other time."

Awkward silence stretched out forever before she turned and walked stiffly into her room. "Okay, I guess I'll see you tomorrow. If we've still got practice."

"Three o'clock this time." By then, he could lock it down. Get his libido under control.

She made a quiet noise—agreement, acknowledgment, he couldn't even tell—and closed the door in his face.

Bren backed against the opposite wall and indulged himself with one light bang of his head against the brick. She was upset, he was an ass—and the whole situation would get worse, not better, if they had to hit Sector

Three *this* twisted up.

No way. It was too dangerous, not to mention unfair to her. He'd fix it.

Somehow.

mad

R ACHEL HAD SLID into Sector Four so smoothly it was like she'd always been an O'Kane, but Mad could have watched her for thirty seconds and known she wasn't sector-born.

She didn't know how to hide her pain. Everyone who grew up in the sectors learned to sooner or later—it was your only defense against bullies, not to mention the cruelty of a world that favored strength over compassion. Not everyone grew up to be a good actor, but you stood a better chance of growing up at all if you refused to let anyone see when you were hurting.

Rachel sucked at hiding. As he approached, he watched her slam more dirty glasses on the counter, her movements so rough she snagged a fingernail under the edge of the plastic tray and snapped it off.

"Perfect," she muttered in a defeated voice that pinched at his heart.

Blood pearled on her fingertip. Mad reached for her

wrist, ignoring her start of surprise as he lifted her hand to examine the damage. Not too bad, but it had to sting like a bitch. "Bad day, darling?"

Her hand twitched, as if she'd barely stopped herself from jerking away. "I broke a nail, that's all."

Liar. Calling her on it wouldn't help, so he rubbed his thumb over her palm and tilted his head toward the remains of the party. "You don't have to clean this all up tonight, you know. Plenty of people'll be around to help you tomorrow, if you want."

"It's got to be done." The words were brittle. Pained. "May as well get it over with."

Alone. It seethed under the words, and Mad would have had to be blind and stupid not to know why. With Jasper stepping up into a leadership role, Ace had been left without a partner. Cruz was the perfect replacement, a steady straight man to play off Ace's lazily deceptive charm.

It had proven a killer combination in the past, and everyone had expected them to put aside their shit and get the job done. No one had expected them to hit it off—least of all the woman they'd been fighting over.

He gave her hand a final squeeze before releasing it to see to the tray. "Well, if you're determined to do it *now*, you'll have to put up with me helping. Besides, I don't get to see much of you these days. Dallas has kept me busy."

She joined him in unloading the tray. "Maybe we can rustle up another regular poker game. Think Jas wants to teach Noelle how to play?"

From what he'd seen of Noelle and Jas lately, any poker game with the two of them would involve betting clothing and eventually sexual favors. Fun as hell, but Rachel was still holding on to too much of that sweet Eden innocence that Noelle had been throwing away with both hands.

"Better off asking Flash and Amira," he suggested instead. "She's going crazy, waiting for that baby to join us. Or maybe Flash is the one driving her there."

Rachel blew her bangs out of her face and sighed. "He's worried about her, that's all. Just scared."

"I know. Hell, we're all a little worried. Babies aren't much of a thing out here."

"Yeah." Rachel picked up a dishcloth and twisted it between her fingers.

He watched her wrench it into knots, her grip white-knuckled, before closing his hand over hers. "What's weighing so heavy on you, honey?"

She didn't answer at first. Emotion played across her face—anger, hurt, bewilderment—and she whispered, "There's nothing more important than the brotherhood, is there?"

Ace and Cruz, then. It must seem like that from the outside, like they'd fallen together and left her behind, and the guys would close ranks behind them. Which was true.

To a point.

Cruz was new, but Ace had been around long enough to know what would happen if the O'Kane women decided he'd done Rachel wrong. "You're forgetting sisterhood."

"Touché." She swallowed hard and looked up at him, her gaze bordering on pleading. "What would you do?"

There was no answer he could give that would fix things, and that hurt most of all. "I always do the same thing. Love everyone who crosses my path. Love 'em as much as I can, for as long as they need." He brushed his thumb over her cheek and tucked a lock of hair back from her face. "You're not me, honey."

She leaned in to his touch. "I could be. Is it easier?"

"It's the easiest thing in the world." He curled an arm around her and tugged her against his side, a little comfort to soften the truth to come. "But it won't heal what's hurting you."

Rachel poked him. "It's not so bad. I'm not brooding,

or anything. Much," she added ruefully.

He poked back, throwing in a tickle to make her smile. "Nah, you're just smashing around and ripping your fingernails off."

"What do I care, anyway?" Rachel hid her face against his shoulder, belying the defiance of her words. "I'm free. I can do whatever the hell I want."

"Sure you can. Lord knows it's a pleasure I've enjoyed to its fullest." He rubbed her back, sliding his fingers along her spine in long, soothing strokes. "You've never done that, have you?"

"What? Thrown myself into affairs?"

"Is that what you want?"

"Maybe." She tilted her head back and met his gaze. "I'm tired of doing things my way. It's not working."

The moment was so delicate, and the familiar temptation rose. Rachel was sweet-natured with a delicious edge of sass, and he was as fond of her as he was of all the O'Kane girls. There was an invitation in her eyes, whether she knew it or not, one it would be no hardship to accept.

He knew how to play a good hero. Sweep in and rock her world, and it wouldn't have to be anything more than the same easy pleasure he'd shared with Trix already that night. Two friends getting each other off.

But she was right. Brotherhood mattered, and Ace was still in love with her.

Smiling, he rubbed his thumb along her jaw. "You're dancing. That's new. Have you got anything else you've always wanted to try?"

She blinked, the moment dissipating like smoke. "I haven't decided yet."

Mad laughed—and put some space between them, just in case. "Well, there's your first step. Put that big brain to work on figuring it out."

"Right." Glass clinked as she lifted another tray and then put it down again. "Did I do something wrong? Did I hurt him somehow? I don't—" She dug her teeth into her lower lip with a wince. "No, forget it."

He couldn't leave that unanswered, brotherhood or no, so he caught her chin. "People always think the broody bastards like Bren are the broken ones, but being tough is how you survive in the sectors. It's the easygoing ones you have to watch out for, because they're the ones so scarred up on the inside that they can't feel, or they're so far past broken they just don't care."

Rachel exhaled on a shaky sigh and reached for him. "Mad..."

He'd revealed too much. He'd only meant to reassure her, but now she was giving him that *look*, the one he was so desperate to avoid that he'd sworn Dallas and his cousin and every damn person who knew his history to secrecy.

"Uh-uh," he said lightly, intercepting her hands. "You've already got one busted old sector bastard on your plate. Don't get greedy, love. I'm someone else's project."

"It's not funny."

It was for him. It had to be. "I know, but laughing at inappropriate things is what I do."

She relented with a soft smile that quickly turned wicked. "Is that why Trix kicked you out of her bed early?"

"Who says I ever got there?" Relieved that they'd skirted dangerous territory, he threw her a rakish wink before turning to gather up stray liquor bottles. "You're not the only one who likes to put on a show."

"Tease."

"Always."

She laughed, and Mad relaxed, safe in the knowledge that maybe he'd helped a little, and he'd only lied once.

Ace might still have a chance, but Mad had promised himself long ago not to let any woman make him her project. Some scars were too deep for another person to heal, no matter how much they loved you.

beyond pain

He was an O'Kane. That was enough.

4

S PARRING USUALLY WENT better when she *wanted* to hit Bren.

It wasn't fair. She'd known that at the start of her restless, uneasy night. She'd known her invitation hadn't been enthusiastic or seductive, so who could blame Bren for not taking her up on it? But her sense of fairness warped in on itself as those tense moments in front of her door replayed themselves over and over, building embarrassment on self-consciousness until she was half convinced she'd thrown herself at him only to be met with disgusted rejection.

It had felt that way, anyway, leaning against her closed door with her body aching for a release she was too tangled up to find. A few futile minutes with her fingers between her legs had made that clear. She'd met people who got off on humiliation, but she sure as fuck wasn't one of them, so now she was frustrated on top of everything else.

beyond pain

It made for great motivation. Unfortunately, it didn't make her faster. Or smarter.

Her back hit the mat hard enough to drive a grunt out of her as Bren circled, as light on his feet as ever.

"Pay attention," he snapped.

She shook off the shock of the impact and rose, staying on the balls of her feet as she pivoted to keep him in front of her. No wasting her breath on excuses or retorts, because she needed every scrap of focus to watch for the tiny signals that would indicate his next attack. But he just stood there, with not a single twitch to indicate which way he'd move.

Until he did.

He lunged for her midsection. This time, she twisted out of his path, jamming him in the side with her elbow to give her more time. She'd drilled enough men in the ribs to know most of them hesitated, but he followed through, pushing *into* the pain to hook an arm around her waist and drag her clear off the floor.

He followed her down to the mat and pinned both of her arms behind her. "You can't always be stronger, so you have to be faster."

She slammed her head back but only managed to knock him in the chin, and frustration lent her snarl a rough edge. "Nothing stops you. Another man would have flinched or winced or *something.*"

"You're the one who wanted to learn."

No, he wasn't tolerating excuses or whining today. It only pissed her off more, because she shouldn't want to whine, but there was a new significance to every touch now. A second meaning. His grip on her wrists wasn't simply an obstacle to overcome, it was a scrap of knowledge some lurid part of her wanted to file away.

This is what it feels like when he pins me to the ground, that part whispered, making her hyperaware of how large his hands were, how easily his fingers encircled her wrists. How even her frantic, determined strug-

48

gling hadn't forced him to tighten his grip to the point of pain, as if he had such finely tuned control over his body and hers that he could judge just how hard to squeeze without hurting her.

Her body was carrying on some lewd conversation with his, one she didn't want to hear and couldn't fucking ignore if she tried.

Gritting her teeth, she forced herself to stop struggling, to lie passively beneath him. "So what do I do next time?"

He released her. "Don't let me get you off your feet, that's—"

She struck before he could finish the sentence, throwing herself up and back while he was off balance, caught in mid-rise. So easy to slam into him, spill him to the floor, but she didn't dare risk losing control of the moment. In a heartbeat, she was straddling his stomach, her knees crushing his arms to the mat as she curled a hand around his throat.

He stared at her, frozen, for a handful of heartbeats. Then the bastard started to laugh.

She was damn tempted just to choke him.

Instead, she dug her fingernails into the side of his neck. "You're a crazy bastard."

"I know." He slipped his arms easily from under her knees and sat up. He caught her as she slid down, locking an iron grip around her waist. "I have a favor to ask. You don't have to do it, though."

This is what it feels like to have him between my legs. She batted the thought away, but not before the feel of straddling his hips had impressed itself on her memory with a vividness that would probably haunt her. She fought to focus on his face, and not on how close it was to her own. "What favor?"

"Dallas is sending me to Sector Three."

That shut her hormones down. Numbness took the place of desire, and it was almost a relief. "Time for me to make myself useful?"

"You know more about the place than any of us." Simple. Straightforward. "Not just the sector, but the people in it."

After five years surviving on the streets, she knew every bolthole and business inside the boundaries that made up her private slice of hell. Wilson Trent hadn't picked her out of the mud by accident. Even at seventeen, she'd known things he could use.

The only thing she hadn't known was how many ways he could use her.

Bren was still watching, quiet and intent, so she nodded carefully. "I know a lot."

"You don't have to go," he said again. "I want that clear, all right?"

She couldn't help her doubtful little laugh. "You sure about that? Why else has Dallas been putting up with me all this time? This is where I pay him back, and that's okay. Better like this than some other way."

Bren glowered as he shifted her off his lap and dropped her to the mat. "I don't lie."

"I know." Scrambling to her feet gave her the advantage of height, if only for a few precious moments. Bren wouldn't lie, but what could she say that didn't sound worse? That she didn't believe the same about O'Kane? That she didn't want Bren fighting with his boss over her? After last night, maybe she was stupid to assume he'd even bother. "I just meant...it makes sense. I can do it."

He watched her, expressionless. "It's not only a fact-finding mission. If bad shit is going down over there, Dallas wants me to clean it up."

Her fingers curled instinctively toward her palms, forming fists she didn't try to hide. Her heart was racing—with hope, maybe, though it was too unfamiliar for her to be sure. She chose her words carefully. "There's bad shit going down over there. Really, really bad shit."

Bren rolled to his feet and nodded. "Then I need your help."

The same words Wilson Trent had spoken to her more than four years ago. She'd believed them, and they'd been true enough. It was all the words that had come after that had been littered with lies and broken promises.

It wouldn't be the same this time. She wouldn't let it be. "When do we start?"

"Depends." A little of his humor returned, tilting his lips up in a smile. "How are you on a bike?"

The ruin of Sector Three was disorienting.

Back when the place had been a hub of electronics production, the manufacturing plants had been right in the middle of it all, with homes and shops built up around them. When Eden bombed the shit out of the sector, they aimed for dead center, intent on destroying those factories. The carnage radiated outward, damn near to the borders, like ripples that gradually faded.

Until you made the trip in reverse, straight into the heart of Three, and the destruction snuck up on you until you were surrounded by nothing but stacks of refuse and dirty rubble.

Not that anyone had put forth much effort to clean it up. Bren pulled his motorcycle to a stop in front of the squat warehouse Wilson Trent had used as his head-quarters. Even here, piles of debris had been pushed into alleys, forming blockades that might have been deliberate but looked haphazard. Haphazard—that was a good word for the whole damn place. Messy, disorganized.

Chaotic.

Not if Dallas had his way. He'd clean it up, all right, in ways the other sector leaders expected, and in others they'd never dreamed of.

Six pulled up next to him and cut the engine on her borrowed bike. She was all hard edges today, severe in borrowed leather, with her hair scraped back from her face in a braid so tight it looked painful.

Her gaze swept that ugly tangle of rubble before she said something really depressing. "Looks like someone's been trying to fix the joint up."

"That's just fucking sad." Bren slid from his bike and rubbed his neck. "Shit, where do we start?"

"With whoever's minding the shop today." She swung a leg over her bike and turned—not toward the warehouse, but to an equally rundown two-story building on the other side of what passed for the street. "They'll be in the bar."

Bren had heard stories of Trent's efforts to reproduce Dallas's success, but by all accounts the nameless strip club was a pale imitation of the Broken Circle. The tales were confirmed when he walked in. The place was deserted except for a handful of nearly naked women clustered around the bar, drinking. No customers, no music, just the bored dancers.

One looked up, her dull eyes barely focusing until Six stepped up at his side. Shock twisted her features as she leaned in to whisper to the other girls. One by one, heads swiveled while Six stood in silence, enduring their gawking stares.

The moment broke when the first girl slid from her stool and bolted through a beaded curtain without a word. The blonde who'd been seated next to her stubbed out her cigarette and rose to face them. "Fuck, woman, I heard you were dead."

"Damn near was." Six's voice was neutral, with the tiniest hint of a tremor. "Got lucky."

"I'll say." The blonde shifted her black-rimmed gaze to Bren and gave him an appreciative once-over that made Six tense. "You guys looking for a party?"

The denial was automatic, but it died on Bren's lips.

Six was wound tight, ready to explode. He wanted to drag her back out of there, away from everyone who remembered the things she wanted to forget. Wrap his arms around her and whisper until that tension melted.

Neither of them had that luxury. Today, they were both soldiers, and they had a job to do. Like it or not, these women had what they needed—information. The real shit, the kind that could matter.

He pulled some cash from his pocket, a single folded bill that he held up between his fingers. "Lead the way."

The blonde snatched the cash and held it up to the grimy light, and Six bit off a disapproving noise. "It's not painted paper, Katie. But you shouldn't be checking where we can see."

"Hey, life ain't as civilized as it used to be," the woman muttered as she tucked away the bill and turned. "You coming or not?"

As they followed the woman through the beaded curtain, Six clutched Bren's wrist and lowered her voice. "This is bullshit. Someone should be here. A bouncer, a guard. *Someone.*"

"I know." At least a bouncer would make sure people paid.

The room Katie led them to was about as subtle as Wilson Trent had been. Ten feet across, with a low couch facing two mismatched plush chairs and cracked, oddly sized mirrors on every wall. Katie nodded to the couch, pivoting her hips in a lazy circle. "Sit down and tell me what you want. Some stuff's extra." A wide, mean-edged smile. "Six knows all the prices."

She didn't rise to the bait, but Bren bared his teeth in a grin. "I'll double your money if you can the attitude."

The girl flicked a look at Six. Her expression quickly settled back into aloof boredom, but there was a hint of uncertainty in her eyes. "It's okay," Six murmured. "He wants information, and he'll pay you for it."

The uncertainty sharpened, but Katie didn't bolt.

"What kind of information?"

Bren pulled more money from his pocket. "I need to know who's been coming around lately, flashing a lot of cash."

"You mean besides you?" she asked dourly.

"Besides me."

She paused, her gaze riveted to the money in his hand, and wet her lips. "Girls with big mouths end up in gutters."

"I didn't," Six said softly. "Trent's gone, Katie."

"Sure, everyone keeps saying that, but for all you know—"

"He's *gone*," Six cut in. "I beat his fucking face in."

Silence. The two women watched each other, seemingly communicating volumes with the tiniest shifts in expression before Katie looked down at the floor. "The Griffen brothers. Those assholes who used to live in the basement of the old church? Rumor is they set up in Trent's old outpost on the border with Two, and they're moving something big. They're in here buying two women apiece every time I turn around."

It was a start. "Thank you." Bren leaned down to meet the girl's eyes as he pressed the money into her hand. "I didn't come here to make trouble. On the level."

Her fingers were thin, fragile and vulnerable as they curled around the wad of bills. "Suz went to find one of the guys," she muttered. "They'll be waiting out front. If you wanna avoid them, you should go out the back."

"Which guys?" Six prompted.

"Riff. Maybe Cain."

"I've got no problem with them," Bren said. They could get on board, or they could try their luck. Either way, it didn't matter to him.

Six pulled the door wide in silent invitation and closed it after Katie slipped away with her money clutched tight. "You've met Cain and Riff?"

"Dallas figured they'd play nice. They seemed more

decent than Trent's lieutenants, at any rate."

"They were outsiders." Six leaned against the door-frame and closed her eyes. "Riff'll probably fall in line if you don't ask him to beat on people weaker than he is. Kids, women, shit like that. But you can't trust him to disobey to your face. He'll agree like he's gonna follow orders, and then you won't see him again for six months. Cain's better. Smarter. He'll talk to you. Not to me, though."

"Why the hell not?"

She laughed hoarsely. "Because I've got tits. Cain is *civilized*. He doesn't let women do dirty work, and he doesn't think anyone else should, either. It's stupid, but his women are the safest girls in Three, so what do I know?"

"No wonder Lex wanted to stab him." Bren clasped Six's elbow and drew her close. "I don't care what he thinks. You want to talk, you talk."

She almost smiled for him. "All right."

The hallway was empty, and the girls had scattered from the main bar. Six followed him out onto the cracked pavement, where a lean man with a dark ponytail and an impressive array of tattoos was waiting for them. Riff.

His gaze snapped straight to Six, where it lingered with an odd mixture of relief and guilt. "You look good."

"Better than I was," she agreed, shoving her hands into her jacket pockets. Her right hand fisted—presumably around the brass knuckles he'd pressed on her—but she didn't pull them free. "You know Bren?"

"We've met." Riff nodded to him. "O'Kane checking up on us?"

"Not exactly." Bren eased over, edging his body in front of Six. "He sent us ahead of the cleanup crews to check out the situation."

Riff laughed darkly. "Situation is that everything's still fucked up. It's taking every goddamn thing we've got to keep O'Kane's grain coming in. We got control of that part of Trent's operation, but we had to let the rest go."

"Like the Griffens? Word is, they're running something big and swimming in cash. Doesn't exactly sound legit, does it?"

"No." Riff leaned to the side and tried to catch Six's eye. "Since when do you let a man talk for you?"

"He's not talking for me." Her voice was cool enough to freeze a man's balls. "I just got nothing to say to you, Riff. But I vouched for you, so if you fuck up and disappoint O'Kane, I'll kill you in your fucking bed."

The threat made him crack a small, bitter smile. "Some things never change."

"And some things do."

"Some things do," he echoed, glancing to Bren. "Weapons," he said, changing the subject abruptly. "Can't say the Griffens are up in it for sure, but that'd be my guess."

Everything could change in the time it would take to call in backup. Nervous amateurs didn't hold on to dangerous goods. The guns—if there were any—could vanish into the wrong hands, and Bren would be too late to stop it.

Bren reached behind him and smiled when Six slid her hand into his. "We're going to pay them a little visit, Riff. You're welcome to come along."

He didn't look enthused at the prospect, but he didn't look scared, either. "The kind of visit that's a warning? Or the kind that ends in dead bodies?"

"If anyone ends up dead, it won't be us. Best I can do."

Riff took a step back and shook his head. "Maybe some other time."

"Suit yourself."

5

T HE GRIFFEN BROTHERS only had one guard, and Bren choked him into unconsciousness.

Six had seen him fight in the cage before, but now she realized how much of that had been an illusion. A show. She'd never entirely believed the whispers that Bren let his opponents beat on him for his own reasons, but now she knew them for truth.

When it mattered, it wasn't a show. The guard didn't see Bren coming, and he didn't have a chance.

He held the man tight even after he went limp. Finally, after what seemed like an eternity, he let his quarry slump to the floor, then stripped off the man's belt and cinched it around his wrists. "They must not have planned on being gone long, to only leave one man behind."

Six thumbed the comforting edge of her brass knuckles. "Could be they don't have the manpower. They don't do teamwork so good in Three."

"No shit." Bren swept the room with his gaze, slow and intent, before heading toward a cloth-draped box in the corner. He peeled away the covering, but instead of prying open the top of the wooden crate, he traced the top edge lightly with his fingers. "They may not play well with others, but they're not entirely stupid."

"Booby-trapped?" Her gut told her Riff would have warned them if he'd known. He wasn't the kind of guy who led you into traps, just the kind who walked away to save his own skin if you got caught.

Funny how that hadn't seemed like a crime until she'd spent a couple months with the O'Kanes.

Bren teased out a wire from beneath the lid and followed it around to the back of crate. "See?" A small bundle nestled at the bottom, something that looked like beige putty wrapped with a Velcro strap. "Trent must have had quite the stash of C-4. Any idea where he got it all?"

"He had some hush-hush contact he was really excited about, but no one was allowed to know who," Six answered, her attention drawn to how deftly Bren's fingers handled the mess of wires and explosives. Her heart should have been pounding, but there was something so casual about Bren's movements. So laid-back.

Efficiency. Confidence. They could have been having this conversation over a car engine instead of a bomb.

Okay, maybe her heart was pounding. Just not with fear.

Bren pulled a knife from his pocket and flicked it open. "Stand back. Just in case."

She obeyed, but only to avoid distracting him. It gave her a better view anyway, the full impact of her quiet, deadly protector as his fingers slowly, surely dismantled death. She watched, hypnotized, as Bren carefully eased apart the tangle of twisted wires. He was utterly focused, so hard on the outside. But he handled the bomb the way he handled her, every movement gentle, every touch precise, as if he knew all the ways she could shatter into dangerous pieces.

Finally, he set aside the jumbled mess and opened the crate. "Random guns. Looks like they raided someone's collection." He looked up and caught her eyes. "Trent's?"

She crossed to his side, unprepared for the gut-punch of memory that slammed into her when Bren lifted an antique pistol.

Staring at the engraved stock, she could almost feel the rough scrape of wood grain against her cheek, the threatening press of Trent's thumb on her jaw as his fingers dug painfully into her scalp. How many times had he fucked her like that? It had been the beginning of the end. Weeks of perfunctory sex with her bent over his desk, refusing to wince at his rough handling as he crushed her face into the unpolished wood.

That was before she started fighting back, when she'd still been convinced his increasing cruelty was her fault, and she'd taken every indignity he dished out. Otherwise he wouldn't have dared to leave his prized antique pistol within reach, where she committed the engraving to memory and—as weeks stretched into months and his touch grew more sadistic—fantasized about grabbing the damn thing and shooting him in the balls.

She'd tried, in the end. And that was when he'd thrown her to the wolves.

Bren didn't touch her. But his voice interrupted her thoughts, wrapped around her like an embrace. "Six."

Her mouth was dry, and she curled her fingers until brass bit into her palm. The discomfort made it easier to focus, and she finally met Bren's eyes. "It's Trent's," she said, proud that her voice came out calm, if a little rusty.

"All of them?"

She chanced a quick glance into the crate before turning away. "Yeah, I think so."

"I'm sorry."

The only other furniture in the room was a make-shift table littered with empty beer bottles, cigarette butts, and a ratty deck of playing cards. Six flipped over a card and studied the glaring face of the king of clubs as if it were the most important thing in the world.

If she had to look at Bren's face, she wouldn't get the words out. "No one ever asks what Trent did to me."

"No."

Her throat ached, but she didn't worry about tears. She knew how to lock herself down before she did something as pathetic as cry. "Sometimes I wish you would. Just so I could pretend everyone doesn't already know."

"That's not why I haven't asked." His voice was closer. Lower. "Maybe...I don't want to know."

She slid her finger over the painted king's face before closing her eyes. "Wanna pretend I'm not all used up?"

"It's selfish, but not like that." He didn't touch her, but she felt his heat at her back. "Trent's already dead, but I'd want to bring him back just to shoot the mother-fucker all over again."

It was her responsibility to bridge the gap, to either reach out or invite his touch. But she couldn't—not here, in one of Trent's hovels, with the memories so close to the surface. Any comfort here would feel tainted, and she didn't want his hands coated in the grime of her past.

So she shook off her pain and turned, putting some space between them as she lifted the hand still clutching her brass knuckles. "If you did, I learned my lesson. No more busting up my own hands on some sorry bastard's face."

"Never again," he agreed softly.

God, the way he was looking at her, with no pity or disgust. *Intense*, with only the slightest softening around his eyes to save his features from harshness. There was something contemplative in his gaze, like he was imagining some future where bad things didn't happen to her.

As if he was silently begging her to imagine it too.

Or maybe she was dreaming the wordless promise, seeing what she wanted to see. It wouldn't be the first time. "Bren—"

He covered her lips with two fingers and cocked his head. Then he turned her with his hands on her shoulders, urging her toward a stack of boxes in the corner. "Hide. Hurry."

She swallowed her protest and hauled ass. She'd been in enough street brawls to know her place when the bad guys came armed.

The roar of bike engines grew louder as she ducked behind the boxes and eased a knife from her boot. Bren closed the crate of guns, leaned against it, and lit a cigarette.

The door crashed open, and Jimmy—the taller of the Griffen brothers—walked in. His scowl was evident even behind his thick mustache and unruly beard, and it deepened when he caught sight of the bound, unconscious man on the floor. "And just who the fuck are you?"

The answer was calm, unwavering. "I'm Bren."

"Is that supposed to mean something to me?"

"Probably not yet," Bren allowed. "But this sector belongs to Dallas O'Kane now, so you'll be seeing a lot of me."

Jimmy reached toward the small of his back, where a pistol butt stuck out of his pants. "Or maybe O'Kane's about to be seeing a lot less of you."

"Maybe." Bren curled his fingers around the edge of the wooden lid. "What's in the crate, Griffen?"

Six had to bite her lip on a swell of wholly inappropriate laughter as Jimmy flung one hand toward Bren, his entire body tensed in sudden, visceral terror. "Don't!"

Bren grinned. "Worried I'm gonna blow that mangy beard off your face?"

"You crazy motherfucker." The man's hand clenched behind his back, his knuckles brushing the gun. "You wouldn't—"

"Don't move!" a second voice screeched from just in-side the door. Will, the other brother.

For a split second, everything was silence. Then the sound of a shotgun round being chambered spurred Bren into a flurry of motion. He grabbed Jimmy by his beard and spun him around in front of him as the shot explod-ed, peppering the room.

The man screamed, and Bren shoved him forward before the other man could pump the slide and prepare another round. As the brothers collided, Bren snatched the shotgun and swung it around like a club, aiming for the knees.

The blow took them both down. Bren lifted the shot-gun, pressed a button near the stock, and worked the pump repeatedly. Unspent shells went flying, and he dropped the gun.

The clatter of it hitting the floor faded, leaving only the pained groans of the Griffen brothers—and Six's hoarse exhalation as she let out the breath she'd been holding.

A handful of seconds. That was all it had taken Bren to take down two armed men.

He was *magnificent*. And he was hers.

He plucked the pistol from the back of the taller brother's pants and unloaded it as well. "I'm not trying to smash you guys up. I'm not even trying to take your business. But shit doesn't go down here until you run it by O'Kane. That's how it's gonna be."

Jimmy hissed out a pained, irritated breath, but he was smarter than his brother. He held both hands away from his body in clear surrender. "We'll pay his cut. We ain't stupid."

"It's not just the money. He knows what you do be-fore you do it."

"Fuck, how are we s'posed to tell him? No one knows who the hell's in charge over here."

Bren shrugged. "For now, you talk to me."

Pride seemed to choke both brothers, but they were subdued enough that Six quietly sheathed her knife. By the time it was nestled safely in her boot again, Jimmy was forcing out an awkward-sounding request. "Can we move the rest of what we've got?"

"Get up." Bren waited until they complied before continuing. "Watch who you sell to, and keep it clean. That's what Dallas wants."

"And a cut," Will interjected with a sour frown.

The taller—*smarter*—man shut his brother up with an elbow in the rib. "What if we need to find you? How do we get in touch?"

"I'll be at the club." Bren didn't glance in Six's direction, but he drifted until he stood in front of the boxes. "Run on down there. Have a good time, and I'll be along."

His body blocked most of her view of the brothers as they groaned their way out the door, but there were worse sights than denim hugging Bren's ass and the strong expanse of his shoulders. Her body was still cranked, oblivious to the fact that danger had passed.

Or maybe it hadn't. Those two dumb fucks were about to disappear, and then it'd just be her and Bren and the taste of violence in the air, and maybe that was a thousand times more dangerous.

She really was a goddamn pervert.

The door slammed shut, but Bren didn't move. "Are you okay?"

His body looked as tense as hers felt liquid. She eased into the open, taking nearly silent steps that wouldn't fool him. She knew from experience that he heard everything. "I'm fine. You weren't gonna let anything happen to me."

"That doesn't make it pleasant for you."

"That bullshit was nothing. It used to be my life every damn day." Reaching out, she grazed the tense line of his shoulder. "Until you."

He whipped around, eyes blazing, and caught her wrist.

Bloodlust, pure and simple. The same unspent adrenaline burning her veins was surging through his, too. He was a predator who'd checked his killing blow and sent his prey scurrying toward freedom. It wasn't hard to read the need in his eyes, the longing to turn all that adrenaline toward a different kind of hunt, the kind that would end with her over the table, begging to come on his cock.

She could stop it in a heartbeat, with fear or hesitation or even a whispered word. But the words that slipped past her suddenly numb lips weren't hesitant. "Watching you beat people down gets me hot. It makes me wet."

His eyes darkened, and he slid his other hand into her hair. "Here? With bullets and casings all over the floor?"

She traced a hand down to palm his growing erection. "This is what I'm used to. Screwing in a dirty warehouse after someone has tried to kill me. A safe bed's a little intimidating."

A quick breath escaped him, along with a soft noise that sounded like a swallowed groan. Then he backed her against the wall and lifted her arms over her head. "Keep them there."

A clear order. Before she had a chance to either agree or argue, he licked her lower lip. Nothing more obscene than that, except that it took forever for him to trace his tongue from one side of her lip to the other, and she was panting by the time he ran his hands down her sides to tease under the hem of her shirt.

He left them there, his fingers warm on the bare skin of her waist, as he tilted his head, nudged her lips apart, and kept licking. Deeper. Wetter. He was exploring her, tasting her, priming her for his touch in a way that made her squirm.

Fucking was comprehensible. Fucking was neat and fast and clean, even when it was messy. This was some-thing else.

Seduction.

Then he kissed her. Really *kissed* her, their lips fused and his tongue gliding over hers, and she couldn't keep her arms helplessly above her head. Not when need had turned so frantic, so sharp.

She grabbed the back of his head, terrified that he'd try to pull away and rob her of the way her body pulsed with each clash of tongue. She was hungry, starving for this feeling, the giddy wanting she hadn't felt in years.

His hands tightened, relaxed. Moved to the button on her borrowed leather pants.

Nervous tension sizzled up her spine, the full weight of what she was about to do smashing down hard on its heels. She was using Bren, pouncing on this fracture in his self-control, dragging him down into the dirt with her. He'd probably feel bad for fucking her like this, against a rough wall in the rubble of Sector Three. He still thought she deserved something better. Softer.

Poor bastard. She barely deserved this.

It wouldn't stop her from taking it, though. His fin-gertips brushed her bare abdomen, and she fought a groan as she groped for his belt buckle. The sooner he was in her, the sooner she could stop thinking about anything but sex and how good he felt, and *God*, she knew it'd be good, so good she might even get off after-wards—

He closed his fingers on her wrists and held her gaze as he guided her arms back up against the wall. "Keep them there," he said again, whisper-soft, then jerked down her zipper and slipped his hand into her pants.

Warm, blunt fingers slid over her pussy, and the shock of it would have driven her head back if she could have looked away. No one had ever watched her like this before, not this close, not with one hand in her pants, stroking and parting, coaxing throbbing pleasure to life.

"Shh." The gentle, questing pressure of his fingers never wavered, even as he leaned in to nuzzle her cheek. "Let me."

That was when she realized he wasn't going to fuck her.

Whimpering, she closed her eyes and twisted her head, distracted by the heat of his breath on her skin. "What the hell, Donnelly, just get in me."

"Yes, ma'am." He shifted her higher, the muscles in his arm flexing against her stomach. He cupped her pussy, and he exhaled against her cheek as he curled two fingers inside her.

"*Bren—*" She couldn't get enough air to say more. All her stupid obsession with the strength and grace and size of his hands, and she'd never imagined this, how huge his fingers would feel, sparking a stretching discomfort only to soothe it with gentle friction.

"Don't." He pressed deeper, the heel of his hand rocking against her clit. "Don't try to stop me."

She'd never let another person get her off. Hell, most of the time she faked it for their benefit, taking the quiet comfort of physical closeness and saving the vulnerability of release for when she was alone. Even when she came riding a man's dick, it was her fingers on her clit getting the job done, her choice to get there or not.

Even if she wanted to come for Bren, she didn't know if she could. Her arms trembled with tension as she fisted her hands and fought the urge to reach for him. The warmth between her thighs was still building, still shocking her with peaks that curled her toes and quiet lulls that let her breathe.

It wasn't desperate, not yet, but she could taste the edge coming—and knew frustration would inevitably follow. "I could help," she offered shakily as her hips jerked without her permission, slave to the rhythm of his thrusting fingers.

His teeth closed in a warning nip at the corner of her mouth.

Groaning, she squeezed her eyes shut and dropped both hands to his shoulders, clutching at him as if that could ground her, but the hard flex of muscle as he rocked his hand only made it worse. Closing her eyes didn't even help, because she could see him painted across the backs of her eyelids, fierce and determined and doomed to disappointment when she couldn't relax enough to give him what he clearly wanted.

His fingers slowed. "Breathe."

She didn't realize she hadn't been, but a whimper rushed out of her as she trembled through a quick exhalation. "I'm trying."

"Then don't." He was panting now, his breath blowing hot on her cheek. "Just feel it." He twisted his wrist, and his fingers inside her, until his thumb brushed her clit in a slick circle.

A hoarse cry rose in her throat, and she pressed her open mouth to his skin to muffle it. But that only brought the taste of him into her, and she wanted so much more because she'd been so, so wrong. Nothing about Sector Three could dirty him. He'd kick aside the rubble and build something beautiful out of it.

Her hips twitched, writhing beyond her control as he brought her higher. More slowly this time, pumping his fingers with the rhythm of her body and adding those dizzying touches to her clit when her nails dug into his shoulders. The tortured rasp of his breath seized her chest tight, a wordless reminder of his self-control even as he stripped hers away.

She was safe. Every second he denied himself to focus on her branded that truth more deeply into her flesh, until her limbs were liquid and she barely felt them as she lifted her hands back above her head, opened her eyes, and whispered his name.

He held her gaze, his eyes locked with hers. "I'm going to do this again," he rasped. "Lay you out where there isn't any damn part of you I can't taste. That's what I want. You."

She came. It could have been the words or the final commanding flick of his thumb—she didn't know and didn't care. The orgasm hit her in stages, as if sheer *relief* traveled the fastest, so fast she was panting with it by the time the pleasure hit her and seized her lungs.

She couldn't cry out. She couldn't look away. She could only come, helpless for terrifying moments as her body contracted around Bren's broad fingers and she couldn't think past how good he felt inside her.

Bren groaned, the sound muffled as he covered her mouth with his. She'd never been kissed like this, so hungry and raw, but she couldn't fall into it because his fingers were still moving, stroking, coaxing little aftershocks of sensation back to roaring life, and she finally had to bite his lower lip with a groan. "Too much," she whispered. "I can't—"

His arm shook, but after a moment, he stopped and pulled his hand away. He kept his mouth on hers, open and hot. "You can. Someday, you will."

A threat wrapped in seductive promise, and she shivered. "Why? Why did you—?" Her words were clumsy, tripping over her tongue. "You could have fucked me. I wanted it, I promise."

"I know." He ground the length of his erection against her hip.

So needy, but he wasn't demanding now, which made it easier to offer. "Tell me what you want."

He shook his head and smoothed her hair back from her forehead. "We have to go."

It didn't make any fucking sense, not with his dick pressed against her, so hard she almost hurt in sympathy. And yet he'd wasted all those minutes getting her off when he could have been pounding out his own frustration.

He could be pounding it out now, instead of tucking the tangled strands of her hair behind her ears with a gentleness that made her legs wobble again. "I think you're a little crazy, Bren."

He chuckled, barely a laugh at all, but it still crinkled his eyes at the corners. "I thought you figured that out the night you met me."

Laughing, she let her forehead drop to rest against his chin. "You were the only one who made any sense at all. And it was nice to have someone treat me like a threat again."

"The very best kind."

Her lips stayed curved into a smile. "The kind you have to gag? And really, Donnelly, who goes around prepared to gag someone?"

"When you run with the O'Kanes, it's best to be prepared for anything."

Maybe he'd been ready for anything, but nothing could have prepared her for this moment in a broken-down warehouse, reminders of Trent scattered across the floor but stripped of their power as her body hummed in remembered pleasure and her heart beat its way into her throat.

Nothing could have prepared her for him.

Bren had never seen a sorrier group of people in his life.

He nodded to the men clustered around one end of the bar. Their rough clothes suggested dirty work, but not what kind. "What about them?"

Six barely glanced up from the whetstone she was using to sharpen her boot knife. "That's Ed's crew. They scavenge, mostly. If you're suicidal, you can tunnel under some of the ruins on the edge of the blast zone and get lucky. Or dead. Ed's brother and half their guys died in a cave-in a couple years back, but he keeps trying."

"Interesting." Ed could probably get his hands on some damn good shit—if he managed to stay alive. "Anyone else I should know about?"

"The blonde on stage?" She nodded toward the thin rectangular block that thrust out between the tables. Calling it a stage was generous, but it had a pole on one end that was currently occupied by a nervous-looking dancer dodging gropes. She was young, with bright pink stripes standing out in her platinum ponytail, and Six watched her twist around the pole before continuing. "She should be managing this place. She's got some kinda perfect memory or something, and she can do math in her head. Any math. I kept telling Trent to let her handle the paperwork, but he said tits like that were wasted anywhere but the stage."

"He would say something like that." The man had had no appreciation for proper resource appropriation.

Six shifted, her thigh pressing against his. "He was stupid. This sector's a mess, but it doesn't have to be as bad as it is. He had to crush anyone successful before they could threaten him, though."

Which meant the place had always been limited by Trent's dubious abilities. "Who else?"

Her gaze drifted over the crowd before snagging on the table straight across from them, one equally hidden in shadows. "Word must have traveled," she said quietly. "Scarlet's here."

All Bren caught was a flash of white hair, the glint of metal. "Scarlet?"

Six gripped the edge of the table. "Riff plays in her band, so he pretty much answers to her. She's got a lot of pull."

"Then why wasn't she at the meeting with Dallas?"

"Didn't see the point. She's not big on answering to men." Six exhaled and resumed her slow strokes across the whetstone. "And I still didn't know Dallas that well. I wasn't sure if he'd have to take her down a few pegs, just to prove he could."

"Yeah." Except Lex probably wouldn't have ended up stabbing tables at the Broken Circle if a woman had accompanied the men. "How does Cain feel about her? He seems to be firmly rooted in some fairly archaic notion of proper gender roles."

"Cain..." Six's jaw clenched. "Honestly, I don't fucking know. But considering what he thinks about me, it can't be good."

"Well, he'll have to wise up if he wants to make it in this brave new world." Bren rose and nodded to the other table. "Shall we?"

The white hair turned out to be a bleach job, pale bangs flowing over the rest of Scarlet's deep black hair. A plume of smoke curled up from her lips, and she watched their approach silently.

Bren nodded to an empty chair. "May I?"

"Nice manners." She shrugged one shoulder. "What's up, Six?"

"Scarlet." Six spun a chair and straddled it, folding her arms across the back. "How's the band?"

"Not practicing for shit, not lately. Things are in a shambles." She eyed Bren. "I guess you're here to fix that, huh?"

"Depends."

"On?"

He mimicked her one-shouldered shrug. "If I can figure out where to start."

"He's solid," Six said, her voice raw. "I know my word doesn't go far, but give him a chance."

The woman's gaze hardened, but her words were gentle. "You sure?"

"Give him a chance."

"I am." Scarlet gestured to the table. "What does this look like? We're talking."

Six's lips twitched. "Yeah? Well, he's about as talkative as you are. But since you both stick to saying what's important without any bullshit, you'll get along fine."

"Uh-huh." Scarlet snuffed out her cigarette. "If you two promise not to make life harder for folks around here, I'll make sure you get the information you need. *All* of it."

"All right." Bren leaned forward. "Who backed Trent's play to blow Dallas O'Kane off the map?"

She shook her head. "That, I can't help you with. Trent took the secret to his grave—if he ever knew at all."

An anonymous partner. It made a twisted sort of sense. A man like Wilson Trent might not have considered that anyone who wouldn't reveal his identity had his—or her—reasons. He would have taken the money and counted himself lucky, not convenient. He never would have wondered if maybe he was meant to take the fall.

"He got reckless near the end." Six rested her chin on her folded arms. "Overconfident. A couple of them wanted him to kill me outright, but he couldn't resist shoving my face in how worthless I was one last time."

He's dead. A reminder, one Bren needed. *Dead.* "So we trace the money and the explosives. Everything leaves a trail."

Scarlet opened her mouth only to close it again. After a long moment, she lit another cigarette. "There might be a way. If I can find him."

Six straightened. "You mean Noah? Is he still around?"

"I said *if,* didn't I? Who the hell knows with that crazy bastard."

Bren reached for Six's hand. "Who's Noah?"

"He's this genius out of Five or Six, no one's really sure." Her fingers curled around his, warm and strong, and she smiled. "Scarlet's right. He's crazy, but he's also some sort of tech genius. He can get into Eden's systems and find or change things."

"Where does he live?"

"Who knows? Sometimes he surfaces to meet people for jobs. Otherwise, he makes them crawl underground to him, but never in the same place twice." Six glanced at Scarlet. "If we put it out there that I want to talk to him, he might show up. We got on okay."

"I'll shake some trees," the woman allowed. "See if he falls out. Where will you two be?"

"Home," Bren told her shortly. "Time to report back to Dallas, see what he wants to do next."

"Riff knows where to find us," Six added as she rose. "You should be proud, by the way. He's the only one who hasn't opened his mouth and said something stupid to one of O'Kane's women."

Scarlet smiled. "He knows better."

Bren laid his hand on Six's elbow as they headed for the door. "Do you need to stick around here tonight?"

"In Three?" She shook her head. "No, I want to go...back. Unless you're staying."

If they left immediately, they'd make it back in time to give Dallas his report before morning. "You can ride with me if you'd feel safer."

She stopped next to his bike and pivoted to stare up at him, her eyes considering as she studied his face. "Won't that make it harder for you to maneuver?"

He could handle the machine in his sleep, so the only danger was to the remaining bike. If it got lifted, Dallas would be pissed, but Bren figured it'd be worth it.

For a few minutes in that warehouse, Six had been open to him, soft and trusting in a way that kicked off a chain reaction of protective instinct. He'd destroy anything or anyone that hurt her, but *her*—

Gentle. Careful.

He wanted it again, the feeling that she would gladly put her body in his hands because she knew it'd be all right. This time, it wasn't about sex. It was about her faith in him, her confidence that he wouldn't let anything bad happen to her. Not now, not ever.

"Ride with me." He pulled her closer and kissed the top of her head. "I can handle the bike."

"Okay." She hugged him, squeezing too tight and then springing away after a nervous moment. Still awkward and uncertain, but she made up for it once she was behind him on the bike. She wrapped herself around him, chest tight to his back, thighs riding alongside his hips.

"Hold on," he murmured, then revved the engine.

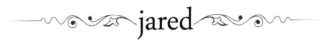

jared

THREE O'CLOCK IN the morning was too damn early—or too damn late—for high-pitched, squawking giggles.

Apparently, no one had ever informed the curvy blonde hanging off Ace's arm. Jared sighed and pushed the door wide. "Come in and introduce me to your friends."

Ace grinned and prowled inside, dragging the woman with him and leaving the other man to trail behind them like a silent shadow. "Jared, this is Sally—"

"*Susi*," the blonde squealed, smacking Ace's shoulder with a delicately beaded clutch that could only have come from Eden. She reeked of the city, of *money*, an adventurous socialite slumming on the arm of a dangerous sector gangster.

Not Ace's usual type, so it was no surprise when he waved a hand at Jared. "Susi, then. Susi, meet the man of your dreams."

Terrific. Jared forced a smile and kissed the back of her hand. "I don't suppose you have a driver waiting for you downstairs, do you, love?"

She beamed up at him, bright and breathless and so very, very drunk. "Yes. Would you like to go for a ride?"

She had a pleasant face and curves that wouldn't quit. Entertaining her wouldn't be a hardship—if she were sober enough to appreciate him. "Another time." He pulled a card from his back pocket and pressed it into her hand. "Saturday night at seven?"

Within minutes, he had her tucked safely into her vehicle, his card still clutched in her hand. It hadn't taken long, but he still returned to find that Ace had kicked off his boots and was rifling through his stash of liquor. "Sorry, brother. It was cold, and the only way she'd give us a ride was if I promised to introduce her to you."

"I see," Jared said absently. His attention was on Ace's other companion, who sat at the far end of the couch, silent and decidedly less bubbly than Susi had been. "Hello."

"That's Cruz. He's one of the new— Aha!" Surfacing with the whiskey in hand, Ace threw himself back down on the couch and didn't quite look at Jared. "Cruz just took ink, but he's from the city. Bren's friend. Cruz, this handsome bastard is Jared. If you ever met a rich lady in Eden who looked sexually satisfied, it was probably thanks to him."

Jesus, maybe Ace was drunker than he'd thought. "The former MP?" Jared asked.

"That's me," Cruz said, offering him a small smile. "Nice to meet you."

"And you, as well." Jared sank into his favorite chair and eyed the two men on his sofa. Last he'd heard, Cruz had snaked Rachel right out from under Ace's nose. So either his friend was playing one hell of a dangerous game, making nice with a sexual rival...

Or things were even more complicated than they seemed.

Ace twisted open the whiskey and took a swig before offering it to Cruz. "I've been showing Cruz around the sector, now that we're partnered up. I took him to one of Gia's parties tonight, and she wanted to eat him right up."

The larger man shifted uncomfortably, the liquor bottle clasped loosely in his hands. "She was very...friendly."

"She was sizing him up for her harem, is what she was doing." Ace nudged Cruz with one foot. "Shoulda seen her pout over Dallas getting to him first."

"I believe it." The man was huge and built, the way Gia liked. "Were you two working security, or merely out for the night?"

"Purely recreational. I was *trying* to get this sorry bastard laid—"

Cruz groaned and dropped his head forward.

"—but he's like that old fairy tale. You know, the one with all the bears. This girl's too nice, this one's not nice enough. And I'm over here telling him that all you need to do is get your clothes off, and it doesn't matter where your dick ends up. As long as everyone's having fun, it's always just right."

The longer they sat there, the more surreal it all got. Jared cleared his throat. "What happened to the bed Goldilocks here *was* sleeping in?"

Cruz blindly shoved the bottle back into Ace's hands and rose. "Can he stay here? I didn't want to leave him alone, not this drunk, but I need to get back."

Jared's first instinct was to apologize, but he bit it back. Better for him to leave than to hear difficult words meant only for Ace's ears. "I'll take care of him. Be safe on the streets."

Cruz leaned down to pat Ace's shoulder awkwardly. "Enjoy the hangover, buddy."

"O'Kanes don't get hung over," Ace replied grandly, but he let Cruz leave without protest, despite his earlier complaints about the chilly weather.

The first thing Jared did was reclaim the bottle. "What are you doing, man?"

"I *was* drinking." Ace sighed and twisted, swinging his legs up onto the couch. "It's not what it looks like. I swear."

"I don't even know what it looks like, so you may as well enlighten me."

Ace stared broodingly at his feet for a solid minute. "Rachel dumped him," he said finally. "I don't know why. He's fucking stupid over her."

Jared had seen the woman look at Ace, her dark eyes covetous and hungry. "Maybe she dumped him for you."

The weirdest part was that Ace didn't even argue. "Maybe. Don't know if that'd be a good thing."

"What, you don't want her anymore?"

Ace shot him a glare—and a middle finger. "Yup, you figured me out. Got it out of my system. Clear skies, bring on the pussy."

Defensiveness and irritation—Jared could work with that. "Hey, I figured there must be some reason you were out drinking with the ex instead of making your move. It's not like you."

"He fought for her."

So had Ace, in his own way. He'd watched Rachel, held back when he wasn't sure what to give her or how. "He's a great guy, big deal. You are, too."

"You're not listening." Ace sat up and leaned forward, resting his elbows on his knees. "She dumped him on his ass, and he still risked everything to drag me into the cage. Not to win her. To *protect* her."

No hint of humor or denial colored his words, just a grim certainty that shadowed his eyes. He wasn't joking around, and he wasn't playing a game.

He was stepping aside.

Jared took a swig from the bottle. "What's your plan? You turn him into the perfect lover, shove them together, and...what? You go back to your cold bed alone and think about what a good, noble thing you did?"

"Stop twisting shit," Ace snapped. "I may not have turned out as fancy as you and Gia, but I got all the same training. You can't play me."

"I don't have to," Jared shot back. "Because I've known you for years, since way before Ace ever existed. And I know all Alexander Santana's secrets."

"Yeah? Well, it goes both ways. Look me in the eyes and tell me you know how to love someone. Not for a few hours or a night. Not for a *gig*. Tell me you know how to really fucking love someone."

He thought of Susi the squealer, and about the woman who'd crawled out of his bed less than an hour before Susi's unceremonious, drunken arrival. He cared about them, all of them, exactly as much as he needed to.

No more.

"I don't," he admitted softly. "But you always were a better person than me. You just have to see it."

Ace reclaimed the whiskey and slumped back. "It doesn't matter. It's not like I have some big fucking plan. Maybe I was thinking that right after the fight, but the truth is stupider. He's...kind of fun."

Jared's breath escaped him on an unexpected laugh. "Fun? You're tragically drunk."

"Nothing tragic about being drunk on O'Kane liquor." But Ace wasn't smiling. He was staring at the bottle, his dark eyes tired. "I gave her a tattoo."

His pain was palpable. Pervasive. "Of what?" Jared asked gently. "More flowers?"

Ace shook his head. "I could have had her. She was still with him, but when she's under the needles... Some people like the adrenaline, but she goes *beyond*."

She liked pain, the kind that came from the buzz of the needle. Maybe that was why Ace couldn't quite shake this obsession, despite his better judgment. "Plenty of women are like that. You can find another one."

"I *have* other women like that. Doesn't help. Beating the Eden out of Cruz so he can be her prince won't help either. You know what'll help?"

Sobering up. A second chance. Another drink. "What?"

"Time, brother. We all keep smashing into each other until we fit right. All of us, even Rachel and Cruz. Even me. Even you."

There was no room to argue with such nihilistic as-surance, nothing to do but nod as Jared snagged a clean glass from the cabinet beside his chair. "Time heals everything," he agreed.

Even me.

6

S HE'D CREPT OUT of a lot of men's beds over the years. Now Six was trying to creep into one.

Not that there was any creeping with Bren. His door was locked, forcing her to wait, barefoot and nervous, praying none of the other doors in the hallway would pop open before he answered her hesitant knock.

The door opened a crack before swinging wide. "Six?"

Her boots usually made her taller. Without them, she was left staring straight at his bare chest, not to mention those damn shoulders she couldn't stop lusting after. For once, she didn't resent the butterflies in her stomach or the quickening of her pulse as she lifted her gaze to his. "My turn."

He stilled, and he exhaled on a slow hiss. "Is that so?"

"Yeah." She inched forward, close enough for her breath to skate across his skin, close enough to feel his warmth even through her tank top. Her survival instincts kicked in, warning her to back away, to meet him on neutral territory. But she'd ignored that warning already, the moment she'd rolled from her sleepless bed prompted by nothing more than vague yearning.

She didn't know why she was here or what the hell she was doing, but she was tired of resisting temptation. So she leaned in, pressed her lips to one of his beautifully formed shoulders, and silently begged him to drag her into his domain.

Bren groaned and lifted her closer with one hand on her ass. Then he stepped back, taking her with him, and kicked the door shut.

Sweet darkness enclosed them both. She moaned and wrapped her arms and legs around him, clinging as she kissed the parts of him she could reach—his throat, his neck, the stubbled line of his jaw.

It was safe to be desperate in the darkness, because no one could see how weak her desire had left her. "Let me," she whispered, and God, she was practically begging. She hated herself for it, even as she used the leverage of her legs around his body to rub her hips against his. "Let me get you off."

Her back hit the wall, and Bren lowered her feet to the floor. "With your hands or your mouth?"

His voice was rough already. She wanted it raw, and she knew the power of giving a man his dirty fantasy. That was the reason she slid to her knees—not because she could almost taste him on her tongue. "Both."

Bren leaned forward with a growl. Just enough light filtered under the closed door for her to admire the flex of his arms and shoulders as he braced his hands against the wall. "Do it."

His loose pants rode low on his hips. She traced her fingertips above the waistband, reveling in the way his muscles tensed under her touch. This had to be the way the O'Kane women felt when they were on their knees, smug and drunk on the power of watching big tough men pretend they were issuing orders instead of begging.

She wouldn't make him beg. Holding her breath, she hooked her fingers over the top edge of his pants and eased them down just far enough to free his erection. He was hard enough to make her heart pound, but metal glinting in the dim light caught her attention. She wrapped one hand around the base of his cock and, ignoring his sharp breath, traced her other up until her fingers reached the crown.

Bren had his cock pierced. Twice.

He laid his hand over hers and squeezed her fingers even tighter around his shaft. "Watch your teeth," he whispered. "Some people don't like how the metal feels on them."

She couldn't help herself. She touched the smooth, curved surface of one barbell and glanced up at him. "Do they like how it feels other places?"

His chest rumbled. "You mean will it make you come harder when I fuck you?"

The jewelry was warm from his skin, but it still felt cool on her tongue as she traced the shape of it, teasing them both. "Will it? Dicks aren't the part of fucking that makes me come."

"We'll see, won't we?"

Nothing ambiguous there. Brendan Donnelly was going to fuck her. He'd probably take his sweet time about it, but the dick straining under her hand would be inside her, filling her more than his fingers ever could, and she was starting to think she'd like it way too much.

Hell, she already did. She liked tasting him like this, circling the crown of his cock in unhurried licks, indulging herself by exploring the intriguing contours the piercing added. She knew how to suck a guy off hard and fast, but as badly as she wanted to see him come, there was something to be said for watching his muscles jump as he groaned and leaned his head against the wall above her.

Then he slipped his fingers into her hair, holding her head still, captive, as he flexed his hips and thrust into her mouth.

Six stiffened before she could stop herself, caught between a dizzying rush of arousal and the instinct to fight his grip on her hair. But it was all so *gentle*, his hands warm and firm, caging without hurting, and the glide of his shaft between her lips, over her tongue... God, it was twisted, perverse, the way Bren could make her helpless and still make it hot.

He soothed her trembling with a soft noise. "Only what you want, sweetness. I swear it."

She believed him. Believed him enough to relax and let her hand fall away from his shaft. The least trusting part of her braced for him to shove deep enough to choke, but he pulled back instead, then slowly thrust forward again.

That was as much as he gave her. Shallow thrusts in and out, with pauses to let her suck, pauses to let her tongue his piercings. She almost made him beg for it, but there was something intoxicating about granting his silent demands. Something desperately illicit, too, about kneeling in the darkness, the only sounds their heavy breathing and his rasping groans punctuated by the lewd music of his cock working in and out of her mouth.

Another thrust, one he held for longer before retreating. "Harder. Show me what you want."

She didn't even know anymore. She'd envisioned pushing him back on the bed and straddling his legs, working him with her hands and mouth until he couldn't help but come. Easy and quick, with her in control, but maybe that had only been the lie she told herself to get out the door.

This was just as good. This was *better*.

He was poised with the blunt tip of his erection brushing her lips, turning every one of her whispered words into a caress. "I want to know what happens next."

The hand in her hair clenched tight. "Then stand up."

She did, lifting her arms when his hands slid under her shirt and shoved it up. She was so turned on she was panting, gasping for air as he tore the cotton over her head.

He stared down at her, cupping her breasts with a satisfied growl. "I want you like this. Ready for my mouth."

Looking down gave her the dizzy visual of her breasts penned by his large hands, as if the feel of work-roughened fingertips against sensitive flesh wasn't intense enough.

She opened her mouth to speak, but he cut off her words with a twist of his wrist, catching one nipple between his fingers and pinching it hard enough to drive her shoulders back against the wall as pain and pleasure smashed into one another.

He soothed her nipple with a slow lick, the warmth of it weakening her knees. Fighting the urge to melt, she dug her fingernails into his shoulders. "This is cheating. It's my turn to get you off."

He laughed, hot breath against wet skin. "You will."

Yeah—when he was good and ready to let her. "You're a controlling bastard, you know that?"

"Don't ever doubt it." He looked up at her, his gaze serious. "I like pain, not submission. I'm in charge, sweetness, or it won't work."

Just like that, all of the things they hadn't said were *real*, taking up the space between them until the air felt heavy. "I know," she whispered, but that wasn't enough. She licked her lips and let her hands relax on his shoulders. "I'm not as careful with my body as I should be, maybe, but it's hard to let it matter when you can't control what people do to it."

"Yes, it is."

No judgment, and that helped. "It means it's not my

fault, you know? It's not my fault if they hurt my body. Not my fault I couldn't stop them."

He tipped her face up with his fingers under her chin. "You're safe here. With me."

If she hadn't known that in her bones, she never would have come to his door. There was probably a seductive way to say what she really meant, something suggestive and sexy that'd make his dick harder, but she didn't like the word *submission* and didn't know another one.

So she blurted out the truth, awkward and raw. "You can have my body. You'll take better care of it than I ever have."

He nodded and lowered his mouth to her breasts again. This time, he didn't stop with licking her nipples, but drew his tongue in long, wet paths over her skin. Each one tugged low in her belly, but that wasn't what had her moaning in confused relief.

Her limbs were light. Her body was floating. A weight she hadn't recognized she'd been carrying was gone, banished by his silent acceptance.

For one night, she didn't have to fight or fail. She could just feel.

And they were moving. She realized it when he urged her down with one hand on her shoulder, and she wound up sitting on the edge of his bed, with him standing in front of her. She'd only have to dip her head to draw his cock between her lips again, but she didn't move. She barely breathed.

And then she couldn't, because he shifted that half-step closer, cupped her breasts, and thrust his cock between them.

She choked back a startled noise and clutched at the rumpled blankets, but her body knew what it wanted. She was arching her back before she realized it, pressing up into his touch, offering herself to him like she only wanted to be used.

"Tilt your head up." His voice had gone harsh. "Your mouth—"

The rasp in his voice did her in. It wasn't the lazy boredom of a jackass who wanted a warm place to stick his dick. It was edgy. Personal. She parted her lips and positioned them, and she didn't feel used at all when he fucked up between her breasts and pushed into her mouth.

He shuddered and did it again, faster this time. "What part of this do you like?"

"I like the way—" He cut her off with another thrust, the slippery head of his cock gliding over her tongue. So she answered without words, wrapping her lips tight and sucking while she licked the underside of his crown, and *like* wasn't strong enough for how she felt when he groaned and slipped one hand up to cup the back of her head.

"Harder." His fingers clenched in her hair. "Suck it harder."

She'd suck him all night if it meant listening to careful, perfectly controlled Brendan Donnelly rasp out crude commands that made his voice shake. Each groan gave her power, even as it hollowed her out. She was wet and aching, half hoping he'd put his fingers in her and get her off.

It'd give her an excuse to come back tomorrow night and get on her knees again.

He watched her, his breathing quick and unsteady. "If I come on your tongue, will you come on mine? Let me taste you?"

She didn't know if she'd be able to get off with his head between her thighs. She'd be exposed, so helplessly on display that even the thought kindled nervous fear.

But she hadn't thought she'd come from his fingers, either. So she held his gaze and nodded, the movement sliding her lips up and down his shaft.

He plunged deep then—deep enough to choke her—

but drew back immediately, as if he hadn't meant to do it at all. A crack in his precise control, and she slipped into it, tried to coax it wider by chasing his cock, struggling against his grip in her hair to take more of him.

Bren gave in, driving into her mouth, far enough to bump the back of her throat but not choke her. Over and over, until his hands were shaking and a sheen of sweat covered his chest, his forehead.

So close, but still restrained. She freed one hand from the tangle of bed sheets and slid it up his hip, over tense muscles. He liked pain, so she gave him a taste of it, raking her nails down his chest with almost enough pressure to break the skin.

"*Fuck*, yes." He covered her hand with his, forcing her nails harder against his flesh. His eyes lost focus, and his hips jerked. "Hurt me."

She did, even if *hurt* seemed like the wrong word for something that dragged a groan of pleasure from him. Just like *pain* was the wrong word for the sensation of his fingers tightening in her hair, pulling until her eyes watered. His other hand pressed tight over hers, urging her to pierce his skin.

Her next scratch left four furrows across his chest. He choked out her name and drove deep, clutching the back of her head with sharp desperation. One heartbeat, two—then he came with a groan and a shudder, his cock pulsing on her tongue.

He was so deep she didn't need to swallow, so deep she couldn't breathe. Panic clawed at her, but she closed her eyes and clung to him. Trusting him wasn't easy, not yet, but there was enough of it there to keep her from struggling against his grip.

He didn't release her when he stilled. He was as controlling as ever, hauling her head back by her hair as he lifted her hand to his mouth for a lingering kiss.

The ache inside her exploded into something desperate and vulnerable, but she didn't know how to ask for relief. She wasn't supposed to need it, because letting him fuck her mouth wasn't supposed to leave her wet and squirming restlessly on his bed.

And it hadn't, not really. But getting him off had, and opening her eyes to meet his lazy, satisfied gaze only intensified the ache.

He held on to her hair as he dropped to his knees, running his fingers through the strands all the way to the ends, and he tickled them over her nipples with a grin. "Are you wet? The truth."

She swallowed, but her voice still came out hoarse. "Yes."

He dragged her pants—and her underwear—down her legs, stripping her completely bare in one smooth movement. "How wet?"

Smug fucking bastard. He had to know she was panting for him, but she wasn't going to admit it *twice*. She pressed her knees together and steadied her voice. "Guess you'll have to find out, huh?"

"Guess so," he agreed easily—but there was nothing easy about his iron hands on her legs, urging them apart. Nothing easy about him cupping his hands behind her knees and pushing them up, up, until her back hit the bed.

She was wide open, exposed.

It was too much.

Nervous anticipation veered straight toward panic, and she closed her eyes and gripped the blankets, fighting the urge to twist away.

"Shh." He didn't release her, only brushed a kiss across the back of one thigh. "Remember. Nothing you don't want."

She hadn't whispered a word of protest, but he still knew. He always knew, and the unfairness of it all made her laugh shakily. "I don't know what I want. And half the stuff I *do* know scares the hell out of me."

"Then trust me, if you can."

"I do. It's just..."

Another kiss, to the inside of her calf. "What?"

How to describe the feeling of floating in the darkness, cut off from anything familiar, exposed and vulnerable with nothing but the touch of his hands and the occasional brush of his lips to ground her? "I'm lost."

"Do I scare you?"

"No." She freed one hand and slid it into his short hair, her nails scoring his scalp. She wanted to drag him up, feel him crushing her into the bed, cutting off the world. "You just feel so far away."

His tongue grazed her exposed clit, but only for an electric moment. He kept moving, up and over her, until he was stretched out, his elbows on either side of her head. "Better?"

His weight settled on her, familiar and not, because it was skin on skin with a bed at her back. But she knew how it felt to be pinned by him, to have him between her thighs.

Safe.

The tension melted out of her body, muscle by muscle, even as instinct had her studying the set of his jaw and the angle of his brow, searching for evidence of irritation or impatience. "Better."

"Mmm." He licked her jawline, up to the spot beneath her ear.

She shuddered and squirmed, rubbing her hips against his. "I'm not scared of you. You know that, right?"

He didn't answer. Instead, he shifted so that the hair on his chest chafed her nipples. Her breath caught, then rushed out on a moan as she clutched at his back.

His teeth closed on her ear. "Do I still feel far away?"

She'd probably feel the heat of him lingering on her skin for days. "No."

His voice was a low, teasing whisper, shivering in her ear. "Even if I slide back down and fuck you with my tongue?"

Oh, God. The nervousness was still there, but now it was wrapped in the faith that he'd come back if she needed him. Her tongue tangled on the words, so she pushed on his shoulders, urging him down her body as she let her legs fall open.

Bren touched her first, the rough pads of his fingertips gliding through the wetness of her arousal, gentling when he circled her clit. Even that brought her hips up, chasing after his touch.

So light. So sweet. And so not enough. It made her cheeks burn to ask, but she was needy enough not to care. "I want your fingers inside me again. Please."

He gave her one, a long thrust all the way into her as he lowered his mouth and licked her clit. She tensed, her inner muscles clenching involuntarily around his finger, and now that she'd had her hands around his dick, she knew how much bigger it would feel. "More," she whispered. "Like you're getting me ready for your cock."

He lingered long enough to make one thing clear— she could issue orders, but he'd do as he damn well pleased. As soon as the thought fluttered through her mind, he pulled his finger free and returned not with two, but three.

Moaning, she jerked her hips back, torn by indecision. The stretch was almost too much, overwhelming, but every sweep of his tongue helped to melt that pressure into something warmer, forbidden but so delicious. She clutched his head and whimpered his name.

Bren kept stroking, kept licking, as if she wasn't wordlessly begging him to give her *more.* He'd shoved her to the very brink, but now he let her hover there, twisting into ever tighter knots until she was biting her lip bloody to keep from pleading with him.

The pressure edged past anticipation, and she groaned and tried to wrench away. He held her still, closed his mouth on her clit—and sucked hard.

beyond pain

It was too much and then not enough and then too much again, reeling back and forth as she yanked his hair and bucked, struggling to get closer in one heartbeat and to writhe away in the next. Pleasure swelled up, crashing through the tension, and she froze, back arched, toes clenched, the word *please* falling from her lips over and over, so tiny and needy and helpless.

And then it was just right. She sobbed out a moan of pure relief as she came.

He guided her through the shudders, his fingers moving, slick and easy, inside her. He trembled, as if he wanted to press her further, but finally his touch eased.

If he'd pushed her up again, it might have killed her. As it was, her limbs felt boneless. Only her fingers had any strength left, but she couldn't seem to unclench them from his hair. "Bren."

He leaned up just far enough to rest his forehead on her stomach. "Yeah?"

She relaxed her hand enough to stroke her fingertips along the edge of his ear. "Are you stopping for me?"

"Mmm." He turned his face to her touch. "For now."

She almost told him he didn't have to, but the words would have been hollow. Sheer habit, telling some guy to take what she wasn't ready to give, because it was the only way to pretend she was in control when it inevitably happened.

Bren didn't need her permission. He knew he could do whatever the fuck he wanted to her, and she should be thanking him for knowing when to stop, not trying to goad him on until he hurt her.

So she brushed her thumb over his lips and savored the tiny hitch in her chest at the intimacy of the contact. "Thanks for taking care of me."

Instead of responding, he crawled up to lean over her. He dropped a kiss to the corner of her mouth, gentle and quick, then stretched out and drew her to his chest.

It shook her more deeply than the orgasm had. "You

want me to stay?"

He combed his fingers through her hair. "Unless you have someplace to be, yeah. I want you to stay."

This was what she'd never known enough to crave before, the thing the O'Kanes exchanged as casually as words. Affection and warmth, the quiet sensual pleasure of warm skin and his hand in her hair. She could rub her cheek against Bren's chest and close her eyes, and every touch would be a reminder that she wasn't alone. "Okay."

He tilted her face up to his. "Is it?"

Probably not. If she twisted logic enough, she could pretend this was just an extension of trusting him with her body. He'd rest better knowing she was safe. It didn't have to mean more. "I might kick you. And hog the covers."

The corner of his mouth curved up in a slow smile. "I'll manage, sweetness."

Her pulse had finally settled, but that damn smile kicked it up again. She covered by burying her face in his shoulder. "And I'm grumpy in the morning."

"Then it's a good thing I already frisked you for weapons."

Could he feel her lips pulling up into an unwilling grin? Funny that she didn't care. "I'd tell you to say that when I'm biting you, but I think you'd like it."

"You catch on quick." His chuckle warmed her temple. "Sleep. It'll be all right."

I know. But that didn't stop her from staying awake long after Bren had drifted off. His heartbeat thumped beneath her ear, steady and soothing, and the warmth of his body wrapped around her, but she couldn't stop trying to memorize the details. The weight of his arm over her, the press of his thigh, the way the hair on his chest felt under her palm as she spread her fingers wide. Maybe if she filled her head with enough good things, the bad ones would topple out the back.

Either way, she wasn't going to take one damn moment for granted.

The single grated window in his room was still dark when Bren woke up. Six curled against him, warm and naked, and he seriously considered ignoring whatever had awakened him.

A soft noise, barely there but rough, like something gliding over carpet. He glanced over at the door and, sure enough, a folded note had been pushed beneath it. He slid slowly from the bed, careful not to disturb Six, and picked up the note.

Meeting at ten, Dallas's office. And I want to see that woman of yours this afternoon.

It was signed with a flourish. Lex, entirely too pleased with herself for figuring out where Six would be this morning.

Bren tossed aside the note and sat at his table, his back to the wall. He'd already broken down and laid out his oldest rifle, his favorite, the one Cooper had lifted off an Eden MP and given him to train with, years before Bren had ever worn the uniform himself. When he picked up the barrel, it slid into his hand like it had been crafted for him. He could break it down in seconds and put it back together just as quickly—in the dark, if he had to.

He knew this weapon like nothing else, and it knew him.

He began to clean it, working silently, his gaze drift-ing to the woman still sleeping under his blanket. In time, he could learn her like he'd learned this rifle. The only question was whether she'd let him.

The sun had begun to rise, and soft purple light fil-tered in through the window. On the bed, Six muttered something and rolled over. The covers slipped away, baring her back in the near darkness.

The shadows only highlighted the scars on her back,

94

rough and raised, marring what should have been smooth skin. He'd known about them already—even if Six had never talked about what had happened to her at Trent's hands, Bren would have known. A woman like her didn't last long without some asshole trying to beat the fight out of her, leaving behind fear and grudging obedience.

No, he'd known about her scars. But seeing them was different, somehow. Worse.

The metal pieces in his hands clinked together, so he set them aside and lit a cigarette.

It took two for his hands to stop shaking.

Six stirred again as he was finishing the second, rolling onto her stomach to bury her face in his pillow. She stretched with a sigh before turning her head to squint at him. "Did I sleep too long?"

"No, it's still early."

Her eyes drifted shut as she smiled sleepily. "Did I drive you out of bed? I told you I kick."

She hadn't, not once all night. "Got a summons. I have a meeting this morning, and you've got one this afternoon."

That brought her eyes open fully. Clutching the blanket to her chest, she twisted into a seated position. "What kind of meeting?"

"To talk about Sector Three, I suppose." He finished assembling his rifle and nestled it into its case. "Debriefing."

Her gaze was fixed on his hands. "Huh?"

"A meeting." Her distraction was blatant—and adorable. "I have other guns I can clean, if you want to watch."

She slipped from the bed and crossed the room, his blanket still crushed to her chest and trailing the floor behind her. "You put it together without even looking."

"Mmm. It was my first. Had it close to twenty years now."

Her finger brushed the edge of the case, but her hair had spilled over her shoulder, hiding her expression. "It fits you. Graceful and deadly."

He pulled her around the edge of the table and into his lap, spinning her so that the blanket wrapped around her first. "Sounds scary when you say it like that."

"Not to me." After a moment of awkward stiffness, she leaned into him, resting her forehead on his jaw. "Because you've got my back."

"Yeah." It helped to soothe him. This was a place of power, of control. He couldn't change the past, but she'd invited him to protect her now.

She turned her face to his neck, and her breath tickled his skin. "You *saw* my back."

"I did."

"Some of it's old. It wasn't all Trent."

"No?"

He felt her shake her head, take a breath, and let it out again. Then she changed the subject. "How many guns do you have left to clean?"

"Fourteen." But he made no move toward any of them. "I was born in Eden, but not in the city proper. In the underground. I don't have a number, the barcode on my wrist was faked, and my name isn't Brendan Donnelly. I don't know what it is, or if I ever had one, really."

"Oh." Six slipped a hand from the blankets and ghosted a finger over the black box on his wrist, where Ace had filled in his barcode all those years ago. "I thought there weren't slums in Eden."

If only. "There are slums everywhere, sweetness. Even in Eden. Another dirty little secret."

She touched the tattoo again. "My father had seven wives. He learned my brother's names, but he mostly called us girls by whatever order we came out. Some of my little sisters never got real names at all."

"I'm sorry." His own story couldn't compare to that. At least it wasn't his family who'd left him nameless, but the loose network of outcasts beneath the city. "It worked out for me. I survived, and then Cooper plucked me up."

"Cooper?"

"Neal Cooper, retired military police. He—" Words didn't exist to explain Coop's unwavering honesty to people used to lies. The matter-of-fact kindness where only cruelty was expected. "He takes care of lost things, people who've been thrown away."

Six twined her fingers with his. "I'm sorry you were thrown away. Whoever did it was stupid."

"Desperate," he corrected. "And it doesn't matter. The hardest shit in my life came early, and I didn't know any better. It just was, and I got through it."

"Everyone's desperate," she whispered. "Everywhere but here. You don't understand how stupid I am. All this tech you have? The running water, the electricity? This is what I imagined Eden was like."

There were places in the sectors that defined *waste-land*, where the land beyond the borders, out in the wilderness, was a less forbidding place to live. "You're not stupid. Life here in Sector Four's pretty damn posh. Dallas keeps it that way."

She huffed in amusement. "No, I'm a little stupid. Girls don't need to read on the farms in Six and Seven. I was just gonna be some old guy's eighth or ninth wife."

"Uneducated is one thing. It means you can learn. Stupid means you can't, even when someone gives you the chance."

"I guess." Her lips brushed his throat, over his pulse. "I know I'm not really stupid, but sometimes I feel that way. Like it doesn't matter if I can learn, I'll never do it fast enough to catch up with everyone else."

Bren had seen burly men—tough men—reduced to tears at the prospect of trials and changes smaller than the ones she'd endured. "You'll be all right, that's a promise. Have I ever lied to you?"

"No."

"And I won't. Even if what I have to say is hard."

"I know." Her laughter tickled his skin. "You're my favorite of all the people who've ever kidnapped me."

It was sweet, in a sad, twisted sort of way—which pretty much described both of them perfectly. "You're absolutely my favorite person I've ever kidnapped."

Six eased her hand from his, only to slide it up his arm and over his shoulder. Her nails pricked his skin. "You're good at fucking, aren't you?"

Bren had never been one for conversational niceties like graceful segues, but her subject change was so abrupt he blinked. "I don't suck at it. People come."

When she lifted her head, the early morning light revealed her flushed cheeks. "I don't know how to do this. I've never wanted to encourage someone to try to fuck me before."

She was so nervous he couldn't tease her. Instead, he brushed her tangled hair out of her face. "We fucked last night. I didn't put my dick in your pussy, but trust me. We fucked."

That tiny furrow appeared as she processed the words, adding the information to whatever mental file she was building. "Then how do I tell you that I want that? Your dick inside me? There should be a word."

His body tightened as he imagined her husky voice tripping over the possibilities. "My dick inside you, yeah. Or I could say I want you to ride me, show me how you like it. Hard and fast, or just hard. Or maybe you like it soft and easy, but I don't think so."

She scratched her nails down his arm, leaving a kiss of pain in their wake. "I don't know what I like best. I hate not knowing."

"You haven't been ready." Her touch shivered up his spine. "Are you now?"

Her answer held no hesitation, no doubt. "Yes."

The morning sunlight streamed through the window, catching the hints of red in her hair and gilding her skin.

It was enough to wash out the scars, but Bren slipped his hand under the blanket to rest in the middle of her back, over the soft, raised skin. "Tonight," he said finally. "You think about it today, what you might like, and you can tell me about it tonight. Then we'll find out."

7

L EX HELD HER meeting in the room typically reserved for Dallas and his men. Tucked away on the second floor of the Broken Circle, the conference room was dominated by a long wooden table ringed with padded chairs. A leather-upholstered seat impressive enough to qualify as a throne sat at the head of the table—Dallas's usual chair.

For the moment, it belonged to Lex. Noelle and Rachel sat on either side of her, passing one of Noelle's fancy tablets back and forth as they discussed something about a brewing business Rachel's family ran in the city. Six had ended up in the chair next to Noelle by virtue of being herded into it like a helpless kitten.

Two other women rounded out the group—Trix, looking as sleekly beautiful as ever, even without being dressed for tips, and Jade, the only other non-O'Kane in the room. Where Trix was pink-cheeked, with the sorts of curves Six envied, Jade looked strung out and half-dead. Which had been mostly true.

Shivering, Six forced her attention back to Lex. She'd take another year under Wilson Trent's thumb before one week drugged into obedience as Jade had been. Bad enough to know you were likely to die if you walked away, but to lose control of your *mind...*

Ten years of Trent's shit would be better than that.

"Our sources in Eden were clear," Lex was saying. "No one on the council gave two shits about Gareth Woods when he was alive, and they're kinda glad he's dead. But they'll be on the lookout for trouble now, and if they find it, things won't be pretty."

"The corrupt will be seeing to their own protection," Jade mumbled in a voice as hollow and pale as her expression. "Perhaps that will serve as a distraction."

"And the devout are probably busy feeling smug," Noelle said, rolling her eyes. "Unfortunately, distraction never lasts with them. Not when they smell money."

Lex lit a cigarette and tossed her lighter on the table. "Which is why we're in disaster cleanup mode in Three. No new ventures means no new profits, and that's fine with me and Dallas. Especially if it keeps Eden off our asses for a while."

This was Six's moment to speak up, and for once she knew exactly what she wanted to say. "Maybe you should fix up the bar first. If you give 'em a glimpse of what things could be like, people will come to you. Faster than if you try to use words, anyway."

"Okay, then. You and Bren can oversee that."

That easy, like Six was really one of them and Lex trusted her to get the job done. It was tempting to leave it at that, but a glance at Noelle's overly encouraging expression gave her another idea. "You said all the furniture you gave me was leftover stuff. Does Dallas need all of it?"

"No." Lex tilted her head. "Why, you want to trade it

off over in Three?"

"People aren't going to trust help," Six explained. "Not if you just give it to them. And if you tell them to come to you with problems, they won't trust that either. But an exchange will make sense to them. They point out problems and get something in return."

"We'll arrange transport." Lex jotted a note on the paper in front of her. "Be sure you run the inventory by Dallas before you take it." She paused and tapped her pen on the table. "Any problems we need to know about, or is it all standard stuff?"

Six hesitated, tracing one finger along the edge of the table. "Maybe this isn't my place..." she said finally. "But are you thinking of recruiting any women from Three?"

"Straight out of the gate? Hell, no." Lex leaned back in her chair. "But I'm listening."

For a silent moment she studied the queen of Sector Four, the woman who so easily held the position Trent had offered Six all those years ago. He'd sworn he needed a partner, and she'd fallen in love with the idea of being more than a vicious street kid. She'd imagined being a leader, a woman strong enough to protect the kids who weren't as tough as she was.

Scarlet had warned her not to fall for Trent's bull-shit, and Six had reacted like the immature idiot she'd been, accusing the woman of jealousy and ulterior motives. Of wanting to keep Six as one of her pretty little pets.

Only one of them had turned out to be a decent leader, and it hadn't been Six. If Lex was going to pull Three out of the rubble, the best thing Six could do to help was step aside. "There's a woman you should meet. I know Three inside and out, but I'm tainted, as far as the people who hated Trent are concerned. They respect Scarlet."

"Will she come here, or do we have to go to her?"

Scarlet probably had the courage to walk into hell, but Six had a different reason for her answer. "I could use some help figuring out how to clean up the club. Maybe we could take care of both at once, someday soon?"

Lex nodded and turned to Noelle. "How's the surveillance coming?"

"Slowly," Noelle admitted, pulling another piece of tech in front of her. It was three times the size of the handheld tablet Noelle had given her, but the girl flicked her fingers over the surface with a speed that made Six dizzy, sending text zooming by as windows popped open and rearranged themselves as if by magic. "When you set me to tracking communications, I figured it wouldn't be that hard. I had no idea how much chatter goes back and forth between Eden and the sectors. I can record it, but even if I scan it all day, every day, I'll never have time to filter out what's important."

Lex rubbed her temples. "All right. We'll add that to the list of shit that needs fixing. Maybe we can find someone."

"Someone who can write code." Noelle settled back in her chair. "I can ask Mad to look at it, but I think he's more interested in the electronics. Hardware, not software. But maybe he'll know someone."

This time it was easier for Six to speak up. "There's a guy in Three, one who can do anything with Eden's computers. Scarlet's already trying to find him for Bren."

"Then we'll get a status update on that when we go meet that chick." Lex capped her pen and looked around. "Okay, that's it. Get out. Not you, Six."

Six stiffened, even after Noelle smiled encouragingly. She and Rachel swept out with Trix lagging behind at Jade's slower pace. But too soon the door was swinging shut behind them, and Six was left clenching her hands together in her lap as Lex watched her.

Finally, the woman spoke. "How was your trip?"

"Okay." Surely Bren had told Dallas everything important, and Dallas would have passed it on to Lex.

Though, for all she knew, that had included Bren getting her off in a warehouse. It wasn't like the O'Kanes were private about sex. "Did you wanna know about something specific?"

Lex finished her cigarette before answering. "I lived in Three for a while, you know. Back before your time."

She'd only heard that Lex had grown up in Two, which was supposed to be a fantasy heaven with luxuries almost as nice as the ones in Eden. "Probably wasn't much nicer back then, was it?"

"It was a pit," she said flatly. "Are you okay?"

Six could sense nothing beneath the words but honest concern, so she forced herself to relax. "I think so. It's still a pit, but the people who hurt me the most are dead."

"You gonna be all right, having to go back again?"

She almost said *Bren won't let anything happen to me*, but that was the easy answer. Her gut was certain that almost nothing in Eden or the sectors could get past Bren, but it was still almost.

The deeper reason made that chance worth it. "You know how I got in trouble with Trent?"

Lex shook her head and poured her a glass of water.

It took two sips before Six could force out the truth. "I wanted to be you. Not *you*, but what you are. Trent convinced me he wanted that too."

"I'm guessing he didn't."

"Oh, sure he did. For a while." Water splashed over her wrist, and Six realized her hand was shaking. She set the glass down carefully. "I was young, but I didn't suck at getting shit done. He thought it was great until I started trying to clean up things he liked dirty."

"Then it's a good thing he's dead, isn't it?" Sighing, Lex flipped her notebook shut and rose. "Some promises weren't meant to be broken. Trent should have known that."

Maybe that was worse—when they didn't *mean* to

break the promises. "Doesn't mean they don't get broken anyway."

"True enough." Lex studied her face. "We don't want to draw attention to ourselves or Three, so we're gonna move slow. There'll be a lot of back-and-forth over the next few weeks. Day trips, overnights, that kind of thing."

"All right." It was more or less what she'd expected, but what she couldn't have predicted was the low buzz of excitement. Lex hadn't laughed at her. She hadn't mocked the idea of Six being more than some guy's piece of ass. "I want to help. I really do."

"I know. And you will."

Six addressed the topic looming silently in the room. "And Bren's looking out for me. So I'll be fine."

"He doesn't fail," Lex agreed. "I don't think he knows how."

"Yeah." The words warmed her cheeks for no good reason, leaving Six to study her boots and try not to think about Bren and fucking and all the things they might be doing to each other in a few short hours.

"Yeah," Lex echoed, gentle humor lacing her voice. "Dallas is sending Bren out with Cruz tonight. If you want to raid my closet while he's gone."

Six had been in Lex's closet before, with Noelle, who'd blithely carried off a small fortune in silk drowning in lace and ruffles. Feeling awkward about the charity, Six had stuck to things that looked cheap—simple cotton pants, beat-up denim, and a couple of plain T-shirts.

She had some clothes of her own now, things she'd paid for out of her slowly growing hoard of cash, but everything was so practical. Tonight, she wanted to feel powerful *and* sexual. And maybe she wanted to shake Bren's perfect self-control.

Smiling, she met Lex's eyes, not minding for once if the other woman read everything she was thinking. "Okay."

Lex's humor grew into an answering smile, and she wrapped an arm around Six's shoulders as they headed for the door. "Okay."

Cruz had been running with Ace for weeks, and it seemed to be working out well. So when Dallas pulled Cruz off the usual runs for a special assignment, Bren had anticipated a quick recon mission into Eden, or possibly across the hostile border into Sector Five.

He didn't expect Cruz to point the car toward the wilderness at the outskirts of their own damn sector.

He stared out the window into the darkness. "We got problems at the outer edge?"

"Rumor is that someone's got a still up and running out here." Cruz seemed more relaxed than he'd been in years—since before he'd been pulled into the upper ranks of Special Tasks. Cruz had never coped well with moral ambiguity.

And there was nothing ambiguous about distilling moonshine in Sector Four. If you made it, you'd damn well better be drinking it yourself, because selling it wasn't an option. Dallas let most everything else slide, but having someone else run liquor through his territory would cut into his profits, make it harder for him to take care of his sector.

And the consequences were clear. Get caught once, he'd destroy your operation. Get caught again, he'd fuck you up good. Everyone knew it.

But Cruz wasn't everyone. "You know what goes down if this turns out to be a repeat offender, right?" Bren asked.

"I know." He flexed his fingers, as if in anticipation of a fight. "They had their warning. What happens next is on them."

They lapsed into silence again. It wasn't new for

them, but the tension was. They'd barely talked since Cruz's defection from the city, mostly because Bren had been responsible for it—and still carried the guilt. "How have you been doing?"

"I'm okay. I'm..." A hesitation, and he caught Cruz glancing at his newly inked wrists. "I'm good, actually. I got something back that I thought I'd never have again."

"A conscience clear enough to sleep at night?"

The corner of Cruz's mouth ticked up. "That too. But mostly? Brotherhood."

"It's true, then? You and Ace are getting along?"

"Most of the time. He's not like anyone in Eden, is he?"

"Nope." Then again, Ace wasn't like anyone else in Sector Four, either. "I wondered if you two would be able to settle your shit."

Cruz shrugged one shoulder. "He still irritates me sometimes, but I misjudged him. I thought he stole Rachel from me, but you can't steal these women, can you? You can't own them."

"Only if they give it to you." Six's face flashed in his mind, her lips parted, cheeks flushed with pleasure. "If they don't hold anything back."

"Doesn't matter," Cruz said, his voice firmer. Like he was trying to convince himself. "I don't have any business wanting to keep a woman, not until I know the sectors. And Ace can teach me that faster than anyone."

So could he, but Cruz and Ace seemed to have a connection that went beyond work. "You'll do good. You already are."

"It's not just him, it's everyone. It's good to belong to a team again."

Bren had had that once, the security of knowing that he was part of something, a team, and that he made it stronger by being a part of it. They'd lived together, fought together, laughed together. And then it had all fallen apart.

Bren cleared his throat. "Did things get so bad after I left?"

Cruz didn't answer at first, not until the car had zipped past the last of the original buildings that had been built at the same time as Eden. They were into the true slums now, dwellings cobbled together from debris and whatever could be scavenged.

"We rotted," he said finally. "From the outside in, I guess. From the top down. The day before you left was the last day we all trusted each other."

A breakdown in trust meant a breakdown in operations. A unit like that couldn't function if you weren't one hundred percent sure the man at your back would have it covered if you dove into the middle of a firefight. And Lieutenant Russell Miller, their intrepid squad commander, wouldn't have been able to fix that dissolving trust.

He was, after all, the cause of it.

"You saw the truth," Bren said simply. "Miller gave me a direct order to plant that evidence, and when it was uncovered, he sold me out. But he betrayed every single one of us."

"He picked the wrong man for the setup." Cruz glanced at him. "You may be crazy as a Sector One preacher, but every damn one of us knew you wouldn't balk at a mission like that. So half of us were left thinking about what loyalty earns you, and the rest broke something inside themselves, trying to believe in Miller."

Bren snorted. "Just glad I can put you in the former category."

Cruz didn't smile. "We all were, to start. But once Miller started talking people around... I can't prove shit, but people who never warmed to him had a higher chance of coming back in a body bag."

"I wish I was surprised." The past was past, but maybe Cruz needed some closure, too. "He comes out into the sectors sometimes. Unauthorized. Uses forged passes."

"And you haven't done something about that yet?"

He could have. He'd followed Miller around the sectors, cataloging his movements...and waiting. "Can't move on it until I can be sure it won't come back on the O'Kanes."

"Understood." Cruz slowed the car and pulled off the road beside a hovel with a collapsed roof. "It's supposed to be a quarter mile past this building. How do you want to approach?"

They could cut the lights, but the sound of the engine would carry out here in the desolate stillness. "Pull up and head in. I'll go around the back and cover you."

Cruz obeyed. "How big a mess are we making?"

"As big as it needs to be."

The drive was short, even at a careful, creeping pace. Their destination was little better than the shack down the road—at least on the outside, and at first glance. A closer look revealed shiny water lines running from a well out back, not to mention not one but two metal chimneys that damn sure didn't lead to fireplaces. Boilers, no doubt, like the ones Dallas used.

Bren cursed under his breath, and cursed again when an inspection of the back door revealed solid steel—and an electronic lock, the kind that cost. A high-dollar operation meant high-dollar weapons, not to mention the muscle to use them. And with Cruz already on his way in at the front, Bren had no time to lose.

He jerked open a pocket on his cargo pants, pulled out his popcard, and jammed it into the key interface. The card activated with a silent flash of blinking lights, and Bren hit the red button on the end. It could take the card up to thirty seconds to isolate the lock's code, but it only took two to overload the circuits.

The lock popped with a sizzle of sparks, and he pushed open the door just as the first shot sounded in the front room. Bren raced down the narrow hall and ran headlong into two men. He took out one with a quick blow to the temple, but the other wheeled back two steps, already groping for his gun.

Bren knocked the pistol out of his hand, caught it by the barrel as it flew through the air, and spun around. He harnessed the force of it into a blow, striking his other attacker in the jaw, using the pistol grip like a club. The man reeled and slammed against the wall.

Gunshots sounded in the next room, two loud retorts followed by a shout and a third, then silence. Bren kicked through the door to find Cruz examining a graze on his upper arm, his booted foot resting on a groaning thug's face. The man's knee had been blown out, and four other bodies lay unmoving, necks at awkward angles, a path of efficient carnage from the front room.

Bren frowned. "I only got two."

"Sorry. You can have this one." Cruz lifted his foot and jerked his head toward a table set against the wall. "I kept him alive after I saw that."

"Oh, *shit.*" Not merely a well-funded distillery, after all. The bottles lining the table all bore identical labels emblazoned with a familiar logo, the same one printed on the sheets of unused labels in a crate at the far end.

The suicidal bastards were bootlegging O'Kane liquor.

Cruz stepped away. "New mission objective?"

"Yeah." Bren hauled the remaining survivor up by his collar. "We drag this piece of shit back to Dallas."

"O'Kane!" the man sputtered.

"O'Kane," he agreed. "My boss. The man you're ripping off."

"But I'm not! I didn't take anything. Every bottle's there—you can count it—"

Bren cut him off by twisting his collar tight, but only for a second. "Who do you work for?"

The man's eyes rolled toward Cruz and back. "For Dallas O'Kane."

"Then why the fuck were you shooting at me?" Cruz demanded, lifting an arm to flash his new ink. "Look familiar?"

The man shook so hard, Bren thought he might piss himself. "I didn't— Shit, if you're an O'Kane, why did you come busting up in here?"

"Because this isn't Dallas's operation." Bren released his captive but stayed ready to snatch him back up, just in case. "He doesn't farm out O'Kane liquor. We make it ourselves."

Confusion knotted his brow. "Buzz *is* one of you. He has the ink."

Cruz stalked back to the front of the room and rolled one body with the toe of his boot. "Which one is he?"

"He's not here."

Through the open doorway, Bren could see four stills, which were powered by the two boilers he'd noticed outside. "We'll let Dallas sort it out," he told Cruz. "Take him out and put him in the trunk. I'll destroy the equipment."

Cruz bit off a curse, but he locked it down and dragged their captive toward the exit.

The larger room had a woodpile in the center, between the stills, but both boilers were cold. A quick tap on the large tanks resounded dully, which meant they weren't empty but full of fermenting mash.

Not for long.

Bren picked up an ax from the woodpile and smashed the first tank, slicing through the thin metal with each swing. Sour-smelling mash flowed out of the holes and onto the floor to splash his boots.

He hit the other three tanks, as well. It was impossible to patch tanks without leaks, and there was no way the bastards would be able to replace them.

Not before he brought Dallas back to see what they'd done.

8

T HE PANTS SHE'D borrowed from Lex's closet were dangerous and sexy, and by some miracle fit Six like they'd been made for her. The leather hugged her skin but was supple enough for her to move freely, and the laces climbing from her knees to her hips flashed enough skin to tease without making her feel naked.

They were hot, and they made *her* feel hot.

And they'd been in a heap on Bren's floor since just after midnight.

Clad in her underwear and a tank top, Six alternated between nervous pacing and restless dozing, mostly trying not to wonder how many ways a job could go wrong. Bren and Cruz could handle anything between the two of them. Whatever was keeping Bren away from his bed—and the woman he'd invited to it—it couldn't be serious. And if someone had been hurt, she'd know. This whole place had boiled up like a hill of fire ants when Lex and Noelle had gotten shot.

She'd given up pacing for another round of fitful half-dreams when the click of the door brought her upright.

Bren came dragging in and dropped his jacket over the chair by the door, leaving him in dark pants, a dark T-shirt, and a worn leather shoulder holster. "Sorry I'm late."

She took a more complete assessment of him, letting her gaze slide from his face down to his boots in search of any sign of injury. Finding none, she exhaled in relief and rose. "You're okay?"

"Tired." He shrugged out of the holster and draped it, pistols and all, on top of his jacket. "Run tonight got complicated. They weren't just selling liquor, they were putting Dallas's name on it."

Then they were idiots. Even Trent had briefly considered—and quickly discarded—the idea of reusing empty O'Kane bottles to sell knock-off liquor. All it took was one inferior bottle getting back to Sector Four, and you'd wish Dallas O'Kane had only crushed your balls.

No wonder Bren looked exhausted. Too exhausted for fucking, which was why it didn't bother her to sink to her knees and jerk at the laces on one of his boots. It wasn't submissive if she only wanted to get his shoes off before he tipped over.

He shook his head in protest, but didn't move. "I can do that."

"Shut up," she muttered, then cursed under her breath at the tangled, mash-splattered laces. Relief had given way too quickly to an unfair buzz of anger. She wanted to drive a fist into his shoulder and demand to know why no one had told her anything, why she'd been left to stew in ignorance and worry.

Stupid. She wasn't his woman. She wasn't even a member of the damn gang. No one owed her an accounting of Bren's whereabouts, and that was the way she wanted it. This thing between them was about bodies and friendship, nothing more.

The laces gave way, and she made a face as she gripped the boot. "These need to be cleaned. I'm not doing that."

"No shit," he said mildly. "Leave the other one and come up here."

She ignored him and set to work on the second boot. "Don't tell me what to do unless we're fighting or fucking."

He wound one lock of her hair around his finger. "So you *are* mad."

"Only if you think you can boss me around," she lied, hauling the boot free. It joined its partner by the door, and she looked anywhere but at Bren as she started to rise. All she needed was an excuse, a few minutes to shove her wobbly-kneed reaction back where it belonged, and she had the perfect one. "I need to wash my hands, and then we can talk."

But he held her, wrapping strong hands around her upper arms. "Look at me."

At first she refused, fixing her gaze on his chest, but that did fuck all good. He was patient enough to stand there all night, and strong enough to keep her there if she tried to jerk free. The only way out was to do her best to shutter her eyes before meeting his.

"I'm sorry," he said gently. "We had to bring a guy back for Dallas to talk to, and it's a huge fucking mess. But I should've sent someone to tell you I was back instead of letting you worry."

She could taste the tears that threatened, and it had been so long since she cared about anything enough to cry. "You don't owe me anything," she told him, the words pleasantly bland. "We're square."

His jaw tightened. "I owed you that much, especially tonight."

"It's just sex," she started, but she could hear the lie when her voice hitched on *just*, as if her body couldn't handle her self-destructive audacity after she'd wasted hours tying herself into knots by imagining his hands on her, his mouth, his cock sliding home as he drowned them both in pleasure.

"I'll make it up to you." The low promise, whispered against her temple, stirred her hair, and she thought her shiver was one of reaction until the shaking grew stronger, and suddenly she was trembling like some virgin out of Eden.

She wanted to tear herself out of his arms or burrow deeper, and not knowing which made her voice waver. "I really do need to wash up. I smell like a still."

"Me too. I need a shower." He reached for her hand. "Come with me."

She tried to think of a reason to say *no*, and a dozen boiled up. She was too raw, too vulnerable to strip physically naked on top of everything else. She wanted to be angry, numb—anything so that the sex that followed was only about bodies. It was too intimate, sharing that private space with him, giving in to the temptation to follow the water over the hard planes of his body.

One reason overrode them all. She wanted to. "Okay."

He led her into the bathroom, turned on the water, and tugged at his belt. By the time he'd undressed, steam clouded the room. But it couldn't cloud the look in his eyes as he pulled at her tank top and her panties— hunger tempered by patience. "Get in."

She stepped into the narrow stall without hesitation and only a brief moment of worry that being naked made it feel natural to obey without question. Then he was there with her, taking up all the space, and she couldn't think at all.

He stretched past her and adjusted the showerhead so the spray hit her hair. Then he stroked his fingers through the strands as the water soaked them. "I like your hair."

She'd always kept it long for sentimental reasons, as

a stupid way of clinging to a memory she wasn't sure was real anymore. But the soothing warmth of the water, the sensual brush of his fingers, and the steam all combined to twist the world into something safe and surreal. A place where it was okay to be silly and sentimental.

"My mother liked to brush it," she said, barely loud enough for him to hear over the water. "It's the only thing I remember about her. They'd call me to chores, and she'd say, 'Hope can't come, I'm not done fixing her hair.' And we'd giggle at fooling the head wife."

"Hope," he echoed just as quietly. "Tell me?"

She closed her eyes as he reached for the shampoo. "She was too young. Six and Seven aren't so different from the communes. They breed you as soon as they can because they need workers, and sometimes it kills you. I think she was fourteen or fifteen when she had me..." And had named her *Hope* because Six was the first child she'd carried to term. No one had expected her to be the last, too.

Bren hummed soothingly and worked the shampoo through her hair.

"That's mostly it. I don't know how old I was when the last pregnancy killed her. Eight or nine?" Too old to be escaping chores—too old to grieve, according to the head wife, especially when she had so many other mothers to respect and obey. "It happened a lot. Getting a doctor or meds might mean not being able to afford the tithe, so if you got sick or hurt..."

"She was important to you."

Tears stung her eyes again, but it was safe to let them slip away with the water as Bren massaged her scalp. "I barely remember her. I don't even know if my memories are real, or if they're daydreams. Almost everything that happened to me before Three is like that. Another life."

He rinsed her hair in silence, then turned her to face him. "It's like rain, sweetness. It can wash some stuff away, but not everything."

Six tracked a drop of water as it rolled over his collarbone. When it strayed toward his nipple, she leaned in and caught it with her tongue. "Help me forget the rest."

His hardening cock nudged her hip. "When I'm done. Soap."

"Bossy," she muttered, but she was smiling as she reached past him for the rough bar. "Remember, you only get to do this when we're naked."

"So you say now." He grinned as he worked the bar between his hands. "But once I have you up against the hood of a car with my hand in your pants, you'll change your mind."

He rubbed one soapy hand across his chest, and her retort died on her tongue. As many times as she'd seen his bare torso, it had never been this close, this intimate. She followed the path of his hands with her gaze before drifting up to his shoulders and back to his flexing arms, trying to look everywhere at once.

He pressed the soap into her hand. "Tease me a little, Six. Show me what I was missing tonight."

This was the part that always felt awkward. Flirtation. Foreplay. It was easy when it was all about groping hands and stroking what you could reach on your frantic path to getting in each other's pants, but this was deliberate, thoughtful, utterly focused on getting someone to crave more of you. She'd spent too much time learning to send out the opposite vibe—*touch me and I'll kill you.*

Of course, that vibe hadn't derailed Bren. Maybe she'd been trying too hard to be someone *else*, sultry Lex or sweet, bratty Noelle. It was about survival, a hard-learned defense mechanism. Imitate the people around you, and you became less of a target.

It felt strange to stop trying altogether as she smoothed the soap up his arm. "I borrowed those leather pants from Lex, the ones that lace up the legs."

"That doesn't seem very sturdy."

"They show skin, Donnelly." She soaped her hand and stroked it lower, over the tense muscles of his abdomen. "But only a little."

He sucked in a harsh breath. "Skin's good."

"Only a little," she repeated. The backs of her fingers almost brushed his shaft before she changed direction and smoothed back up. "That's how I'd dress up. A little skin and big knives, so anyone who wants to see more knows I'll probably cut their fingers off."

"Anyone else." Bren lifted her suddenly, backing her beyond the spray so that it beat down on him, rinsing him clean. "You'd cut anyone else. But not me."

His hands on her skin stole her breath. "I might. But only 'cause you'd like it."

"Try me," he urged. "Try it now. You don't need a knife."

Her nails were longer than they'd ever been before, and still glittery with what was left of Nessa's last attempt at girl bonding. She raked them down his chest, leaving thin white lines the water seemed to follow, but that was too tame. Too easy.

So she turned her face to his throat and closed her teeth over his pulse hard enough to bruise.

Bren pressed her against the tile with a groan, then spun her around by the shower door. "Towels are on the shelf," he rasped as he shut off the water.

She groped for a towel, but her hands shook as she tried to dry off. Bren took over, sliding the soft but rough fabric over her skin as he edged her toward the sink.

He draped the towel over it, locked an arm around her waist, and lifted her onto the porcelain. "Here?"

It was hard to take a full breath as he wedged himself between her thighs, pushing them wide. Panic gripped her, an inexplicable certainty that she'd built this up in her mind so much that nothing could live up to her fantasy. She countered it by scratching another set of welts down both his arms. "Damn it, Donnelly, I thought you were in charge. Go on and fuck me already."

He splayed one hand across her lower back, just above her ass, and held her still as he nudged the head of his cock between her pussy lips. She had only a moment more to choke on panic before the sensation caught up to her, a shivery pleasure that made her clench in anticipation.

That tiny touch shouldn't have been so good. She tried to blame it on the piercings, but that wasn't why she felt like her nerves had multiplied, and each one was laid bare.

This must be what it felt like to want someone.

She was wet, so wet that he slid all the way into her in one hard stroke, and she really couldn't breathe now. She tangled her arms and legs around him and moaned as the movement shifted him inside her, made her *feel* how thick he was. His fingers had been an intense stretch, but this was more, better, because he was so, so deep...

Bren groaned and flexed his hips. "That's right, baby. Squeeze my cock."

"Arrogant ass," she rasped, but it sounded like a whimper and was muffled against his shoulder anyway. She let her head fall back and closed her eyes as her body melted and reformed, hungry and eager. "Do you want to know how you feel?"

"I know how I feel." His hand hit the wall behind her, and he leaned in until the only thing balancing her on the edge of the sink was him. "My neck aches like a son of a bitch. So does my dick. And I like it."

She could still see the imprint of her teeth on his throat. Tomorrow there'd be a bruise, a claim as undeniable as any of those women wearing their men's ink, and it heightened her satisfaction as he somehow pushed deeper.

They'd both feel each other in the morning.

Bren drew back, but only a little. Then he slammed

home again, harder this time, driving a choked noise from her lips. His hand was steel at the small of her back, anchoring her hips in place even when her shoulders thumped back against the wall.

There was no escape. He had her pinned, penned, his body stretched over hers, one hand braced above her head. Everything was *him*, around her and inside her, and oh God, her tilted hips had him rubbing against some greedy spot that hollowed her out worse and worse with every touch.

She couldn't get enough.

What if she *never* got enough?

"Bren—" Her voice broke with his next advance. She clutched at him, completely adrift in the twisting, aching hunger he'd created with a few lazy thrusts. If he could do this to her when he'd barely gotten inside her, she wouldn't survive. "I can't— I need, I *need*—"

"You need," he growled. Then he was fucking her.

Fucking her, hard and intense, every bit of him wholly focused on being inside her. Maybe if he'd pulled all the way out, she could have gathered her wits, but his cock kept working that same spot until her skin felt so tight she thought she'd scream.

Orgasm didn't slam into her. It built in slow motion, the promise of it hanging sweet in the air as she clenched in anticipation. Then Bren groaned, and she knew she was squeezing him again, but she needed more than the slick sound of him plunging into her and their panting breaths. She needed that voice, stripped of its bland control, growling obscenities about the things he'd do to her.

She dug her nails into his back until the skin broke and begged him, the words tumbling end over end in a confused jumble as she began to shake. "Say something, please. Tell me what you want. What to do."

"Open up. Feel it." He punctuated each command with another hard thrust. "You can come all over my dick, but I'm not gonna stop. Not this time."

It should have been impossible to feel *more*, but his words shattered the building pressure. Her entire body seized for one dizzy moment of bliss, and then she was falling, writhing through impossible spasms. She wanted to laugh, to cry, to *scream* because it felt so good, so fucking good—

Bren gripped her chin and growled. "Don't stop. Not yet."

"I can't," she moaned, even as her hips lifted greedily, her body shameless in its need to be filled.

She tried to twist away from the intensity in his gaze, but he forced her back, forced her to stare up at him as he rode her until she couldn't tell if she was still coming or strung out on the edge of another orgasm.

Then he released her chin, reached down between them, and pressed his thumb to her clit.

No, she hadn't been coming, but she was now, sobbing his name as pleasure wrecked her. It was like being caught out in a storm, the friction of his cock dragging her one way as the sharp pulsing of her clit slammed her in the other.

Too much. Too fucking much, and *still* not enough, because now she was wet and open to him, and the sweet edge of discomfort that had made the rest bearable had vanished.

Whimpering, she fought to spread her thighs wider, to let him go deeper. No, not just deeper. "Harder," she pleaded, scratching desperately at his arms. "Fuck me harder."

Bren clutched her closer with a groan. Harder and faster, every plunge slamming his hips against hers. There was no room for his hand between them, not like this, but he tangled his fingers in her wet hair and pulled.

Hard.

The third orgasm didn't even build, just crashed over

her, sweet and brutal. It washed away everything else only to linger as a fuzzy, dreamy bliss. Everything seemed distant, disconnected.

Everything except Bren. His muscles flexed under her hands as he bucked and shuddered, driving into her wildly. Something crashed behind her, almost drowning out the sound of her name, torn from him on a tortured groan as he thrust deep one last time and stilled.

It took all the strength in her shaking limbs to wrap them around his body. Burying her face against his throat was easier. His pulse pounded in time with hers, and she parted her lips, tasted the salt on him as she pressed a kiss to the rising bruise.

She'd marked his skin. Only fair, since he'd marked her *world*.

"You'll have bruises too," he mumbled, as if he could read her thoughts from the kiss.

Probably, though her body still tingled so pleasantly she couldn't begin to guess where. "I get 'em from sparring all the time. This is more fun, I think."

Bren hoisted her against him and walked into the bedroom. "Why do I think you'd like it best if we did both?"

Her sleepy libido stirred just imagining it. All-out warfare, fighting to see who got to be on top. "Were you ever imagining it? All those times you got me beneath you?"

He hesitated. "No. But I think only because I wouldn't let myself."

Her heart pounded. There'd been a trap under the words that she hadn't meant to set—not consciously. Answering *yes* would have stripped away Bren's careful protectiveness, turning him from a source of safety into some sort of pervert in waiting.

But he'd passed. And now her pulse raced as she tilted her head back to meet his eyes. "What will you think about if you get me under you tomorrow?"

He didn't answer until he'd laid her down on the bed and stretched out behind her, one arm around her middle. "You'll have to fight me and find out."

 lex

DALLAS WAS WASHING blood off his hands. Again. Lex watched him, only speaking when he looked up to meet her eyes in the mirror. "How'd it go?"

"Not so good." He grimaced and turned his attention back to the sink. "Most of the blood is from the gunshot in his leg. I didn't have to hit him. I didn't even have to *frown*. The bastard heard my name and spilled every secret he knew, straight back to the time his grandpa screwed the neighbor's wife. And not a damn bit of it was useful."

It was pretty much the worst-case scenario. "So we don't know who's behind the bootlegging, and all we can do is shut down this operation and then...wait."

"Pretty much. Whoever set these sorry bastards up sure isn't coming to look for them." He slammed off the water with a sigh. "What a fucking mess."

She handed him a towel and rubbed at the knotted muscles between his shoulders. "We'll find them. We'll track down every case of bogus liquor and trace it back."

"Eventually." Once he'd dried his hands, he tossed aside the towel and dragged her from the bathroom. "But all that takes time, plus men on the ground. Goddamn, we're still spread thin. And too many people know it."

Inarguable facts. Lex rubbed her face and dropped to the bed. "Do you have a better plan?"

"No." He slumped beside her and fell back to stare at the ceiling. "You don't think Dom has anything to do with it, do you? It's a long shot, but he's carrying a big enough grudge, and he knows my operation."

Dom was an idiot, barely capable of tying his own shoes, much less aspiring to beat Dallas O'Kane at his own game. "I called in a few favors to see if our intel on Dom was accurate, and it seems to be. He's still over in Five, sucking up to Mac Fleming."

Dallas huffed out a laugh. "That's one bastard I should have killed. *Two* bastards."

She soothed him with a kiss to the temple. "Slow and steady," she breathed. "It feels like there aren't enough of us right now, and it's true. But it'll turn into legitimate weakness if we take on new members just to have more warm bodies. You know it."

"I know." He sighed again and looped an arm around her, hauling her close to his side. "Time. As long as I can keep buying us time, it'll shake out."

"Uh-uh." Lex propped her head up on her arm and turned his face to hers. "You'll make it work, because you're Dallas fucking O'Kane. You're good at this, you work hard, and you're the smartest damn man I've ever met in my life."

He smiled slowly. "Keep going. What else do you like about me?"

"Not *like*," she corrected softly. "Love."

Growling, he twisted a hand in her hair and dragged her into a long, deep kiss. "What else do you love about me?"

"How much you worry." She rubbed her cheek against his and relished the burn of his stubble on her skin. "How much you care."

His chest rumbled beneath her. "I was hoping for something a little more lewd, love."

A lie, revealed not only by the warmth of his voice, but the tenderness of his touch. "You'll figure it out, Declan. We'll do it together."

"That's the word I love the most."

Together. "Good, because you're stuck with me now."

He pulled her head back far enough for him to kiss the ink winding around her throat. "For life."

The seductive lure of his lips on her flesh was tempting, but Lex steeled herself against arousal as another idea hit her. "What if they tried to peddle their booze under their own label first? They might have approached some of your buyers."

His fingers loosened, and he frowned. "That'd be fucking stupid of them, but what about this situation isn't? I'll put out the—no, I'll have *Jas* put out the word," he corrected grumpily. "See? I know how to delegate."

"Mm-hmm. It gets easier, I promise."

"Might get even easier if you were naked."

"Lech. I'm trying to work here."

"You can keep working. I'll just have a better view."

Lex arched an eyebrow and sat up to kneel astride one of his legs. "It's my turn to watch. You forgot, didn't you?"

His lips curved into that slow, lazy smile that made her heart skip and stutter. "Then open my pants."

"You're supposed to jerk off for me, and I have to do all the prep work?" She unbuckled his belt with a single rough tug. "That doesn't seem right."

He moved without warning, not so much as a flex of muscle to give him away until it was too late. She wound up on the bed, on her back, with him straddling her waist. "Well, if that's how you feel about it..."

"You wouldn't," she breathed, even though she knew damn well—he *would*.

"What's wrong?" His fingers toyed with the button on his fly. "Don't like the view, love?"

His cock was already straining his pants, and Lex licked her lips and scratched her nails over the back of his hand. "Could be better. Get them open."

His grin widened as he batted her hand away and cupped her breast. "You didn't want to do the work, so now you're on my timetable. Maybe I want to talk business after all. How'd your meeting with the girls go?"

He already knew it had gone fine. He only wanted an excuse to hear her voice crack and her breathing hitch while he played with her nipples, pinching and tugging until she was squirming beneath him.

Delicious bastard.

She gave it to him, the same way she gave him everything—with a little fight, and a lot of attitude. Dallas took it all and demanded more.

And then gave her back everything.

9

F IGHT NIGHT WAS still her favorite part of Sector
Four.

Once a week, the Broken Circle closed early, and
Dallas's employees packed up the liquor and hauled it
across the cracked parking lot to the original warehouse,
where they'd sell it at marked-up prices to the bloodthirsty spectators.

Supposedly, this building had been the heart of the
O'Kane empire in the earliest days. Now it was a cavern-
ous empty space dominated by the cage in the middle,
with the crowd jostling for good vantage points in a
three-quarter circle around it.

The northwest corner of the warehouse was privi-
leged space, made up of a scattering of tables and seats
and a raised dais reserved for Lex and Dallas. Six headed
in that direction, toward the collection of plush couches
that made up the gang's unofficial cheering section.

She didn't feel awkward about being an unofficial

O'Kane tonight. She'd rescued Lex's pants from Bren's floor, had even let Noelle braid her hair around her head in some ridiculously complicated style that looked like a crown.

She didn't have the ink, but for the first time, she felt like she had the attitude.

Noelle clearly agreed. The pretty brunette clapped her hands together and let out a delighted noise. "Oh my God, those pants. Lex, look at her. She's *hot*."

"I know." Lex sat on a long, low table in front of the couch, leaning back against it with her elbows digging deep in the cushions. The position stretched her tiny T-shirt across her tits, her nipples showing through the thin white fabric. "Bren'll have to keep a tight lock on you tonight, honey."

It was the sort of statement that would have scared her before she knew Lex. It went without saying that no man here would lay a hand on her without her permission, because if any man dared, Lex'd be the first to rip that hand from his body.

Well, maybe not the *first*. "I think Bren's fighting tonight," she said, dropping to sit next to Noelle. "A few of the guys from Three will be here. Probably won't hurt to remind them not to piss him off."

On the other end of the couch, Rachel finished her drink and laughed. "Sweet, but beside the point. I think Lex was talking about herself."

Lex tilted her head back with a smile, her dark hair flowing over the deep black velvet covering the sofa. "Guilty."

Oh. Six's cheeks heated, and not only from embarrassment. Lex had the same magnetic quality that Scarlet always had, a larger-than-life personality that radiated strength and confidence. Dallas's queen could be hypnotic, and sometimes Six couldn't tell if she was jealous of her, or just a little turned on.

"Be nice," Noelle scolded, throwing an arm around

Six's shoulders. She managed not to stiffen at the embrace, though being hugged still felt awkward. More so when she let herself remember that the woman hugging her was Edwin Cunningham's daughter, a legitimate princess out of Eden.

It was kind of absurd for a sheltered city girl to protect *her* from flirtation. Her lips twitched, and maybe she'd gotten used to smiling, because it didn't even hurt. "Bren's not the boss of me."

"But he'd have to be part of any games you play." Lex tilted her head. "I know how it is."

"I'm glad someone does," Six muttered without thinking, setting off another round of hugs and sympathetic sounds, and she could see why Jasper had gotten Noelle a kitten to cuddle. It was probably the only way he could go fifteen minutes without being smothered in adoration.

Against all odds, Six was starting to believe it was earnest. Weird and painfully naive, but how could Noelle be anything else? She *was* from the city.

And Rachel apparently knew how to distract her. "Is Jas climbing in the cage tonight?"

"I hope so." Noelle released Six only to drop a hand to Lex's hair, stroking her fingers through it absently. "If he does, I'm tempted to climb right on in with him after he wins."

"That's not his thing," Lex teased. "It's Bren's."

"I bet I could convince him. You don't think he'd get off on having everyone watch me blow him? On playing the victorious, conquering barbarian?" Noelle shivered, her expression dreamy. "Delicious."

"Is that what it's about?" Six asked, unsure she wanted to know the answer. Everyone talked about how Bren liked to bang women in the cage after a fight, but she had yet to see him do it.

"Could be about the rush." Rachel stretched out on her side, her head propped up on the heel of one hand as her other joined Noelle's in combing through Lex's hair. "They get all worked up for the fight, and that doesn't magically fade the second someone taps out."

A vivid flashback seized Six, the memory of Bren's eyes and the way they'd looked with thwarted violence pulsing through them. He'd turned that intensity on her, and her mistake had been assuming he would burn through it by fucking.

Now that he'd been inside her, Six knew the truth. Bren didn't fuck. He *possessed*.

"She's blushing again." Lex nudged Noelle. "Should we congratulate her, or get all the dirty details?"

Six fisted her hands to keep from covering her cheeks. They *were* burning, but considering how often Noelle turned pink, maybe there wasn't any shame in that.

But she still couldn't make the mental leap. Rachel and Lex and Noelle were sprawled together, touching one another in a casual, comfortable way that had plenty of the outside cage fighters casting them appreciative looks. There was a belonging there, an easy trust that made Six's skin prickle in warning.

And envy. God, so much envy. She wanted to lean into Noelle's hugs—return them, even. She wanted to share the wonder and giddy confusion of Bren's touch instead of hoarding it away.

But her jaw wouldn't unlock, not until she saw Noelle's brows pull together and her lips part, and she knew she was about to get another one of those supportive hugs as the Eden princess chided Lex, and her pride wouldn't survive it.

"I need a drink," she blurted instead, rocketing off the couch and out of Noelle's well-meaning reach. She plowed through the crowd and ducked between two fighters, only to smash headlong into one of the last people she wanted to see.

"Whoa." Elvis steadied her with heavy hands on her

shoulders. "Slow it down, sweetheart."

Of the three men she'd vouched for, Elvis was the simplest—and the least civilized. He was good at crime, a veritable prince of Sector Three's black market, and a lecherous asshole. But he didn't have a taste for murder or unwilling sex, which was a glowing fucking character reference compared to most of the men Trent had gathered around him.

Six knocked his hand away and glowered at him. "Still not your sweetheart."

"Okay," he said easily. "Hey, you and the O'Kane girls are tight, yeah?"

She glanced back to the couches, where Noelle was watching her with big, heartbroken eyes while her fingers traced meaningless patterns across Lex's bare collarbone.

She felt like she'd kicked a puppy in the face, which made her even less patient with Elvis. "I guess."

"They look pretty close."

She'd thought Trent had beaten it out of her, but Elvis's transparent, glassy-eyed approval stirred protective anger. "Don't have too much fun looking."

He snorted. "Well, that's the point, right? Show us all the good things we can stare at but never touch?"

Her nails bit into her palms. "I dunno, Elvis. Maybe the point is that they like it?"

"Do they?" He said it almost too casually, his gaze fixed on the women in the corner.

He didn't give a fuck. Oh, he might stroke his dick a little faster at the idea of Lex and Noelle and Rachel being enthusiastic, but only because in his imagination, it was all about *him*. A show for him, or a tease as punishment, and nowhere in his pea-sized brain did they register as people with their own desires.

Her temper slipped free. He had to be half a foot taller than her, but she still grabbed his chin and wrenched his face around, forcing him to meet her eyes.

"You leave them alone, you hear me? Something *good* might finally happen to our sector, and I'm not gonna let you ruin it because you're a pervert."

"Jesus Christ, Six." He shoved at her hand and glared at her. "What the hell's your problem? I'm not doing anything."

Her problem? Her problem was that the comfortable shell of numbness that had allowed her to deal with Elvis and the other men from Three was cracking, and rage was bubbling up in its place.

They'd all watched Trent abuse her. Elvis, Cain, even Riff. They'd never participated. Cain had quietly disapproved, and Riff had vanished from the ranks of Trent's men in silent, reproachful protest. Elvis had gone so far as to discourage others from taking advantage of her at Trent's invitation.

That had made them decent in her mind. Hell, it had damn near made them heroes.

But they'd never tried to stop him.

She felt exposed all over again, humiliated and enraged, without the comfortable lie of imagining no one else would have done more. A few weeks in Sector Four had stripped away that delusion. "Why are you here?" she demanded. "To gawk?"

"I came to fight." He said it as if it was obvious, his tone underscored by his mockingly upraised brows. "Fight night?"

It should have made her feel better. The chances were good he'd face an O'Kane, and most of them had protective bullying down to an art. They'd beat some manners into him, make it clear he needed to stop leering at women like every breath they took was for his benefit.

It wouldn't be half as satisfying as beating that lesson into him herself.

Six shoved past him, ignoring the smug laughter that followed. She wasn't tall enough to see through the surrounding crowd, but she knew where Dallas would be. She ducked past fighters and dodged one or two friendly grins before breaking free of the crowd on the far side of the cage.

Her stomach did a funny flip when she saw Bren standing with his leader, already shirtless and barefoot in anticipation of a fight. She'd woken up wrapped around that hard, merciless body, and he'd murmured with sleepy affection as she explored every flexing muscle in the soft light of dawn.

It'd been different, that second time. He'd held back, letting her slide on top of him and set the tempo. But even flat on his back with her riding him to her own orgasm, he managed to seem utterly in control. *Indulgent*, as if he'd give her anything, but remain effortlessly dominant.

He started to smile, but the expression faded as he studied her face. "Everything okay?"

With a deep breath to steady her—not to mention the comfort of Bren's presence—she crossed the space between them and planted herself firmly in front of Dallas O'Kane. "I want to fight in the cage tonight."

Dallas raised both eyebrows, but Bren was too busy surveying the warehouse to catch the man's quizzical look. "Did something happen?" he asked, stepping closer.

So protective, and she didn't know if it soothed her anger or stoked it higher. This was what she'd never had through all those terrible months of Elvis and Riff and Cain sitting by, doing nothing. Someone who gave enough of a shit to *do* something. "It's not like that."

"But, all of a sudden, you want to fight?"

She didn't point out that she'd always wanted to fight, because he'd still want to know why tonight was the night she stood up for it. "Someone's going to kick Elvis's ass tonight. I want to do it."

Dallas spoke. "I'm sure Bren'll do it for you, honey. Free of charge."

Ignoring him, Six held Bren's gaze. "I can do this," she told him softly. "It's how you guys clear the air, isn't it? Elvis and I have a hell of a lot of air to clear."

His jaw tightened. "You climb in the cage when you're pissed, and things can go south real quick. I've been there. You make mistakes."

Out of the corner of her eye, she caught Dallas waving toward the corner. Summoning Lex to wrangle her back into place, no doubt, so Six grabbed Bren's arms and stepped toe-to-toe with him, digging desperately for the words to convince him. "I'm pissed," she admitted hoarsely. "But this isn't all temper, I swear. They took something from me, and if I don't get it back on my own, it won't matter. It won't be *mine*."

"They?"

"Trent. All of them. They made me a victim." Lex was already heading their way, and Six's seconds were numbered. "Help me be something else again."

Lex walked up and slipped her arm around Dallas's neck. "What's up?"

Bren spoke, his eyes still locked with Six's. "The lady wants to fight."

"That so?" Lex whispered something too low to hear in Dallas's ear.

Whatever it was, it drew a heavy sigh from Sector Four's king. Six braced herself for disappointment, the only thing that kept her from bristling when Dallas snapped his fingers at Bren. "Has she got a chance in hell?"

"Against the pretty boy? You bet your ass."

"And when that pretty boy lands a hit or two on her? It'll look bad if you climb in after her to dismember him."

But Bren shook his head. "I'm square. Besides—it wouldn't be a fair fight, a *good* one, if he stood there and let her whale on him."

Six's heart lurched painfully. "You believe I can do it."

136

"Because you can." He brushed a stray lock of hair from her forehead. "Watch your ribs while you're swinging, don't telegraph your moves, and get this out of the way. He looks like a hair puller."

Dallas groaned. "Jesus fucking Christ, it's the end of fucking days all over again." He moved Bren aside with a hand on his shoulder and forced Six to face him. It was hard—Dallas O'Kane had what Wilson Trent had only dreamed of, the kind of sheer presence that carried easy power. He took up too much space and radiated the sort of danger that made you want to roll over in pure animal submission, anything to keep him pleased with you.

He didn't look pleased right now. He watched her like she was a splinter shoved under his thumbnail, and he didn't know if he could dig her out. "I knew you were gonna be a pain in my ass," he said finally. "You kick the shit out of that fucker, you hear me? I don't have time for Bren to go swearing blood vengeance on my new sector."

She'd mostly wrapped her head around the notion that Bren would protect her. The idea that he cared enough to go on a rampage after the damage was already done was strange and intimidating, but she didn't hate it. "You heard him. He wants a fair fight."

"So he's telling himself." Dallas shook his head and jabbed a finger at Lex. "You better be right."

For a moment, Six thought the woman might just bite him, but she only smiled slowly. "Does it ever go well when you doubt me? A king should have a little faith in his queen."

Laughing, Dallas sank a hand into Lex's hair and dragged her to him. "This is more than a *little* faith, love." Then he was kissing her, hot and rough and wild, and for once Six didn't avert her gaze.

Lex lingered before breaking the kiss with a sharp bite at the corner of his mouth. Then she ran over to the cage, using the momentum of her speed to hop up on a crate beside it. "I hope you bloodthirsty bastards brought your betting money tonight. We've got a fight night first—a lady in the cage."

Hoots and cheers greeted her words, along with one punk at the fringes of the room who yelled, "Cat fight!"

"You wish, you stupid fuck." Lex's cool smile shut him up, and a new hush fell over the room.

It wasn't a joke, the kind of show put on for money next door at the Broken Circle. No naked mud-wrestling, but a fucking *fight*, with blood and blows—and wagers.

Six stripped off her boots and dug into her pocket for her precious wad of cash. Not all of it—she'd found a dozen hiding places to squirrel away her valuables, all of them readily accessible if she ever needed to run. But the largest bills she kept on her, and she pressed them into Bren's hand. "Make me some fucking money, huh?"

"I'll place the bets. You win the fight."

"Done." And because it meant that much, she rolled up on her toes and kissed him once, quick and fleeting, before spinning away. There was too much excitement roiling through her already to add the taste of him to the mix. Besides, Lex was watching, waiting for her to climb into the cage and call Elvis out.

Pulse racing, she hauled open the cage door. The concrete was cool under her bare feet, and the audience seemed oddly removed, their faces bisected and obscured by the crisscrossing metal. She was the object of everyone's attention, as scrutinized as she'd ever been on a stage, but this was different.

This was where she felt strong.

Twisting in a slow circle, she scanned the crowd until she found the familiar blond hair and pretty face. "Elvis," she called out. "You're here to fight. Let's fight."

He held both hands out to his sides. "You've got to be shitting me, Six."

It didn't matter that smiles were still awkward for her. One came easily now, and she knew how she must look, grinning wildly in Lex's leather pants. Dangerous.

Untouchable. "Don't worry, it's not to the death or anything. You can tap out when you've had enough."

"No way. You've lost your fucking mind." But he kicked off his shoes and tugged at his shirt in spite of the denial.

The crowd erupted in cheers and shouts as money flashed and bets were laid. Elvis climbed in the cage, and Lex slammed the door shut behind him.

Just like that, the crowd was gone. Everything outside the ring ceased to exist, leaving her and him and the unforgiving cement that one of them would be kissing before too long. "How 'bout a wager, El? Just between you and me."

He eyed her warily. "What kind?"

"If I win, you go a month without saying a single lewd thing to any O'Kane woman. Or leering at them, either."

"Done. We don't even have to fight."

It didn't make her feel better. It made her feel naked, because the emotion lurking behind his eyes wasn't fear or dislike, it was *pity*. A few years ago, he would have faced her with anticipation and determination and wary respect, because Trent had picked her for a reason. She'd had a reputation.

No one remembered it. They looked at her now and saw a victim, and as long as she had to face that reflected back at her everywhere she turned, it was all she'd ever be. They'd smother what was left of her pride in well-meaning sympathy.

Words wouldn't change it. Action would. So she feinted, just enough of a swing to give him a warning, because she didn't want anyone saying she'd taken a sucker shot. He brought his hands up, ready to block, and she twisted in under his arms and drilled him in the ribs.

"Ow, fuck!" He staggered back with another, harsher curse.

Her body shifted, ready to press the advantage on instinct, but she held back. "Fight me. Don't you fucking dare hold back."

"I don't *want* to hit you, you crazy bitch!"

"Why not?" She swung again, smacking him in the side with only enough force to irritate, not injure. "You watched other people do it for months."

"You think I liked it?" He deflected her third blow with a sweep of his arm. "You think we didn't sit around and try to think of ways to get you out of there, me and Riff and Cain?"

"Yeah, I'm sure it sucked for you." She rammed her shoulder into his, pushing him against the cage bars. "Did you sit around and think about ways to get all the other girls out, too?"

He finally struck back this time, shoving her toward the center of the ring. "We should have fought him, right? Easy way to get dead."

"Then you made your choice." He blocked her next jab, smacking aside her wrist hard enough to bruise. Bren would be pissed if she ended up with too many, but she didn't dare spare a moment to look for him.

Instead, she aimed the next punch straight at Elvis's perfectly chiseled jaw.

He took the blow and struck back, hitting her hard in the midsection. It knocked the air out of her lungs and sent her stumbling back, but the pain had another meaning this time. It prickled through her, awakening every nerve, and left a wicked clarity in its wake.

Not pleasure, but something better. Purpose.

Maybe she couldn't be like Bren and push toward the pain like a lover, but she knew how to weather it. So Elvis was still pulling back when she swung around and knocked his face in the opposite direction.

A roar rose in the warehouse, loud enough to penetrate the blood rushing through her veins.

No, not just a roar. Female screams of approval cut

above the noise, and she saw a swell of movement over her opponent's shoulder. The O'Kane women, standing on the couches and cheering her on like she was their champion.

Like she was one of them.

She was gonna kick Elvis's fucking ass.

Sometimes, the hardest thing to do was nothing.

Bren held his ground during the fight—not because he'd promised Dallas, but because Six deserved it. A turn to test herself, to do battle against the shadows of her past and emerge not only triumphant, but bloody enough to know she'd *earned* her victory. It hadn't been handed to her. She'd claimed it in a fair contest, which meant no one could take it away. And if they did, she'd just fight for it again.

But oh, it was hard as hell to *watch*. He felt every blow in his bones, every scrape of concrete and burn of knuckle on hard bone, and only the knowledge that this was what Six wanted kept him from interfering when it looked like the tide was turning in Elvis's favor.

Then she laid him out, riding him down to pin his face to the cement until he tapped out in weak defeat, and Bren still had to do nothing, because the other O'Kane women swept Six away to celebrate.

"Well, I didn't have to have Jas or Flash sit on you," Dallas drawled beside him. "That's something."

Bren's hands ached from clenching them. "I've been teaching her. It's not like I threw her to the wolves."

His leader regarded him seriously for a few seconds before lowering his voice. "That's not what I meant, Bren. Not even close."

"Yeah." Then, because he had to, he confessed. "If he'd fought dirty, even a little..."

"I know." No judgment in those words, and no disapproval. "Hell, I would have helped."

Across the warehouse, Six accepted an open bottle of whiskey from Rachel—and smiled. Bren relaxed his hands and flexed his fingers. "I'm still going to kick his ass one day, but not tonight. Six took care of that."

"She sure did." Dallas slugged Bren on the shoulder. "Don't know how much of that was your training and how much was her, but the girl's got moves."

"Told you. So did Lex."

"So she did. She'll be insufferable tonight."

He seemed so pleased about the prospect that Bren had to laugh. "I better collect Six's cash. The odds were against her, you know. She won big."

Ace was sprawled at a table in the O'Kane section, counting a ridiculous stack of cash. The artist grinned and kicked back a chair in invitation. "Got your girl's money. And mine. I haven't made this much on a fight since Mad put a beatdown on the Armstrong brothers."

Bren sat, but his gaze kept tracking back to Six. She was wedged between Lex and Rachel, her eyes bright as the women toasted her. "She did good."

Ace laughed and nudged most of the cash across the table. "I was gonna point out that she looked good too, but I'm in no mood to get my teeth knocked down my throat. You've got that look, brother."

"Do I?"

"Mmm. Maybe it's because you finally got laid. I was starting to worry about your poor dick, all neglected and unused. You haven't exactly been partying hard since your girl showed up."

As if Ace had any worry left to spare after seeing to his own overtaxed libido. "I didn't before Six got here, either."

"But you burned through the tension." Ace swept his winnings into a haphazard pile. "If you need an outlet, I'm here. I know you two are punching each other in the face and all that, but just in case it's not enough."

Ace worked pain with a whip or a flogger the same way he did with his needles—skillfully. "I don't know, maybe. If Six is into it."

That sent Ace's eyebrows up. "Like, you want her to watch? Or...?"

"Or whatever she wants."

A slow nod, and Ace grinned. "Sure thing, brother. Lady's choice."

They didn't have to take him up on the offer right away. But Six was curious about it, the mingled pleasure and pain, and there was no better way for her to understand than to experience it firsthand.

"Yeah." He folded her money into his pocket, reached for the nearest bottle, and poured Ace a drink. "Lady's choice."

By the time Dallas chased the outsiders back into the night, it was clear to Bren that the O'Kane women had claimed Six as one of their own, ink or no.

They were out on the floor, dancing to the smoky melody pouring from a small set of speakers hung from the cage bars, smooth pre-Flare jazz instead of the usual hardcore bass rhythms. The music was different, and so was the dancing, swaying hips and closed eyes and low laughter.

Six was swaying too, crushed between Noelle and one of the newer girls—Ace's apprentice, Emma. It made a hell of a picture, Noelle sweet and soft and Six with her stark, hard edges and Emma a mixture of pretty and punk, covered in ink.

They looked like they came from different worlds, but they laughed like they were family. And when Six twisted around to meet his eyes, the slow smile that curved her lips was drunk on a feeling he recognized all too well.

Belonging.

He almost sat to wait for her to finish the dance, but he'd been patient enough, so he held out his hand.

Noelle whispered something in Six's ear that brought a flush to her cheeks, but she broke free of the giggling dancers and curled her fingers around his. "Hi."

"Hi." Her knuckles were still red and swollen, and there was a splotchy mark high on her left cheek that would bruise by morning, but otherwise she looked fine. Unscarred. "Congratulations on winning your first fight."

She *glowed*. "I kinda thought you'd be pissed I didn't flatten him at the beginning. I had to goad him into fighting back."

"Chivalry isn't dead. It's just misplaced."

"Whatever that means." Six shifted closer, until his chin brushed her temple and the tiny strands of hair that had escaped her braid tickled his cheek. "I don't know, maybe it's unfair to be mad at him. If he'd tried to stop Trent, he would've ended up dead."

Alone, probably—but he hadn't been alone. All it had taken to keep Trent's power base secure was for Elvis and the others to sit back and do nothing. "If that were true, not a damn thing would ever change. It's something he tells himself to sleep at night, sweetness. That's all."

"I guess." Another step and she was pressed against him, her lips brushing his throat with her next whisper. "Knowing you might get dead hasn't stopped any of you crazy fuckers yet."

The grazing touch sparked heat in his blood, and he pulled her closer with one hand splayed across her lower back. "Welcome to Sector Four."

"Are you my prize for winning?"

Things were heating up on the dance floor. An even sultrier song had rolled over on the radio, and the women had paired off into slow dances. Emma and Noelle were still whispering and laughing, but Lex and Rachel had a whole different vibe going, serious and charged.

Bren spun Six so that her back nestled against his chest. "If you're ready to leave the party."

Tension rolled through her body, but it wasn't the usual awkward stiffness. She felt restless underneath his hands, coiled tight. Alive. "I don't know," she whispered, low and husky. "Not—not yet."

Dallas was in the corner, talking to Jasper as people continued to drift out of the warehouse. But his gaze was on the women. On Lex. He was still high on the success of the evening, on their joint rule and shared, seamless power.

"There's nothing Dallas wouldn't give her tonight." Bren murmured the words in Six's ear. "If Lex wants Rachel, he'll do it."

Her breathing hitched. "What would you do if she wanted me?"

Does she? It didn't matter. His hand clenched in Six's shirt. "She can't have you. Not tonight."

"Possessive, aren't you?"

"She can't have you." The words ripped free of him again, rough and raw. "Maybe not ever."

Six shivered, all teasing gone from her voice. "What about everyone else?"

She liked to watch, but she'd never given a single hint that she wanted to join in anyone's sexual revelries. "We look," he said finally, "but I'm the only one who touches you."

She slid her hand over his, pressing his palm tight to her abdomen, and there was something almost soothing in the way she stroked his wrist. "I don't need anyone else."

Not a concession, but a promise. A vow. "Only me, sweetness."

She laughed and twined her fingers with his. "I hope that doesn't apply to friendly touching, too. I promised Lex a dance."

Lex already had her hands in Rachel's back pockets.

Bren released Six with a kiss to the shoulder. "Better go make good on it before things get naked over there."

She squeezed his hand and slipped away, and Rachel and Lex welcomed her with smiles and soft kisses to her cheek.

As the three of them swayed and whispered, Dallas appeared at Bren's side. "She's as good as in, you know," he said. "If I don't offer her ink after tonight, none of us will ever get our dicks touched again."

"Sure you would." Bren couldn't stop the grin that curved his lips. "You've got two hands."

Dallas shuddered. "That's the most depressing thought I've had in a decade."

"Then we'd better make it official, after all."

"I'll talk to Lex. *You* keep your mouth shut on the topic, unless you want to risk a little queenly wrath. The women are her domain."

Bren watched Six's hand graze the back of Lex's. "Will she make her wait?"

Dallas shrugged. "If she thinks that's what the girl needs. Lex knows people better than they know themselves."

Better to wait than offer her something she might not be ready to accept, not just yet. "Trent did a number on her. Lex'll understand."

"Trent screwed them all up. Her, the men, the whole damn sector. They're like a pack of whipped dogs who don't know when to stop biting."

Six would have a place here, and ink of her own. "It can't be because of me. You know that, right?"

"Yeah." Dallas crossed his arms and spent a silent moment watching the three women dance before tilting his head. "Lex is cooking up a little fantasy for Rachel tonight. Am I imagining it, or is your girl into watching? Because Rachel sure seems to get off on having an audience."

Noelle and Emma had already drifted toward the

back door with Jasper in tow. Only the five of them were left, and Bren eyed the couch on the dais. "Here?"

"Mmm." His gaze fixed on his queen, who'd wrapped one arm around Rachel's waist, her thumb gliding under the denim at the small of the woman's back. "Lex has a filthy imagination. The floor lights'll be off, so Rachel won't be able to see you, but that's kind of the point."

A fantasy, all right. It shouldn't have worked so well, a perfect chain reaction of lust and need, but it did. Rachel had been exploring her exhibitionist tendencies, Lex got off on joining in that exploration, and Dallas got off on Lex.

But a show wasn't a show without an audience. Six would say yes—she was hopped up on adrenaline, riding the rush—which left him to decide. And sitting in the shadows, Six's bare skin heating beneath his hands as a fantasy played out before them?

"Hell, yes."

10

R ACHEL WAS DANCING again...and this time Lex was dancing with her.

Snuggled against Bren's side in the darkness, Six watched the two of them move together, watched Lex's fingers slide up under Rachel's shirt as the other woman moaned softly. They swayed in front of the couch where Dallas sat, all three illuminated by lights that seemed stark in comparison to the shadows surrounding the dais.

Not *quite* a stage, but Lex was turning it into one. For once, Six couldn't look away.

The hem of Rachel's tank top rucked up, baring pale skin as Lex cupped her shoulder beneath the fabric. "Soft and sweet. You've tried to harden up, but that's not you."

Rachel swayed and blinked before clearing her throat. "Isn't it?"

No, it wasn't her. Six could see it a mile off, a gentleness wrapped around her that no one else possessed, not even Noelle, with all her city innocence and open affection. Maybe that was why watching Rachel on the stage was so difficult—something that precious should be cherished, not thrown to the wolves, naked and unprotected.

She was protected now, with Lex in front of her and Dallas sprawled behind, and Six had no doubt the man was aware of everything. Of Lex and Rachel, of the area beyond their circle of light, of every possible variable. Hell, he probably knew how many breaths Six had taken since she sat down.

Not enough to keep her head clear. She exhaled gustily and slid her fingers over Bren's leg in search of his hand.

He wrapped it around hers, leaned closer, and whispered, "Anytime you need to go, say the word."

Lex smoothed her fingers toward Rachel's breasts, and Six shivered as she imagined the phantom touch on her own skin. Not Lex's hands, though. Bren's, work-roughened and sure, scraping sensation in their wake. "As long as they want us watching—"

On the dais, Rachel hissed in a breath as Lex stripped off the tank top she wore, exposing her to sight as well as touch. "Is this what you like?" She accompanied the question with a gentle sweep of her thumb over Rachel's nipple. "This?" A quick flick of the hardened peak.

Even Six could see she wanted more. Dallas apparently agreed. His laughter rolled across the room, low and lazy, as he stretched out his legs. "I think she likes it rougher, darling. Those sweet nipples are aching to be pinched. Make her lick your fingers first."

"Yes, sir." Lex traced her fingers over Rachel's mouth but pulled them back just a little when she parted her lips. Her tongue darted out, but she still had to chase after Lex's hand.

She licked Lex's fingertips slowly, leaving them wet and glistening. "Like that?"

"Mmm, so obedient." Instead of dropping her hand, Lex wound it into Rachel's hair with a wicked grin. "But I like to misbehave." Then she dipped her head and sucked one pink nipple into her mouth.

Dallas laughed again, watching with no hint of disapproval. Six fidgeted on the couch, as if that would change the fact that her nipples were tight enough to ache.

And she was starting to ache other places, too.

She didn't *have* to imagine Bren's mouth on her nipple. She could summon the sensation from memory—the rough suction, the hint of teeth, the way it shot pleasure straight to her clit. And he was right there beside her, his body warm and hard against her left side. He seemed relaxed, his expression remaining the same even when Lex switched to Rachel's other nipple and yanked at the woman's jeans.

A moment later, she slipped her hand into the denim and straightened just in time to catch Rachel's ragged moan with her open mouth.

Bren shifted beside Six, his hand stroking over hers.

Her focus narrowed to those precious inches of skin. Dallas was talking again, saying something about fingers and making Rachel come, but even the most obscene words tripping out of his mouth couldn't compete with Bren tracing a leisurely path from her knuckles to her nails and back.

She wet her suddenly dry lips and whispered the first thing that popped into her head, anything that would distract her from how badly she needed him to stroke her everywhere else. "Lex isn't very obedient."

"No." The side of Bren's hand brushed her thigh. "But Dallas likes it."

That didn't make sense. Nothing made sense about these men and their indulgent idea of dominance. Dallas had tried to explain it at the first party she'd attended, claiming he didn't need to prove he was the strongest, because his people trusted him to make life good.

He didn't bully, he seduced.

Just like Bren. "You said you like being dominant, too."

"It's what I am," he corrected. "I've tried to submit. It doesn't work."

Submit. The word still tightened her chest with fear, and not the kind she liked, the kind that heightened an experience. This lodged in her throat like a lump of tears, no matter how hard she fought it down.

In the darkness, watching Rachel writhe on Lex's fingers, everything seemed a little surreal. Distant enough for Six to whisper her confession. "I don't know what submission means here, but I'm scared I won't be able to give it to you."

"It doesn't mean one thing to everyone." He nodded to the dais. "Watch."

Rachel shuddered and made a frustrated noise as Lex slowed the pace of her hand. "Don't stop," she begged. "Let me come—"

"Shh." Lex licked a delicate line of ink tracking across Rachel's collarbone. "Not this quick, honey. Up and down a couple times first. You'll come so hard you can't see straight. Right, Declan?"

"Mmm." Dallas and Lex exchanged a look, and he smiled as he stroked his thumb along his belt. "Why don't you get her out of those pants so we can do the first time up right?"

"Hear that, honey?" Lex bit Rachel's earlobe and shoved the loosened jeans off her hips. "We."

Another shudder, and she clung to Lex's shoulders as she stepped free of the denim and her white lace panties. "We?"

"Dallas can't let me have all the fun." Her voice lowered to an inviting whisper as she pushed her still-wet fingers between Rachel's lips. "You have no idea how deep he can fuck a woman."

Jesus *Christ*.

"Slow, I think." Lex spoke lazily, her words matching the rhythm of her fingers. "Until you get off at least once. Then I want to watch him ride you so hard you can't even scream."

Rachel groaned and twisted one trembling hand in Lex's T-shirt so roughly the thin cotton tore.

"Uh-uh. I didn't say you could take her clothes off." Dallas patted the arm of the couch. "Darling?"

Lex steered Rachel to the end of the couch and bent her over it. The position put her face-to-face with Dallas, and she braced one hand on his chest. Six held her breath until her lungs burned, but she couldn't *breathe*. There was something terrifyingly intense about this moment, about Rachel, naked and vulnerable, bent between two clothed bodies, as open and helpless as she'd ever been on the stage.

Dallas touched Rachel's cheek, so gentle Six's breath exploded from her in a relieved sigh that almost drowned out his words. "You wanna be a good girl, darling?"

"I want—" The words cut off in a cry as Lex bent and licked the small of her back. "I want to be good."

He rewarded Rachel with a smile and slipped his hand into her hair.

The first time he'd fucked her, Bren had grasped Six's hair the same way. Now, she reached up to the braid coiled around her head, and she half-wished she'd taken it down so she could feel that tingle in her scalp.

Bren took over, pulling it down easily and without a word. He unraveled the braid the same way, with silent, practiced ease. Twisted locks of hair tumbled around her face and over her shoulders, tickling her throat as he eased his fingers through the strands.

It was hotter than the hand-holding.

Lex smoothed both hands up Rachel's back and down again, over the swell of her bare ass. "Legs apart, honey," she murmured, rubbing her knuckles over the outer lips of Rachel's pussy.

She obeyed with a whimper, coming off the floor onto her tiptoes, and Six felt the first stirrings of envy. What would it be like to trust so effortlessly? Even when Dallas guided Rachel's cheek to his thigh, leaving her balanced precariously—her ass in the air, her legs spread wide enough to bare her completely to Lex's touch—she looked so damn unconcerned. Starving to get off, maybe, but not the least bit worried about anything else.

"She makes it look easy." Six pressed her thigh more firmly against Bren's.

"Yeah." He took her hand and brought it to his mouth for a slow kiss.

"She's wet." Lex paused long enough to drag her shirt over her head and let it fall to the floor. "Already wet enough for my fingers, if you want me to fuck her."

"Bring her up," Dallas ordered, stroking Rachel's spine with his free hand. "But not all the way, not yet. She's putting on a show, after all."

There was no way Dallas could see them in the darkness, not with the lights glaring down on the dais, but for one moment it felt like he was staring straight at Six as his thumb followed the curve of Rachel's ass. "You want to give everyone a good show, don't you, honey?"

Her desperate nod turned into a shudder as Lex rocked her hand, sliding her fingers deep. She pulled them free to circle Rachel's clit, then did it all over again. One thrust, followed by a slow, wet tease.

Rachel fidgeted helplessly, arching her back and try- ing to move against Lex's hand until Dallas pinned her in place with a palm on the small of her back.

It was too much for Six. The shamelessness of it all, the intensity, and Bren's lips were still touching her skin, kindling a fire she didn't know how to manage.

She clenched her thighs together and closed her eyes, but that only made it worse. Rachel was panting and moaning, and Dallas whispered filthy encouragement to Lex, things like *is her pussy as sweet as she is?* and *let me see you lick the taste of her off your fingers.*

Too easy to imagine those words directed at Bren, and herself in Rachel's place. It was a fantasy she shouldn't want. Pinned, *bound*, trapped while he worked her and worked her, used his fingers and his tongue and tricks she couldn't imagine, because her part of Sector Three wasn't the kind of place where people sat around dreaming up ways to get a woman off.

God, Bren probably knew them all.

Rachel cried out—sudden, strangled, hoarse—and Lex moaned. "Ride it. Squeeze my fucking fingers and ride it."

Bren exhaled sharply against the back of Six's hand. His mouth opened, and his tongue flicked over her skin.

Biting back a moan, Six slammed her head against the back of the couch. It was a struggle not to lift her hips in a silent plea. She was so turned on, so wet, so *empty*—

"Give her another one," Dallas rasped, the rough tone twisting Six's brain into knots. So she spun it into her fantasy, made it Bren's voice against her ear, demanding she take more.

Leave it to her to need a fantasy with the real thing right next to her, but she couldn't ask. She couldn't even unclench her jaw, or she'd whimper.

A soft tug—Bren's free hand on the zipper of her leather pants.

Her nails scraped the leather cushion as she struggled for breath. "I don't know what I'm doing."

"I do." He pulled the zipper down slowly, the sound eclipsed by another volley of sharp moans from the dais. "Open your eyes and watch them fuck her."

It was more than a command. It was *permission*, and her eyelids drifted open in time to watch Dallas pin Rachel's arms behind her back, his hand massive around her slender wrists. Her expression was pure pleasure, lips parted, eyes clenched shut, and it felt like a lesson.

Trust led to bliss.

Lex kissed the back of Dallas's wrist and reached for her own pants. "Did you know she got drunk once and told me she'd always kinda wanted to have sex with me?" She paused. "*Kinda.* What's that all about?"

Dallas chuckled and stroked Rachel's hair with his free hand. "Not everyone is as forward as you, Lexie."

And that was all Six heard, because Bren's fingertips grazed the bare skin of her abdomen, and it was her turn to lift her hips in a futile attempt to nudge a caress where she needed it.

"Relax," Bren whispered. "Trust me to give it to you."

Trusting wasn't the same thing as relaxing. Hell, it felt like the opposite, her hands clenching as she concentrated on stilling her movements, on waiting for his touch.

She tried not to be jealous that *Rachel* was writhing as much as Dallas's grip on her wrists would allow. Freedom by restraint, a concept that had made no fucking sense until this moment, where holding herself motionless seemed like the hardest thing she'd ever done.

Her body trembled, but she trusted him, and as Lex tugged Dallas's pants open, freeing his cock to press against Rachel's lips, Bren eased his hand lower.

Lower, parting her beneath the leather until his finger brushed her clit.

Glancing contact, too gentle to do anything but twist her into tighter knots, but she still hissed out a breath and let her head fall back, staring blindly at the darkness above them as Dallas's low voice drifted past her. "That's right, honey. Lex is gonna get a good grip on your hair and show you just how I like it."

The murmurs subsided, replaced by the distinct, wet sounds of an enthusiastic blowjob, and Bren teased Six with an even lighter touch.

Her hips began to move, and she groaned and stilled

again. "My body's not listening to me."

"Maybe it doesn't follow orders well." His thumb swept over her hipbone.

A lower moan broke through the silence, and Six rolled her head to one side, her gaze swinging automatically back to the stage. Dallas was the one making the noise this time, as Lex and Rachel kissed around the head of his cock until their mouths met in a joyful tangle of clashing tongues.

He still had Rachel pinned in place, and Six wanted to squirm along with her as Lex twisted her fingers in the blonde's hair and guided her to take his cock deeper.

Six wet her lips and skated her nails over Bren's arm. "Doesn't look like Rachel's body follows orders, either, but that's not stopping Dallas."

"Because he knows what she wants." His hand eased lower. "They both do, or they wouldn't have started this."

Rachel's lips slid down Dallas's shaft until they bumped the fist Lex had curled around the base, and the visual was so raw Six gave up. She pushed her hips up toward Bren's hand, and hissed in a relieved breath at the momentary pressure. "Well, it's fucking hot."

Bren shuddered wordlessly, pushing one finger inside her while rocking the heel of his hand against her clit.

Gasping, her body clenching tight, Six shoved her hand against her mouth. Too late to muffle all sound, and that was when her buzz of adrenaline shattered.

Reality slammed into her, sharpening every sense until the reality of it overwhelmed her. She was in a warehouse, sprawled on a couch with Bren's hand in her pants, his finger *inside* her, and it wasn't some frantic, rushed thing like in Sector Three. This was slow and lazy and deliberate, *public*. She was rubbing against him like a cat in heat, eager for an orgasm she hadn't even doubted she wanted, because watching Rachel come on Lex's fingers had gotten her wet.

And she didn't want to stop. God, she wanted *more*.

On the stage, Lex nuzzled Dallas's cheek and said something, something that had to be about Rachel, who was bobbing up and down, her cheeks hollow as she sucked with a bliss that pushed Six's arousal higher.

Closing her eyes didn't help. Dallas's strained voice chased her there, pitched to carry in a way meant to remind her that he knew she was here, watching, and he wanted her to hear every word. "She's sweet as sugar, Lexie, hot and eager. You'll see when she's got this clever tongue in your pussy. I think I'll reward her every time she makes you come all over her face."

"See, Rachel?" Six could imagine Lex cooing the words against the woman's ear, her breath stirring blonde hair. "He'll take care of you. All that hunger. Want to know what Dallas's idea of a reward is?"

A gasp, a shuddering sigh. "Yes."

Christ, Six did, too.

"Not just fucking you," Dallas rumbled, his voice so roughly compelling that Six's eyes fluttered open. He had Rachel's head tilted back at a precarious angle, her throat stretched in a pale, vulnerable arc. "Fucking you together. The first time, I might just impale you on my cock and hold you still while Lex sucks your clit."

Rachel's hands flexed in his grip, and her reply came out husky and challenging. "I thought you wanted me to eat her pussy."

He laughed. "That's how you earn the reward, darling." Then he pushed her back down and watched in heavy-lidded approval as she willingly parted her lips to accommodate his cock, and Six wondered hazily if Bren was taking mental notes about what made her clench around his finger.

Just in case he wasn't, she turned her head to his, leaning her forehead against his chin without sacrificing her view of the stage. "You could do that to me sometime."

"Fuck your face?" He thrust a second finger into her pussy along with the first. "Or make you go down on Lex?"

Grinding against Lex on the dance floor had been fun. Watching her fuck was, too. But any attempt to put herself into the action happening on the stage morphed into Bren's hands, Bren's cock, just... *Bren.*

His fingers pumped into her, and she lowered her voice. "No one touches me but you. But you can do whatever you want to me."

"Can I?" His free hand grazed her breast, and he pinched her nipple until she had to bite her wrist again.

Lex was wiggling out of her pants, and Six considered doing the same. Hell, if Bren wanted to bend her over the arm of the couch and fuck her to the sound of Rachel going down on Lex, she'd let him. "Yes."

Lex urged Rachel up until Dallas's dick slid free of her mouth, then pulled her around to the front of the couch. She stood there, keeping her wrists crossed behind her back, as Dallas hauled Lex to kneel astride his lap, her legs folded beneath her, her back snuggled against his chest. His hand drifted down to cup her pussy, his fingers rubbing until her back arched.

Six bit back a whimper and clutched at Bren's arm. "That," she whispered hoarsely, imagining her back pressed to the solid wall of his chest, his arms around her, caging and protecting her as he worked his fingers deep. "I want that."

His breath hitched, and he pinched her harder. "Now?"

The pain short-circuited something in her brain. Her hips twisted off the couch, as if she could ride his fingers just by driving up against them. If he got her out of these damn restrictive pants— "Yes. Yes, yes, yes."

It was dizzying how quickly he pulled away and tore his shirt over his head. Then he had her bent in front of him, dragging her pants low enough for her to kick them away.

He closed his arms around her, his chest hot at her back. "Say it again," he rasped.

She couldn't breathe. Even in the shadows, she felt exposed, her knees forced apart by the width of his strong legs. For the first time, there was a tiny thrill in that. Not in the exposure, but in the darkness, the secrecy of Bren's hands on her body, stroking her in time with the scene playing out before them.

She was supposed to say something, only she couldn't remember what it was. So she said the one word that mattered, chanted it in a rough whisper as she clutched Bren's wrist and tried to guide his hand between her legs. "Please."

He wrapped one hand around her throat—no pressure, just the light weight of his hand. "Shh."

Shivering, she stilled and watched Lex's head loll back against Dallas's shoulder. Those big hands of his had smoothed down her body, his fingers parting her pussy lips, holding her exposed as Rachel knelt before her.

Arching, Six mirrored Lex's pose by folding her arms behind her, trapping them between Bren's abdomen and the small of her back. This was a message she could deliver in silence, a reminder. *You can do anything to me.*

His chest rumbled, and he stroked her hair, tickling one lock over her nipple. Before she could recover from the brief tease, he reached down, sliding two fingers against her, one on either side of her clit.

On the dais, Rachel moved slowly, licking a path up Lex's inner thigh before reaching her pussy. Lex exhaled sharply, only to do it again a heartbeat later, when she should have had no breath left.

"Slow," Dallas commanded. "Lick her up and down, but not her clit, not yet. Fuck her with your tongue instead."

Lex stilled for a moment, then clenched her fingers in Dallas's hair as she rolled her hips against Rachel's mouth. "Oh, *fuck.*"

Six echoed the motion with a slight rock that rubbed her against Bren's fingers. She squirmed, unable to sit still but unwilling to break the moment by speaking, either. The furtive frustration cranked her higher, as if her body were drunk on being denied.

She was a freak, and she'd never given less of a fuck.

Rachel lifted her hands from behind her back, curled them around Lex's thighs, and pulled her closer. Dallas caught Lex's chin in his hand and turned her head, forcing her to meet his gaze.

His lips curved up in a gentle smile that he never gave anyone else, and Six almost looked away. Watching them fuck was less intimate than that soft-eyed smile, even if Dallas dirtied it up by murmuring, "Suck her clit now."

Rachel obeyed, and Lex held his gaze as she began to shake and moan. She touched his face and mouthed words, silent but unmistakable. *I love you.*

It was too raw, scraping at hollow, hungry places inside Six, places Bren had already laid bare. She tilted her head back against his shoulder and concentrated on the brush of his fingers over her clit to fight off a fantasy where Bren gripped her chin and mouthed those words to her.

"More?" Low and intense, but Bren didn't wait for an answer before pushing into her again, two fingers deep in her pussy.

So good. The stretch of those inner muscles, the sound of his fingers slicking into her, the heat of his breath on her ear, of his chest against her back. If she'd felt lost the first time he'd gone down on her, this was the opposite. She was surrounded, embraced, pinned in place so the rising pleasure couldn't sweep her away.

Even with her eyes clenched shut, her body tensed

with the need to come, a moan from Lex painted vivid pictures across her imagination. Maybe Rachel was using her fingers now, pushing them as deep as Bren had. Or maybe it was Dallas, unable to keep his dick out of the woman he loved. "What's happening?" Six whispered, shuddering as Lex moaned again. "Tell me."

"Rachel's touching her." Bren rocked his hand in a rhythm he'd never used before, and Six knew he was mimicking what he saw. "Lex is trying to ride her fingers."

"Oh, God." It was worth forcing her eyes open to watch Lex's hips move in a tempo she'd already matched by instinct. For a dizzy moment, she felt connected to her, bound by the experience they were sharing, even if Lex was oblivious to it.

No wonder they all got off on fucking in front of each other. How much more intense would it be to meet Lex's eyes across the room, to know they were both shuddering under the same caress, fighting the same rising edge?

"Deeper," Dallas commanded, reaching around to twist one hand in Rachel's hair. "Fuck her with your fingers as hard as you want me to fuck you with my cock."

Rachel groaned, and Six didn't have to see her fingers driving into Lex to know she obeyed. Lex bucked so hard Dallas had to grip her hips to hold her down, his fingers framing the intricate tattoo of his name that spanned her abdomen.

"That's it," he whispered, so low Six had to strain to hear him. Bren's fingers thrust lazily, stringing her along the edge, and it was bliss and goddamn *torture* just to hang there, panting, and watch Lex fall.

The woman's skin flushed, and every muscle tensed, right down to her feet where they rested on Rachel's back. Her shaking had turned into an all-out quake, and a low noise escaped her, somewhere between a moan and a cry.

Her eyes snapped open, dark and unfocused, and her movements took on a primal sensuality—not the desperate pursuit of release, but something lazy and languorous. She slid her fingers into Rachel's hair and held her in place while she circled her hips, riding the last waves of pleasure.

Shivering uncontrollably, Six opened her mouth, prepared to beg, but Bren stole her words with a flex of his arm, his fingers plunging into her deep and hard and perfect.

"So sweet." Bren's words were quiet but harsh. Hungry. "You want it. Show me how much."

"Bren—" Her back bowed, arching her body away from his, but he still held her tethered with that gently unyielding grip at her throat as everything started to unravel, spinning out of control.

She closed her eyes. "Don't let me scream," she begged, her last coherent thought because it was hotter in darkness, in silence—

His hand moved from her throat to fold over her mouth, muffling her hoarse cry as a final twist of his clever fingers shattered her. She came in shuddering spasms, irrationally turned on by his hand clamped over her mouth, especially when she dug her teeth into his fingers and he growled like she'd wrapped her lips around his dick.

"I'll fuck you right here." He drew out her orgasm by curling his fingers firmly inside her. "But you have to be quiet."

She whimpered at the thought of his cock inside her, stroking all the places that were still untouched, still hungry.

On stage, Dallas rose. He left Lex sprawled on the cushions and pulled Rachel up to lean over, her hands on the back of the couch and her tits in Lex's face.

"Think she's ready for me?" he asked as he dragged a hand down Rachel's spine, but he didn't wait for an answer. He fisted his cock, stroked it once, and smiled as he positioned the head and pushed into Rachel's body so smoothly, she had to be wet, so wet—

Six nodded jerkily, silently answering Bren's question. *Fuck me, please fuck me.*

Bren released her mouth, and his hand brushed the small of her back as he unbuckled his belt. "Say it. Say yes."

She'd kicked ass in the cage. She'd beaten down her past, reclaimed her pride, proven to all the people who'd seen her shamed that she wasn't a victim anymore.

If she wanted to have sex in a warehouse while a filthy threesome played out in front of her, she fucking well would.

And she did. She so, so did. "Yes."

To an outsider, it would just look like fucking.

They'd see naked flesh, bodies joined, and no more, nothing beyond the sheer physicality of the people writhing on the brightly lit dais. They wouldn't notice the things that caught Bren's eye immediately—the protectiveness inherent in Lex's hand on Rachel's cheek, or the way Dallas spared a moment to rub her back, soothing and petting.

She was safe here, and Christ knew she needed that. In some ways, she was even more of a princess than Noelle. Though her family back in Eden was solidly middle-class, Rachel had been sheltered. Cherished.

When she'd taken the fall for her father's liquor smuggling, she'd protected her family *and* Dallas. If she'd been willing to roll over and give the investigators in Eden insider information about the O'Kane operation, she might have been spared banishment. Instead, she'd kept her mouth shut, and that gesture had earned her an instant place within the gang.

She'd never lived on the streets. Never wandered the sectors, struggling to survive, and that innocence showed in more ways than she realized. But Lex and Dallas knew what she needed, just as they knew someone had to guide her through this experience.

No, an outsider wouldn't recognize how much tenderness accompanied every rough caress any more than they could understand the sort of gift Six had offered Bren. Here, now, she was trusting him to take her, to give her pleasure she'd never considered possible. To indulge her fantasies and her body's very real needs, all at once.

He stripped off her shirt and laid her on the couch, facing the others, before stretching out behind her. Sweat had begun to pearl on her skin, and he relished the heat as he pulled her hair aside and licked the back of her neck.

It had to be even hotter up on the dais, under the lights. Rachel's skin gleamed, damp and flushed, as Lex ran a hand down the front of her throat. "You burn so bright, honey. Next time, we'll fuck you in front of mirrors so you can see the show, too."

Rachel moaned, and Six shivered again. That seemed to get to her the most, not only Dallas's dirty words but the noises torn from Rachel against her will, sounds of pure, helpless pleasure.

"Close your eyes," Bren whispered. "Don't look. Listen."

Her hand slipped back, nails scratching over his hip, but her eyelashes drifted lower until they were dark smudges against her cheeks. "You have to tell me what they're doing."

"If you're quiet, you can hear them." He lifted her leg up to rest on his, opening her to his touch. "The grunts, the moans, even the little sounds they don't have words for."

She tilted her head, straining toward the stage as

Dallas landed a playful slap on Rachel's hip. Six squirmed at the crack of an open palm on flesh, rubbing back against Bren's cock as if seeking relief.

He stilled her hips with one firm hand. "Rachel's so turned on her thighs are wet. Can you hear him fucking her?"

Six bobbed her head in a jerky nod, but he caught the gentle flutter of her lashes.

She was peeking.

Bren dug his fingernails into her skin, just for a moment, and made her wait, untouched, while he unbuttoned his pants.

She squeezed her eyes shut once more. "Where's your gag when you need it, huh?"

"If you can't stay quiet, I'll cover your mouth again." He didn't need to feel her skin turn hotter to know she'd like it. She'd come hard before, shuddering in his arms, but he'd make her come harder before he finished with her.

He eased his pants down just far enough. Six liked contrasts, the starker the better, and there was nothing else as blunt as rough denim on sensitive skin. She shivered as he rubbed his cock against her ass and turned his gaze back to the couch on the dais.

Dallas had stopped teasing and started *fucking*, and it had Lex squirming on the cushions. She wrapped her hands around Rachel's waist, urging her back into a low bend that canted her hips before his next deep thrust.

"Fuck!" The word ripped free of Rachel on a shudder, and her hands slipped on the back of the couch. She wound up pressed against Lex, her face buried in her neck.

Lex hissed a curse. "Harder, shit."

At first, Bren thought she was talking to Dallas, but then she gripped the back of Rachel's head, and the look on her face sent a bolt of heat rocketing to his cock.

He wrapped his fingers loosely around Six's throat.

"Rachel's biting Lex, trying to keep from screaming."

She swallowed before whispering, "Are you jealous?"

"Of what, the pain?" He flexed his hips, sliding his cock between her open legs to nudge her pussy.

Groaning, she twisted, fighting his grip in an attempt to writhe closer to him. "Inside," she whimpered instead of answering. "Please, Bren, just be *inside* me."

"Like this?" He pushed between her inner lips, gritting his teeth against the need to drive into her, to sheathe himself fully in the hungry, wet clasp of her body.

"*Bren.*" She slapped her hand over her mouth almost as soon as his name escaped, as if the trio on stage was likely to hear over their own noises.

He didn't start slow. Instead, he plunged into her in time with Dallas's next thrust, trusting that the visual combined with the sensation would drive her higher. Harder.

She went a little wild, her cry muffled behind his hand. Her hips bucked, and she was so tight, squeezing down around him like she might be close to coming again.

He rolled her beneath him and pinned her there, her cheek pressed to the cushion so she could watch as Lex slid her hand between Rachel's thighs.

"Fuck yeah," Dallas growled, catching Rachel under the shoulders. He hauled her body up, trapping her with a hand across her throat and the other anchoring her hips. "You want Lex to let you come, sweetheart? You want her to suck your sweet little clit?"

"Please." Rachel ground out the word. "Please, let me—"

"Shh, no begging." Lex licked a circle around Rachel's navel. She eased up and did it again, this time around one of her nipples, coaxing it to an even tighter peak. Then she stretched up on her knees, high enough to lick the corner of Dallas's mouth.

He caught her in a kiss, rough and wild. Dallas ended it with her lower lip between his teeth, and he growled as he released her. "She's been such a sweet girl, Lex." He tilted Rachel's face up to his. "Time to reward her."

"I know." Lex licked her way back down—neck, tits, hip—before sliding to the floor at her feet.

The first touch of Lex's tongue made Rachel jerk in Dallas's arms, though her sharp cry was lost to his mouth. Then it was his turn to groan, and Bren knew Lex was licking his cock, teasing him with quick flicks at the root of his shaft.

Six knew it, too. She clenched around him, but Bren held her still. Trapped, though she didn't struggle or fight against him. Her body was pliant beneath his, warm and soft and as relaxed as he'd ever felt her, even as she clutched at the couch.

Watch. Bren almost said it aloud, but he didn't have to tell her. She was spellbound, her gaze riveted to the scene before her, to the helpless ecstasy they could almost taste in the air.

Lex's nails flashed, black and gold, as she stroked a hand over Rachel's hip and up to Dallas's wrist. A fleeting touch, half a heartbeat before he clenched his jaw, and from the look of sheer determination on the man's face, he was fighting a swift battle for the self-control not to ride the orgasm Rachel couldn't even vocalize yet.

But when she did, the cries from before paled, quiet and reserved, next to the way she screamed and bucked and scratched, pulling Lex's hair and leaving welts on Dallas's arms. She was surrounded by them, caught between the hard thrust of cock and the soft, sinuous heat of tongue.

And she fucking loved it.

Six was squirming again, tiny furtive movements that pushed her ass up and drew Bren deeper inside her. She was trying to get a hand beneath her to toy with her clit, so he dragged both arms over her head and pinned them there. Then he eased his free hand beneath her and gave her what she wanted, fingers moving in a quick, rough circle.

That was all it took. She turned her face into her arm, muffling her cry as she came on his cock in shuddering spasms that rocked her slight body.

Not yet. He pulled free before he could give in to the lure of her pussy convulsing around his dick and spun her to face him. "Look at me, sweetness."

It took forever for her eyelids to flutter open. Her gaze was dreamy and unfocused, but it still slid toward the stage with the next cry, as if she couldn't help herself.

Rachel slumped to the couch in Lex's arms, her chest heaving and her hair damp with sweat. Dallas dropped beside them, murmuring in Lex's ear and caressing them both as Rachel recovered.

A furrow crinkled Six's brow, confusion mirrored in her still-dazed eyes as she shifted her attention back to Bren. "They stopped. You stopped."

"Not for long. Just a minute, so everyone can catch their breath."

The furrow deepened as she shifted her hips. "It doesn't hurt you?"

His shaft was still slick, and the smooth glide tightened his balls. "Don't worry about my dick. It'll be back inside you soon enough."

"Oh." Smiling, she touched his lips. "Good. I like you there."

He echoed the gesture, tracing her smile with his thumb before pushing it between her lips. Her gaze stayed locked on his, so open, so *trusting*, as she swirled her tongue around the tip and then sucked.

His cock twitched, and he thrust his thumb deeper with a groan. Her cheeks hollowed out, and she bobbed her head, her eyes all but daring him not to imagine pushing something else between her lips.

He couldn't stop.

Bren straightened. "On the floor, Six. Now."

She slipped from the couch and hit the floor on her knees, her hair a wild tumble around her shoulders. "I won't be able to see."

"I will." He sat and stretched out his legs, caging her between them. "Got a real good view from here."

Her breath caught, and she slid her hands up his legs, pausing hesitantly on his thighs. She wet her lips and stared at his cock. "Tell me you want my mouth."

He took his erection in hand and pumped it slowly from base to tip, just to see her lick her lips again, to watch that pink flash of tongue and imagine it on his aching cock. "I want you to take it this time," he whispered. "Fuck me with your mouth. Show me how good it is."

Almost shyly, she slid her hand over his, working her fingers between his until he could feel the contrast, the soft warmth of her skin alternating with the rougher brush of his. Her breasts rubbed against the coarse denim he still wore as she leaned in and closed her lips around the crown.

A voice broke through the buzz of pleasure in his ears. "Six and Bren are out there." Lex looked mellow under the harsh lights, relaxed as she toyed with Rachel's hair. "Think they're fucking yet?"

Rachel answered in a low, satisfied purr. "I hope so."

Six tongued his piercings, exploring the ends of each barbell as Dallas's laughter rang out. "Not even stone-cold Bren Donnelly could keep his pants on through you coming, sweetheart. Tell her how good she looked, Lexie."

"Like an angel."

Rachel's back stiffened, but after a moment she kissed Lex's open mouth. "Show's not over, though. Is it?"

"Not yet," Dallas agreed. "Do you wanna help me fuck her?"

That quickly, the fire returned, burning in Rachel's

eyes. "Show me what to do."

Dallas silently swept Lex up, and Bren had to clear his throat before describing the scene to Six. "He's laying Lex out. Pushing her legs up for Rachel to hold."

Six hummed her approval, her tongue vibrating delicately against the sensitive underside of his cock before she sucked him deeper.

"Fucking hell." Bren bit his tongue. "Again."

She slid up slowly, her gaze locked to his, and repeated the entire thing over again. The sucking, the humming, the way her hand squeezed his and her eyes danced with mischief and newfound power.

Words. He dragged his gaze back to the dais. "Dallas is in his favorite place—between Lex's thighs. But I think Rachel gets off on it, too. On pinning her down."

Lex whimpered as she tried to wiggle free, and then moaned as Rachel held on so tight she left red marks on the woman's golden skin. Dallas pushed deep, fucking fast and hard from the first stroke, his face a mask of tortured intensity.

Rachel stretched out on the other end of the couch, keeping her face close to Lex's as she held on to her legs and spoke, low and satisfied. "You were right. He can fuck you so deep it feels like you'll never stop coming."

The words drove a moan from Lex's throat, and Rachel soothed her with a teasing lick to the lips—but she didn't stop with her mouth. Instead, she kept exploring, drawing a wet path down past Lex's collarbone to her breasts.

Rapt, Bren watched as she sucked one rigid, peaked nipple between her teeth. It should have looked lazy, like Rachel was entertaining herself while Dallas drove Lex closer and closer to orgasm.

But no, her hands on Lex's thighs trembled, and an aroused flush colored her cheeks. She was as invested in this pleasure as she had been in her own.

As invested as Six was in sucking Bren's dick, in tak-

ing tiny caresses and building them to a blinding cre-
scendo.

He reached down to tangle his fingers in her dark
hair and pulled her head up. "You've seen Lex come," he
rasped.

Breathing heavily, she nodded. Laughed. "Everyone
has."

"Then look." He turned her face with one rough hand
on her chin. "What do you see?"

"She's close." Six swallowed. "God, she's so close. Her
skin's all flushed, she's tense, I think she's biting the hell
out of Dallas's hand. We both like to bite something when
we come."

"But he just started." Bren hauled Six into his lap
and bit her ear. "You think she got off that hard on
fucking Rachel?"

Six squirmed. "I got off that hard watching."

He slid back inside her, angling her hips for maxi-
mum friction. "Can you come before she does?"

"I don't—" She shifted, shuddered, and tilted her
head back. "You can make me if you want to. I know you
can."

"But can you take it?" He ran his hands down to her
thighs and rubbed his thumbs over her bare skin. "Ride
me."

She hesitated until he slapped a hand against her
hip, and then she was moving, the strong muscles of her
thighs working as she rose and fell, taking him deep and
hard and frantic.

It shot through him like a shock, but a string of curs-
es drew his attention back to the trio on the other couch.
Lex arched and writhed, pinned down now not only by
Rachel but by Dallas's hand around her throat. Caged
and wild—and on the verge of an explosive orgasm.

No time for Six to find her rhythm and ride him to
completion. Bren gripped her hips and held her suspend-
ed above him. She made a single noise of protest that

turned to sheer pleasure as he drove up into her, pumping his hips in thrust after desperate thrust.

She came with a cry everyone must have heard, not
just a cry but his name, broken and desperate. He fucked
her through it, fucked her until the tight, rhythmic
clench of her pussy drew him over the edge, too.

The room blurred, everything but the thump of Six's
heart as he hauled her close for his last frenzied thrusts.
Nothing touched him but her. It had been true for
months, but never so much as here, now, when she'd
given him so much.

Nothing else mattered.

11

S IX WOKE UP sore, a little hung over, and still floating.

Bren was a solid mass of warmth around and over her, though his breathing lost the easy rhythm of slumber as soon as Six began to stretch.

After a lifetime of jerking away every time a board so much as creaked within a dozen yards of her, the previous night's blissful, uninterrupted sleep was a slightly guilty pleasure. "Did I keep you up all night?"

"Keep me up by sleeping?" He stifled a yawn. "How would that work?"

She squirmed onto her back and studied his sleepy eyes and disheveled hair, unprepared for the jolt of innocent affection that made her heart wobble. "You always seem to wake up whenever I so much as twitch a toe."

"Mmm. Maybe I'm getting used to it."

God, she could get drunk on that, on being so far beneath Brendan Donnelly's skin that his instincts simply accepted her presence. "Good." She gave in to the temptation to touch him, tracing her fingertip along one eyebrow and down to the shell of his ear.

He turned his head until her fingers brushed his cheek. "What about you?"

"I'm getting used to lots of things." Like his naked skin against hers, and this warm, relaxed feeling that shifted to delicious tingles when she remembered the previous night. She scraped her nails lightly over his cheek and smiled teasingly. "Like coming more than once. I'm getting used to that."

A ghost of a smile curved his lips, but then vanished. "No regrets?"

"No." She let her own smile fade as she flattened her fingers to cup his cheek. "It was...intense. Maybe a little confusing. I wish I knew why some things get me off when they feel..." If there was a word to sum up the feeling, she didn't know it. Something to explain how it felt to be pinned by him, his hand over her mouth, adrenaline and pleasure spinning her into a dizzy mess, all while an angry, guilty part of her protested that it shouldn't feel good.

"When they feel like they should be wrong?" he prompted.

Sudden tears stung her eyes, and she squeezed them shut as words bubbled up in a rush. "I should be more broken, right? That's how the other girls act sometimes. Like I should be afraid of fucking or hate it or something, because Trent and some of the others fucked around with me. And I wonder who they are, and where they grew up that they thought they'd go through life without people using their bodies in ways they didn't want. As long as you survive it, what the fuck does it matter? It's a *body*."

He drew her closer with a soothing noise. "They're looking at it the way they would, but that doesn't make them right. They don't get to decide for you what the worst shit was. That's yours."

It should have helped, but another fear lurked beneath it. A deeper one, one she barely dared admit to herself, much less to anyone else. Even trying made her voice come out in an uncertain whisper. "But what if they *are* right? What if I'm so broken that I only think I like some things *because* someone did them to me?"

Instead of denying the words outright, he shifted and sat up, with her still in his arms. "I know how that goes. Everyone assumes that's why I like pain—because I got hurt so much that my mind twisted it into something good out of self-defense. But they're way off the mark."

Sitting like this was another thing she was getting used to. She liked leaning into his chest, burying her face against his throat, surrounding herself with the warmth and scent of his skin. "So why do you like it?"

He exhaled. "I told you Cooper got me off the streets. What I didn't tell you is that I went back to them. I mean, Coop's place was home, but I didn't stay there a lot. I ran with a pretty rough crowd."

"Street kids usually are," she agreed. "I know I was."

"So was Chey." His expression turned thoughtful, almost nostalgic. "Her brother was a friend of mine. He kicked my ass when he found out I'd been messing around with his sister."

He fell silent again, and she almost wanted to give him an out. A chance to laugh it away as a joke instead of baring his past to her, especially when there was so much she still hadn't told him. "So he got you into pain? Or she did?"

Bren poked her in the side. "Chey was hardcore. Into a bunch of shit I don't mess with anymore—barbs, branding, even blades. It's hard to explain, except...I'd never met anyone who only got off on inflicting *welcome* pain. Most of the assholes you run into who like hurting people aren't exactly looking for willing partners."

It was a distinction that had never mattered to her

before, because she hadn't imagined it was possible. "How did she know? How did *you*?"

He shook his head. "I don't even remember. But when it happened, it was like I knew I'd needed it all along."

No one had broken or twisted him. He wanted what he wanted and didn't seem to feel guilty about getting it. "The shit with Trent, it wasn't black and white. Obvious. It's not like we went to bed happy one night, and I woke up with him beating on me. I'm not sure when it got bad, only that by the time I realized it was, it felt like it had been bad forever."

"And then you fought back."

"That gun you found in the warehouse. It was his." The memory was still crystal clear, after all this time. The scent of fresh ink on his paperwork. The rough grain of the wood under her cheek. "He liked to fuck me over his desk. He wasn't all that into it *or* me, didn't even just need to get off. And every time got meaner, like he wanted to see how far I'd let him go. So I finally told him I didn't feel like it..."

He'd thrown her over the desk anyway, hard enough to bruise her face. Not that she hadn't ended up bruised before, but it had been the first time she'd said *no*, and some stupid part of her had thought it would matter to him. That he'd only been roughing her up before because she'd been letting him, not because he didn't give a shit whether she wanted it or not.

"I went for the gun," she continued, before Bren could interrupt, before he could try to comfort her. Comfort would feel like pity, and she'd never make it through these words. "I told him no and he still tried to fuck me, so I went for the gun. I was gonna blow his balls off."

Bren swallowed hard, but he waited, silent and watchful.

She took a careful breath and focused on a spot just

beneath his left eye. A small scar, a reminder that he had plenty of his own bad memories and wouldn't judge her for hers. "The fact that he beat me half conscious and fucked me anyway wasn't the part that really hurt. Until that moment, I was still so goddamn deluded I thought he loved me."

Bren closed his eyes, but his hand found her cheek anyway. "Trent is dead. He can't hurt anyone anymore."

Trent was dead, all right. At her hands. Her knuckles had been split and sore for weeks, and she'd cherished every throb of discomfort as a reminder that she was finally safe. "I shouldn't be making you listen to any of this. It doesn't matter."

"No, look at me." He slid his hand around to cup the back of her neck. "He can't hurt you anymore, but he hurt you plenty already. That doesn't go away just because he did."

"I know." She swallowed around the lump in her throat and got the last words out. "The twisted part is that everything that happened after that? It hurt. God, it hurt. But it's easy to shrug off, because I know none of it was my fault. I said no. I fought back. Hell, I killed some of them. None of that's on me."

"Neither is what he did before."

"I didn't try to stop him."

"Do you think that makes it okay? That it means he got to be as big an asshole as he wanted?"

He said it like the idea was silly, *absurd*, but he'd lived on the streets, too. He knew the answer. "It doesn't matter if it's okay. People'll take as much as you let them get away with."

"Yeah, they do. Doesn't make it right." His jaw clenched. "What would you say to someone else? To Trix, or Noelle? Would you look them in the eye and say it was their fault, that they should have fought harder?"

The bottom of her stomach dropped out as she imagined sweet-faced Noelle trapped in a room with Wilson

Trent. Or God—Trix, who'd let a member of Dallas's gang hit her and hadn't muttered a word of protest, because she'd believed she wasn't worth defending.

He would have eaten either one of them alive, hurt them and twisted them and made them think it was their fault from start to finish. They weren't broken and mean inside like Six. They were people who cared.

"It's not the same," she said weakly, even with her rationalizations crumbling beneath her feet. "I knew better. After the farms, and the—" Panic tightened her chest, and she stumbled past the final secret, the one she didn't ever think about. "The streets," she said instead. "After all that, I *knew better.*"

"Knew better than to trust someone." It wasn't a question.

Put that way, it was so stark. It made her sound broken, feel it too, because it was nothing but truth. "I know better than to trust you," she whispered, bracing herself for him to pull away. "I know better, only I can't stop. And that scares me a little, but not as much as not wanting to stop."

"You don't have to stop," he offered quietly.

She choked on a hysterical laugh and buried her face against his shoulder. "Thank you."

Bren wrapped his arms more tightly around her. "I don't know if I can help. *Really* help, I mean. But you can talk to Lex."

Lex seemed so fucking tough that it was hard to imagine her like this, hurt and scared and clinging to a man. Then again, maybe that was reason enough to ask. Weeping on Bren was easy and safe, but the pity in Elvis's eyes was a fresh wound. If she ever saw that reflected back at her from Bren...

She turned her face to the warm, bare skin of his shoulder. "You just keep telling me I'm not a pervy freak, okay? I'll figure the rest out."

"You got it."

He had bruises on his throat again, bruises she'd put there with her teeth. She traced a fingertip over the edge of one. "You never told me what happened with that girl. The first one."

He breathed out a soft laugh. "Nothing tragic. Chey wasn't just a sadist, she was one hell of a dominant lover. I got tired of fighting to be on top, and we parted ways."

"Did last night count as you being on top?"

His voice dropped to a growl. "Would you have said no to anything I told you to do?"

She struggled to hold back a smile as something giddy rose, wiping away her lingering pain. She loved being able to put that rough edge in his voice with a few simple words, like she had the power to drive unflappable Bren crazy. "Only if you told me to do something that didn't seem fun."

His lips brushed her ear. "Liar."

Her heart beat a little harder, and her breaths came faster. She wasn't the only one with power, and now her voice held the same rawness. "I'm never going to be a submissive person. But if what you wanna do is be in charge of getting me off a million times a night, I'm not about to argue."

His hand drifted down between her shoulder blades, strong and unyielding. "You won't just let me, will you? You'll love every second of it."

"Probably." She touched the bruise again. "But I want more. I want to be what you need, too. All of it."

He tipped her face up to his. "Six."

She tensed. "I'm not going to let you be in charge of getting me off if getting *you* off isn't important, too."

"I need you to be you," he said firmly. "Beyond that, you'll have to trust me."

"I do, but I want..." She couldn't think of an easy way to explain, so she let the words come, awkward and jumbled, and trusted him to sort them out. "I want to understand. The pain and how much of it I like and how much of it *you* like and how it's so different for everyone."

"There's only one way to know that." He stroked a path from her chin across her jaw. "You try it."

"With you?"

He hesitated. "Ace offered. It could be good for you to see it outside of sex."

After watching some of the things the O'Kanes liked to get up to, she wasn't sure watching Ace beat Bren into a state of emotional release could be anything but sexual—for her, anyway. "Is it that easy to separate them?"

"Nothing easy about it. But Ace and I have done it before."

It was her turn to meet his gaze. "Can we try?"

He pulled her hand to his mouth before answering. "Maybe I should ask if *you* want it to be about the sex or the pain...or both."

That led right back to the thought of Ace and Bren and tension-laced touches. Her cheeks heated. "Lex is a bad influence on me."

The corner of his mouth kicked up, and he nodded, as if she'd answered the question. "I'll talk to him."

"You don't mind putting on a show for me?"

His eyes lit at her teasing. "No. But what about you?"

He still had one hand on her back, splayed across her scars. There'd been nothing sexual about the beatings that had left them, not for her. But getting whaled on in the cage last night had riled her up, and she got off harder when Bren added an edge of pain to her pleasure.

"I trust you," she ventured, pressing her thumb to his lips. "I don't want to try anything too rough. Just a taste. We have time, right? Time to go slow."

"Yeah." His fingertips traced one raised ridge of flesh, and he nipped at her thumb. "Real slow."

Oh, *God.*

Given time, Six might get used to sitting across a desk from someone she'd watched scream her way through a couple orgasms the night before.

She wasn't used to it yet.

It was hard not to fidget as she sat in Lex's office, waiting for the woman to get around to telling her why she'd been ordered to stay behind while Bren went out to help clear the roads in Three. But Lex only lit a cigarette and watched her, studying every flinch and wriggle.

Finally, she spoke. "You feeling uncomfortable, honey?"

Six could only hope she wasn't blushing. "First time for everything, right?"

"Uh-huh." Lex grinned slowly. "Don't worry. I'm not gonna lay you out on the desk and have my wicked way with you."

At least that sounded teasing. Six relaxed and pulled the straightest face she could. "Not even if I ask nice?"

"Oh, you're not ready for me, sweetheart." Lex propped her elbows on the desk. "Question is, what *are* you ready for? Dallas thinks a little ink might be in your near future."

Her heart stopped beating.

Ink. Her gaze dropped to Lex's wrists, tracing the lines around the O'Kane emblem, the one Rachel had tattooed across her chest in a symbol of pride and pleasure. It meant security and safety. Belonging. It meant having a family again. Hell, maybe for the first time.

And it meant trusting more than just Bren. She'd have to trust everyone—first and foremost, Dallas O'Kane.

She wet her lips. "Bren wants me in?"

"I haven't asked him. And I'm not going to."

"Oh." She sounded stupid, and she felt it, too. "So it's not because he and I have a thing?"

Lex's dark gaze sharpened. "Becoming an O'Kane

isn't about being some guy's old lady. If that's all you want, you've got it already. But I thought you were after more. Something that's yours."

"Yes." The word escaped on its own, raw and hoarse. "But I kinda stopped believing in that."

"So had I, once upon a time." Lex arched an eyebrow. "Do you know how I ended up here?"

There were so many rumors and conflicting legends it was hard to tell which one might hold a shred of truth, so she shook her head.

"Dallas caught me with my hand in his safe. And before you start thinking that's a clever euphemism..." Lex finished her cigarette and crushed it out. "I was ripping him off."

Of course she was. "And he put up with that?"

"Put up with it?" She snorted. "He got off on it, once he realized I wasn't going to snivel—or worse, try to pacify him with a half-hearted blowjob."

It was a common thread, but not because of Trent. Bren was the one who seemed to like Six violent and rough around the edges. "So Dallas let you into the gang?"

"Not hardly. But he let me stick around, and that was a start."

"I guess." She didn't want to ask the next question, but she had to. With her heart so fragile and messed up, it'd be foolish not to be careful. "So if I take the ink, I get to stay no matter what? Even if Bren and I don't work out?"

To her credit, Lex's reply was far from glib. "It might not be easy, but you'd find some way to coexist. The gang comes first. Rule number one."

And you'd still want me? The question balanced on the tip of her tongue, but it revealed too much. That was the kind of question a victim would ask, some broken-ass bitch who didn't think she was worth shit unless a guy was sticking his dick in her.

She was more than that. She was all the things she'd wanted to be for Trent, all the things he'd never let her be. She was tough, she knew Sector Three, and she was willing to get her hands dirty to get things done. Dallas O'Kane didn't need to *want* her. He could use her. And he could give her something in return.

"The gang first," she echoed. "Does that mean I can keep helping in Three?"

"If that's what you want," Lex allowed. "That's not really a paid position, though, so you'll probably want to keep up your shifts at the bar."

Half the gang was over in Three now, busting their asses dragging rubble out of the roads to clear enough room for trucks to get through. It wouldn't be fun, but it might be more satisfying than hauling drinks. "Is anyone getting paid to work in Three?"

"What, you mean the road work?" Lex shook her head. "You get paid for things that pull in cash. Three doesn't qualify—yet. But most of the guys understand we can't make any money over there until we get it in order."

Oh. Cash still meant security, which meant finding a way to get it. The windfall with the cage match could only work so many times—she couldn't beat everyone, even if Dallas let her fight again. And the more she managed to win, the narrower the odds would be.

Dancing wasn't an option. Neither was fucking on stage, not in this lifetime. And no matter how much Bren made her smile, she wasn't going to be able to fake it for tips. "Is bartending the only paying gig for women? I mean, if we're not dancers."

"No hard-and-fast rules, honey. I'm the queen, remember?" Lex shrugged and held out both hands to her sides. "You want to do something else? Convince me."

Six felt her brows rise. "Even if what I want to do is dangerous? You'd back me?"

"Sure, why not? I'd hope you'd have enough sense in

your head not to take on a job you can't handle just to prove something."

She couldn't help her laugh. "If I wanted out of this life, I've had more than my share of chances. It's not that I mind working the bar, but I'm not good at it. The only guys who tip me decent are the ones who get off on women glaring at them. I'd be more useful doing something where I'm not supposed to put men at ease."

"Such as?"

Six grinned. "Throwing them out on their faces if they cause trouble? Lord knows they won't see me coming."

Lex leaned back in her chair. "We could use another bouncer," she mused. "It's not very glamorous, but you'd get to smash a few heads now and then."

Excitement sparked, the kind Six hadn't felt in months. *Years*, maybe. "I don't need glamour. I get that even if you and Dallas and every guy wearing ink thought I was tough enough, it'd still be stupid to send me out to do what they do. It's image, right?"

"Partly. The rest is about being able to back up the promise of that ink." Lex's expression turned serious. "If you think you'll have an easier time dealing with dickheads just because you're inside these walls, think again. And you've *got* to be able to back it up, or someone'll end up dead."

It was a solemn statement, and it deserved the same in return. "Ask Bren. He knows what I can do, and what he's teaching me to do better. If he doesn't think I can do it, I'll work until he does."

"That's fair—" A knock interrupted her words, and Lex gestured toward the door with a nod. A queen, expecting her minion to jump at the wave of her hand.

Six jumped.

It was Emma, nervously playing with the end of one bleached-blonde lock. "Is Lex in there?"

Six glanced over her shoulder and, at Lex's nod,

pulled the door wide. "Come on in."

"Thanks." Her nervousness didn't fade. If anything, it cranked higher as she faced Lex. "I hear you guys have been looking for someone who might be in Three. Some tech guy named Noah."

"We are," Lex confirmed.

"I know him," Emma blurted. "I mean, I used to. He was friends with my brother back in Sector Five."

"Seriously?" Six asked, swinging around to study Emma again. She was one of the newer O'Kanes, one who'd taken ink not long after Six's arrival. They had to be around the same age, but something about Emma seemed young in a way Six had always assumed meant she was from a sheltered family, maybe even from inside Eden itself.

Five might not be the shithole Three was, but the man who ran it was a scary motherfucker.

Emma crossed her arms over her middle. "If I get him a message, he'll come. He'd do that much."

Lex studied her before rising with a sigh. "You know why Dallas wants him, don't you?"

"Information." Emma swallowed. "Noah can get him that. Noah can do anything."

"Okay, then. We'll put out word that you need him."

Six wanted desperately to pry, to demand to know Noah's story. Who he was, how he'd ended up smart and crazy and living in the tunnels under Three while thugs ransacked the sector, trying to find him. But she recognized Emma's posture all too well. Defensive and wary, pain edging her eyes.

And the words. *Noah can do anything.* So rawly confident, despite her sadness. That was probably how Six would sound about Bren, if things went to hell. And he *could.* Bren could do so many things.

But there was one thing she could only do for herself. So Six pivoted back to Lex. "About that other thing—I'm ready for all of it."

Lex rubbed her temples. "I'm on it. Both of you, out."

Six felt sure enough to give Lex a grinning salute before following Emma into the hallway. And though talking had never been her thing, the hurt lingering in the other woman's eyes made her hesitate. "Hey, you okay?"

"I'm—" The words cut off as Emma swung to face her. "You're from Three, and you seem like you know him. Noah?"

"Kind of," Six answered honestly. "We were never friends or anything, but he was nice to the street kids. Helped them find safe places to live sometimes."

She squeezed her eyes shut. "Of course he did."

Wishing she knew what to say that would make things better, Six touched her arm. "Emma?"

When she opened her eyes, it was with a calm smile. "Never mind. Hey, congratulations on your match last night. That asshole had it coming."

"Thanks." It was easy to smile back. No, to *grin*. "I guess we'll see if he polishes up his manners, huh?"

"He'd better." Emma jerked her head toward the end of the hall. "I've got to go. See you around?"

There was nothing to do but nod and watch Emma bolt. Six caught herself rubbing her thumb over her wrist again, and she stared down at the bare skin, trying to imagine it circled with ink.

It was still mostly a dream. Lex hadn't offered the ink outright or told her it was definitely coming soon. But she'd talked like Six belonged, like she could be more than some girl slinging drinks. Like she could be anything she had the wits and strength to become.

A home, if she was brave enough to believe in it. A home no one could take away from her.

Not even Bren.

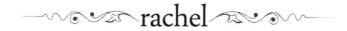

rachel

THE LAST PERSON she expected to barge in on inventory day was Cruz.

She blinked up at him, setting aside her clipboard as she fought to cover her suddenly galloping heartbeat with nonchalance. "Can I help you?"

His expression was just as bland, though he looked rough around the edges. "Someone said the medkit was in here."

Her nervousness slipped away in the face of a potential emergency. "It is. What happened?"

"Nothing bad," he assured her quickly, then pulled up his shirt to reveal the chiseled muscles of his abdomen—and a large bandage. "Need to change this."

Rachel peeled back the edge of the bandage and winced. It was a nice-sized slice, one that had been neatly but inexpertly sutured. What concerned her was the blazing heat of his reddened skin. "What did you do, sew this up yourself?"

His long pause was answer enough, but he clearly felt her disapproval because he tried to justify it. "We're stretched thin, trying to clear those roads."

"It's not so dire you can't spare ten minutes," she protested. "A little gel, and I could have had you fixed right up. Now, you'll need antibiotics."

She could almost hear him grinding his teeth. "Then I'll take the antibiotics."

It stung. Had he cared so little for his own well-being that he'd neglected to care for a simple cut, or had he needed so desperately to avoid her that he'd decided to chance infection?

She jerked open the cabinet and pulled out the medical case. "If you need med-gel, you don't have to come to me. You can get it from Dallas's office."

He reached out to brace the heavy box for her. "His office wasn't any closer."

"Then I really don't understand." She unzipped the case and snatched up a bottle of antiseptic. "Don't you give a shit?"

"I wasn't trained to give a shit. I was trained to stay alive long enough to get the job done, and deal with the consequences later." His arms flexed as he dragged his shirt over his head and tossed it aside. "It worked better when I had access to a regen lab."

Remorse stabbed at her. "I'm sorry," she mumbled, dabbing at the cut. "We don't have the same kind of resources around here. You'll have to be more careful."

He didn't flinch, didn't give any indication her touch hurt, though it must have. "I know. I didn't mean to upset you."

Such perfect control. But she'd seen a different side of him, felt him tremble beneath her hands and mouth when that control had failed him. There, in the dark, for those few stolen moments, he'd been hers.

Not that it mattered now.

She tried not to stare at the muscled expanse of his

abdomen as she struggled to find an innocuous answer. "I'm not upset," she said finally. "You're the one who gets a needle to the ass cheek now."

That got his attention. All those glorious muscles tensed as he jerked back. "A *what?*"

"A shot. The antibiotics that were no big deal a minute ago?" She capped the antiseptic and reached for a single-use gel applicator. "If you're worried about flashing your ass at me, don't be. It's nothing I haven't already seen."

It should have flustered him. A month ago it would have, but now his eyes narrowed in what looked like suspicion. "You still use needles to administer antibiotics?"

"Oh, for Christ's—" Rachel bit her tongue. "Yes. Yes, we do."

His lips twitched. "If it helps, all the doctors hated me. I'm not a biddable patient."

"No shit." A laugh bubbled up and, for a moment, it was as if nothing had changed. They were just two people, laughing at each other and themselves, discovering one breath at a time what it meant to be special to someone.

But it was an illusion. Because of her, things *were* different, and they couldn't go back. So she swallowed her laughter, fell silent, and busied herself with squeezing the med-gel onto his wound in a thin, careful line.

She'd almost regained her composure when he shattered it. "Ace says I owe you an apology."

Oh *God*, she couldn't handle the thought of them sitting around, talking about her. She'd have expected both men to have the common courtesy to pretend she'd never happened—to either of them. "Ace says a lot of things."

He caught her hand, his fingers folding around hers, enclosing them. Trapping them. "This is important. And more about me than you."

He was always so cautious, the sheer heat and size of

him only highlighting the tenderness of his touch. "Cruz—"

He exhaled roughly. "I came out of Eden with some twisted ideas about sex and how to treat a woman when you want her to know you respect her. You got the worst of it."

Her throat ached. "You didn't hurt me. That's not—"

"Just let me finish." He touched her chin, tilted her head back. "I had a lot of stupid, bullshit ideas about right and wrong. I was acting like you were too pure to fuck, even though all I could think about was getting inside you and getting you off. I was a bastard."

She exhaled. It was all she could manage with him touching her, gazing at her—and casually talking about how much he wanted to fuck her. He'd always been considerate, a true gentleman—and the bit of careful distance his strict sense of decorum provided was the only thing that had ever allowed her to keep her head around him.

How the hell was she supposed to do that with him talking dirty to her?

When she didn't respond, he rubbed his knuckle along her jawline. A soft brush, but devastating when combined with the serious look in his eyes. "I wanted to be a hero, but there aren't any heroes out here, are there?"

The tightness in her throat migrated to her chest, and she pulled his hand away from her face. "If this place changes you, it should be because you're waking up. Not because someone else said you were wrong."

His laugh was tinged with something she'd never heard from him before: darkness. "I woke up all on my own, it just took a while. If it'd been Ace's doing, this apology would have happened a long time ago."

Yeah, Ace moved fast—when he wanted to.

Rachel looked away. "Apology accepted."

Cruz was silent for so long that she might have suspected he'd left, if his presence hadn't prickled over her skin with constant, tantalizing heat. "Do you want me to find someone else to stab my ass?" he asked.

"That's stupid." She reached for the vial and a syringe. "Turn around."

She was left staring at the broad, chiseled expanse of his back as his belt clicked, and his pants sagged, dipping lower and lower and dragging her gaze with them.

His ass was as perfect as the rest of him, of course. She'd seen some beautiful men—the gang was fucking full of them—but something about the way Cruz carried himself elevated that beauty to damn near supernatural levels.

He had an awareness of his body that spoke of his complete control, as if he never made a move or a sound without meaning to. So when she touched the small of his back to hold him still, his quick, indrawn breath hit her like a rough caress.

Jesus Christ. She wanted to keep going, see where else she could touch him to elicit more gasps, so she administered the injection and stepped back. "All done."

Even when he hauled his pants up, they still settled low on his hips, inviting her gaze to linger on the intriguing play of muscle under his skin. "Thank you, Rachel."

"You're welcome."

Cruz turned, still fastening his pants, only to freeze when his gaze fell on her. "Hey. You okay?"

"No." Every time she thought she had her feet under her, something happened to send her spinning again. "I mean, yeah. No worries."

He stepped close, crowding into her space. He took up too much room, but he didn't touch her. He studied her, his expression impossible to decipher. "Worrying about you is my right, isn't it? That's what the ink means."

He sounded like Ace, and it pissed her off. "Well, that

depends. Are you worrying because you care? Or do you do it so you can say how noble and giving you are, looking out for me when there's no reward?"

Two steps. He took two fucking steps and had her back against the shelves, his hands on either side of her head, his face hovering over hers. "I've always cared, and that didn't stop just because you decided you were done with me. You can be pissed at Ace for being Ace, but you don't get to pretend you couldn't have me any fucking time you wanted."

"I'm not *done*," she ground out. He was too big, too close—too everything. "I was trying not to hurt you."

He laughed, like she'd said the funniest thing in the world.

Tears stung her eyes. "I'm glad that I amuse you."

"Life amuses me," he corrected, but his gaze softened as he cupped her cheek. "He's trying not to hurt you, you're trying not to hurt me, and all I want is to protect you both."

She couldn't bring herself to move away, so she closed her eyes and spoke past the lump in her throat. "Save it for Ace. He needs it more."

"Does he?" His thumb brushed her lower lip before pressing hard enough to coax her lips apart.

She reacted out of instinct. Her tongue touched the rough pad of his thumb, and she opened her eyes in time to see him lowering his mouth to hers.

He stopped, so close she could feel his heat. "You should tell me to go, because I'm done protecting you from myself."

Rachel took a deep breath, but all she managed to do was draw in his scent. His breath. It wasn't fair that she still wanted him to kiss her, just plain *wanted him*, after all that had happened.

"Ace," she whispered, a warning and a reminder. "You two seem happy together."

His brow furrowed. "We're not *together*."

"Bullshit."

"We're partners."

"You're more." Someone else should have had to break it to him, someone without painful ties to both him and Ace. "I see it. So does everyone else."

His expression didn't change beyond the slightest tightening around his eyes, but she was close enough to sense his sudden tension. "Not everything is about fucking."

It hurt. With only a few words, he'd managed to belittle so much—her perceptions and jealousy, Ace's affections, and maybe even his own feelings. What it meant to be an O'Kane, and all the ways they could care about one another, ways that could never be reduced to *fucking*.

Her throat burned, but she bit back her angry words and gave him ice instead. "You were right. You should go."

He opened his mouth, but it wasn't his voice she heard. It was Ace's, echoing from just beyond the door. "Cruz, where the fuck are you?"

Cruz lunged away, but even his reflexes weren't fast enough. He'd barely snatched up his shirt when Ace rounded the corner. "I told Gia we'd pick up her payment..."

He stopped and stared at Rachel, his gaze tracking over her flushed cheeks, but she knew he hadn't missed Cruz's disarray, either. Shirtless, his belt hanging open—

It looked bad. But the worst part was feeling like *she'd* come between *them*, and this was all her fault.

Cruz started to speak, but Ace lifted a hand. "I hope she kissed it all better, brother, because we've got twice as many stops tonight with half the men over in Three."

She'd heard him fake cheerful before, but never with this much manic intensity, as if his life depended on the two of them buying his lighthearted, breezy words.

She couldn't look at him.

12

ITH THE ROADS cleared, the trip across the border and into Three took half the time, not to mention half the attention.

No longer having to dodge debris, Bren guided his motorcycle into the heart of the sector. There, with fewer stone walls to magnify its rumble into an echoing roar, the engine sounded almost quiet. Tranquil, a sharp contrast to the lingering destruction surrounding them. At one time, these streets had housed the factories and shipping warehouses that made Sector Three a power to be reckoned with. Now, crumbling brick and dusty, pitted concrete were giving way to the grass pushing up through the wreckage.

He pulled to a stop next to the squat building Six had described. "Is this it?"

"Yeah." She slid from the bike and nodded to the corner. "Around this way."

Her apartment was underground, straight down two

flights of cracked cement steps and hidden behind a padlocked steel door. There were no windows Bren could see, nothing but gloomy shadows and darkness, despite the early hour.

"Doesn't look like anyone's broken into it," she said, lifting the undamaged padlock. "How good are you at picking locks?"

The ancient lock in her hand was sturdy but simple. He tugged the small set of picks out of his back pocket and slipped a tension wrench and a small hook free of the case. "It might take me a minute."

She took the case from him and shifted aside before running a finger over the S-rake pick. "These are really nice. I bet you can get into anything."

"They come in handy." He turned the tension wrench a little and flicked the hook across the pins inside the lock. "Only three pins."

He cocked his head as he worked, listening for the telltale clicks as he set one pin, then another. With the final click, he turned the wrench and the lock fell open.

"Damn." Six took the tools from him and slipped them back in the case. "If you ever get bored with cleaning guns while I watch, you could open locks instead."

"I'll remember that." Bren slid the lock free, but this door wasn't his to open. "After you?"

Six drew in a deep breath, squared her shoulders, and dragged open the creaky steel door.

Inside was pitch black. Six flicked on the flashlight he'd given her and swung it toward the wall a few steps inside. "If the wires to the solar panels are still in place..." She flipped a circuit breaker, and lights flickered on.

Christmas lights.

They were everywhere, tacked to the walls and running across the ceiling, mostly cheap white bulbs mixed with a few strings of color that started to fade in and out as they warmed up. The strings illuminated a snug room just big enough for a mattress piled high with blankets and pillows, a coffee table, a couple of rickety chairs, and a few cluttered shelves.

"It's silly." Six poked one of the dead bulbs in a string of lights draped by the door. "But they were pretty cool when I was a kid."

They still were, because they reminded him of her—tiny glows in the darkness, determined but struggling. "I like it."

"So, this is it." She sat on the edge of the mattress and leaned forward to run a hand along the bottom surface of the coffee table. "I think everything's still here."

"Doesn't look like it's been ransacked..." His words trailed off as she pulled out a wad of cash bound by tape. "When were you last here?"

"A couple months before Trent threw me to you guys. I haven't lived here full time in a few years, though. Even after I started running with Trent, I liked knowing I had somewhere to go." She waved the cash. "Somewhere to stash things."

Someplace safe. "Lex did the same thing in the early days. Drove Dallas nuts."

She tilted her head and studied him. "Would it drive you nuts? Knowing this place is here?"

"If you kept it, you mean?" So tempting to give her the easy answer, the one she probably wanted to hear. "A little, but not because you shouldn't have your own space. If you needed it to be away from the O'Kanes."

After another silent moment, she nudged aside the coffee table and reached for his hand. "Come here for a second."

It skirted dangerously close to *we have to talk*. "Shit, what did I do?"

"Shut up and come *here*."

At least she was laughing. Bren dropped to the closest chair and wrapped his fingers around hers. "What is it?"

She shifted to her knees in front of him, her gaze suddenly intense. "Lex talked to me about joining. I mean, she didn't flat-out offer me ink, but...she asked if I was ready." Six exhaled. "And I told her I was."

He quelled his reflexive relief and took a deep breath. "Ink is for life, Six. Are you *sure* you're ready for that?"

"I don't know," she admitted softly. "I don't think anyone *can* know. But she wanted me, Bren. And not to sling drinks or give you a friendly place to stick your dick. Lex believes we can be more than some guy's bitch. I still don't get Dallas, but I'll follow her into hell for that."

She might never understand Dallas, or realize that everything his queen did was because he had her back. But Lex *was* O'Kane, just as much as Dallas was, and if Six could trust in her...

That was enough. "Congratulations, sweetness."

"Yeah?" She lunged upwards, sliding astride his lap fast enough to rock the rickety chair back and threaten a total collapse. "Don't speak too soon. Lex said I could switch from bartending to bouncing, as soon as you think I can handle it."

He'd have to teach her how to move drunken assholes twice her size with pain instead of leverage, but she'd be good at it. Protective, attentive. Smart. "Sounds right up your alley, if you ask me."

Her eyes lit up, and she wound her arms around his neck before pressing her forehead to his. "You sure you don't mind sharing your home and your family with me?"

His. She still thought of it all that way, and it was time for that to end. "Until I took these cuffs, none of it was mine, either. You're a little late to the party, that's all."

Six laughed, tightened her fingers on the back of his head, and kissed him.

Slow and soft, so sweet that he felt clumsy for the first time as he wrapped his arms around her waist. It hit him square in the gut—the kiss of a woman opening up, not just to him, but to a world of possibility.

She caught his lower lip between her teeth, then released him to whisper against the corner of his mouth. "I never brought a boy here, you know. I never brought *anyone* here. You're the first to see all of me."

A gift, greater than any control she'd ever given him over her body. "Thank you."

"Mmm." She kissed her way up his jaw, stopping to feather a kiss over his earlobe. "Wanna screw around? Over the clothes only."

The tiny caress splintered through him. "No fucking?" he asked lazily.

She rolled her hips, grinding on his lap in a move worthy of a Broken Circle dancer. "That depends, I guess."

He had to force his hands to relax, to hold her hips lightly. "On?"

"How long you can take it." Another roll, and this time it was her teeth on his earlobe, the barest tease as her fingernails pricked his scalp. "How long you can grope and grind and let me touch you before you'll do whatever it takes to get in me?"

His dick swelled, but shifting beneath her didn't relieve the pressure. It made him harder. "Take off your shirt."

She lifted her head long enough to grin at him, wild and unrestrained, her eyes dancing. "No," she said, and leaned in to nip at his other ear. Her breath raced across his skin as her voice dropped to a hoarse whisper. "But you can rip it off."

Too easy. Bren twisted his hand in the fabric and pulled it up slowly, stopping just before the ribbed cotton slipped off the hard peaks of her nipples.

She hissed in a breath—and hissed it out when that

rubbed the fabric against her breasts. Shuddering, she pressed her next openmouthed kiss to his throat.

He flicked her nipple through the cotton. "Can't take it?"

"Whatever," she growled, and closed her teeth on his throat.

Not hard enough, not yet. Bren urged her hips closer to his and rocked her against his erection until she shuddered, her teeth clamping down on his skin.

Yes.

"Show me how you'd fuck me," he invited.

She lifted her head and caught the back of the chair before rocking up, rolling her hips in a slow, taunting grind as she stared into his eyes. "Like this. Slow. Because you're big, and I love that feeling when you're first pushing into me."

He could fuck her like that, withdrawing with every stroke just so he could drive into her all over again. "Can you feel my piercings when I'm in you?"

"I feel something..." Her eyelids drooped as she gave a little shiver. "When you had me on my stomach on the couch that night, every damn thrust felt like coming all over again."

Her nipple tightened even more under his thumb, as if merely saying the words turned her on. "Your G-spot, sweetness."

She frowned and studied him through narrowed eyes. "I thought that was a story guys made up so they could talk you into bending over a table."

"I'll show you." He twisted his hand slowly, until he could catch her nipple between his thumb and index finger in a hard pinch. "I'll fuck it until you come all over me."

Her mouth dropped open on a silent moan, and she squeezed her eyes shut. "I'll come faster if you keep talking," she whispered, the words as unsteady as the sudden rocking of her hips.

He wasn't usually a man of many words, but motivation like that had a way of changing things. "You know what to do, Six."

Breathing heavily, she jerked her shirt out of his hands in her haste to haul it over her head.

Bren caught a lock of her hair as it tumbled down her bare back. "Are you wet?" He tugged sharply. "Tell me."

"You wanna know if you get me hot?" She reached for his shirt next. "You do. Sometimes just by breathing."

It was a different sort of power, a need that transcended obedience. "I don't need submission, not the way you think of it. This is better."

Her fingers fanned wide on his chest as she stilled her squirming and stared down at him. "You don't want to own my body," she said, the words hesitant, almost a question. "You want me to give it to you, every damn time."

The expression of gentle wonder made his dick ache. "Every time."

"Because it belongs to me." She scratched him, streaking gentle lines of pain in her wake. "It's *mine*."

"Yours." He pulled open the button and the zipper on her pants and urged the fabric down, off her ass. "Give it to me."

"Tell me what you're gonna do with it," she challenged. "It better be dirty. It better be filthy."

"Here? Fuck you 'til you can't breathe." He squeezed her ass. "But I talked to Ace."

"Yeah?"

Casual, too casual for the way she squirmed over him. "Yeah. We can show you a little pain, sweetness. Mine *and* yours, if you want it."

"Will it turn you on for me to watch?" she demanded breathlessly. She freed her hands from his shirt only to slide them up his arms, fingers digging into muscle. "Would it turn you on if I let you fuck me in front of him?

He couldn't help, not with the fucking. I only give my body to you."

Excitement edged her voice, and Bren shuddered. She'd be hot around him, gripping his cock, while Ace rained a different sort of heat on his back. Blow after blow, but the thing about the fantasy that truly rocked him was her hunger, her anticipation.

His pleasure would spark hers.

He kissed her, dragging her mouth to his with a groan. Her pants were in the way, and he had to lift her to push them down and kick the denim free. The chair wobbled as she crashed down against him again and snatched at his shirt.

She jerked at it hard enough to tear a seam, snarling in frustration until he helped her take it off, then guided her hands to his pants. She fumbled with his belt, her fingers trembling, but then she had it open and his fly down and she moaned as she closed her hand around his cock, like she was already imagining him inside her.

Bren groaned and wrapped his hand over hers, squeezing her fist around him. "Now?"

"Now," she echoed, leaning close enough to kiss him. "Take my body. I'm giving it to you."

Open and wet, so eager that one thrust took him all the way inside her. He froze, her hips clutched to his, as her head fell back and her lips parted.

She didn't speak, but the hands that settled on his shoulders, fingernails digging in, said plenty. She clung to him and squirmed, her throat working, her eyes clenched shut. "Like this," she whispered. "I love this part. When all I can feel is you."

Her body surrounded his, warm and inviting. He released her, letting his hands fall to his sides as she squirmed harder. "Push me."

It took forever for her to lift her head and meet his gaze, and even longer before she began to move. Just a slow, experimental rock at first, her eyes unfocused. "I figured something out."

His voice came out hoarse. "What's that?"

"I don't give a shit what I'm *supposed* to want." She rose up on her toes only to drop down hard enough to drive moans from them both. "I've never let anyone tell me what to do before. Why should sex be different?"

"Good girl." He tilted her hips with one hand at the small of her back, and she sucked in a breath and clutched at his upper arms until her nails broke skin.

"I was going to come up with fantasies," she continued unsteadily, "but I kinda just have the same one over and over."

He couldn't really slam into her without lifting her and taking over her movements entirely, but he thrust up once, sending the chair skidding a few inches across the floor.

This time she whimpered, scratching down to his elbows before gripping his arms as if to hold them both still. Her gaze found his, eyes already hazy with pleasure and so trusting, so *open*.

She held nothing back, not with her eyes *or* her words. "In my fantasy, I ask you to make me feel good. That's all. Because I trust you, and whatever you do with me, you'll make it feel good."

The words jolted through him in a shiver. "How far will you go, Six?"

"What does *far* even mean?" Her hands framed his face, and she smoothed her thumb over his lower lip. "Nothing you could do would take more trust than me bringing you here. This was my safe place, and I'm giving it up. I don't need it anymore."

"Are you sure?"

She bit his lower lip with a laughing growl. "About this place, or what you can do to me?"

"I'm serious." He stilled her head with one hand wrapped in her hair. "Keep it if you need to."

After a torturous moment, she nodded as much as

his grip allowed. "Okay, but not because I *need* to. Because we'll be here, working, and it'll be nice to have a private place for just us."

Us. She'd talked so much about all the parts of his life he was letting her into, and this was hers, the only thing she had to share with him.

Bren kissed her again, his mouth crashing into hers as he dragged her down for another hard thrust. The chair cracked, and he staggered to his feet as it gave way under them.

He backed her up to the wall instead, hitching her high against the paneling with her legs around his waist. She slammed her head back with a choked noise, digging her heels into his thighs. "Make me—make me feel—" Another groan. "Oh God, *Bren*—"

"Shh. Your safe place," he panted, closing one hand loosely around her throat. "Right here, with me."

"Safe." Six stopped trying to move, stopped trying to force *him* to move. She twisted her arms around his neck and shuddered in his grasp. "Show me."

He tightened his hand, just enough to cut off part of her air as he sped his thrusts, pounding her pussy until he was gritting his teeth against slick pleasure.

And through it all her gaze never left his. Trust, naked trust, so much of it she let him take her to the edge, to where her body clenched tight and her lips parted on a silent scream, and then she was coming, hard, the orgasm abrupt and intense.

He jerked his hand away from her throat to slam against the wall. One ragged breath and she was screaming, *screaming*, loud enough to cut through the roar of blood pounding in his ears. He followed her over the edge, thrusting until he was spent, and the desperate grip of her pussy eased into gentle flutters.

She slumped forward, limp, and mumbled something against his throat. He combed her hair from her face and tilted her head back. "You with me?"

kit rocha

"I don't know," she whispered, blinking at him a couple times before her eyes drifted shut. "Are you somewhere tingly?"

Not dizzy from lack of oxygen, then, but drunk on
pleasure. "We broke your chair."

"Buy me a better one." She let her head fall forward
again and nuzzled his cheek with a laugh. "Buy me one
sturdy enough for you, you hulking lug. I'm gonna ride
you on it all the time."

"Home away from home?"

"Will you buy me a real bed?"

"I'll build it with my own two hands, if you want."

Her head popped up, and she smiled as if he'd offered
her the world, gilded and wrapped in a bow. "You can
build things?"

"Maybe." And for the first time in years, he felt like
it might be true.

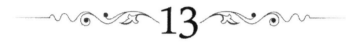

13

I F SIX HAD possessed a little less pride, it would have been tempting to let Bren tackle her to the floor just for the pleasure of feeling him stretched out over her, warm and hard and as turned on as she was.

Evading a feint and riding him to the floor was almost as good.

They hit the mats with a thud, her body astride his. His grin was quick, but not as quick as his movements as he flipped her over using sheer strength.

He was still grinning when she smacked her forehead into his nose.

Bren rolled away, rubbing his nose. "You might want to save that move as a last resort."

"Sorry." Wincing, she scrambled to her knees and reached for his face. "It's a bad habit. I know you've taught me new ones, but sometimes instinct gets me."

He let her poke and prod at his nose for a moment before waving her away. "I'm all right. Nothing's broken."

beyond pain

She dropped her hands to rest on her lap. "I've got to get new instincts. Right now, I'm fine until you startle me, and then it's like I'm fifteen again, breaking noses and trying to ram a guy's balls into his rib cage."

"That won't fly if you're working the door at the Broken Circle."

It wouldn't, and she knew it. She'd expected Bren's acknowledgment to be disheartening, but there was a thrilling sort of focus in having a *goal*. It gave her the energy to shake off the discomfort and rock to her feet. "So I do it again."

He stretched his neck and squared his shoulders. "First lesson—don't let things get to the point where you have to headbutt someone. Try to stop the trouble before it starts."

Zan was good at that, but he was huge and had a face that made his scowls extra intimidating. She'd have to be better. Quicker, more efficient. "Show me?"

Bren shook his head. "It's about control. You're the bouncer, so you have it, and you can't ever forget that. You have to *breathe* it."

Like him. "Have you always been able to do it, or did you learn?"

He took his time answering. "I didn't come from a place where many people had control over anything. I guess I learned it once I joined up."

The story of how he'd gone from a street orphan to the ranks of the most terrifying elite soldiers in their world was one she desperately wanted to know, but the way he mentioned it made her think it had to be as laced with pain as her own history.

She knew what it was like to not want to talk, but just as familiar was the certainty that no one cared enough to listen. So she settled on a middle route, inviting him to talk without pushing. "The MP, you mean?"

"It was Coop's idea," Bren murmured. "Said it was the best way to make something out of my life. So he fronted me the cash for a bar code and a brand-new identity."

"How old were you?"

"On paper? Eighteen. But I don't really know."

All those times she'd joked about him being old, and he didn't even know how old he was. Her chest ached as she shifted closer, until they were knee-to-knee. "What was it like, being in the military police?"

"Structured," he said thoughtfully. "There's comfort in that, I suppose, especially for a kid from the streets. I always knew where to go, what to do. What was expected of me, and what I'd get in return."

"You got to learn things." She couldn't quite keep the hunger out of her voice. The hacked tablet Noelle had given her made it easier to work her way through books, but now the struggle was to focus on learning the words at all when listening to the tablet's soothing female voice was so much easier.

"Yeah," he said wryly. "I learned the art of assassination. The most effective silent kills. How to line up a two-mile sniper shot, accounting for wind shift. Your basic Special Tasks education."

"How to be strong," she countered. "How to hurt evil bastards, so they can't hurt anyone else. How to be a protector."

"No." Bren's smile held a tinge of sadness as he reached out and ran his fingers over an escaped lock of her hair. "All those things, I learned right here in Sector Four."

She wanted to turn her face into his hand and kiss his palm, but she couldn't look away from his eyes. "So teach them to me. I don't have to fight for survival anymore, but I can protect people."

His smile widened, and he brushed his thumb over her cheek. "You'll be better at it than I've ever been. Just wait."

Biting back her smile, she gave him her sternest

look. "So stop being mushy, Donnelly, and throw me around this room."

"Yes, ma'am." He climbed to his feet and stretched again. "Want to come at me? Want me to come at you?"

She bounced to her feet, to her toes, watching him warily. He could lunge into sudden movement without the slightest tensing muscle to give warning, but sometimes she caught tiny hints in the crinkling around his eyes or the set of his mouth. "I wanna see that arm lock one more time."

"Oh yeah?"

If it had been anyone else, she would have asked if he was ready. But Bren was always ready, and when she came at him, driving hard for his ribs, he swatted her wrist, knocking it aside without apparent effort.

He must have slowed the progression down so she could see it, but it still happened so fast. His wrist slid up to slam against the inside of her elbow, forcing her arm to bend as he twisted behind her, somehow getting his other arm threaded through hers and his hands linked together.

A few seconds, that was all it took for her to end up against his chest, her arm bent out to her side at an awkward angle, her wrist trapped in the crook of his elbow and his other hand gripping her shoulder.

It would take very little force to drive her to the floor now, and even less to cause so much pain that she'd beg to end up there. But he hadn't thrown a single punch, hadn't smashed his nose into anyone's face. He'd simply moved to take control of the situation—and her—with minimum fuss.

Quick, efficient, deadly.

It turned her on.

She inhaled slowly and tested the limited range of motion she had within the lock. "I bet you could move a pretty big guy with this."

He increased the pressure, but only the tiniest bit.

"He'll go where you point him, all right."

Easy to believe, since she was up on her toes, her fingers twitching, as if her body was ready to tap out whether she wanted to or not. "Do you think I can pull this off on someone a lot taller than me?"

"There are other locks that might work better for you." He released her and rubbed her shoulder. "We'll go over them."

"Okay," she murmured, distracted by the warmth of his fingers soothing away the lingering ache.

His eyes darkened, and his fingers slowed to a sensual caress. "Six—"

Someone rapped on the door, the hollow sound still echoing as it swung wide, and Emma poked her head in, dark and bleached-blonde locks swinging. "Amira's having her baby!"

Instead of taking a step back, Bren pulled Six into the circle of his arm. "How long?"

"What do I look like, a fucking psychic? It's a baby, Donnelly, not a shipment of booze." She slammed the door behind her.

Six laughed, and it didn't even feel awkward anymore. "Unless your Doc has some fancy city tricks, it's probably going to be a while."

"Christ help him if Flash starts getting pissed." He kissed the top of her head. "First O'Kane baby. Want to go wait with everyone else?"

Her wrists were still bare, but with Lex's offer on the table, Six didn't feel nearly as hesitant to take him up on it. She'd have her ink soon. She'd be one of them in a way outsiders would have to acknowledge, a way no one could take from her.

For now, the fact that they included her was enough. Hell, it was everything. "Yeah, let's go."

The first time Flash punched Doc, Jasper had to go in to run interference.

Bren would have volunteered, but his experience with pain and blood was far less helpful than Jas's years on the farm, where he'd assisted with numerous births. No, Bren was better off with the others, gathered around the makeshift bar in the warehouse, waiting for news.

"God, how long does this take?" Ace demanded as the fourth hour rolled around. He'd given up making jokes and was sprawled in a chair next to Six, staring broodingly at the door.

She patted him on the arm. "I'm sure everything's fine. I've seen it take all night."

Ace shuddered. "Flash'll pound us into the ground one after another if it takes much longer."

Lex shoved another beer into his hands. "Relax. Doc's under strict orders—nothing goes sideways. This kid's an O'Kane."

"Still, maybe I should go check on—"

"No." Noelle wrapped both arms around Ace's neck and rested her chin on his head. "Amira doesn't need everyone hovering, and Jas can handle Flash. But you're adorable when you're worried, Ace."

He scowled. "Oh, shut up, princess."

It drew a round of laughs, and Six grinned. Bren found himself matching her expression as he wove his fingers with hers and gave her a reassuring squeeze.

Lex caught his eye and winked, though her amusement faded as Dallas walked in from the back office, tablet in hand.

He shook his head slightly at Lex before pointing to Bren. "I need you for a minute."

Trouble. He recognized the look on Dallas's face even before he released Six and followed his boss to a quieter corner. "What is it?"

"Word from Three." He tilted the tablet, showing the curt message. "Emma's suggestion worked. Noah surfaced. And reading between the lines, he's pissed."

"About us looking for him?"

"Could be." He glanced across the room, his gaze set-tling on the cluster of O'Kanes. "Could be he'd take any mention of Emma as a threat. Lex thinks there's some history there, and I don't want this whole thing blowing up in our face. I need you to meet him and explain the situation."

Which likely meant heading over into Sector Three, or at least to neutral ground. "What do you want me to offer him?"

"Money for services. And if he asks to see Emma in-stead..."

She would have made the offer to unearth this Noah character, even if he presented a personal danger to her. She was an O'Kane—she'd do whatever the gang needed, and trust them to keep her safe. "If he asks after her, I'll tell him he has to see her here, and only after he meets with you and Lex."

"If you think he's more trouble than he's worth?" Dallas met his gaze, eyes serious. Unyielding. "You take care of it."

The real reason Bren was the best choice to take the meeting. His involvement in Three aside, he was unique-ly suited to tackling the potential danger this hacker represented. "Quick and clean," he promised. "If I have to."

"Good." His lips twisted into a grimace. "From what Doc tells me, you can leave now and still maybe show back up before this kid does. Which is good, because we'll all be taking turns sitting on Flash by then."

"Doc's got plenty of drugs. If he can't find anything in his case, make him front Flash some shit from his per-sonal stash."

Dallas's laugh was far from amused. "Just as long as he's not dipping into it while he's taking care of our girl."

The man had seemed sober, the surest sign that his

rampant death wish apparently didn't involve having Dallas dump him in a shallow grave for endangering Amira and her baby. "Don't worry, I think he's straight tonight."

"Damn well better be. I only got so much time for crazy motherfuckers—" A wail from beyond the room drifted through the walls, and Dallas started before breaking into a wide grin. "Well, thank fucking God."

Relieved murmurs gave way to cheers as people laughed and hugged, already toasting the newest O'Kane. Then the door at the far end of the room swung open, and the celebration halted as Jasper walked in.

He grinned, an expression at odds with the fresh shiner darkening one eye. "It's a girl."

"A girl." Dallas clapped Bren on the shoulder. "You got this? Lex and I have to check on Amira and Flash."

"Yes, sir."

Bren stopped beside Six to squeeze her shoulder and whisper in her ear. "Got to run an errand. I'll be back soon, though."

She tensed as she peered up at him. "Everything okay?"

No need to borrow trouble. Coop's voice rang in his ears, and for the first time Bren understood the warning. So he smiled and tucked her hair behind her ear. "Yeah. I'll see you soon."

Smiling, she grazed his jaw with a quick, shy kiss. No one was paying attention—there was too much excitement for that—but even if they had been watching, Six didn't seem to care. She only blushed softly, with no uncomfortable squirming, no hiding.

Damn, he hoped he didn't have to kill that motherfucker from Three. A life just had begun, and it seemed wrong to end another so soon, with the baby's first indignant cries still ringing in his ears.

Besides, nothing stood to upset the fragile balance he and Six had found like executing a hit on someone from her old sector. Especially someone she actually *liked*.

Scarlet's directions to the meeting site were something out of a pre-Flare spy movie—*He'll meet you under the bridge. Come alone.*

By itself, the location was enough to make Bren nervous. At one point, the bridge had served as an overpass, part of the system of shipping roads that ran in and out of the city. One end had disintegrated in the sector bombings, rendering it unserviceable, but Wilson Trent had found other uses for it—namely hanging people he felt had betrayed him, letting them swing from the girders as a reminder and a warning.

The place was quiet, and the bits of frayed rope still swinging above him only heightened its sinister air. A thin layer of fog clung to the ground, swirling around the plants that had burst up through the concrete in a ghostly dance.

The whole place gave him the goddamned creeps.

"Brendan Donnelly." The rough voice echoed off stone, and Bren tilted his head, trying to pinpoint his location. "Former military police, burned for falsifying evidence. All those years working for the smartest men in Eden, and they never realized you were a fake from the start."

Bren turned just as Noah Lennox materialized out of the darkness. "Did you know I was coming, or have you memorized dossiers on all the O'Kanes?"

"Not all." Noah stopped a few paces away and offered a smile that would have chilled even Dallas. "Only those of you with a digital footprint, real or fabricated."

"I certainly have one of those," Bren agreed.

Noah met the words with silence, tense beneath his battered leather jacket. He was tall and lean, built more like Ace than Bren, with the kind of deceptive strength that might fool someone into thinking he wasn't a threat.

Bren knew better.

After another moment of studying him, Noah narrowed his eyes. "Where's Emma?"

"I was told to come alone."

The man gritted his teeth. "I know what the note said. I want to know where she is."

Bren shrugged. "She's back in Four."

"Guest or hostage?"

"Member." He held up his wrist and flashed his ink. "She's an O'Kane."

"Bullshit."

For all the force of his denial, Noah Lennox looked rattled, and Bren pressed the advantage. "You can see her any time you want—back on the compound, after you meet up with Dallas and Lex."

"Then what did—?" Noah bit off the question and ran a hand through his short red hair. "Fuck. If this isn't about her, then what the hell does O'Kane want?"

"Scarlet didn't tell you?"

"She said you want intel, but..." His gaze drifted to the side. "Tell me what you want to know. When I've got it, I'll send word. But I won't hand it over until after I've seen Emma."

The quiet confidence of the demand raised the hairs on the back of Bren's neck. "Who backed Wilson Trent's play to kill Dallas and take over Sector Four?"

Noah laughed abruptly. "Oh, just that. That doesn't come cheap."

"You can take the job or leave it, Lennox." Bren hesitated. Playing the hard line was smart if the guy was a creeper from Emma's past, but if he really had simply been a friend of her brother's... "She's all right, you know. She's doing okay."

"Is she safe?"

A deceptively straightforward question, edged with lethal challenge as well as hope. "I saw her right before I left. She was having a drink with the others."

Noah seemed to process that. "How serious is O'Kane about cleaning house over here?"

"Pretty goddamn serious."

"Then we'll be in touch." The man vanished into the fog.

Bren rubbed his temples and headed back toward his bike. No new answers about Trent, but putting Lennox on the trail was progress.

It didn't answer Dallas's other questions, the ones about Emma's relationship to this elusive hacker. Ace could get the truth out of her easily enough, though Bren was starting to think it didn't matter. For all Noah Lennox's intensity and mystery, he didn't act like a man driven to reclaim something he'd lost and believed to be rightfully his.

Then again, maybe that was the point. He'd asked all the right questions, shown just the right amount of concern for her well-being—like a man telling the truth, or a consummate sociopath.

So which was he?

14

THE NOTE WAS simple, so simple she struggled with only a few of the words, mostly due to Bren's harsh, slanted handwriting. Abrupt and efficient as he was, the note directed her to climb the stairs at the end of the hallway.

Mysterious.

Most of the O'Kanes lived in converted rooms on the first floor of the building. In fact, Six had only been upstairs on the nights Dallas threw his extravagant parties. She hesitated on the stairs, trying to imagine what the next one would be like. All those naked bodies, all that pleasure. For once, she'd feel free to watch, to take in the joy and the lust and let her imagination run wild.

Until Bren dragged her someplace quiet and fucked her cross-eyed.

With that thought sparking a flutter in her belly, she followed the directions up the stairs, past the party room, and down a narrow corridor toward one corner of the building. The hall ended in a simple wooden door, slightly ajar.

Anything could be on the other side, but in her gut she already knew. Bren, and Ace, and God knew what else. Whips and chains and all those things she'd never thought much about until she'd started thinking about Bren and what he might do with them.

What he might want *her* to do with them.

She took a deep breath to settle her nerves before pushing open the door. Inside, Bren was sprawled on a huge cushion in the middle of the floor, a drink held loosely in one hand.

He was the only familiar thing about the room.

Since he was watching her, assessing her reactions, she lingered in the doorway and took it in slowly—the chains along the wall and hanging from the ceiling, the oddly shaped furniture whose purposes she couldn't quite figure out, and the solid wooden shelves along the far wall, where Ace stood testing the weight of a leather flogger.

If the party room was expansive debauchery, this room was...distilled. The hard liquor of fucking. Sin on the rocks.

Bren nodded to the couch behind the cushion. "Sit."

She took her time pulling the door shut, but that *click* did more than shut out the world. It triggered something inside her, something that recognized this moment for what it was.

This wasn't simply another night in his room or hers or even Ace's. This was a stolen moment, set apart from the others. A fantasy, where reality could be what they wanted, with no past or future or baggage or worries, just now.

Her heart beating faster, she crossed to the couch and sank down on the middle of it.

Bren lifted his glass to his lips for a leisurely sip.

"We have some things to talk over, starting with the basics. Who touches you?"

Six glanced at Ace, who gave her his wickedest smile in return, the one that had sent panic racing through her in the past. It still made her nervous, but the good kind, the kind that shivered over her skin with the same prickling pleasure as Bren's fist in her hair.

She wet her lips and returned her attention to Bren. "Would you let him touch me?"

It was Bren's turn to smile. "No."

"Harsh, brother." Ace didn't seem upset as he ran the flogger's tails over his fingers. "But I don't think she minds."

Six didn't realize she was smiling too until she tried pressing her lips together. Bren was watching her, so intent, so *protective*, and she couldn't help it. "He gets a little possessive," she murmured, nudging his leg with her foot.

Bren nudged her back. "So do you. Ace might not have much to do tonight with his hands. Or his mouth."

But Ace would have to wield the whips, and for one moment, that did make her jealous. Anything her body wanted, Bren found a way to supply, but he had needs she couldn't meet.

Yet. "I want him to show me how."

"You mean the flogger." It wasn't a question.

She still answered. "If you'll let me. If you want me to."

He held her gaze—and licked his lips. "Ace?"

"It's her night, brother. Hers and yours. I'll show her anything you want me to." The words were more serious than any she'd ever heard from the man, so solemn her gaze jumped to him again. He'd picked up a different flogger, one with wider tails. "But I did bring the deer-skin, in case you want it."

Bren rose slowly, set his glass aside, and reached for her. He combed his fingers through her hair, pulling just a little, and kissed her cheek. "Deerskin is soft," he murmured. "You should know what it feels like before Ace shows you how to use one."

She shivered and turned into his cheek, inhaling shakily. "I thought you weren't going to let Ace touch me. Or is that different?"

Bren hummed softly. "If you were like Noelle—if this *was* sex for you—then I'd want to be the one to give it to you. But the leather doesn't fit in my hands like it does in Ace's. He can show you better."

"It doesn't have to be about pain," Ace said, his voice closer than it had been. "Some people like the adrenaline. Lex is like that. It gets her warmed up, floating, but it doesn't get her off."

Adrenaline. God knew Six had a thing for that, like the illicitness of fucking where she might get caught, or the dangerous thrill of Bren's hand around her throat, cutting off her air. So careful, so controlled that it didn't feel like danger, not exactly, but she'd come so hard she'd been woozy for hours.

She lifted a hand to touch Bren's cheek. "What will you do while he's flogging me?"

"We talked about how it can be part of sex or separate," he whispered. "Which do you want it to be?"

It was an impossible question to answer, because she still couldn't imagine it. "I don't know if I want to keep them separate, or if I'll be able to."

"Hey, fighter-girl." The couch sank as Ace settled next to her, close but not touching. "Anything you want to try is okay, anything you don't is off the table. Bren and I understand the rules in this room. He's the boss. That's it, start to finish. If something I do gets you wet and tingly? Well, that's because *he* told me to do it. You don't even have to remember I'm here."

She turned just enough to study him, but nothing in his dark eyes or easy expression indicated distress. Being considered an extension of Bren's will didn't seem to bother him, but that didn't make it fair. "You really don't mind?"

"Not even a little." Ace winked. "I can't promise not to get hot watching the two of you, but I know plenty of girls who'll be more than happy you sent me over already warmed up."

Bren shifted on the couch, sliding his hand down her back. "Yes or no?"

Curiosity might have been enough to motivate her, but this was more than that. More than Ace's jokes about tingles, though sitting between them with the promise of lust in the air was enough to set anyone squirming. Bren was offering her a peek into himself, a chance to experience something as profoundly important to him as her little bolthole in Three was to her.

She had meticulously strung Christmas lights. He had this. Pain.

Meeting Bren's eyes, she nodded. "Yes."

"If you want it to stop—*any* of it—you say so."

Her smile widened. "Not a problem."

"And if you don't want it to stop..." Bren's fingers spread wide at the small of her back. "It's like the man said. What I say goes, and you have to trust me to make you feel good."

Saying *no* came easily to her. *Yes* was still new, but not as new as the knowledge that her consent mattered. They'd moved past some invisible line where Bren was willing to serve as caretaker for her body, a body she didn't know how to own. It had become *hers*, in a way she'd never understood was possible, and he never wanted to take it away.

He wanted something more precious, something she'd always guarded closely even though it was so shattered she didn't know where all the fragments had ended up.

Her fragile, wounded heart beat too fast, and she knew when she opened her mouth that she was offering it to him. If she was lucky, he'd be too distracted to realize it was busted until she'd jammed enough of the pieces back together to make it worth a damn. "I trust you."

She barely got the words out before his mouth descended on hers, quick and hard. He pulled her up, into his lap, her hips nestled to his as he slid his hands into her hair, and her heart slammed into her rib cage so violently it was amazing it didn't break all over again.

The first rush of pleasure from his mouth knocked her senses sideways, and it wasn't until she was closing her teeth on his lower lip that she remembered they weren't alone. Pressing her forehead to Bren's, she tilted her face enough to catch a glimpse of Ace, sprawled against the corner of the couch a few feet away.

He met her gaze with a slow smile that crinkled the corners of his eyes and made her stomach flip-flop. "Don't mind me," he murmured, stretching his legs out in a way that made it impossible not to notice his dick straining his fly. It could have been lewd, except that Ace didn't leer or rub at himself like a creeper. He stared at them, obviously turned on by their pleasure, his eyes full of as much fond affection as hot lust.

Being watched wasn't so bad when the person watching just wanted to see you get off.

Shuddering, she turned back to Bren and licked his lower lip until he eased his hands under her shirt. He cupped her breasts, flicking her nipples with his thumbs, and she couldn't hold back a moan of protest. "Harder."

He smiled, his thumbs maintaining their easy rhythm, caught the front of her shirt between his teeth, and dragged it up to bare her breasts.

She wasn't all that exposed, not with his large hands cupping her tits. But Ace's gaze still pressed in on her, a hint of danger scraping her nerves and heightening every touch.

And he could tell. Either she was transparent or he

was a lot damn deeper than he let on, because his voice smoothed over her, low and soothing, inviting her to laugh off the tension. "I've never seen Bren so damn possessive. I don't know which of you I'm more jealous of."

"He's a liar." Bren's voice was hoarse. "He's always wanted me."

"Who wouldn't?" But words weren't enough, so Six crossed her arms and caught the edges of her shirt, jerking it up and over her head before she could think too much about stripping half naked in a room with two men.

Trust.

"You're beautiful." The words whispered over her skin, followed by the wet heat of Bren's tongue. He stroked her breast, his fingers pinching and then parting so that he could lick her nipple.

The gentle touch jolted straight to her pussy. She *was* wet and tingly, a second from squirming even as she cupped the back of Bren's head. "Harder," she whispered again, punctuating it with a whimpered, "*Please.*"

He sucked her nipple into his mouth and opened her pants with his free hand. Her gasp turned into a groan when his knuckles brushed her abdomen, a groan Ace echoed.

She tilted her head and found Ace digging his fingers into the leather couch. "You need some help, brother? Or are you the only one who gets to undress her?"

Bren was panting already, his broad chest rising and falling with each quick, rough breath. Instead of taking off her pants, he jerked them low on her hips, low enough to slip his hand into her panties. His wide fingers parted her, one fingertip nudging her clit, and the tingles exploded into buzzing warmth all the way to her toes.

Finally, he answered Ace's teasing question. "Get the flogger."

Ace vaulted off the couch, leaving Six to hover over

beyond pain

Bren, her body pulsing with the need to grind against his hand until she tipped over the edge. "You want him to flog me while your hand's in my pants?"

"In you." His hand shifted until one finger pushed inside. "I want to see if it turns you on."

It was so calmly obscene she had to bite her lip to keep from moaning, but she couldn't stop her body from tensing, clenching around the finger rocking so hot and deep inside her. "That's stupid," she said unsteadily. "What wouldn't turn me on while I'm riding your hand?"

"You're not riding it." He thrust a second finger inside her, almost distracting her from the steely hand he laid on her hip, stilling her furtive movements.

Panting, she put more effort into moving, but he had her fixed in place, trapped with two fingers filling her, stretching her. Arousal constricted around her, and now she was aware of every damn way her body reacted. Her tightened nipples, her flushed skin, her pussy clenching around his fingers, every reaction betraying how hot he was making her.

And the smug bastard knew it.

Footsteps sounded behind her, and she tensed again before twisting to peer at Ace. He'd lost his shirt somewhere, revealing that the tattooed sleeves covering his arms spilled onto his shoulders, though his chest was smooth and bare of ink.

But he didn't meet her eyes. He was too busy looking at her back.

At her scars.

She tensed, but before she could do more than part her lips, Ace raised his gaze to hers. She'd braced herself for pity, and was unprepared for the flash of fierce anger that disappeared beneath another of his easy smiles. "Scars can change how this feels, but yours aren't so severe, and everyone's different. I'm only going to ask you for one thing, fighter-girl."

Nervousness pricked her at his uncharacteristically

228

serious tone. "What?"

He twirled a finger in the air. "Keep your eyes on Bren, and don't try to hide what you're feeling. Because I know your type, sweetheart. You're like Lex, always wearing some kind of mask, and this won't work if you hold back."

It was the longest she'd ever heard Ace go without profanity, and that was a stupid thing to realize when she was mostly naked and shivering at the sensation of Bren's fingers inside her, but Ace was watching her so intently, waiting for her promise, and that was when she realized how very, very seriously he took what they were about to do.

A hazy memory surfaced, from what felt like a lifetime ago even if it couldn't have been more than a handful of weeks. Standing with Bren, watching Ace whip a woman for a captivated audience. Struggling with the mixture of fascination and horror.

At the time it had seemed so casually obscene, the sort of unrehearsed show you threw together with a girl who was willing to fake it and a guy who could make swinging a whip look good. But nothing about this was careless.

That was what would make it good.

She nodded once, turned back to Bren, and braced both hands on his shoulders. "No hiding," she whispered.

He rewarded her with a quick twist of his fingers, one that rocketed pleasure through her body. "Show me how it feels, sweetness."

"Oh God, it feels—"

Leather brushed her back. Softly, so softly, just a tease that kissed her skin. She tensed against a blow that didn't come, not until she'd relaxed again. That was when the deerskin slapped against her skin, the sound startling her more than the sensation.

"Easy." Bren steadied her, rubbing her hip soothingly. "Ace knows better. He won't land a blow if you're dreading it. Let it come."

Exhaling slowly, she forced herself to unwind. Not so difficult with Bren stroking her inside and out, setting off tiny trembles as arousal made everything bright and blurry. The next blow thudded against her back, warming her skin.

When she didn't tense, he did it again. And again.

It wasn't pleasure, not really. But it wasn't pain, either, even when the deerskin fell harder the next time, turning warmth to heat. Bren's gaze roamed her face, watching for the slightest twitch of reaction, and *that* made her clench tight around his fingers, impossibly turned on by being the center of so much intensity.

His chest rumbled, and he reached up to gather her hair, winding its length around his fist. "It's not the flogging getting you this wet, not yet."

"N-no—" Another thud, and her eyelids fluttered shut. She could imagine Ace behind her, as alert as Bren to the slightest hint of distress. Two people utterly focused on her, on something beyond mere pleasure. Bren was building an experience for her, managing every possible detail, and every time the deerskin tails thwacked against her skin, it reminded her how far beyond her control this moment was, and how utterly safe she still felt.

"Lower," Bren commanded, and the next blow landed across the top of her ass, teasingly light again but somehow more sensual. Or maybe it was the reminder that her ass was bare, and even with her pants clinging to her thighs she was more on display than she'd ever been.

But not for Ace's gratification. For her own, and that made all the difference.

He hit her again and she moaned, squirming on Bren's hand.

"It's illicit, isn't it?" Bren whispered, rocking his hand to slowly pump his fingers in and out of her. "That's why you're this damn wet."

The gentle friction sparked colors behind her eyelids, colors that danced as the fall of the flogger settled into a hypnotic rhythm, one she felt in her bones. "You have me," she choked out, hating that they weren't the right words, but knowing he'd somehow understand. "It's for me."

"Every fucking bit of it."

All for her. All about her, about this fuzzy feeling spreading out toward her fingertips, a welcome sort of giddiness. After so many fucking years of constant, exhausting *fighting*, it was bliss to close her eyes and trust someone else to give her all the things she was too afraid to reach for herself.

Bren's hand twisted harder in her hair as he sped his movements, fucking her with his fingers, and his voice buzzed in her ears. "Don't stop when she comes."

Firm and commanding and perfectly in control. She opened her eyes for long enough to meet his gaze, and the heat and intensity there were all it took.

Bren had control, so she lost hers.

Her body must have remembered her promise on some level, because she screamed when she came, and not all sexy, breathless noises. She was lost in a full-fucking-body orgasm, and the noises ripping free of her throat were loud, raw, and so relieved, like she'd been holding in a lifetime's worth of moans.

She wasn't holding anything in now.

A strong hand wrapped around the back of her neck—Bren, pulling her close to his chest to stop her writhing. "For both of us, Six." His breath blew hot on her ear. "You don't have to fight. Let me do it for you."

Let him fight. Let him—

The soft deerskin tails smacked against her skin, scattering her thoughts. It didn't matter, she didn't need to have thoughts. She turned her face to his neck, rested her cheek on his shoulder, and let the aftershocks build toward another wild peak. She wallowed in the rhythmic pressure against her back and Bren's broad, twisting fingers, and she rewarded both men with abandoned moans and whimpers.

They deserved them. They'd earned this, the only thing she'd always selfishly held back because it was the one thing that was hers. Her reactions, naked and on display—even when Bren flexed his fingers inside her and murmured a single word of encouragement. "More."

She didn't know who the command was meant for, but she was so close to the edge that she snapped. She came longer this time, deeper, wailing through the pleasure and sobbing when it started to fade only for Bren to bring it back with another turn of his wrist.

Sobbing—but not telling them to stop. Part of her hoped they never would, that she could spend the rest of her life floating in this moment, the first moment in her life made of nothing but pleasure and safety.

The rest of her only wanted it to end so she could do it all over again.

She was still trembling through the aftershocks of a hard, powerful orgasm, but she wasn't done. "One more," Bren whispered, dizzy on her pleasure, high on the fact that she'd writhed, screamed, clung to him—

But she hadn't pulled away.

She made a choked noise, small and wild, and her fingernails bit into his shoulders. Ace met his gaze over the top of her head, giving Bren a moment to anchor Six against his body before landing another gentle blow with a practiced flip of his wrist.

"Harder." She was spinning, off in the clouds, and *gentle*—from either of them—wasn't going to cut it anymore. "You can take it now, can't you, sweetness?"

She panted, hips twitching restlessly as her pussy clenched tight and sweet around him. "Yes, yes. *Yes.*"

Ace nodded and adjusted effortlessly, increasing the strength of his blows in small enough increments for Bren to judge her response by her strangled breathing and trembling limbs, and the noises—Christ, the noises. He'd never known she could make so many sounds. They only intensified as he waited for Ace to lift his arm. Just as the flogger was coming down to strike, Bren pressed his thumb to her clit in a hard, slippery circle.

She cried out, the sound cut off abruptly when she twisted her head and bit his shoulder, sparking a different sort of pleasure. She came like that, muffling her screams against his skin as her pussy soaked his hand, tight but so damn wet he could have easily worked a third finger into her.

Instead, he eased her through shudders that didn't end, not until he fell still and then carefully slid his fingers free of her body.

But she was still shivering, so Bren petted her and kissed her temple while Ace dropped a blanket around her bare shoulders.

Afterward, he settled on the couch beside them, the flogger resting across his knees. "Gotta admit, brother, I wasn't quite expecting that."

"Which part?"

The corner of Ace's mouth twitched up. "Maybe you wouldn't see it. You're as stone-faced as she is...usually."

Usually. "I'll give her anything she wants. All of me."

Ace absorbed that as Six murmured and pressed closer. But she didn't lift her head, and when she nuzzled her face against Bren's throat again, Ace smiled. "Dallas said I'd be laying ink on her soon enough."

"Her cuffs." It was too soon to talk about marks—too soon to *think* about them, especially when Six could still feel trapped if he moved too fast. "Plenty of time for the rest of it, right?"

"Plenty of time for what?" Six mumbled, her lips tickling Bren's throat.

beyond pain

He tilted her head back and couldn't help but smile at her flushed cheeks and sleepy eyes. "To find out what else you might be into. Pain might not do it for you, but plenty of other things do."

"You do it for me." Her gaze flicked to Ace and back. "And I still want to see what does it for you."

She already knew—all the bites and scratches, every time her eyes had darkened at his indrawn breaths. But the look in her eyes said she wanted to see it taken further, as far as he would go. "Not the deerskin," he murmured. "I like something heavier. Something that stings."

Ace was already rising, but Six ignored him, tracing her finger along Bren's lower lip instead. "Tell me what it feels like for you."

"Heat." The word escaped him without thought. "That adrenaline rush you get when it starts to hurt? It's like a green light. Everything gets going."

She pulled back and clutched the blanket around her shoulders. "Show me?"

Bren swallowed—hard. So far, she'd seen him relish only the tiniest hint of pain, and what he craved was nothing like the careful blows Ace had rained on her back.

The moment of truth.

He climbed off the couch and reached for his belt. "It's not always pretty, sweetness. Not like you were just now."

Six tilted her head back and lifted her hands, nudging his out of the way to work the supple leather of his belt. "If I wanted pretty, I'd be fucking Ace or Mad. Pretty doesn't get me hot."

"Poor Ace. He can hear you, you know." The skin just under her chin was soft, so soft, and Bren stroked it with the backs of his fingers until she slid his belt free of the loops.

He took it out from her hands and stepped back, all

the way to the heavy steel frame on the other side of the room. It had built-in leather shackles, but Bren ignored them and slung his belt over the top of the frame instead.

"The braided bull hide," he told Ace, who was hovering by the racks, waiting on the instruction. The leather was heavy, with edges sharp enough to sting.

With a nod, Ace retrieved the flogger and gave it a few lazy test swings before slapping the tails lightly against his palm. "How much warm-up do you want?"

The fingers on his right hand were still slippery from Six's pussy, and he rubbed them over the leather as he gripped it. "Not much. My dick already fucking hurts."

"Yours and mine both, brother," Ace drawled good-naturedly as he moved to stand behind him. "Say the word."

Six watched them, fascinated, from her perch on the couch, and a rumble rose in Bren's chest. "Now."

The first hit was slow, a heavy thud that vibrated through him until his teeth clacked together. The second was just a little bit faster. With every swing, Ace sped his arm until the flogger whistled through the air to strike with stinging precision.

Bren had to close his eyes against the rush. Not pleasure, not exactly, but arousal of the most primal, primitive sort—his body preparing itself to engage the most instinctive of drives.

Survival. Sex. For him, in these moments, they were the same damn thing.

Sweat broke out on his lip, his forehead. It sheened his back, and the stinging intensified as it mingled with leather falling on existing welts. Not cuts—Ace was too careful for that—but just enough abrasion for the salt to burn.

Bren drew a shuddering breath and jerked with the next blow. He'd never hit the wall this fast, careening straight to the plateau where the pain swirled around him in a heady rush.

Ace's voice broke through the fog, low and careful. "How about a breather, brother?"

Don't stop. He didn't realize he said the words aloud until he heard the harsh grind of his own voice. It brought some things rushing back into sharp focus—the bite of leather around his hands, his unsteady breathing—

And Six.

He opened his eyes. She'd kicked free of her pants at some point and was curled inside the blanket, watching him with flushed cheeks and parted lips. When her gaze locked with his, heat greeted him, heat and wonder and need.

She wet her lips and shifted to her knees, ignoring how it made the blanket gape wide. "Can I touch you like you touched me?"

The lash at his back, and her mouth— "Get over here."

Her eyes sparked with something fierce as she rose and stalked to him, utterly naked and not the least bit vulnerable. She stopped so close she had to tilt her head back to meet his gaze, but she didn't touch him.

She waited.

If she had her way, she'd already have her hands on him—he could see it in every trembling line of her body, in the way her hands flexed at her sides.

But she didn't have her way. She had *his.*

"Suck my cock," he rasped. "I want to fuck your face before I fuck your pussy."

Six folded her knees, sinking to the floor without looking away. Her hand came up, fingers curling hot and firm around his shaft, and she stroked him once before leaning in until her breath shivered across his cock.

"You dirty fucker," she murmured, the words hoarse with approval.

Then she sucked him into her mouth.

His head swam with dizzy pleasure that redoubled

when the flogger whistled through the air again. He'd had just enough time to settle, for the nerves in his skin to stop singing, but the sharp strike of leather brought them roaring back to life.

Six drew him deeper, slowly at first, but as Ace resumed his pace she began to match it, sucking hard in the stinging aftermath of a strike, watching his face as if riveted by his reaction.

Arching away from the wicked leather tails thrust him farther into her mouth, harder. The first time she gagged, the sound twisted up with the pain and the pleasure and the *moment*, jolting through him like a shock. She'd asked for this, watched Dallas choke Rachel with his cock and begged for the same damn thing.

He couldn't hold the back of her head, but he leaned into the thrust, lingering instead of drawing back. She pushed into him, gagged again, and only then asked for respite with a soft brush of her fingers against his hip.

It sent him spinning, that single, gentle touch, and Bren groaned as the heat and pain melted into something else entirely, something warm and vague. It crashed over him like a storm, loud thunder and gusts of sensation that threatened to blow him off his feet.

Enough. This time, he couldn't hear the word through the pounding in his ears, wasn't sure he'd managed to say it at all.

But Ace knew. The flogging stopped, and he spoke a moment later, quiet words Bren barely registered. "Give him a few seconds. He doesn't like to go too far up."

Her touch vanished, only to return as a warm cheek pressed against his hip.

Bren let go of one end of his belt. It slithered off the frame, and he swayed at the sudden release of the tension in his arms, his body. Ace and Six both steadied him as he drew in one deep, bracing breath after another.

Ace murmured something else, and Six wrapped both arms around Bren. Wood scraped across the carpet, and one of the padded benches bumped the backs of his legs. "Sit," Ace advised, managing to make it sound like a suggestion instead of an outright order.

"Too wobbly," Bren muttered, then laughed and dropped to the bench. Of course he was—weak as a newborn, shaking like a leaf. He'd taken it too far and almost slipped into the gray haze beyond pain.

"Wobbly, but still amazing." Six's fingers smoothed over his forehead, brushing his hair back. "You're better than pretty. You're...everything."

"I can't stand up straight."

"I know." She laughed and leaned down to kiss the top of his head. "That's why I'm being all mushy, Donnelly. You better enjoy it."

A little high on endorphins, maybe, but not helpless. He drew her down across his lap, smiling when his erection nudged her hip. "I enjoy it. But I'm not done with you yet."

Her breathing hitched as she pressed her forehead to his. "You mean getting me off a million times wasn't enough for you?"

The truth was stark, blunt—and there was no going back from it. "It'll never be enough."

She stilled, silent for long enough for his head to clear. Her lips parted, and she whispered two words, soft and shy, like an offering. "Me too."

Her mouth was hot and open beneath his, and he fell into kissing her. Even when Ace touched him again, smoothing cool gel over his back and shoulders, Bren took his time lifting his head.

"I can stick around for a while if you need me," Ace offered as he finished his work. "You were pretty cranked up, brother."

The dazed rush had already begun to fade. "It's all right." Bren turned his head to meet the other man's gaze. "I'm solid now."

They both understood the rules, but this was one

where Ace was unwavering and more than willing to overrule Bren. The artist studied him in silence before nodding abruptly. "If you need anything, I'll be in my studio."

Presumably after he'd made a detour to take care of his sexual frustration. "I owe you one, man."

"Not even a little." Ace winked at Six. "It was our pleasure, wasn't it, fighter-girl?"

She refused to laugh it off. Her voice still husky, she said, "We both owe you one."

Ace snorted and shook his head. "Have fun, you two." The door slammed behind him.

Bren rose, Six still in his arms, and crossed to lock the door again. "Did we answer your questions tonight, sweetness?"

"A lot of them." She locked her ankles at the small of his back and hissed in a breath as his cock ground against her pussy. "My flogging didn't really *hurt*, but I don't know if I'd have wanted it much harder. But for you..." She tilted her head back to look at him. "Do you really think Ace would teach me?"

"In a heartbeat."

"Then I'll learn." Her legs tightened as she lifted herself high enough to catch his mouth in a quick kiss. "I mean, I'll suck you off while he's beating you if that's your favorite thing, but I'm a possessive bitch. I want to be the one who makes you wobbly."

She already did, with every smile and wondering touch. "You might find out that you like it."

"Of course I will. It'll get you off." Her mouth found his ear. "And I'll look badass with a whip."

"Smartass."

She laughed and bit his ear. With his entire body sensitized, the nip made him shudder, and he gripped her hips harder. The sharp edges of her teeth vanished, replaced by the soft press of lips. "Will you bend me over something and fuck me already?"

beyond pain

Flippant words, but there was a very real plea behind them. So Bren stopped by the end of the couch and let her slide slowly down his body until her feet hit the floor. As soon as they did, he turned her and bent her upper body over the padded arm.

She went up on her toes, nudging his erection with a groan. "You've got too damn much self-control."

He bent over her before answering, sliding his cock against the small of her back. "You love it."

That earned him a snarl as she slammed her head back into his shoulder. "Do not."

He shifted his hips so that his cock slid between her legs this time, against the slick heat of her pussy. "Feels like you do."

"*Bren.*"

It was worth waiting to hear that desperate edge in her voice. "Yeah? You want something?"

She panted and let her head fall forward, baring the back of her neck as her hair swung down to shield her expression. "I'm the one who's already gotten off. I can outlast you."

Maybe she was right—but he didn't have all that self-control for nothing. "You might," he allowed in a rumble, then licked a path up the delicate line of her spine, from her shoulder blades to the base of her neck.

Her whole body was shaking by the time his tongue swiped across her vulnerable nape, but she dug her fingernails into the couch and fought back with words. "I know how turned on you are. I had your cock in my mouth, in my fucking throat. Tell me you weren't thinking about grabbing the back of my head and making me swallow all of you."

"Dirty words, sweetness." Her hair was soft and heavy as he wrapped it around his hand, and he relished the stifled moan that vibrated in the back of her throat when he jerked her head back. "I was hard before that, when you were coming on my fingers. I can wait."

240

She sucked in an unsteady breath. Another. A shudder, and the tension melted from her body as she closed her eyes. "Make me feel good?"

He guided his cock until the head barely pushed between the inner lips of her pussy. "It won't be soft or easy."

"Nothing good ever is."

Soft and easy. That wasn't him, and he was starting to understand that it wasn't *her*, either. She didn't need it, only him. Like this.

He plunged into her, releasing her hair to grip her hips instead. She moaned her approval and pushed back, never passive even after she'd given in. "Like this," she said hoarsely. "Rough. I'm not fragile, damn it."

"Shh." One more kiss to the center of her back, just under the shallow network of scars that crisscrossed her skin, and he straightened. Her hips arched in his hands, enough delicious friction to send shivers through them both.

And her voice came, soft and shaking. "Please."

Slow and deep, every thrust harder than the last. The rhythm did little to distract him from her choked noises, especially when they grew into moans, into pleas. Pleas to make her feel good, to make her feel *everything*.

But she didn't fight his grip. She didn't ask for more or faster or rougher, even though he knew she wanted it.

She gave him something far more fragile than her body. Her trust.

So he sped his thrusts, his hips slapping against her ass, and let his own words come. "Take it deep, baby. So fucking deep."

She grabbed on to the back of the couch, gripping hard to brace herself, to make it easier for him to drive home. "I can—" She moaned with his next thrust, throwing her head back. "I can take more."

He caught her shoulders in an iron grip, arching her back. "Harder?"

"Yes. *Always.*"

His next pounding thrust drove her feet off the floor, and she moaned his name as her pussy clenched. "Only once," she gasped. "I can't—God, I don't know if I can—"

"You can," he ground out between gritted teeth. "You will."

And she did, even though he had to ride her G-spot hard to get her there. After an endless climb, she slammed into orgasm, gasping his name again and again in a raw voice almost as impossible to ignore as the tight clasp of her pussy.

It went on and on, until nothing could have kept him from coming. The helpless clutch of her inner muscles dragged him straight up to that trembling edge, and one last desperate plunge sent him tumbling over it. He pulled her to him, an arm locked across her chest, as they shuddered together.

She stilled long before she spoke. "Are my feet on the floor? I can't tell."

Bren couldn't tell where his *own* goddamn feet were. He loosened his grip, and she slid down his body. "Better?"

"I don't know." She exhaled shakily. "I think you turned me into a sex junkie or something. Fucking *hell.*"

A far cry from the first time, when she'd insisted she didn't need to come and it probably wouldn't happen, anyway. "This is Sector Four, sweetness. No such thing as too much sex."

"So you say now." She tilted her head back enough to grin at him. "Think you can keep up with me, old man?"

She'd spent her first night in the sector chained to a chair, and nearly every night since in varying stages of fear and healing. Now, here she was, open and trusting—

His.

Bren returned her grin, lazy and confident. "Don't worry. I've got a few secrets left. I might surprise you."

Just like she'd surprised him.

 ace

E MMA HAD PAINTED her ceiling blue.
Ace tucked a hand behind his head and studied it as he listened to her crash around in her bathroom. "When'd you have time to decorate, junior?"

"When?" She emerged, still naked, and grabbed a half-empty bottle of whiskey on her way back to the bed. "First chance I got. The color helps me sleep."

It wasn't a bad choice. Not ultramarine or navy, but a little more vibrant than denim. Cobalt, maybe, though God knew the colors you could get now weren't anything like the pre-Flare bounty. The mouth-breathers slogging away in Sector Eight's factories wouldn't know cyan from cerulean, and the snobs in Eden contented themselves with art made from pixels and code.

Emma sank onto the mattress, and he shifted to give her space. "It's nice. Where'd you get the paint? Walt's place?"

"Yeah. He likes to pretend he's a hard-ass, but he's

fair enough with his prices."

Ace lifted her wrist with his free hand and admired the cuff he'd laid there barely a month ago. "This doesn't hurt," he reminded her, rubbing his thumb along the intricate framing. He'd been plenty smug the day he'd tattooed it onto her skin, pleased that he'd finally talked her into signing on as his apprentice, pleased he'd avoided having Cruz flatten his face in the cage, and *really* damn pleased that Lex and Dallas had worked out their shit.

Everything had been looking up.

Emma turned her wrist—and wrapped her fingers around his. "What's wrong, Ace?"

"Not a goddamn thing," he replied easily. "I just got a dirty-hot show followed by an enthusiastic fuck, and you brought me whiskey in bed."

"Liar." She uncapped the bottle and took a drink before offering it to him. "You heard the rumors, I guess."

His gut tightened, and he almost told her he didn't want to know. It didn't matter that he'd had some hazy, half-cocked plan to throw Cruz and Rachel back together. That had fizzled the second he'd walked into the storeroom and seen them—

Christ, he hadn't *seen* anything, just Cruz, shirtless with his belt hanging open. Then again, Cruz was the next best thing to a fucking prude. Ace had had an easier time getting into the pants of city virgins.

Not that he was trying to get into the man's pants. No, he was trying to get someone *else* into them, someone who could shake a few of those Eden hang-ups—

"The other night, after the fights? Word is that Rachel hooked up with Dallas and Lex. I don't know if it was a one-time thing or what, but that's what I heard."

His mind shuddered to a halt, and he stared at Emma. "She did *what?*"

"Yeah, that's what I said." Emma tilted her head. "Shit, you really didn't know?"

"No." But there was no way Rachel would lead Cruz on if she'd been jumping in between Dallas and Lex. Which meant whatever he'd walked in on couldn't have been the two of them scrambling to hide sexual evidence.

"If that's not why you're brooding in my bed, what gives?"

He took the whiskey and downed a healthy swig, letting the familiar burn settle him. "I'm an artist, Em. We brood. It's why all the chicks wanna fuck us. You should know, since Jas has to pry Noelle off you with a crowbar."

"Or I'm just that good." Emma shrugged. "I don't know, you're taking this awfully well. I thought Rachel was your big unrequited, deathless love. Your favorite thing that was never gonna happen."

The word *unrequited* stung, but not as much as the word *never*. Combined, they pissed him off. "What, so she fucked Dallas and Lex. Who hasn't?"

"Well, *I* haven't. That doesn't seem fair."

Her sincere irritation was adorable enough to slice through his, and any opportunity to change the damn subject was a gift. "Next time you're playing grab-ass with Noelle, tell her that. You haven't lived until you've gotten all up in between those four."

"Really?" Emma leaned closer and flashed him an impish, knowing smile. "Who ends up on top?"

Ace laughed and tugged at her hair. "You've been around long enough to know the answer to that, kid. Whoever the ladies decide they want on top."

"In a pile like that? I'd be hard-pressed to choose."

"You already did." He nodded to her wrist. "O'Kane for life, eh?"

"For life," she agreed, then smiled softly and snuggled down into the crook of his arm. "You're not going to tell me what's got you so down tonight, are you?"

"You're talking like I even know," he said lightly, leaning over to set the whiskey bottle on the floor. "Maybe it's just weird, seeing Bren act like he's in love.

beyond pain

You have no idea what he was like when he first showed up. Concrete was more sentimental."

Emma laughed. "I think it's sweet. Like there's someone for everyone, and it's Fate they both wound up here."

The hell of it was, it *had* been sweet. Intense. That moment after they'd driven Six over the edge, when Bren's gaze had met his—that was always Ace's favorite part. The shared sense of accomplishment, the feeling of working together to bring a woman outside herself. He got off on it almost as much as the sex.

All of the intimacy, with none of the responsibility.

But today Six had lifted her face to nuzzle into Bren's neck, totally possessive and totally possessed, and Ace had felt...

Envy. Longing. *Something.*

Emma stroked a soothing hand over his chest. Finally, she spoke, quiet and serious. "You don't have to listen to me, but I think maybe wanting something isn't enough sometimes. You have to wait until you need it so bad nothing else matters, and that's when you're ready for it."

Until he needed what? To try to shoehorn himself in between Jas and Noelle? Or Bren and Six?

Or Cruz and Rachel?

Fuck his imagination, anyway, because the image didn't even form. It was just *there*, fully realized, hot enough to stir his cock. Cruz, all those fine-as-fuck muscles flexing as he held Rachel in place and told Ace how hard the next stroke should fall, both of them reveling in her cries, her writhing. Or Christ, pumping his fingers into her pussy while he watched her blow Cruz.

Helped her.

No.

He shoved away the thought and forced himself to laugh. "Don't you go getting all philosophical on me, junior. You're my apprentice, and that means you have to live up to my reputation. We're hot, we're shallow, and everyone wants to fuck us because we know all the best tricks."

"Right." She stretched across him, reaching for a sketchpad on the nightstand. "Want to take a look at some drawings before you split?"

Okay, maybe that had been *too* defensive. He let his hair fall over his brow and gave her big eyes. "You kickin' me out?"

"Oh, please. You're not gonna stay." She gave him a pointed look over the top of the sketchpad. "I might get my *feelings* all over you."

So much for that. He slapped a hand over his eyes and groaned. "Why did saddling myself with a smartass sidekick seem like a good idea?"

"Because I keep you humble, and Lord knows you need it?"

Even better, she kept him distracted. Slamming the door on fantasy, he flung his arm wide. "Yeah, yeah. Fine, show me the sketches."

It'd do. For now.

15

"CHRIST, DID THIS twitchy bastard pick the creepiest place in the Sector to meet?"

Bren grinned. The railyard was a mess of ripped-up steel and graffiti-riddled train cars, but it was open, with plenty of spots to take cover—just in case. "You should have been here last time, Dallas. I had to chat with him under Wilson Trent's murder bridge."

"Someone's been watching too many old movies." Dallas checked his watch and sighed. "Not much for punctuality, either, is he?"

"He has a flair for the dramatic."

"Great. He and Ace can start a club."

"I don't think—" A barely audible crunch on the gravel behind them interrupted the words. Bren spun, one hand already on the pistol beneath his jacket. "That's a good way to get shot in the fucking face, Lennox."

Noah stopped, both hands held out to his side. "Bad habit. I'll work on breaking it."

Bren relaxed, his heart still racing, and waved in introduction. "Dallas O'Kane, Noah Lennox."

"Lennox."

"O'Kane."

The two men sized each other up, both careful to keep their expressions bland. The silence grew heavy, until Noah broke it by running a hand nervously through his hair. "Scarlet tells me you're trying to clean house in Three."

"He is. *We* are," Bren corrected, edging closer. "She sent us a message, said you had information about something going down. Something big?"

"The what is bad enough. It's the who that I think you'll be real interested in."

"So spit it the hell out," Dallas growled. "I don't have time for games."

Noah's gaze flicked to Bren. "Russell Miller."

The name sent chills down Bren's spine and raised the hair on his arms—and, judging from the look on Noah's face, he'd already made the connection. "My commanding officer from Special Tasks."

Dallas's head whipped around. "The bastard who burned you?"

"Yeah." Bren took another step forward. "What's Miller up to out here?"

Noah reached inside his jacket, moving slowly, and pulled out a small tablet. "Dealing in the kind of merchandise you'd better put a stop to," he said seriously, holding the tech out to Dallas. "People."

Dallas's eyes narrowed. "You're telling me some MP big shot is engaging in human trafficking in Three?"

Lennox shrugged. "Ask him if Miller's capable of it."

After claiming the tablet, Dallas slanted a look toward Bren. "Is he?"

Russell Miller was capable of torture, rape, murder—any goddamn thing you could think of, and probably a good handful of things a decent person couldn't imagine.

"A hundred and ten percent."

Dallas's face hardened. "Is everything on here?"

"Everything I could find."

"And how much is it gonna cost us?"

Noah waved a hand. "The information is free. The price is dealing with it."

"All right." Dallas handed the tablet to Bren without looking away from Noah. "Bren?"

"Watch yourself," he found himself saying. "Miller's not just another asshole out to make a buck. He's Eden-trained. He knows better than to run an operation without proper intel, which means he's got someone local. Someone who probably knows your face."

"Oh, I'm taking care." Noah met Bren's eyes, serious and a little wary. "I know the sorts of things an Eden-trained soldier is capable of doing."

For once, Bren welcomed the condemnation. "Good. Then you might stay alive."

As much as she was starting to enjoy waking up with Bren, Six still loved having her own room with a door that locked, even if it was full of furniture someone else had picked out for her.

No, especially because of that.

She never would have chosen a bed with a solid, elegant headboard carved from real wood. She wouldn't have dared go for all the shit that had come with it, either. A dresser and mirror, table and chairs, solid pieces that had been dusted and shined, any one item worth more credits than she'd seen in a year as a teenager.

At first, every damn thing an O'Kane had given her had felt like a weight around her neck, a debt she'd have to repay before she could begin squirreling away enough money to build a new life. Now, they felt like something else. Gestures of good faith.

Or gifts from family.

Her favorite gift was on the couch. She kicked her boots into the corner and swept up the tablet, activating it with a quick swipe across the screen as she curled up on the couch, ready to continue the latest book Noelle had helped her download.

But her book didn't open. Instead, a message appeared, one the tablet began to read in its friendly, feminine voice. As the words rolled out of the tiny speakers, her stomach sank.

Six—

Maybe the good's worth the bad, but everyone deserves full disclosure. Watch it all before you make any choices you can't take back.

Noah

Before she had a chance to wonder what she was supposed to watch, a video popped up, filling the screen. Bren's face stared up at her, at least a decade younger. Some of the rough angles and scars she'd traced with her fingertips were gone, and his nose looked a little straighter.

A man behind the camera's field of view spoke. "What was your mission objective?"

"To stop the trafficking, sir," Bren answered immediately.

The unseen man cleared his throat and repeated the question. "What was your mission objective?"

Bren shifted in his chair. "Sorry, sir. Our objective was to find the subjects wanted for trafficking and eliminate them."

"Did you?"

"I terminated one of the targets. My team took care of the other three."

"And yet you fired..." paper rustled, "...twenty-two rounds. For four targets? That sounds like a sloppy operation, soldier."

"It was—" Bren swallowed hard and looked away from the camera for the first time. "They had captives, sir. Lieutenant Miller told us we had to leave them."

"So you executed them."

"He told us we had to leave them."

Six slapped at the tablet. The video paused, leaving Bren frozen, his gaze fixed somewhere off camera, his face turned away.

Her gut churned. The air in the room felt stale, stuffy. She rasped in a breath and then another, forcing herself to breathe slowly, forcing herself to *think*.

She barely knew how to operate tech, but she'd seen Noelle and Nessa run enough movies. Placing her finger on the slider along the bottom, she dragged it backwards, until it was flush against the left side of the tablet.

When she lifted her finger, the video started again.

It was no easier to watch the second time. The word *trafficking* echoed inside her skull, banging against her temples and scraping at mental doors she'd bolted firmly shut. Bren's voice came again. *"They had captives, sir. Lieutenant Miller told us we had to leave them."*

Shuddering, she silenced the screaming in her head and dragged the marker back to the beginning, as if listening a third time would change the content.

"Do you know how much each of your rifle rounds costs this city, Officer Donnelly?"

Silence.

"Was that an appropriate and necessary allocation of resources?"

"No, sir." Then Bren's chin rose, and a quiet sort of defiance lit his eyes. "But I'd do it again."

She smacked her palm down on the tablet, silencing the voice and obscuring Bren's face. The walls were pressing in, making her room feel too small, too dark.

It had been dark in the back of the trucks, too. Endless dark, with only the crying of the younger children to remind her she wasn't alone. It had taken years before she could stand the dark again, even more before she'd learned to love it for how easy it made to hide.

"So you executed them."

Bren had come across captives. People snatched from their lives, kidnapped, lost in the dark and doomed to God only knew what fate. And he'd shot them.

She didn't know what horrified her more—that her stomach could roil at the thought, or that her mind skipped instantly to rationalizations. If she let herself, it would be all too easy to conjure the feeling of chains around her wrists and ankles, of staring into the darkness where the door should be, throat parched, stomach empty, scared the captors would come. More scared they wouldn't.

Faced with the choice between leaving those people to a slow death or making it quick, he'd chosen mercy. And the city had chastised him for it. He'd been defiant.

But not defiant enough to try to save them.

"Fuck." The word slipped free, and she moved in a rush, shoving the tablet down between the side of the couch and the cushion before lunging to her feet. Pacing didn't usually help, but it did remind her body that the room wasn't small and she wasn't trapped.

Most of all, she wasn't a helpless kid. And she wasn't going to let Noah Lennox fuck up the only good thing to ever happen to her.

Leaving the tablet and its damning video, she flung open the door and stepped into the hall, intending to stalk to Bren's room to wait for him. She'd taken only two steps before the echo of gunfire jerked her to a halt.

It was close, and *loud.* So loud that she spent a few tense moments wondering why O'Kanes weren't bubbling out into the hallway, weapons in hand, ready to defend their territory.

She spun in the opposite direction and whirled around the corner so fast she almost slammed into Trix.

"Hey." Trix laid a hand on her arm. "It's all right.

Just a little target practice."

Six listened to round after round, each echo leading into another shot. "*That's* target practice?"

"It is when Bren does it." Her carefully curled red hair bobbed as she jerked her head toward the back of the building. "Closed-off alley in the back. You can watch from the roof or take the fire escape down."

"Thanks." Six stepped aside so the other woman could pass, too unsettled to manage small talk. "See you at the bar tonight?"

"Double shift. Wouldn't miss it." Trix rolled her eyes a little and laughed. "See you."

Six held her easy expression until the redhead was gone, hating that it felt awkward, that she wanted to drop her masks and let someone else see her distress, even comfort her.

Christ, right now, she'd take one of Noelle's hugs.

She had to backtrack to get to the stairs, climbing past the second floor and its party room and the third floor with its echoing rooms that still seemed in various stages of construction. They'd be in use soon, if the O'Kanes kept inking new members.

The final flight of stairs ended in a small landing and a door propped open with a garbage can. A huge sign covered the middle third of the door, its message conveyed in cheerful pink letters and profanity.

The door locks behind you, dumbasses. Quit trapping yourselves on the fucking roof (ACE) because I do NOT have time to keep hauling ass up here to rescue you.

Nessa had signed her name with a flourish and a heart.

Biting her lip, Six pushed through the door, careful to ease it back against the garbage can. The shots were so much louder up here, thundering from the west side of the roof, where the barracks formed a blind alley with the long, L-shaped building that Dallas used for storage.

She reached the edge of the roof and saw Bren in the

alley below, a wickedly large pistol in his right hand. He pulled the trigger almost continuously, firing until the gun clicked uselessly. He flicked his thumb across the release, dropped the empty magazine, and replaced it before switching the weapon to his left hand and continuing to fire at the shredded target at the end of the alley.

It was magnificent violence. Raw, skilled, the kind that usually cranked her up good when it was Bren causing the mayhem. And it did, even with his words slamming around in her skull.

"I'd do it again."

By the time he'd emptied the second magazine, there was nothing left of the target, only ragged bits of paper on a battered straw backstop. Instead of reloading, Bren lowered the gun and stood there, unmoving.

The stillness shattered a moment later with a bellow of pure anguish as he exploded into movement, hurling the pistol down the alley. It skittered across the cracked asphalt, and he stalked after it, only to snatch up a board that was leaning against the wall. He smashed it into the bales with another roar, swinging again and again, sheer desperation radiating from him like heat. Like flame.

She'd seen cracks in his control, tiny slips. Roughness in his voice, his body jerking toward hers, groans he couldn't hold back. This was a hundred times worse. A thousand. Bren's control had shattered...and shattered her heart with it.

God fucking help her, she was in love with Brendan Donnelly.

Bits of straw floated in the air, landed on his shirt and his hair, but he finally stopped swinging. The board clattered to the ground, smudged with red—blood, she realized, as he looked down and flexed his hands.

Wounded, just like he was.

Fuck Noah Lennox. Fuck Eden and the terror churning in her gut, the instinct born of a lifetime of avoiding danger. He wasn't some unknown threat, and he wasn't the cold-blooded bastard Eden had trained. He was *Bren*, her lover, her protector. Hell, he was the one who'd told her Sector Four had changed him, taught him to be better. Whatever they'd made him do, it was in the past.

She'd make herself believe it. She had to, or else she was just a stupid girl who couldn't stop falling in love with psychopaths.

So move.

Shaking, she reached for the fire escape—and jerked back when the door creaked behind her.

It was Jasper, who approached with a sigh. "He finally stopped?"

"Yes." Her voice cracked, proving she was a coward. "His hands—I think he hurt himself."

Jasper held her by the arms as he leaned over and peered into the alley, then cursed softly. "It's not easy to see him like this, I know. But he'll be all right."

Like this. Jasper seemed concerned, but not worried. Not like the sight of Bren having a violent meltdown was unfamiliar. Which shouldn't matter, and maybe it wouldn't have, if she'd *known.*

Swallowing hard, she looked away. "I was going to check on him, but maybe he'd rather be alone right now."

Jasper didn't argue. "I'll head down and make sure he's square, okay?"

She took a step back when his hands fell away, then hesitated. Whatever had triggered this must have wider implications than her feelings, because she couldn't believe Bren had just come home and lost his shit. "Did something happen while he was in Three? Something bad?"

But Jasper only shook his head. "It's not my shit to talk about, Six. Give Bren some time to cool off, and you can ask him about it."

He was closing ranks, protecting his brother's back, and Six would have as much luck dragging the truth out of him as she would beating her fists against stone.

beyond pain

No shortcuts. She shouldn't have expected one. She'd told Bren the truth the other night, the only truth that mattered in this world.

Nothing good came easy.

16

H IS HANDS ACHED like a son of a bitch.
Bren toyed with the edge of one bandage as he watched Cruz enter another set of coordinates into the oversized tablet mounted on his wall. "Any patterns yet?"

"Nothing obvious." Another point appeared on the map sketched out on the tablet. "But there wouldn't be, would there?"

No, the bastard wouldn't make it that easy to catch him. "Everyone makes mistakes, even Miller."

"Mmm." Cruz slid the coordinate list aside with a swipe of his hand and pulled up another box, one that spun out the raw data on the various locations. "He has one vice that's only gotten worse since you left. He hates going without his city comforts."

"Yeah?"

"He'll tell his team to catch some shut-eye on dirty concrete when it's five below and half of them have holes in their hide, but God forbid he has to spend a night outside the barracks. Or his whore. It's made him sloppy more than once."

Bren leaned over, bracing a hand on Cruz's desk despite the pain. "Tell me where to find him, and those days are over. Truth."

His friend pinned him with a sidelong look. "Have you got it locked down? If we do find him, I'm in no mood to let you get us dead because your head's somewhere else."

Rage burned in Bren's gut. "You'd better not be saying you don't want him dead, because that's exactly what he is. He just doesn't know it yet."

"Of course I want him dead." Cruz returned his attention to the wall, drilling down through the scrolling lists of data with practiced ease. "You're the one I'm hoping to keep in one piece, Donnelly."

"I'm not getting crazy or careless."

"Good." Cruz flicked his wrist, and four new spots lit up on the map, all of them ringing the main blast zone. "We're lucky Three is a fucking disaster. Not a lot of places fall within the common parameters with regards to resource access."

If these shipments had been as regular as Noah Lennox believed, there were even fewer places they hadn't used recently. "We'll hit them all if we have to."

"We should start here." Cruz stabbed a finger down on a dot glowing near the border of Two. "It's got tunnel access, it's close enough to leech off Two's power grid, and it's far enough west that no one's likely to notice the traffic."

No one but the people they'd snatched off the street to sell into servitude—or worse. Bren started to unwrap his left hand. "So let's check it out."

"Can you use those hands?"

He needed another application of med-gel and a few more hours of healing time, but it seemed like a luxury when Russell Miller could take his cargo and slip out of

Sector Three, right under their noses. "I'll let you do the heavy lifting. Happy?"

"Oh, you can do the lifting." Cruz flexed his hands, and finally Bren saw his own rage reflected in the man's eyes. "I'll do the punching."

"Deal."

The place was deserted.

Not just empty, but thick with a layer of dust that told Bren no one had been there at all, maybe not for months. They hadn't missed their prey by hours or days; they were on the wrong fucking trail entirely.

He kicked an empty bottle with a frayed, faded label and swore. "Shitty luck of the draw, or did someone tip him off to our search?"

Cruz crouched in the doorway, his gaze fixed on the street beyond. "I'm working this with a fraction of the data I usually have. Shitty maps, no access to Eden's cameras. Could be nothing more than that."

Bren forced himself to take a deep breath. "Okay. Forget the number-crunching, then. You don't have cameras, what do you do? Talk to people, right?"

"Will people in a shithole like this tell the truth?"

"Maybe, maybe not. But we can't track him like an animal, and he's sure the hell not going to leave us a trail of breadcrumbs to—" The words caught in Bren's throat, colliding with his heart as it kicked up out of his chest. "It's backwards. We're doing this backwards."

Cruz rocked to his feet and turned. "Explain."

"We know how he operates. In a situation like this, he's bound to have help. The kind that comes straight off the streets of Sector Three."

"Thugs," Cruz agreed. "Disposable thugs."

"Thugs who know which poor bastards won't be missed if they up and disappear one day."

"Who do we know who could help us pick out the likeliest suspects?"

Six. Bren shoved the thought away. "There are a few men I could ask." He hesitated. "It's a riskier route. Might not lead us to Miller unless we time it right."

"But it could upset his operation," Cruz countered. "Fuck, Bren, I want him dead too, but shutting this down needs to come first. Worst-case scenario, you climb the walls someday soon and put a bullet in him from a mile away."

"No." He had things to say to Miller's face while he lay dying. Confessions to make. "I want to kill him close."

Cruz stilled. "Even if it risks your life?"

"It won't."

"If you're sure." He jerked his head toward the street. "The bar's mostly fixed up now. We can track down Riff, or maybe Elvis. Isn't he the one with all the black-market contacts?"

"Better to let Dallas do it." Everyone in Three had been wondering what price they'd have to pay for O'Kane's patronage and protection.

Might as well let them know.

When Bren finally dragged himself back to his room, Six was waiting for him.

She wasn't wearing sexy pants this time or thinking about jumping him. She'd been sitting cross-legged on the foot of his bed so long her legs had fallen asleep, but she was sure he'd make his way home sooner or later, and then they'd *talk*.

She hadn't expected the frustration that rolled off him in waves, or the way he slammed the door shut behind him. Everything about him had always screamed *control*, but now he tossed his jacket carelessly across a chair and didn't even notice when it slithered to the floor.

Even his greeting was distracted. "Hey."

"Hi." She straightened her legs and told herself she wasn't getting ready to bolt. "You okay?"

Instead of answering, he rubbed his hands over his face. "Who knows Sector Three best? You? One of the guys who worked for Trent?"

"Depends on what you want," she replied carefully. "I know the inner streets, the good places to loot or hide. But Elvis knows shit about the black market no one would ever tell me, and Cain knows about the outskirts of the sectors, and some of the closer farms."

Bren circled the bed and sank down on the mattress. "Elvis, then."

"For what? Do you need something black market?"

"What? No, it's—" He sighed and turned to face her. "Lennox uncovered a human trafficking operation in Three. He brought it to us so Dallas can stomp that shit out."

Her stomach twisted, the coincidence of it too much to wrap her mind around. But of course it wasn't coincidence at all—Noah had found the traffickers. For all she knew, setting Bren and Dallas on their trail was some sort of test. A way for him to judge how far to trust them.

A way to judge whether or not Bren had changed.

She wet her lips. "What are—*who* are they moving? And to where? Do you know?"

"Not yet, but I've seen things like this before. They snatch people off the streets in the sectors and ship them into Eden." His jaw tightened. "You don't want to know why."

There it was, the perfect, effortless opening. All she had to do was stumble into it, like she'd blurted out a hundred awkward, stupid things before. "I already know."

But he didn't notice. He just rose again and paced the length of the room. "Right next door—no, *in* Dallas's damn sector. He's fucking pissed."

She was sure Dallas was, but Bren was the one prowling the room. For the first time, she realized how completely she'd held his attention. Since the moment Trent had dragged her into his life, chained and fighting—always *fighting*—she'd been at the center of all that intense focus.

Now she was invisible.

It stung, but hurt feelings were bullshit compared to what was going down. If she had to give up the comfort of his attention to save people from the hell of being sold, he could ignore her all fucking night. Whatever he needed to get the job done. "Do you know anyone involved? Any of the guys in Three? I know where people like to hide."

"No," he said firmly. "If Elvis knows his way around this shit, we'll work with him. I don't want you involved."

That did more than sting. It wedged under her skin, an echo of all the times Trent had shut her down. "I'm not going to get in your way. I can help."

"I know that." He leaned over to cup her shoulders, his gaze intense. "I don't want you putting yourself in danger. I mean it."

"Some things are worth it, Bren."

"Agreed. And if we need you, I won't stop you from helping. I promise."

He was looking at her now, *seeing* her, and she braced herself to dig into his past, to do the one thing they never did—push for secrets.

She ended up giving him one instead. "That's how I ended up in Three. My family sent me to the man I was supposed to marry so the wives could train me in my duties, and I ran. And I was young and I didn't know how to live off the farms—"

Two days. That was how long she'd lasted before blundering into a trap no street kid would have fallen for. She'd been twelve, already an adult in some ways, but so hopelessly ignorant in all the ones that mattered.

Bren pulled her close, into the strong circle of his

arms. "It's okay."

She closed her eyes and pressed her forehead to his shoulder. "Are they kids? Do you know?"

"There may not be anyone right now, all right? They're probably between shipments, that's why we didn't turn anything up."

"Bren?"

"I won't let them slip past us."

"And we'll get them free?"

"Every single one, sweetness."

She exhaled slowly and pushed Noah's message aside. Digging into the past was stupid when she had the proof she needed in the present. Bren, warm and solid and as gloriously dangerous as ever.

Easing back, she reached for his hands. "You hurt yourself. Do I need to get the medkit?"

"A couple of scratches. Jas took care of it."

She turned his hand over in her own and traced his palm. No sign of cuts or scars. The med-gel the O'Kanes possessed in seemingly limitless quantity was the kind of thing people killed for on the streets. Wounds disappeared like magic, leaving nothing behind.

Her scars were on the surface, where anyone could see. She'd never know how many Bren had. "Are you sure you're all right?"

He gave her a reassuring smile. "I'm sure."

But the smile didn't reach his eyes, and Six was left alone again, even with him in the room, less sure than she'd ever been.

17

N O ONE HAD invited her to the meeting.

Six polished shot glasses that were already too clean for the drunks who'd be tumbling in after the bar opened and tried not to look like she was listening in.

"Thirty-two people," Elvis was saying. "They've got 'em locked up tight in a warehouse close to the city border. Best I can tell, money's exchanging hands some-time soon. Two, maybe three days."

Six's heart slammed into her ribs as Mad spread out a meticulously drawn map and ran his finger across it. "Cruz flagged a couple of likely locations, but there was nothing there when they looked."

Elvis leaned over the table and tapped one marked spot. "It's this one." He squinted up at Cruz. "You called it, huh? That's pretty slick—for a city boy."

Cruz ignored the jab and tilted his head. "It's the first one we checked out," he told Bren. "I remember enough about the layout to plan a rescue."

"From seeing it once?" Dallas asked doubtfully.

"Training." Cruz shrugged. "And I had a hunch."

Bren finally spoke, his gaze riveted to the map. "You don't underestimate this bastard. If you do, you're dead."

"No one's underestimating him," Dallas drawled, leaning back in his chair. "He trained the both of you. That's warning enough."

Six's fingers clenched so hard the rim of the shot glass dug into her palm, and she couldn't hear whatever Mad said next over the blood pounding in her ears. The last few days clicked into place with stark, painful clarity. Bren's rage, his distraction, his mounting obsession—

They were chasing the man who'd made him. The man who'd thrown him away.

And he hadn't told her.

He looked up, his gaze clashing with hers, and she knew his silence hadn't been an oversight. He hadn't *forgotten* to tell her.

She pivoted, putting her back to him. Row after row of O'Kane liquor stretched out in front of her, some of the bottles perilously close to empty. She should be checking them now, figuring out what needed replenishing, and hauling ass into the storeroom.

Her feet wouldn't fucking move.

"The building is built for optimal stealth, not so much defense." That was Cruz, sounding as calm as if he were making small talk about the weather. "Unless the guys guarding it are professionals..."

Elvis snorted. "These knuckleheads? Not hardly."

"Then this is an easy job. Hell, toss a gas grenade through the window and wait for them to drop. It'd only take one."

Six tensed, and she wasn't even sure why until Mad voiced the sick feeling in her gut. "Only if you want to gas the captives, too."

"They'd recover."

"They *might*. That shit can kill, you know."

"So can a bullet."

"So don't let them get shot, city boy. It's an easy job, right?"

"Enough!" Dallas barked, slamming his hand down on the table so hard it rattled. Six glanced out of the corner of her eye and saw Mad glaring at Cruz, whose blankness had faded to a hint of confusion. "Bren? You wanna weigh in on a plan of attack here?"

Silence. Then, "We should wait. Hit them when Miller's there. Take care of the whole damn thing in one strike."

"No."

Heads swiveled to face her, and Six realized the word had escaped her lips. God knew they felt numb enough, but with everyone staring at her, she wasn't going to back down. "That could take days. Do you know what they can do to someone in that time?"

"They won't damage the cargo," Bren argued. "They want to get paid."

Her blood chilled. "They're not cargo. They're *people*."

"And we're going to get them out of there. But we need to shut down the operation, not just this one run."

Cool logic, so reasonable it twisted her gut. "Don't you know who it is? You can get him any time."

His eyes flashed with annoyance. "It's not worth the risk of letting Miller get away. Not if we can end it now."

He was pissed at her, and it was pissing her off, too. Her fear was bleeding into anger—at herself for wanting so fucking badly for him to be a hero, and at him for holding so much of himself back when she'd given him everything, showed him the most vulnerable, broken places in her heart.

Maybe that had been her mistake. She wasn't his partner. She was his *project*.

Her hands ached as she braced her fists on the bar.

"What would be worth the risk? Anything? Anyone?"

"It's not a sacrifice, Six. It's strategy. A choice."

A choice to corner the motherfucker who'd taught him to kill, and to do it in a building with thirty-two helpless, frightened people. Staring into those hard, intense eyes, Six almost believed he'd consider the death of every last one of them an acceptable loss.

She opened her mouth again, but Dallas cut her off with a snarl. "I don't have time for bickering. Six, if you can't keep your mouth shut while you're stocking the bar, then you need to leave."

Her teeth clacked together as heat flooded her cheeks. Humiliation was too fucking familiar, and for one terrible moment she was back in Three, raising her voice to be heard over the greedy babble of Trent's men, trying to exercise what tiny influence she had to make someone safer.

Shut up and pour the drinks, bitch.

"*Declan.*" Lex's protest was firm and quiet, but it lashed through the silence like a whip.

Dallas flinched.

Mad slid into the awkward silence. "I agree with Six. Rescue should be our priority, not to mention that this whole thing gets a lot more dangerous if Miller's there."

Bren crossed his arms over his chest. "I can handle him."

He wasn't even looking at her anymore. She was invisible again, irrelevant to his mission objective and therefore unimportant. He stared at Dallas, who rested both elbows on the table and sighed. "Cruz? Can you still pull this off with Miller sitting on top of the captives?"

Cruz hesitated, glancing at Six with a pity that stuck in her throat like glass before he nodded once. "The risks are within acceptable parameters."

"Fine. Bren and Cruz, draw up a plan of attack." He jabbed a finger at Elvis. "I want you and Riff sitting on top of them for the next forty-eight hours. These fuckers are *not* sneaking anyone out past us."

Elvis nodded. "We can do that."

More of the men snuck glances at her, enough pity and sympathy to make her queasy. With her throat burning, she pushed through the employees-only door behind the bar and stumbled into the darkened kitchen.

A hand wrapped around her arm, and she knew it was Bren even before he spoke. "Six, wait—"

She snatched her arm away. "You've got plans to make. And I'm supposed to keep my mouth shut, didn't you hear?"

"Dallas didn't mean that."

"Yeah, you men say a lot of things you don't mean."

Bren heaved a sigh and dragged both hands through his hair. "Russell Miller is a nasty piece of work, okay? If I don't get him now, while I can, he could fall off the face of the motherfucking planet. *Gone*, all right?"

Something about the words felt off, but he was looking at her again, *seeing* her, and he was so strong and intense and certain that doubt wormed its way into her heart. "Those people will suffer," she protested, and it sounded weak to her own ears. "You should know how much damage you can do to someone without leaving proof."

"I do," he allowed quietly. "I also know what Miller's capable of. That's why we can't miss this chance. We have to get him."

"And this is the only way? Leaving them—" Her voice broke, and she steeled herself. No more tears for him, no more moments of vulnerability. "I probably know some of them. Most of them. The people in Three no one would miss? Those are *my* people. So don't ask me to be okay with this, because it's not going to happen."

"You don't have to love it." A muscle in his jaw ticked. "You just have to understand."

"No, I don't. I just have to shut up and fall in line." She turned toward the door that spilled from the kitchen

into the side alley. "Don't worry, I've got plenty of practice knowing my place."

Bren slammed his hand against the wall, blocking
the door. "Don't. Don't fucking compare this to Wilson
Trent's shit."

The barely contained violence of it kicked her heart
into her throat and prickled warning over her skin.
Worst of all, it brought guilt roaring to life. Bren had
never hurt her. He cared about her, about the people
they were trying to help. And she was so brittle inside, so
broken and wary, so ready to find an excuse to shove
someone away.

Déjà fucking vu.

No, this couldn't compare to Wilson Trent at his
worst. But this was the beginning of the journey, step by
tiny step into the darkness, while she made excuses and
beat on herself for being so suspicious, so distrustful, so
damaged that she couldn't recognize a good thing.

Trent hadn't bothered fucking up her body until he'd
bored of playing with her head.

Staring at the rigid muscles in Bren's outstretched
arm, Six gathered the tattered shreds of her pride
around her. "Am I not allowed to leave?"

He stood there, trembling with tension, and finally
stepped back. "Fuck it. Think what you want to think."
He turned on his heel and stalked out of the kitchen,
leaving her alone.

It was better that way. She'd tried, she'd fucking
tried, and this was what came of it. Humiliation, pain,
feeling so small and stupid. And she couldn't even blame
Bren when Noah had provided the first push, and she
was the one who couldn't make herself believe.

Maybe she was too broken to deserve being loved.

18

BREN NEVER TAPED his hands when he hit the practice bags. Some of the men did, but he was as used to fighting outside the cage as he was to the brawls inside it. Assholes on the street didn't stop long enough for you to grab some gloves or brass knuckles, so he went after the bags bare-handed.

Today, it wasn't helping.

Those people will suffer.

The words haunted him, but not nearly as much as the haunted look in Six's eyes. The betrayal. The disbelief.

And this is the only way? Leaving them—

He growled to drown out the echoes and hit the bag harder.

Leaving them—

Bren's fist slipped off a slick spot where a rip in the heavy canvas had been patched with tape, and the force behind the blow pitched him forward. He hit the bag and shoved it away, ignoring the ache in his hands. If he burned off all this nervous energy, he could sleep—exhausted, dreamless—and he wouldn't have to hear her words anymore.

He'd get it done. Free the captives and end this shit with Miller, once and for all, because failure wasn't an option. And afterwards, Six would understand.

"I thought you and Cruz would be planning."

Mad, as sneaky as usual. Bren hit the bag one last time and turned, stopping it with the bulk of his body as it rebounded against his shoulder. "Too much planning for a mission is counterproductive. You know that."

Mad watched him, gaze dark and unflinching. "I know a lot of things. I know you. I just don't know what in hell you think you're doing."

"Letting off steam?"

"Don't play dumb. I thought you gave a shit about that girl."

For the first time, his hands ached—not from hitting the bag, but from the sincere desire to punch Mad's face in. "Careful, Maddox. I'm not in the best fucking mood."

"Nothing you could do to me scares me, *Brendan*." Mad crossed his arms and leaned against the wall, deliberately casual. "She's right. We should be over there right now, hauling those people out of there. If it was the only way to get to Miller, fine. Another couple days probably won't kill anyone. But it's not, and you know it."

"It's the best way. The surest one."

"Says the sniper who can kill a man from the other side of the sector. Fuck, man. I've seen you take shots that should have been impossible. You could drop that bastard at his dinner table or in the fucking bathtub. We could free those people and have you set up to blow his brains out when he shows up. So why aren't we?"

Because it wasn't *enough*, not for someone like Miller. He should have to confront death, stare it in the face and know it was coming for him. "Too many variables."

"Liar."

Bren's temples throbbed, and his hands clenched into fists. He relaxed them and shook his head. "You don't know Miller."

"I know men like him don't get less dangerous when you're face-to-face and they know you're there." Mad held his gaze. "It's okay to say it, Bren. It's okay to just fucking admit it. You want his blood on your hands."

"If you knew what he'd done—what he made the men and women under his command do—you'd want it too."

"That depends on the cost." Mad pushed away from the wall. "Anyone could see Six was worried about the people in her sector, and you and Dallas shredded her."

Guilt didn't sting—it burned through Bren, closing his throat. "Dallas was harsh, and Lex'll give him hell for it."

"Dallas made the wrong fucking call because you're lying to yourself. He really thinks the only way to get Miller is to wait." Mad stopped a few feet away, burning with unfamiliar intensity. "Have you ever been there, Donnelly? Have you ever been the one in chains? They're worse than helpless, less than human, and if you corner Miller because you're so hungry for blood you can't think straight, they're as good as dead."

"I want to kill him slow." Admitting it felt like admitting a lie, even though that wasn't what he'd done—was it? "I can do both, Mad. I'm *good* at this."

"It's revenge, man. I feel it, I know it. But you have to own it and know it's eating you up inside, or you'll make stupid decisions and maybe get more than yourself killed."

Revenge. It called to him. He'd waited for it, waited for *years*—all for Dallas, because risking the security of the O'Kanes wasn't worth nailing Miller to the wall. All the while, he'd comforted himself with the knowledge that, one day, he'd have his chance.

This was it. His moment.

"I can't," he muttered. "I've spent half a fucking decade, Mad. I've followed that bastard before, trailed him right through the sector streets—did you know that? Close enough to kill, but I held back, because the gang didn't need that trouble." The bag swayed behind him, bumped into his side, and Bren slammed one fist back into it and stepped forward. "The second he knows his deal went bad, he'll vanish."

"Why the fuck would he do that?"

Bren stumbled over the question. "If he gets word that I'm coming for him, I mean."

"And who's gonna tell him that?" Mad pressed. "Besides, before you said he'd set up a new operation, not disappear. Which is it?"

Both. Neither. Trapped by the scattered rationalizations, Bren scrubbed his hands over his face. "I need this, Mad. *Me*, all right? Is that what you want me to say?"

"Yes." Mad squeezed his shoulder. "Christ, man, do you think anyone here would judge you for that? Did you think *Six* would?"

"Judge me? No." He spun away. "But you sure the fuck expect me to set it aside."

Mad moved without warning, without sound, slamming into him so hard he put Bren face-first up into the wall. He twisted his arm behind him, holding him still with a lock far meaner than the one Bren had been teaching Six.

"How about you check that fucking attitude and consider the facts?" Mad ground out. "Everyone here wants Miller dead, for what he did to you and what he's doing now. Between all the brains in that room, we could have come up with a damn good plan to rescue those people *and* give you a chance to bathe in that motherfucker's blood. Your bloodthirsty little girlfriend would have probably been first in line to help. But you didn't give us a chance, and now your leader's making stupid, dangerous decisions because you lied to him."

Red. Rage throbbed through Bren, hazing his vision. He twisted, breaking the hold to catch Mad in an identical one, reversing their positions. "You don't know. You don't know *shit*."

Mad didn't struggle or fight back, but his words landed like blows. "I know you feel something for that woman that I've never fucking seen in you before. And I know you're going to lose her if you don't snap the hell out of it."

The words shredded Bren's justifications, all his safe reasons why this had to work. His plan was solid—take out Miller and free the captives—and the aftermath was equally simple. Once he'd managed to get it done, Six would understand. She'd forgive him, because what would be the point of staying angry after everything had turned out all right?

But Mad's words were so certain, so sure. What if he was right, and this was something she couldn't move past?

What if she didn't forgive him?

Reeling, he released his hold on Mad. "You believe that."

Mad turned, his expression serious. "Did you tell her any of this? That it was Miller doing the kidnapping, and how fucking much you needed this revenge?"

Bren couldn't even remember. It hadn't seemed as important as making sure he could deliver on all his promises, as an ironclad end result. "You've been there—in the chains. Would you forgive me for it?"

The other man paused. Groaned. "Jesus fucking *Christ*, Donnelly. Tell me she wasn't kidnapped by traffickers."

"I never said I wasn't an idiot," Bren growled. This was what he did—he tore down, ripped apart. Destroyed.

Only Six had ever expected anything different from him, and now he'd fucked that up, too.

Mad seized both of his shoulders. "All right, listen to

me. That girl came in here fucked up and scared, and I get it. She triggered something in you, and you want to protect her. Am I right so far?"

Six was a lot of things, but not helpless, and the urge to protect her had melted into something else a long time ago. She didn't need a hero.

She needed someone to love her.

"I have to go," he blurted in a rush. "Tonight. Those people matter to her, and she matters to me."

Mad released him with a sigh. "Good. I was starting to think I'd have to lead you there by the damn hand."

"Close." Bren reached for his shirt and dragged it over his head. "You up for it?"

"Of course." Amusement sparked in Mad's eyes. "If you hadn't come around, I might have taken care of it myself."

Before he could answer, Rachel rushed through the open doorway leading toward the living quarters. "You're here," she said breathlessly. "Shit, you've got a problem."

Bren tensed. "What happened?"

"Six didn't show up for her shift, so I went looking for her." Rachel pressed a hand to her side and panted. "She's gone."

Mad sucked in a breath and let it out on a groan. "Oh, fucking *hell.*"

Gone. The word tripped through Bren's mind, and every time he thought he had a handle on it, it threw him for another disbelieving loop. *Gone* meant danger, risk. *Gone* meant she'd set out for Three, determined to fix his fuckup.

Gone. A rumble drowned out the word, and it took Bren a moment to realize it had come from him, from someplace so deep in his chest it was a wonder Six had managed to touch it in the first place.

Fuck Miller. Fuck everything.

All he gave a damn about was Six.

19

EVEN CROUCHED NEXT to Scarlet on a litter-strewn roof, Six couldn't stop rubbing her thumb over the inside of her opposite wrist. It was like scratching an itch, touching that bare skin and aching at what she was about to give up.

No way would O'Kane give her cuffs now, no matter what Lex said. He may not have meant to shut her down in the bar, but this was something no leader would tolerate. She'd gone rogue, and Dallas wouldn't appreciate that it was Bren's words that had driven her here.

"I don't know, maybe it's unfair to be mad at him. If he'd tried to stop Trent, he would've ended up dead."

"If that were true, not a damn thing would ever change. It's something he tells himself to sleep at night, sweetness."

She wasn't putting the gang first, but at least she'd be able to sleep tonight.

"That's the place," Scarlet whispered. "You sure you

want to do this?"

"No," she admitted just as softly, watching the warehouse. There was only one guard visible now, his shaved, tattooed head making him easy to place. Zip had been one of Trent's low-rent thugs, one of a dozen who'd scattered when the O'Kanes started making their presence felt. "But I'm sure I have to do it."

"You really don't." Scarlet laid a hand on her arm. "Let us—me and Elvis and Riff."

Six shook her head. "If it's worth doing, I need to stand behind it. I'm done leaving you to fight this shit on your own."

Scarlet nodded and edged toward the rickety iron ladder on the opposite edge of the roof. Some of the bolts securing it to the brick façade had come loose, and Six braced herself for the precarious climb down.

Scarlet's boots hit the cracked concrete with a thump, and she pulled a pistol from her jacket. "Around the back," she whispered. "Then we wait."

As much as she preferred her fists, Six eased her own gun free and checked it, telling herself not to think about Bren's scarred hands as they slid over the pieces of his rifle, fitting them together with casual efficiency.

He'd never forgive her for this, either.

She'd figured her heart would be numb by now, but it still hurt so much she had to struggle to breathe as she followed Scarlet around the side of the building. From the crumbled wall at the back, they could hear every noise the guards made, from the murmur of conversation to the crunch of boots on gravel and broken glass.

Scarlet's brow furrowed, and she tilted her head. After a moment, she shrank closer to the wall and laid one finger over her mouth.

Someone had walked up to the blown-out window opening above them.

"I ain't doing it," the man rumbled. "You feel free, but don't expect some fucking bonus for it. Even if you managed to knock one of 'em up—"

Rough laughter spilled out, sadistic and vaguely familiar. "Who needs a bonus? A chance at some Eden pussy is all the reward I need."

Six frowned and mouthed *Eden?* to Scarlet, but the woman raised both eyebrows and shook her head.

"You forget who's lording it over Three now? Dallas O'Kane'll make you wish you'd kept your pants on."

A third man chimed in. "Yeah, if his bitch doesn't get to you first."

"I ain't afraid of a fucking woman," the familiar voice blustered, but the lie under the words pinged a memory, and a face to go with it—another of Trent's scummy thugs, Warner, a jackass who'd tried to climb on top of her one night by holding a knife to her throat.

He'd been real tough until she bit off part of his ear and shoved the knife into his leg. He'd cried as the other guys hauled her off him, and he hadn't been stupid enough to get within arm's reach of her again.

Killing him might restore her good mood.

"You do what you want," the third voice said. "I ain't taking any damn chances. I heard O'Kane's woman cut off a man's balls and made him eat them."

God, she was going to miss Lex.

A door clicked, rebounded against the wall. "Too much blood on the carpet," Elvis declared, his self-assurance strong enough to waft through the walls. "I'd watch my ass if I ever ran into her carrying a bunch of plastic drop cloths, though."

Adrenaline pulsed through her veins, and Six tightened her grip on her weapon. She could be through the window in a few seconds, if needed, but if Elvis pulled off the first part of their plan, she wouldn't need to. Bren's mentor might be some scary fucking enigma, but she knew the scum of Three. They were lazy, they were dumb...

And they were greedy.

"What the hell are you doing here?" Warner de
manded, and Six had to resist the urge to peek over the
sill.

"Heard you had something big over here. Wanted to
see it for myself."

"What, and report it back to O'Kane? Everyone
knows whose boots you're licking now."

Elvis snorted. "You can't win a game you refuse to
play, Warner." A pause. "This one's cute. How much?"

A rattle of chains accompanied a terrified whimper,
and Six steeled herself against memories and a renewed
surge of horror. At least it strengthened her resolve. The
captives inside that building were trapped, helpless,
listening to cowards like Warner bicker over whether or
not to rape them.

Two days was too fucking long to wait. Hell, an *hour*
was too long. And if Elvis didn't hurry along with this
plan...

*Just offer them the fucking money so we can get on
with killing them.*

"This lot's not for sale," one of the unnamed men replied. "But if you want to take that one for a ride, be my
guest. You could settle our debate. Would O'Kane cut
your dick off for it?"

"Probably," Elvis said, and Six could easily picture
his affable shrug. "If they're not for sale, what're they
for?"

"Not for sale to *you*," Warner sneered. "This isn't sector trash. These're fresh from Eden, and the communes'll
pay top—"

A crack cut him off, the unmistakable sound of an
open palm against flesh. "Boss won't like you spilling
your guts to an O'Kane lackey," a voice drawled, and Six
absently identified Zip. Most of her mind was churning
over the implication of Warner's words.

These weren't her people.

They were Bren's.

"Lackey," Elvis repeated. "I take offense to that, Zip. Especially when I come bearing a business proposition—and more cash than you assholes have ever seen in your miserable lives."

Six's whirling thoughts kept swinging around to the same possibility—if these people were coming *out* of Eden, Miller's part wasn't to drop off money and collect his cargo. He was the one doing the selling.

He could be in there right now, guarding his investment.

Scarlet had obviously come to the same conclusion. Her eyes went wide, and she mouthed a silent curse, but there was nothing they could do. Elvis was already in play, and there was no way to signal him to get the fuck out. They could abandon him, and even he might agree they owed him nothing more—

But he'd agreed to this. He'd risked O'Kane's ire and his own life to do the right thing, and maybe she wasn't the only one atoning for past sins.

Logic said the bastards from Three wouldn't have been bickering over raping their captives with their boss in the room, but Six had been in this warehouse before. There was an entire second floor, not to mention a back corner walled off from the rest, some sort of office with cheap metal furniture too ugly and rusted to steal. Too many places Miller could have settled.

And that wasn't even considering what kinds of city tech he might have brought with him. For all she knew, he had cameras on this damn alley, was watching them and laughing.

"Get the fuck out of here, Elvis, before I have to—"

"*Now.*"

Not a subtle signal, but they hadn't expected to need one. Riff would be plowing through the door now, gun at the ready, expecting that Elvis had accounted for everyone. It was all happening too fast, seconds smashing into one another as the first gunshot sounded. Six only had time to exchange a brief glance with Scarlet, no words, but it didn't matter because she wouldn't have come this far if she wasn't willing to go all the way.

Scarlet planted a boot on the edge of the window and vaulted through, Six hard on her heels and laughing at the irony as fear sent her adrenaline through the roof. Bren's training had ensured she was more dangerous than ever. She should have been less scared, not more, but that was Bren's fault, too.

He'd made her want to live. It would suck to die now.

She made it through the window in time to see Riff drop one of the guards. Scarlet strode right into the chaos, ignoring the clatter of bullets and chains, firing high to avoid hitting the men and women cowering on the floor along the walls.

Warner caught sight of Six, and his eyes bulged. She lifted her pistol, but not fast enough. The coward lunged for the nearest woman, dragging her up by the throat to use as a human shield, and Six exhaled and snatched for the calm Bren had been slowly teaching her.

Control herself, control the situation.

Warner lifted his gun—pointed at her, not the woman—and that was his mistake. His grip on his hostage loosened, and the girl thrashed, kicking at his knee. He cursed and dropped her, and Six hit him with three shots to the chest.

"Look out!" Elvis slammed into her, knocking her sideways with a low grunt. They skidded across the floor, the rough concrete scraping the skin from her arm and ripping her shirt.

Ears still ringing, she tried to shove Elvis off her and swore when her fingers slipped on blood. He was bleeding from the bullet that had almost hit her, bleeding all over her as one of the guards lined up another shot. Trapped, she could only lift her arm and do her best to take aim.

Her first two bullets went wide, digging into the ceiling. The third struck the guard's shoulder just as one of

Riff's caved in the side of the man's face.

A heartbeat later, an even louder shot rang out, crashing through one of the few remaining sections of low-hanging ceiling tile. A man stood at the foot of the stairs, one hand tangled in a female captive's hair. "What the fuck is going on here?"

Six pushed at Elvis's shoulder again, and he rolled off her with a hiss of pain. His blood was all over her, sticky on her skin and her torn shirt, but she ignored it just like she ignored his moan.

Instead, she focused on the man who had to be Miller.

She knew better than to think evil always came in an ugly package, but Miller wasn't handsome *or* hideous. He was...bland. A generic man whose face you'd forget the instant he was gone, his coloring not dark or pale, his hair not long or short, his clothing nice but not fancy.

But his *eyes*. Looking into them, Six knew he'd done things she couldn't imagine and hadn't merely slept fine afterward. He'd enjoyed every moment.

"A rescue mission?" His tone was just shy of polite, and he dragged the woman up to stand beside him. "None of you are from the city."

Six shifted to her knees. Slowly. "Guess we're equal opportunity heroes."

"Three of you. Four, if you count the one bleeding out on the floor." Miller stared her down, his gaze riveted to hers even as he thrust the barrel of his pistol into his hostage's mouth. "Not very heroic."

She could see the next few minutes playing out as if she'd already lived them. His finger squeezing the trigger, the horror as he blew off the back of the woman's head, the sick knowledge that her death would be on Six's hands.

How many bullets did she have left? Enough to make Miller's death a sure thing? Maybe, if she was willing to let that one woman die. Six met her eyes without meaning to, and the terror there made the room swim.

God, she was no fucking hero.

A clink and a hiss startled her, and a small, sleek grenade rolled out into the middle of the floor. Lush white smoke began to billow up from it, and Scarlet shouted something Six couldn't hear through the roaring in her ears.

Don't breathe, don't breathe— It was the only thing she could think, with Cruz's casual mention of knock-out gas so fresh in her memory. She moved on instinct, rolling to one side so she wouldn't be in the last place Miller had seen her. Boots scuffled at the door, and Six squinted, trying to make out some familiar feature in the bodies flashing through the smoke.

A shot. A scream. Her lungs burned, and she had no choice but to gasp in a breath. But it smelled like smoke, not gas, and she had one second to indulge her sheer relief before a blurry figure loomed in front of her.

She lifted her gun and found herself pointing it straight at Bren's face.

He knocked it away and lifted her off the floor, holding her up when her knees would have buckled. "Are you hurt?"

Getting enough breath to answer involved inhaling smoke, but Bren didn't seem to notice. His hands were everywhere, sliding over her body like he'd forgotten he didn't own it, but the panic in his eyes as he wiped away Elvis's blood silenced her protests.

"It's not yours." He cupped the back of her neck, pressed his forehead to hers. "It's someone else's blood."

The fact that Elvis didn't speak up to point out it was his was enough to force her away from Bren. She turned, almost grateful for the excuse to pull free when every instinct in her traitorous body was screaming at her to wrap herself around him.

"I need a medkit," she rasped, sinking to her knees beside Elvis's unmoving body. His pulse fluttered under her fingers, weak but still there. She jerked her knife free and cut through his shirt. "Scarlet and Riff—"

Cruz appeared out of the smoke, towering over her. "They're fine. No casualties among the captives. But Miller's gone."

Every muscle in Six's body tensed as she braced herself to become invisible, but Bren ignored the words and knelt beside her. "We'll patch the wound and send for Doc. He'll make it."

Shock held her immobile as Bren took over assessing Elvis's wound. All of his focus was on the task at hand, all that intensity pulsing in the air between them.

Even Cruz watched him with a frown of confusion. "You don't want to mount a pursuit?" he asked. "We could still catch him in the tunnels."

"I don't give a fuck," Bren barked. "Clear the smoke and get some gel—lots of it."

Cruz vanished, and even though Bren and Six were crouched in a room surrounded by hysterical captives and dead bodies, the smoke shut out everything but the two of them.

She didn't know how to reach out, didn't know if she wanted to. But she knew his heart was as wounded as hers, and one thing might fix it. "They're safe now," she said, her irritated throat turning the words into a rasping whisper. "You should go after him. I know how much it means to you."

Bren tore a strip off Elvis's already ripped shirt and pressed it to the man's wound before meeting her eyes. "You're more important."

Then he looked away.

He couldn't have shoved her harder off balance if he'd said *I love you*—though that practically seethed under the words, the unspoken assumption, the only logical conclusion.

If she could believe him.

Not that it mattered either way, since she was about

to vanish from his world in all the ways that counted. She could build a decent life in Three, she honestly believed that now. She'd survive, and maybe she'd do some good.

It would never be the same as being an O'Kane.

Six helped Bren bandage Elvis and pretended it was the smoke making her eyes sting and water.

dallas

D ALLAS O'KANE WAS a king with a pissed-off
queen and a mutiny problem, and he wasn't stupid
enough to think the two were unrelated.

He paced past her again, trying to walk off the edge
of tension since he hadn't been able to sweat it off, and
Lex was still way too upset to offer to relieve it any other
way. "I can't give her ink now. When you go rogue, I look
tougher for having a tough queen. Six running off on her
own ain't so neat and tidy."

"That's true." Lex poured two drinks and handed him
one, which was definitely progress. "Though, if you think
about it, who really knows what Six did?"

Reason. That was the blessing and curse of venting
to Lex. "Me and you. Bren. Cruz. Mad. The people from
Three."

"No one with anything to gain by talking about it."

"And if she gets her ink and decides she doesn't like
my next order?"

beyond pain

"Ah." Lex sat on the couch and crossed her long legs. "Now, that's another question entirely."

Dallas drained the whiskey in one gulp and slammed the glass down on the sidebar. "Will she?"

"Don't know. I guess that depends on a lot of things—including you."

"You're gonna make me say it, huh?" This part wasn't a blessing. Sometimes they both knew the ugly truth, and all he wanted Lex to do was drag it into the open so he could pretend it was a surprise. It was hard enough to be wrong. It was a thousand fucking times worse to have to admit he'd known it—and had taken the easy way out.

Lex set her drink down with a thump and shifted on-to her knees, tucking her legs underneath her. "You've never been that asshole, Dallas. The guy who just wants his people to follow orders, no matter what their con-sciences dictate. Why start now? Because she doesn't have her ink yet? Or because you feel guilty?"

He sighed and put the truth out there so they could both stare at it. "I knew Bren was lying."

"Not only that," Lex whispered. "You let him get away with it."

"Because it was simple." Admitting it hurt worse than scraping his nerves raw. "Because if Miller got away, I knew what I'd have to do. What I'm *going* to do."

Lex watched him, sympathy tempering the tough love in her dark eyes. She held open her arms. "Come here."

He probably didn't deserve to get off this easy, but he sure as fuck was selfish enough to take it. He gave up pacing, slumped to the floor in front of Lex, and buried his face on her lap with a groan. "I've never been good with Bren. He's like this perfect fucking weapon someone handed me. He doesn't know how to be disloyal, even when I'm fucking him up."

She made a soothing noise and stroked his hair. "I

know, baby. That's why you have to let him go, just a little."

"To her."

"Would it be so terrible? You let Noelle have Jas, and the world didn't end."

Laughter clawed its way into his throat, and he huffed. "You think I'm jealous?"

"No, I think you're worried." She guided his face up until his eyes met hers. "But I also think you shouldn't want a man like Bren, not if he has to shut down everything but the job."

"No, I don't." Sighing, Dallas lifted his head. "Go get her, then. Let's get her wearing ink before she tears this place down around my ears. And then I'll deal with Miller."

The corner of Lex's mouth kicked up. "She's right outside."

Presumptive, brilliant, *maddening* woman. "I hate you when you're smarter than me."

"No, you don't." She hesitated. "Those people—they were headed out to the communes. Workers and breeders. Since when are they so short-handed? So desperate they'll kidnap people from the city?"

"I don't know, but those were street people. Maybe someone figured they could clean up a problem and make a little cash, to boot."

Lex frowned. "And Miller?"

"I'll turn him over to the one person who hates corrupt Eden officials more than I do," he drawled. Even though he'd been loath to take this step, the familiar excitement was building again. This wasn't the move of an insignificant sector thug. He was about to cross a line that would drag the O'Kanes to the next level when it came to power and influence.

Heady shit—and dangerous. When Lex's eyes widened in understanding, he grinned. "What did they used to say? The enemy of my enemy is my friend?"

She sat up straighter and leaned forward to drive her fingers into his hair. "Careful, Declan. It's a risky game."

"I know. But someone came along and infected me with this fucking urge to make things better, and that means using all the advantages I can get."

She brushed her thumb over his lower lip. "Sure, blame it on me."

All the good things were her fault, and later he'd make sure she knew it. For now, he sprawled next to her and lifted his voice to a roar. "Six, get your ass in here!"

The door clicked open. The girl slunk in, somehow looking wary and regretful and defiant, all at once. Dallas stretched his arms across the back of the couch and let his queen do what she did best.

"Well?" Lex asked lazily, retrieving her drink from the table. "What do you have to say for yourself?"

Six glared at her feet. "I fucked up and almost got us all killed because Elvis's intel was incomplete. But I don't regret trying. Saving them was the right thing to do."

"Fair enough." Lex drained her drink. "You didn't apologize, which is promising. So I just have one question left."

Dallas bit the inside of his cheek to keep from smiling as Six's head jerked up, her face awash in confusion. "What's that?" she asked cautiously.

"Can you handle being an O'Kane if it means seeing Bren all the time?"

So much for the urge to smile. For one terrible moment, the girl's face was nothing but naked pain and shattered hope, and he bore some of the blame for that, for letting Bren lie to her and himself because he wanted the easy path.

He'd have to make it up to both of them.

Six donned her mask, her expression smoothing out, and her voice only trembled a little. "The good things in life never come easy. But they're worth it."

Lex rose, walked over to Six, and grasped her shoulders. "You'll be fine, honey." She kissed her cheek, then sighed. "But if you go running off again, it'd better be because you came to me first, and I told you to go for it. Understood?"

The girl hesitated. "What would you have told me to do this time?"

"Take a bigger gun."

Six laughed, shocked and abrupt, and then she was hugging Lex for all she was worth, clinging to her as she stared at Dallas over Lex's shoulder. "I changed my mind," she said thickly.

Alarming words, but the pleasure in her eyes was enough that Dallas didn't tense. "About what, darling?"

"I get why you're still in charge."

He didn't have to work hard to call up the memory—everything about the night he'd collared Lex was branded into his mind. Six had given him big, baffled eyes and admitted she couldn't understand how he was still in charge when he didn't beat people into place, and he'd told her the truth she wasn't ready to hear.

This is my family. These are my people. I'm in charge because they trust me to make life a hell of a lot better for them than it would be without me.

Now he had to live up to that challenge. "Welcome to the family, Six."

20

W HEN BREN RAN into Noelle on his way to Six's room, he knew he was in for a world of hurt. What he didn't know was how effectively the damn woman could strike—and with nothing more than a cool glare.

He stepped forward. She planted herself in front of him. "Bren."

He sighed. "I could pick you up and move you, but I'd rather not."

One of her perfectly arched brows swept up. "If you can't even talk your way past me, then I'm doing you a favor by keeping you away from her."

"So that's how it is." He shoved his hands in his pockets. Making his apologies to Six was one thing— necessary, the least he could do—but having to convince Noelle he should be allowed to offer them... "I just want to tell her I'm sorry."

Noelle kept staring at him. "That's all?"

"That's all."

"Bren, she *hugged* me."

He couldn't imagine how badly Six must be hurting, to seek a comfort so foreign to her. He closed his eyes and nodded. "I get it."

"Maybe not all of it." Noelle stroked his cheek, her fingers warm and gentle. "I love you, but so help me, Brendan Donnelly... If you screw this up by not admitting you need her, I'm going to let my cat pee in your bed every night for the next ten years."

Bren bit his lip, torn between laughing and something darker he couldn't even define, something like the wail of a wounded animal. "As threats go, that's pretty fucked up."

"We use the weapons at our disposal," she replied. As light and breezy as the words were, there was a dangerous edge under them. "The hardest thing I ever did in my life was learn how to start fighting. And that was easy compared to what Six is having to learn."

How to stop.

They stood in silence for a tense moment that stretched out until Noelle sighed and stepped aside.

Six's door was ajar, but he stopped and knocked on the jamb. "It's Bren."

"Come in."

She had her hair up and was wearing a halter top. It was so unlike her usual T-shirts and tank tops that his gaze lingered—long enough to catch the telltale shimmer of drying med-gel on the tops of her shoulders.

Bren tensed, ordered himself not to reach for her. "What happened?"

The corner of her mouth kicked up—not a smile for him, but one for herself. "Ace happened," she said, lifting her wrist to flash a shiny black cuff at him. Before he could process the implication, she turned to show him her bare back.

Only it wasn't bare. The scars were still there, crisscrossing her spine, and the tattoo didn't try to hide them.

It simply overwhelmed them, stretching across her shoulders in a delicate tangle of dark swirls, forming a detailed frame for the O'Kane emblem emblazoned between her shoulder blades.

Her ink, *her* way. Breathtaking, a celebration of overcoming the hardships and scars of her past. Of belonging.

Bren swallowed past the lump in his throat. "It looks good. It's beautiful."

"It stung like a bitch," she said, facing him again.

Words failed him, so he reached for something, *anything.* "How's Elvis doing?"

"Clean exit wound," she answered carefully. "Doc says he'll be fine."

"Good."

She was tense, a little awkward, but at least she wasn't glaring. She simply watched him, her dark eyes shuttered.

And Bren had no idea where to start, except at the beginning. "I was wrong. I should have listened to you."

Her expression didn't change. "Why? I didn't know all the details, because you hadn't bothered to tell me."

"I thought it didn't matter—no." If he was going to do this, he had to do it right. No hesitation, and no lies. "I didn't tell you about Miller's involvement because I guess...on some level, I knew it wasn't a good reason. And then I was too busy coming up with reasons—excuses— that I couldn't unravel what was true anymore."

"You were hurting." Her fingers curled toward her palms, the first sign of pain. "I know I'm fucked up, I know I'm ignorant, but I'm not a pet. You didn't give me a chance to take care of you."

An idea he could still barely wrap his head around. "No one does, Six. Not like you mean."

"Because you have to let them. And it's *hard.*" Her hands trembled, and she crossed her arms over her chest, as if to hide it. "You have to trust someone to see you when you're weak. And you have to trust yourself to leave if they break you."

The way that he'd broken her. "I'm sorry."

"Do you know what hurt worst?"

Everything? "No."

"You made me feel crazy. You made me doubt what I knew was right." Her voice rose, losing its calm edge. "Why didn't you just *tell me* you needed him dead?"

The truth was stark, unforgivable. "Because I knew it wasn't enough." He wanted to touch her, slide his hands over her skin and feel her melt into his embrace— so he took a step back. "I'm not asking for another chance, Six. I wouldn't. I don't deserve one."

She hugged herself tighter. "Then what are you asking for?"

"Nothing." But that seemed too simple, too evasive. "I was an asshole. And you're right. I didn't realize I was doing it, but I took everything you'd shared with me, and I used it against you."

"Oh." She wet her lips and looked away. "What happened to Miller?"

"I don't know."

Her gaze jumped back to him. "What do you mean? I thought Dallas said he was taking care of it."

"He must be, yeah." But Bren hadn't asked. It wasn't so vital anymore, not after facing the fact that he'd lost Six.

He'd lost her.

The room was too small, with walls that were pressing in on him. He had to get out. "Anyway, that's all I wanted to say—I'm sorry. And I'm glad you're sticking around, for the gang's sake. For yours."

"Bren—" He saw her waver, saw the fracture in her defenses, that hint of vulnerability. But she dug her teeth into her lower lip, and it vanished behind a tough, polite mask. "Thank you."

He turned away. He didn't trust himself around her

anymore, not even his voice, not until he'd reached the door and had his fingers around the handle. "Least I could do, sweetness."

He closed it firmly behind him without waiting for an answer, dismissive or comforting. Any closure between them belonged to Six. She was the one who'd opened up, risked herself in so many ways.

She was the one who'd earned it.

21

RIX STARED AT the bundle in Flash's arms. "She's so *tiny.*"

It wasn't the first time Six had heard the words. It seemed to be all any of the O'Kanes could say when confronted with the sleepy newborn. Everyone except Jasper, who'd grown up on one of the communes and had probably seen as many babies born as Six had.

To the rest of them, little Hana was a strange and wondrous creature, mysterious and fragile. Flash was watching her with awed fascination, as if he couldn't believe she existed and didn't know what to do with her—and didn't care a bit.

It was adorable. "She's not that small," Six said, fighting to keep her expression serious. "She only looks it because Flash could hold her in one hand."

Flash's brow furrowed. "Nobody better hold her in one hand."

"No one's going to," Jas assured him. "Congratulations, man."

"She's beautiful," Mad added, leaning closer to the couch. Amira and Flash had a new, larger suite of rooms, supposedly to make space for a nursery. Six suspected it had been to make room for the endless parade of aunts and uncles who cycled in and out, perching on the extra chairs Dallas had dug out of storage.

That she was included as one of them still stunned her.

The baby squirmed and blinked, her lingering sleepiness melting away. In a heartbeat, her features screwed into a grimace, and she whimpered.

Flash's calm vanished. He was on his feet before the first hungry cry rang out, rocking Hana and making soothing noises tinged with panic. "What's wrong?" he demanded, as if Noelle and Trix weren't staring at him with equal alarm.

Jas answered before Six. "She sounds hungry, that's all. Better take her back to her mama."

Six bit her lip as Flash seemed to struggle between the urge to rush and to take careful steps. He disappeared through the door to the bedroom, and Doc emerged a few moments later.

His clothes were rumpled, wrinkled shirt sleeves rolled to his elbows, his dark hair disheveled. But it was his expression that stopped them all, a scowl of disgust tempered by disbelief, as if he couldn't believe their audacity in being there. "Get out."

Mad frowned. "C'mon, man, we're family. We just want—"

Doc cut him off with a quick shake of his head. "Frankly, I don't care what you want. I care about what Amira and her child need. Hell, Flash too, for that matter. They need to rest. So get out, all of you."

Noelle slipped from Jasper's lap and dragged him up. "Trix and I should be checking inventory in the bar anyway."

"Way ahead of you." Trix's lips curved into a smile as she hurried toward the door with a little wave at Six. Noelle rose on her toes to kiss Jasper's cheek before following her.

That left Six to be herded out the door with Mad and Jas. Doc snapped the door shut behind them, and they stood there in awkward silence.

The women had been welcoming her for so long that the ink seemed like a formality. The concept of sisterhood that had baffled her so completely only a few months ago was reality now, a truth she felt in her bones. Brotherhood must be the same, and the men towering on either side of her were Bren's friends, his brothers. For all Lex's promises, it was hard to believe a little bit of ink could change that.

Jas watched her for several long seconds before finally shoving his hands into his pockets. "Tomorrow morning, eleven o'clock."

It was a struggle not to blink stupidly at him. "What's at eleven?"

"Lex says you're gonna work the door at the club. You need to train, right?"

Still guarded, she nodded.

"Jas'll do it," Mad said, hooking his thumbs into his belt. "I'll help. It'd be good for you to practice with different people who've got different styles."

Goddamn, she had to stop underestimating the O'Kanes. A lump formed in her throat, but at least she could pretend she was moved by the offer and not mourning those quiet afternoons with Bren. "That'd be good. Thanks."

"Yeah." Jas rubbed her shoulder, his expression neutral. "I'll see you then. Come prepared to kick ass."

It was hard to remember how rare her smiles had been when they came so easily now. "I always am."

"That's what we like to hear." He slung an arm around Mad's shoulders, and they headed down the hall toward the warehouse, unaware that they'd tilted her world on its ear.

She hadn't let herself think about working the front door, not from the moment Ace had started her tattoos. Dallas and Lex were offering her the world, safety and family and a place to belong. Without Bren to train her and vouch for her, she wouldn't have blamed them for sticking her back behind the bar until she proved herself in other ways.

But no one was punishing her for standing up to Bren. Instead of beating her back into the dirt, his brothers were reaching out a hand to pull her up. To pull her as high as she was willing to climb, as high as she *dared*, out of the grime and fear of her past, out of being afraid and alone.

First, she had to learn how to dream.

The garage was a safe haven.

Bren swabbed sweat and dust from his forehead with a swipe of his arm, then wrapped a fresh sheet of sandpaper around the rubber block in his hand. If he kept going, he could get the left fender finished and primed before collapsing into his bed.

"There you are. I've been looking all over for you."

He paused just long enough to glance up at Dallas. "Need something?"

"I wanted to check on you." Dallas leaned back against the workbench and studied him. "I haven't seen you in and out of Amira's room like the rest of 'em."

"I'm not good with babies." Or people.

Dallas scoffed. "None of us are good with babies."

"True enough." Bren set aside the sanding block and sat back on his heels. "I'm fine, Dallas. Working."

"Hey, I'm not here to force you to spill your secrets. That's not my thing. But if there's anything or anyone you'd like to avoid, I need to know so I can work that into my plans for what we do next in Three."

Christ, he hadn't even thought about it. "Is Six—will she still be helping out over there?"

"Probably. It's important to her, and she's useful." Dallas hesitated before heaving a rough sigh. "I'm sorry, man. For my part in what happened."

"I'm a grown damn man." Bren rose, wiped his hands, and reached for a beer in the open bucket of ice by the worktable. "You're not responsible for making sure I don't fuck up. That's on me."

"You're *my* man," Dallas said quietly. "My brother, my friend. I let you get away with it for my own reasons—lazy, cowardly reasons. We've gotta draw the line between right and wrong, because no one else will."

"No one else," Bren agreed. Which meant it was up to him to make amends. "I need to do something good, Dallas. Build things instead of tearing them down. But I also need to stay out of her way, and that means staying out of Three."

Dallas nodded. "We can figure something out. Just—" He shook his head with another sigh. "If I thought you might push her, I'd beat you into the ground. But don't make the opposite mistake. Don't give up on her."

Every cell in his body screamed at him to grab on to Dallas's words. But the truth wasn't nearly so simple. "It'll take a while for her to get it, really understand that she doesn't have to be with me to be an O'Kane. Safe. Until I know she believes it, one step in her direction is too many."

"You're a good man, Donnelly."

"Not good. Honest. Usually," he added with a snort. Time to do some tough self-examination, figure out how and when he'd first let that honesty fail him.

Dallas caught his shoulder, his fingers digging in hard enough to bruise. "Bullshit. You're a *good* man. You don't let those bastards in Eden, or me, or even that girl convince you otherwise."

"You didn't." More of the truth he'd rededicated himself to. "I managed fine on my own."

"You made a mistake. Good men do that all the damn time. I have it on the highest authority that what makes them good is that they can admit it. And fix it."

Lex's words, no doubt, and Bren had to smile. "Sounds like a smart authority."

Dallas laughed. "You better fucking believe it, man, or she'll take you apart."

In the grand scheme of things, he could see how Dallas wouldn't think he'd fucked up irreversibly. He hadn't murdered anyone, and everything worked out all right in the end. How could he explain an invisible wound? A betrayal made all the more devastating by the fact that he knew—he fucking *knew*—Six would forgive him, even at her own expense?

On second thought, perhaps Dallas did understand. "Lex lets you off the hook way too easily, you know that?"

"Of course I do." No laughter now. Dallas's expression was deadly serious. "Why do you think being a better man matters so damn much? The sex, that's good, but it's not the prize. Trust is the prize, and the fight's not about winning it or keeping it. It's about deserving it, and that's a fight a man's got to have with himself. Every fucking day."

"Point taken." He twisted the cap off the beer and handed it to Dallas. "I'll get there. Someday, huh?"

Dallas lifted the bottle in a salute that felt more like a reprieve than anything. "Maybe sooner than you think."

22

I'M NOT ASKING *for another chance, Six. I wouldn't. I don't deserve one.*

Six dragged her pillow over her face to muffle a frustrated snarl, but the lack of sound stole all the satisfaction. Bren's words had wiggled into her mind, repeating in an endless, taunting refrain.

I'm not asking for another chance.

She'd wanted him to. She'd *needed* him to, every bit as much as she'd dreaded it. Her feelings were still a sick tangle of guilt and hurt and wounded pride, but as wary as she was of her urge to forgive him anything, she couldn't shake the feeling she was missing something deeper.

Bren was no Wilson Trent. They'd both lied to her. They'd both made her doubt herself. But what Trent had done out of childish cruelty, Bren had done out of...

That was the question, wasn't it?

I don't deserve one.

Impossible to imagine those words coming out of Wilson Trent's mouth. He'd been unerringly confident in the truth that he deserved everything. Six's body, her emotions, her secrets. Her mind, heart, and soul. He'd picked them apart, pushing her across the line in steps so small she was already broken before she realized what was happening.

Six threw the pillow away, rolled to her feet, and stalked toward the couch. The tablet was where she'd left it, rammed down beside the cushion. Maybe Bren was telling the truth. Maybe he'd done worse things, horrifying things, things he could never fucking come back from.

There was one way to find out.

The video list picked up right where it had left off, with Bren in a plain, brightly lit room.

This time, the voice that spoke from behind the camera was lower. Angrier. "Your CO reported that you disobeyed a direct order."

Instead of answering, Bren stared down at the table.

"Insubordination is a capital charge, son. You'd better answer the question."

Bren spoke, his voice flat. Lifeless. "I didn't hear one."

The video cut to Cruz. He looked different, younger and clean shaven. His hair was cropped close to his head, his eyes hard. "Donnelly attempted to fulfill his orders, but the mission parameters were—"

"You're saying he couldn't deliver the package?"

Only a moment's hesitation, but Six could tell he was on the verge of lying, and so could whoever was on the other side of the camera. Cruz's jaw clenched, and he ground out a grudging, "The circumstances weren't optimal."

A hand slammed down on the table from outside of the frame. "Miller's orders were clear."

"We achieved every other mission objective. We disabled ninety-two percent of Nevada City's weapons resources. Poisoning their water supply when they were no longer a military threat—"

"Take him to the stockade."

Two stone-faced soldiers stepped forward and lifted Cruz out of his chair. He didn't struggle, though from the tensing of his shoulders, Six thought he was considering shaking free of them.

But he didn't. He went along, enduring the rough handling as they dragged him off to face punishment for refusing to poison an entire town—or maybe just for refusing to pin the blame on Bren.

Her stomach twisted, imagining what they'd done to *him* for his disobedience.

The video jumped again. The same room, and Bren looked older.

Exhausted.

"I didn't miss the shot." He said it as though he'd said it before, like he was trying to explain to someone who wouldn't listen. "I flubbed it. Harrison hasn't done anything to merit a proper arrest, much less an execution. And I don't do personal hits."

A woman sighed. "If I put that on your evaluation, do you know what will happen to you?"

"I know. You should ask me if I give a shit."

Six thought back to Noah's note. Noah's stupid, vague, misleading note. *Make sure you watch it all*, he'd said, and she'd ignored it because she'd been so sure he was setting out to show her Bren's descent from man to monster.

This was so much better and so much worse. A progression, all right. Eden, breaking Bren's spirit. Breaking his heart.

A monster waking up because he knew he could be a better man.

"They won't execute you, if that's what you're after." Papers rustled, and the woman sighed again. "You're too valuable a resource to squander, even when you're bucking orders. But if they ever need someone disposable—"

"Yeah." Bren nodded slowly, understanding in his eyes. "I can live with that."

Six stopped the video. Bren's face froze, that terrible choice clear in his eyes. If she'd had a mirror in the moments after Wilson Trent had thrown her to Dallas O'Kane, she probably would have seen the same thing.

Death is better than more of this.

Russell Miller was the man who had shattered Bren. The man who had pushed him, used him, hurt and discarded him. Yet with that betrayal shredding his heart, Bren hadn't reached out to her—to anyone—and asked for help, for vengeance.

He'd made up a hundred reasons, because he'd truly believed his own broken heart wouldn't be important enough.

I'm not asking for another chance. I don't deserve one.

She'd forgotten the one advantage she had over him, over so many of them. Daydreams or not, she could close her eyes and remember soft hands running through her hair and the warmth of her mother's voice, the feeling of being loved and cherished.

Bren didn't have that. He didn't know how to be loved, maybe didn't believe he deserved it.

Tossing the tablet aside, Six lunged for the door.

"I want Miller's head."

Lex arched an eyebrow without looking up from the papers on her desk. "Yeah? Get in line."

Six slammed her hands on the scratched wood and leaned down. "Bren doesn't think any of us give a shit how bad that bastard hurt him. He thinks his feelings don't matter enough."

"No, he thinks they don't matter to *you*." She focused a mild look at Six. "He usually knows better than to bring that shit to the table when he's dealing with me and Dallas. We all have our traumas and our skeletons, honey, but we check them at the door when shit gets tricky. We have to."

It hit hard, and no doubt Lex had meant it to. So Six took a careful breath, dragged her emotions back into line, and straightened. "You told me Dallas was taking care of it. Does that mean Miller's dead?" If not, there had to be a way to get to him. A way to end him.

"Miller? He's getting something better than dead."

There were fates worse than death, but this wild, protective rage gathering inside her wouldn't be satisfied with less than blood. It had clicked into place somewhere between her room and Lex's office, something that transcended forgiveness and love and even words.

Bren was *hers*. He could forgive the hurts Miller had done him, could decide his pain wasn't worth it. That he had to move on. She never would.

"Tell me," she whispered. "I need to know."

"Banished," Lex said simply. "I don't really doubt Miller was operating with the approval of someone in Eden, but that seems to have dried up. And human trafficking is enough to get his ass kicked out into the sectors."

Six blinked. "Dallas got *Eden* to kick him out?"

"All Dallas did was tip off some concerned citizens to Miller's crimes. They decided their own punishment."

She couldn't think of a single *concerned citizen* who would give a shit what a sector gang leader thought, much less listen to one, until she remembered all the hugs she'd been drowning in over the past week.

Noelle's father. The most moral fucking man in a city terrified of sin. "Cunningham?"

Lex waved away the question. "It's been taken care of. That's all you need to know."

"Just tell me he won't last long in the sectors."

Lex grinned. "You've got our ink now, girl. You should know better."

She should, and she did. Her fire was newly formed, awkward and uncertain. She was still learning how to love people, how to belong to a family and protect them. And Dallas and Lex wouldn't take chances.

The rest of her temper dissipated, and she sank into a chair. "Learning how to care shouldn't be this damn hard. Are normal people born knowing how?"

"Hell, no." A pause. "But some people are lucky enough to have someone to teach them."

Six stared at the cuffs on her wrists. The O'Kane emblem was the same for everyone, but she'd noticed that Ace got whimsical with how he framed each person's ink. Twisted barbed wire curled around her wrist, the same that edged Bren's. But hers was a mesh of intersecting lines, like the cage where they held their fights.

She'd reclaimed her pride here, reclaimed her body. "I have a whole family to learn from now."

"Yeah, you do." Lex dragged open a drawer and pulled out a small ring loaded with keys. "If you're gonna work the door at the Broken Circle, you'll need these."

She leaned forward, unable to hide her eagerness. The weight of the keys felt like trust, and she folded her fingers around the hard edges with a smile. "Thanks."

Lex covered her hand, holding her still as their eyes locked. "You're right about Bren. He needs to know he matters. But you don't take that on unless you need it too, okay?"

"We're both broken." Saying it out loud sounded stark and rough, but the realization changed everything. "I didn't get it before. Maybe that should make it worse, but it doesn't. If I'm not the only broken one, maybe I can be good for him, too."

Satisfied, Lex released her and sat back. "Then remember that you're an O'Kane now, and don't give up until you have everything you want."

Six uncurled her hand and stared at the ring of keys, the symbol of what she could have when she had enough faith in herself and her abilities to go after the impossible. "I guess that's the part I've got to figure out."

"You'll get there. Trust me."

She did, and it wasn't even scary anymore.

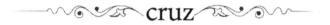

cruz

WITHIN HOURS OF watching the light fade from Russell Miller's eyes, Cruz had a woman sucking his dick.

Not just a woman, a prostitute. And she wasn't just sucking. She was going down on him with the sort of enthusiasm money couldn't buy, her tongue slick and hot, her moans so low and real they vibrated in his bones. He had both hands buried in her masses of curly hair, but not to guide her movements.

Someone had to keep it out of Ace's way.

Leather slapped against the woman's back, the sound as hypnotic as the noise that always followed, a throaty groan rising up from deep inside her. The flogging was turning her on.

It was turning them all on.

No heroes here, he thought darkly, letting his gaze drift down the woman's spine and up Ace's body. His chest was leanly muscled, but it was his ink that always

beyond pain

caught Cruz's attention, a riot of color from his wrists to his shoulders, the patterns shifting with the flex of his arms. Dark hair swept over his brow, but did nothing to cover the intense set of his eyes as Ace landed another precise blow, and his lips curved into a pleased smile at the groaning response.

He was living, breathing sin, and Cruz was tired of resisting temptation. What was the point of scraping through a proper life here, in the barbaric, uncivilized sectors? There had to be a reward for living without the comforts he'd grown up with.

This was a start. A filthy, illicit, too-fucking-hot start.

The woman lifted her head, the firm stroke of her hand taking the place of her mouth. "Harder," she pleaded.

"No," Ace drawled, dragging the falls across her shoulders teasingly instead. He looked up and smiled. "Jeni always asks for it harder. Don't you, pretty girl?"

"Ye—" The word cut off in a throaty squeal. "Yes."

Cruz followed Ace's arm down to the hand between Jeni's thighs. He stroked her like he'd done it a thousand times, working his fingers just right, making her squirm and wiggle.

He snapped his gaze back to Ace's, and there was something there—a challenge. A question. Ace's smile had melted into a little smirk, the kind that said *I know your secret* and maybe *just let go.*

The dark hunger Cruz had spent so long choking into silence swelled, testing the bonds of his self-control, straining the cage he'd built around it. It seemed so pointless now. Trying to live up to the ideals of the men in Eden, men who'd never followed them, never really believed them. He was a weapon, built to kill on command. He'd done that tonight. He'd do it again.

It was his fucking turn to issue the commands.

He tightened his grip in Jeni's hair, savoring her

316

sweet noise of approval. She liked it rough and hard. He'd seen her on the stage at the Broken Circle, screaming in pleasure as Ace worked her body. He knew enough to take control of this moment.

"Tell Ace what you want," he whispered, a quiet command that he half expected her to disobey.

Instead, she *melted*, the tense lines of her body softening into lush submission. "I want him to help me."

The words were deceptive. He almost misunderstood them, but Ace's sudden laugh held a sharp, dangerous heat as he swatted at Jeni's hip. "Be more specific, or he'll think you want me to move some furniture."

Jeni laughed too, scratching her nails up Cruz's chest as she rose to her knees on the bed. Close enough to kiss, yet she bypassed his mouth and dipped her head to lick the hollow of his throat. "I want him to help me get you off."

The bed shifted as Ace moved closer. Jeni was small for all her curves, fitting neatly under his chin. Nothing stood between his mouth and Ace's except half a foot of empty space that suddenly seethed with obscene promise.

The hunger inside him pulsed. The cage cracked.

"Do you want to help her get me off?" Cruz asked, the words screaming into the tension. He couldn't take them back, so they hung there, rough and demanding, a challenge that could change everything.

But Ace didn't answer. He rocked forward, closing the distance. Four inches.

Three.

The tension between them wouldn't fit in so small a space. It pressed against Cruz's chest, made it hard to breathe. Jeni had gone still against him—maybe she was aware of the stakes of this endless, terrifying moment.

Two inches. Ace stopped so close, Cruz could feel his breath as he spoke. "That's not what you wanted to say, brother."

No, it wasn't, and he hated Ace for seeing through him, for *knowing*. All these damn weeks, leading him down the path of temptation, step after step. Ace didn't seem like the type to have a strategy and a mission, but Cruz still felt like he'd stumbled into a trap.

Two damn inches.

Cruz had climbed fifteen-story buildings without a safety rope. He'd jumped out of helicopters. Hell, he'd started a riot once, a full-scale fucking riot that had torn apart what was left of the city of Las Vegas. He could conquer two inches of empty air.

He freed one hand from the silk of Jeni's hair. Ace's was shorter, he couldn't get a grip. That didn't fucking matter. He curled a hand around the back of the other man's neck and wrenched him across the empty space.

Their mouths collided, and it wasn't anything as pretty as a kiss. Teeth dug into his lower lip. He growled and pressed harder, taking control, kissing Ace the way he'd never let himself kiss Rachel. Rough, violent, *starving*, biting and needing and not worrying about what was gentle or right.

The cage inside him shattered, flooding him with endless hunger, and he jerked back, his chest heaving.

Jeni shuddered and bit his earlobe so hard it hurt. Her words were even harsher, hoarse and low. "You're so fucking hot together."

Together. Just like Rachel had said, and he wouldn't be the bastard who pretended Jeni's pretty red hair was blonde and straight, that her husky pleas belonged to another woman.

Ace was still watching him. Still waiting.

That's not what you wanted to say, brother.

He fisted his hand in Jeni's hair—her red, curly, not-at-all-blonde hair—and guided her back down. His gaze never left Ace's, not when she moaned her approval, and not when she slid those talented, hungry lips around his aching cock.

That's not what you wanted to say, brother.

No, it wasn't. "Help her," Cruz rasped, putting a harsh command behind the words. Giving in to the darkness. "Help her suck my dick."

Ace's smile was pure, smug victory. "I thought you'd never ask."

23

H IS NIGHT IN the cage started off slow—some brand-new, wet-behind-the-ears punk who had no idea who Brendan Donnelly was. He almost felt sorry for the guy, but nowhere near sorry enough not to whoop his ass.

One lucky hit left Bren spitting blood, so he ended it quick. *Welcome to the club, kid,* he saluted silently as Jasper and Mad dragged the kid out of the cage.

He didn't know who Brendan Donnelly was anymore, either.

A charitable man would have given up the cage to other fighters, but Bren was in the mood to *brawl*, damn it. Five days of brooding and drinking and working himself to death hadn't taken the edge off the ache in his chest, so it was high time he tried fighting it out.

He chanced a glance at the cluster of couches where Lex and the other women had congregated. Six was among them, dressed to kill in a short leather skirt, tank top, and boots. She'd pulled her hair back into a sleek ponytail, and the harsh lights overhead glinted off the dark strands.

Looking at her was torture, and he welcomed it. It beat the hell out of the pain of *not* looking at her.

She had an arm around Noelle's shoulders, but she was watching the cage. Her eyes met his, and she didn't look away, didn't blink. He stared right back until the cage door clanged again, and he turned to face his new opponent.

Riff stood there, his shaggy hair pulled back into a short tail, his shirt discarded to reveal a lean body laced with scars. "Bren."

"Riff." Maybe he figured he'd have to fight sometime. Maybe he just didn't like Bren's face. Either way, it didn't matter.

Another silent moment. Then Riff rushed him, fierce desperation lending him speed, and his first swing came in low and fast. Bren blocked it, but didn't strike back. Instead, he jogged back and waited.

Riff groaned and circled. "Fuck, are you going to play with me? I'm not in your league, Donnelly."

"Then why are you in my face?" He was in the mood to do some damage, not pop a guy's fight night cherry.

"Absolution." Riff took another swing, and Bren barely had to dodge. "Make it good and humiliating. She deserves to watch it."

Six. "You're assuming I *want* to hit you. I don't."

"Then I guess I'll kick your ass." Riff slammed into him again, jabbing for his jaw.

Bren let the blow land. It snapped his head back, and he embraced the pain. He embraced the pain of the fist that dug into his side, and the follow-up blow that sent him stumbling into the side of the cage.

He spun and caught Riff's wrist, using the momentum to twist it up behind the man's back in a brutal hold. "Tell me what you did."

"Nothing," Riff spat. "I walked away."

Walked away—and left Six alone to deal with Wilson Trent's increasingly sadistic torture. Bren remembered damning Riff and the others for that, telling her they should have done something, *anything*.

He didn't feel so fucking high and mighty now.

He let Riff go. "You can't have your absolution. Either she understands and forgives you, or she doesn't, but it's up to her. You can't do shit about it, not now."

Riff wiped blood from his lip and circled Bren. "Then let's just punch each other until it stops hurting."

It hadn't been working out so well for Bren, but he shrugged anyway. "I've got nothing else to do."

They came together in another clash of fists, and Riff was right. He wasn't in Bren's league. He wasn't a bad fighter, but his style was reminiscent of Six's, fraught with dirty tricks. It probably worked well against someone who'd been trained, who expected combat to have rules.

Bren knew better. He'd been fighting dirty since before landing in the sectors, and he unleashed that on Riff. A distracting punch to the gut, a feinted jab, and a hard right to the jaw sent him tumbling to the concrete.

Instead of retreating to the other side of the cage, Bren held out a hand to help him up.

Riff took it and limped out of the cage. When he was gone, Dallas caught the side of the door and lifted a brow at Bren. "You done yet?"

He had his own guilt to work off, and two easy fights would never do it. "Not yet."

"All right."

Dallas stepped aside, and one of the Armstrong brothers filled the door. This one had a reputation for being brutal in the cage and out. His sneering face and cheap tattoos contributed to his aura of menace, though his sheer size was enough to intimidate most fighters.

He and his brothers had always been unpleasant,

but they'd gotten downright ugly and mean since Lex had stopped letting them near her. It would be a good fight, a tough one.

Exactly what he needed.

The silence on the couches was painful.

The O'Kane women weren't made for quiet, especially not when two men were pounding each other against the sides of the cage in an orgy of flexing muscles and rage. But the one thing stronger than their enthusiasm was their sense of solidarity.

As long as she was sitting there, none of them would point out that Bren was losing his shit.

In the end, she gave them freedom by vaulting out of her seat and away from the tangle of sympathetic glances. The whispers started as soon as she melted into the crowd, and she supposed she should just be glad Lex was standing with Dallas. Lex's definition of solidarity didn't involve holding back.

Bren *was* holding back. The hulking, mohawked brute in the cage slammed another fist into his gut, and Bren took it. He took the next hit too, even though it crashed him into the cage, and Six didn't think he was taking any pleasure in the beating.

He was seeking oblivion, but she was the only one who could give him what he needed.

The problem was making him believe. She'd been working on the words for days, trying to string the ones she knew together in some order that might convince him. But neither of them was good with the words that mattered, and Christ, she of all people knew how hard it was to trust the words you wanted to hear, because wanting to believe was the scariest fucking thing of all.

She couldn't tell him. She had to *show* him.

If he didn't get himself killed first.

The crowd parted where people noticed her tattoos, but most of the spectators were riveted, completely engrossed in the fight. Bren had had enough, apparently, and the balance of power tilted between two beats of her heart. He went from up against the side of the cage to slamming hit after hit home on his opponent, driving him across the concrete, punishing him for every punch he'd landed.

By the time Six made it to Lex's side, Bren had laid the bastard out cold.

He gestured blindly, an encouraging flick of his hand, but Lex stopped Dallas before he even moved. "No, it's enough. Tell him."

Jasper and Mad were already dragging the cage open to retrieve Bren's fallen opponent. "Wait," Six said, catching Lex's arm. "Let me go in there."

Lex snorted. "Have you lost your mind?"

Maybe. Or maybe she knew the one thing she could give him that would cut through his pain, would show him the sort of trust he'd have to believe. Loving Brendan Donnelly was never going to be passive, but neither was she.

She tightened her fingers and forced Lex to look at her. "Trust me."

After a tense, endless moment, Lex gave in. "All right. Go."

Jasper and Mad dragged the unconscious man past her, leaving her with a clear view of Bren. He was standing by the opposite side of the cage with one hand raised, braced against the chain. His attention was fixed on the couches as the crowd screamed and cheered and shouted at one another over bets made and lost.

When she stepped across the threshold, silence spilled outward. The clang of the door swinging shut was too loud, but Bren didn't turn. From here she could see his bruises, the scrapes and cuts and the blood and pain. So much of it she ached in sympathy.

She didn't let any of that show in her voice. "If this is some jacked-up way of punishing yourself, Donnelly, you should have just let me beat on you."

His spine stiffened. "Is that why you're here?"

"Depends."

He turned to meet her gaze, and his face looked even worse than the rest of him. "On what, sweetness?"

She couldn't help it. One step, two, and then she had his face in her hands, her heart pounding as she wiped blood from his lip with her thumb and swore she wouldn't kill him for letting himself get injured. "I was gonna fuck you, but now I don't know if you can get the job done."

He closed his hands around her wrists, but it was the sudden flare of hope in his eyes that held her still. "Don't joke about that," he whispered thickly. "It's not funny."

"I'm not joking," she replied just as softly. "But we can't do this unless you get who I am. I could peel Russell Miller's skin off for how bad he hurt you, and if you can't wrap your head around that, I'm gonna pound it into something hard until you give up and admit you deserve to be loved. And that I'm the one who gets to do it."

He lifted one hand to her mouth, touching her lower lip with a gentleness that didn't belong in a cage like this. "Did you just say you love me?"

The words spilled out into the uneasy silence, and she knew the closest part of the crowd was straining to hear. Whatever she said next would ripple out, a message passed in whispers until every person in the warehouse knew.

She'd never been more exposed. She'd never cared less.

She slid her hands into his hair and gripped the strands, smiling because it was finally long enough for her to pull. "I love you, Brendan Donnelly," she said clearly and loudly. "And you are *mine*. Don't you fucking forget it ever again."

"Yes, ma'am." The words barely made it past his lips before his mouth crashed down on hers. She tasted the blood of his split lip and didn't care, not when her body was shaking and her blood was roaring in her ears.

Except that wasn't her blood but the crowd, scream-ing now in anticipation of a different kind of show, the kind encouraged as Bren's hands slid down her body to clutch at her hips. She couldn't forget the gossip she'd heard when she'd first arrived, the whispers of how women would fight to climb into the cage with him after a victory.

Too bad for them. He was hers now, and she issued her final ultimatum as she tore her mouth free. "I'll let you fuck me right here, up against the cage. I'll let you get me off as many times as you want while everyone listens to me scream. I'll give you my body and my heart. But only if you need me. Not want me or like me. *Need* me."

"I do—" The clank of bars and chain drowned out the rest of the words as he lifted her against the side of the cage. "I love you."

No one would have been able to hear the words over the cheering of the crowd, and that suited her just fine. The admission was hers, something she wasn't ready to share, even though she was ready for damn near any-thing else.

She wrapped her legs around his hips and raised both arms, weaving her fingers through the wire of the cage. "Make me feel good, Bren. Make us both feel good."

He kissed her again, and his hand eased under her shirt—a careful exploration, like he was rediscovering all the things that made her moan and rock against him. But when he reached her breast, his fingers twisted tight around her nipple with just the right amount of pressure to make her groan.

The catcalling spectators melted away. They didn't disappear—no, that edge of adrenaline was still there, the one that sizzled over her nerves and whispered that she was being reckless, so reckless—but they didn't matter. Bren did, his teeth against her lip, his fingers tugging at her other nipple until a zip of pain slammed through her and turned to pleasure.

"Say it again," she whispered, arching closer to his denim-clad erection and wishing her underwear was already gone.

"I love you." His hands dropped, one to push up her skirt and the other to jerk at his pants. His cock sprang free to rub against her, closer when he dragged her panties aside.

The fabric ripped, but she barely heard it with Bren's words echoing in her ears, barely felt it with the blunt head of his erection nudging between her pussy lips.

She shuddered, savoring the anticipation, the knowledge that any moment he'd drive home. "How much do you want to be inside me?"

He didn't answer. He stroked his thumb over the corner of her mouth, then edged it between her lips, pushing deep. His gaze locked with hers, and she watched his face as she teased him with soft licks and gentle suction and finally the warning edge of teeth. *Get in me, Donnelly.*

He smiled, slow and soft, and thrust into her—hard, unyielding, his hips crashing against hers.

God, she'd missed him. It wasn't as though they'd been apart for long, but it felt like forever since she'd savored this moment, when he took all of her at once, no hesitation, no working his way in. She loved it because it was raw and real, with just enough discomfort to make the pleasure feel well-earned, and because this was the only thing Bren did without care.

Without control.

He could finesse a lock or spend hours setting up the perfect shot, but when it came to sliding into her body, he needed her so much he couldn't wait, couldn't plan, couldn't handle not being as far inside her as he could possibly go, as fast as he could get there.

She tightened her legs, digging the heels of her boots into the backs of his legs as she held him there, deep and hard and *everything.*

"I'll show you," he promised, already panting in her ear. "Every day, I'll show you how much."

Shivering, she freed one hand from the cage and twisted it in his hair, hauling his head back so he had to meet her eyes. "You deserve love. Say it."

"I deserve better." He pressed closer with a grind of his hips. "I deserve you."

The words slipped under her skin, igniting a warmth unrelated to the friction of his cock. She pulled his mouth to hers for a hungry kiss, one that mingled their panting breaths and tangled tongues and left her shaky, squirming for more pressure, just *more*—

He gave it to her, one hand behind her head and the other behind her hips, protecting her from the cage bars even as he slammed her against them with rough, driving thrusts, each one shoving her higher, twisting her tighter, making her need the next that much more.

She forgot to be nervous about getting off until the first shivers of orgasm snaked up her spine. It cut through the bliss, thrusting her back into her body, into the gritty reality of the cage and the crowd, their hollers and whistles and glee.

They were watching her, watching Bren, captivated as he brought her to the brink of release. For one breathless second, she wondered if she could really be this fearless woman, one who loved hard enough to forgive, who was strong enough to be vulnerable in front of the whole world.

Bren saw it, just like he saw everything. "It's okay," he growled. "I've got you."

He had her. Beautiful, dangerous, flawed, lonely Brendan Donnelly had her, and she was going to give him everything.

Closing her eyes, she lifted her hands to the bars overhead, wrapped her fingers around the cool metal, and clung to the cage as he fucked her into bliss.

ABOUT KIT

Kit Rocha is actually two people—Bree & Donna, best friends who are living the dream. They get paid to work in their pajamas, talk on the phone, and write down all the stories they used to make up in their heads.

Beyond Pain is the third book in their dystopian erotic romance series. They also write paranormal romance as Moira Rogers.

ACKNOWLEDGMENTS & THANKS

Eternal thanks for the support and tough love to all the usual suspects—Vivian Arend, Alisha Rai, Ann Aguirre, Lauren Dane, and filthy-minded ladies of TLTSNBN. If we ever open a bar, we'll name drinks after the people who made this book better: Jay AhSoon Samia, our trusty beta reader; Lillie, the Keeper of the O'Kane Series Bible; Sasha Knight, lovingly sadistic editor; Fedora Chen, eagle-eyed proofer; and Sharon Muha, our last defense against typos and formatting bloopers.

And first, last, and always—thanks to the readers who have embraced the O'Kanes and make us excited for the end of the world. If the apocalypse comes, meet us at the Broken Circle.

Turn the page
for a sneak peek at

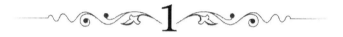

S HE'D TURNED INTO a creeper, and it was all Ace's fault.

Rachel drained her third shot of tequila and fought a losing battle to drag her covetous gaze away from the cage—and the man inside it.

Of course, everyone was watching. It was hard not to when Cruz was setting a Sector Four record by taking on three opponents at once. And he'd apparently decided to go big or go home, because not a single one of the poor bastards had managed to land a solid shot on him.

It wasn't fair, when even three-on-one odds couldn't bring a man down.

Rachel half wished she'd laid money on the match, just to have an excuse for her galloping pulse, not to mention the tiny drop of sweat that rolled down the small of her back. But she'd never been good at lying to herself, so there it was. The truth, in mesmerizing Technicolor.

Lorenzo Cruz, stripped to the waist and fighting like

his life and dark mood depended on it, was a beautiful sight. Damn near enough to make a woman come from thirty feet away.

A tug on her shirt pulled her attention away from the cage. "Show me where you want this?"

Shit, she'd forgotten all about Gunner, their conversation—and, frankly, anything that didn't have to do with licking a path straight down the center of Cruz's chest. "Uh, yeah." She lifted her hands automatically, allowing Gunner to pull her shirt higher. "I know the ribs hurt, but I was thinking my left side?"

"Sure, sure. No problem." He grinned at her. "I can put it anywhere you want."

"A tattoo," she said firmly. "Don't go getting your hopes or anything else up."

Gunner winked, the gesture more playful than it was suggestive. He knew better than to push his luck with an O'Kane, especially in the heart of their compound. "I'll be a perfect gentleman," he assured her, crouching to get a better look at her side. "So you want a fallen angel right across here?"

"Falling," she corrected. Not just an angel, and not one lying on the ground, her wings broken. That wasn't her. What she wanted to capture was the journey, the dizzy, spinning descent. "I want—"

Someone reached around her waist and jerked her shirt back down into place. Even before she looked down at the brash, beautiful sleeves of ink covering those arms, she knew who it was from the zing of awareness that rocked her.

Ace.

She slapped his fingers and turned to face him. "Hands off, Santana. I'm having a conversation here."

Ace's gorgeous face twisted into a scowl. "Not with him, you're not. *Hell* no."

It wasn't enough for him to dominate her thoughts, her fantasies. He had to own her skin, too. "Seriously? You think I'm gonna come to you for this?"

He ignored her, shifting his gaze to Gunner as if she hadn't spoken. "I thought we had an understanding, man. You got a sudden death wish?"

Gunner raised both hands in clear surrender, and Rachel shoved him out of the way. It wasn't about him anyway, not really. "If you have a problem with my life choices, Ace, have the respect to take it up with *me*."

Now she had his attention, one hundred and ten percent of it. Ace was usually so easygoing that she forgot how intense he could be when he fixed that dark gaze on a person. "Letting that bastard ink you isn't a life choice. It's a *fuck you*."

"Even if that were true, don't you think you've earned it?"

"Maybe, but there are better ways to say it." He leaned in, the air between them heavy, electric, and even the roar of the crowd around her couldn't shatter the illusion that they were trapped in their own tiny world. "Did you think past sticking it to me? About how long it would take, how much it would sting? How high you'd be flying, with only some fucking outsider there to catch you if you fall too fast?"

"I hate you." The words slipped out, and she immediately wanted to snatch them back. Not because they weren't true—he'd hurt her, more than once, in ways that couldn't have been accidental—but because they revealed too much. How much she cared, when she shouldn't have, not at all.

Her cheeks burned. She turned on her heel and fled, heading for the back hallway and its maze of rooms and exits. Plenty of places to hide until the waves of mortification settled. She'd blame it on the tequila, laugh it off the way she did everything else—

"Rachel, wait."

"No fucking way."

Ace caught her arm and hauled her to a stop. "Fucking hell, woman, *stop* for a second!"

"What?" She jerked away and smacked her shoulder

against the hallway wall—hard. At least the darkness would hide the sudden tears of pain that stung her eyes, even if it did nothing to conceal her stupidity. "What do you want from me, Ace?"

"Fuck." His hand hovered over her shoulder. "I want to stop hurting you. But it's the one thing I manage, no matter what I do."

Did he stop to wonder why? To think about all the ways he was in her face, every day, showing her there was nothing he couldn't have if he wanted it. Nothing and no one, including Cruz.

Including her.

"I don't—" Her voice failed her, and she fought to speak past the thick, painful lump in her throat. "I don't want to do this anymore. We should just stay out of each other's way, okay?"

"Easier said than done," he whispered, dropping his hand to her wrist. He slid a fingertip over her wrist and the cuff obscuring her city bar code, the first tattoo he'd ever given her.

The moment was burned into her memory. Ace had set her at ease with his friendly jokes and warm smiles, turning a terrifying moment into something simple, almost sweet. She'd clung to it, the only solid thing in a whirling storm of uncertainty.

He pulled away. As light as the caress had been, its absence was a punch to the gut. "If you don't trust me with your ink anymore, all right. But Emma's got more talent in one toe than that bastard will ever have in his life. And she's one of us."

"Okay, you win." The words caught on a hitch, and Rachel shook her head. "You always win."

"Sure as hell doesn't feel like it, angel."

"That's your own damn fault." She looked away, toward the low red light glowing at the end of the hallway. "You didn't even ask me why."

"Would you have answered?"

He was leaning closer. She could feel it, and she

steeled herself against the seductive tug before she looked up and met his gaze. "Anything."

The space between them was too precise not to be deliberate. He should be touching her somehow—an accidental bump of his hand, his chest grazing hers when she dragged in a breath—but the prickle along her skin was pure anticipation.

He let her hang there forever before closing his eyes. "Maybe I don't want to hear you say how much you hate me again. Once a night is all my wounded, delicate heart can handle."

His words should have sparked her temper again, not a tiny frisson of guilt. "I meant it. But not the way you think."

The corner of his mouth kicked up. "My mistake. It's the good kind of hate."

"The frustrated kind." He always found a way to hide behind his joking words. Exasperated, Rachel reached down and grabbed his belt buckle, curling her fingers beneath the warm metal. "I know what sorts of games you and Cruz are playing these days. How come you two haven't knocked on *my* door yet? Think I can't handle it?"

"And what do you think you know?" Ace demanded, his eyes snapping open. His hands hit the wall on either side of her head, caging her. Trapping her. "Don't skimp on the filthy details. You know how I love dirty talk, angel."

She'd lost her mind—it was the only explanation for why she didn't retreat. "You've been sharing your women." She leaned closer, her mouth next to his ear. "Is it about pleasure or conquest, Ace? And do you take turns, or fuck them at the same time?"

"Conquest?" His eyes narrowed, and a new expression darkened his features, one she'd never seen directed at her before.

Anger.

Good. She could work with him hating her, too. At least that made sense.

Rachel snatched her hand back. "Sorry, I forgot the rules. Everything's a joke until it's not, and words don't mean anything until you want them to."

The arms on either side of her tensed, muscles flexing under ink. "We fuck them at the same time, because that's what they want. What *he* wants. Is that what you really need to know? What your city boy's doing now? How filthy he's gotten? Because you sure as fuck don't seem to give a shit about me."

If only.

Her eyes burned, and she bit the inside of her cheek until she tasted blood. It didn't stop the first hot tear from spilling down her cheek, or the ragged sob that tore through the knot in her throat.

"Fuck. Fuck, fuck *fuck.*" Ace cupped her cheeks, a warmth on her skin that lingered for only a heartbeat before vanishing. "Ignore me, angel. You're sweet and you're perfect and Cruz is in love with you. You're both too good for the likes of me, so don't cry."

The only thing that hurt worse than his censure was his pity. Desperate for escape from both, Rachel stumbled blindly toward the door. Any place was better than standing in front of Ace, hearing awful, hurtful words spill from her lips, when all she'd ever wanted was—

It doesn't matter. She repeated it like a mantra, a tiny whisper under her breath until she was outside, her breath puffing out into the frigid night air. She was heading in the wrong direction, toward the warehouses instead of the living quarters, but she didn't give a damn.

She had to get away.

It wasn't difficult to track down Rachel. Cruz had successfully stalked more elusive prey across far more expansive terrain, and had done so with less intimate knowledge of his quarry. When Rachel was rattled, she fled to higher ground, to fresh air and open skies.

So he wasn't surprised to find her on the roof. She sat with her back to the low wall edging the rooftop, a nearly empty bottle nestled between her knees. "Emergency tequila," she explained, holding the bottle aloft. Her teeth chattered, and her lips were several shades darker than their usual pink. "To keep me warm."

Liquor didn't work that way. It opened the capillaries, flushed the skin with what seemed like a rush of warmth, but in the end it only hastened the loss of body heat. Especially now, when they were well on their way to winter. It got cold in the desert at night, and for all that Eden had fought to hide the fact with irrigation and reservoirs and carefully cultivated greenery, that was exactly where they were.

"Here," he said, slipping out of his jacket. His blood was still pumping from the fight, but the icy wind cut easily through his thin T-shirt. He could only imagine how chilled she was, huddling against the stone.

She relaxed into the fabric with a soft moan. "You're so warm. And I'm so stupid. I shouldn't have come up here, but now I can't leave."

It didn't make sense, but she was so wasted it probably shouldn't. Rachel could match any O'Kane drink for drink, which made him wonder how full that bottle had been when she'd come up here. She might have even started drinking while he was still in the cage, before he'd claimed victory only to discover a guilt-stricken Ace, hitting the whiskey hard enough for it to hit back.

It wasn't a surprise that the two people he cared for most couldn't exchange two words without shredding each other to ribbons. That had been his life forever—the agony of divided loyalties. His orders or his conscience, the sectors or Eden...

Rachel or Ace.

Ace would have to fend for himself tonight. Cruz crouched and held out a hand. "Share the tequila?"

"Take it. My head is spinning." She passed him the bottle, then pressed her palms over her closed eyes. "You talked to Ace."

"He didn't have much to say." It wasn't a lie, because he hadn't needed words to know. The pain in Ace's expression had told Cruz who, and enough of what. Only a fight with Rachel could put *that* look in the man's eyes.

She changed the subject. "Congratulations on your win. That's a record, you know. I hope you were smart enough to bet on yourself and clean up."

"I've got some cash now, yeah."

She leaned her head back against the brick. "Good."

"Rachel, honey. It's too damn cold to be out here. Why don't you go back to your room?"

"I don't want to be alone." Her eyes fluttered open and fixed on him. "Up here, I'm killing time. If I go home, I'm alone."

The offer hung heavy on the tip of his tongue, but he bit it back. It would be too easy to cross this line. He'd crossed so many others lately, stumbling across them in blind pursuit of pleasure.

He could stumble into her, too, but not like this. Not drunk and sad and shivering from the cold. His words had to be careful, precise. Comfort with no hidden strings, no temptation. "You don't have to be alone. There are plenty of places you could crash tonight."

She smiled—slow, with no hint of amusement. "Everyone feels sorry for me these days."

"I don't think that's true."

"Maybe not. Fine." She reached out. "If you're not going to let me sit here and feel sorry for myself, the least you can do is help me up."

Now it was safe to smile as he straightened and took her hand. "You promise to go somewhere warm, and I'll let you brood all night long."

"I don't *want* to." She tripped over her feet and pitched against him, bracing her free hand on his chest. "I don't know what else to do. This isn't how things were supposed to turn out."

The line always blurred when she put her hands on

him. But this was the first time she'd touched him in the days since he'd killed Russell Miller, and that had been a turning point. The moment he'd given up on some impossible idea of being a hero.

Of being *her* hero.

He gripped her shoulders to steady her and ignored the way even that small contact stirred arousal. "Turn out? That's awfully final."

Her fingers tightened in his shirt. "Yes, it is."

Careful. "Your life's not over. Anything could happen tomorrow. You and I both know that better than most."

She looked up at him, her expression serious. Her eyes clear. "I'm glad you're happy. Doubt anything else, but not that, okay?"

He wasn't happy. He was falling, losing himself in vice because fucking and fighting were the only things that gave him a taste of pleasure. But she looked so somber, so fucking *sad* that only a monster would take that small comfort from her. "All right."

She huffed out a laugh and hid her face against his chest. "You're a terrible liar. Just wretched."

It wasn't funny, but his lips twitched as he gave himself permission to touch her hair. He'd missed running his fingers through it, feeling the slippery blonde strands slide over his skin. It was longer than it had been during their brief time together, long enough that he could imagine wrapping it around his fist—

No. "I'm actually a damn good liar," he said, mostly to distract himself. "Just not with you, I guess."

"Not with me." She arched closer, rubbing her cheek against his shirt. "I miss you."

"Yeah?" His heart kicked into his throat—an amazing fucking feat with all the blood rushing to his cock.

But Rachel didn't respond, and she wasn't just leaning into him for support anymore. He allowed himself a single sigh before scooping her off her feet. She barely murmured as her head tucked itself neatly under his chin.

She'd be feeling the tequila tomorrow, and the chances were good she wouldn't remember a damn thing she'd said to him tonight. That was the only reason he let himself speak at all as he carried her toward the stairs.

"I miss you, too."

Coming in March 2014